SIRENS

You're going to love Anthony. You'd better.

SIRENS

Simon Messingham

Derelict Space Sheep

First published in Australia in 2017
by Derelict Space Sheep
www.derelictspacesheep.com
Please direct all enquiries to the publisher at:
maxmooney@derelictspacesheep.com

ISBN 978-1-925270-04-4 (print)
ISBN 978-1-925270-05-1 (electronic)

Typeset in Britannic Bold; Garamond.

National Library of Australia Cataloguing-in-Publication entry

Creator:	Messingham, Simon, author.
Title:	Sirens / Simon Messingham.
ISBN:	9781925270044 (hardback)
Subjects:	Science fiction.

Cover illustration by Emily Coelli:

- emilycoelliart.org
- facebook.com/EmilyCoelliArt/

To my family: Julie, Ralph, Oscar, and to Jacob Edwards

For what each individual wills is obstructed by everyone else, and what emerges is something that no one intended.

– Friedrich Engels

Book One

THE GLAMOUR

Chapter 1

You know I hate telling people what to do. So it is with a glad heart that today I give Emma Raynor her free will. We meet outside the Tate Modern at a Turkish place I use; a family restaurant on the way to the hospital. I like the convenience.

Emma tells me she'll be fine. She says she will be very happy. I think so too.

She looks at me across the table as I scoop more figs out of my silver bowl. Love is in her eyes. The sun is shining through the tinted glass, causing the strings of golden syrup hanging from the spoon to glow. I remark upon this. She is very happy.

Emma's face is remarkable; a perfect oval. You wouldn't forget that face if you saw it. I certainly never forgot her. I always dreamed she would be mine and now she is.

Emma is wearing an expensive summer dress I picked out in the designer department at Selfridges. Olive green suits the tone of her great skin. Emma smiles and her teeth are perfect. She used to have a yellow stain on her upper left incisor. I saw to that. I saw to all her blemishes.

'I hope the weeks haven't been too hard,' I say. 'You look great.'

She blushes, suddenly coy. 'I missed you so much.' A furrow grows between her eyebrows. 'I'm in the right place mentally now. Exactly the right place.'

'That's terrific,' I tell her.

You see, I sent Emma away. For six weeks. I've had her in this health spa somewhere in Hampshire. Body and mind relaxography or whatever they call it. I can't tell you exactly where the spa is because I asked the doctors not to let on. I wanted to miss her.

Anyway, Emma's been undergoing intensive psychotherapy treatment to prepare her for today. Physical therapy too; just in case that makes a difference. Nobody knows for sure.

I raise a finger. 'Now,' I adopt a stern, fatherly tone, 'giving you your free will back isn't something I do lightly. In fact, when I've tried before… well, the people haven't always been happy.'

The crease of doubt reappears on her high forehead and I can't help it: I lean over and kiss her right there, the cute skin over her nose. She holds my arm and looks at me.

'You know my doctor?' I ask.

'Conor, oh yes.'

'He's not convinced. He says there are too many unknowns. Risks and variables. Conor knows. He knows a lot about these things. Much more than me.'

Tears of gratitude glisten in Emma's eyes. 'I'll do whatever you think is best.'

Can you believe it, I'm embarrassed! I'm like a little schoolboy. Come on, Anthony, get a grip. I swallow and continue.

'I just want you to know…' I say. 'I want you to be absolutely clear, that I'm giving you your true self back because I love you. I want you to be my companion. A real companion. Perhaps later even…'

'Yes, Anthony?' Emma pushes her chair back with a scrape and stands, barely able to draw breath. A counterfeit Turkish folk song, arabesque they call it, rings round. A traditional tune cheapened into counterfeit pop. Melody simplified with the rough edges smoothed out. I know all that but to me at this moment, in this afternoon light, the swirling female vocals are magical. Perfection frozen in time.

'If it works out,' I say, 'if you're okay with the situation, I want you to become Mrs Anthony Graves.'

'I love you, Anthony.' We look at each other.

Emma flings herself across the table. I tell the staff to piss off. They do and Emma and I make wonderful love spontaneously right there in the restaurant. And to think at college she never knew I existed. I have come a long way.

Emma's great. She loves me. She said so. It took her three years to find me and I hadn't seen her for twelve. That's dedication.

One Sunday, completely out of the blue, Emma rang my buzzer. She was standing cold and shivering outside my Hampstead mansion. I hadn't told her to find me; I knew nothing about it. She said she was living with her husband and daughter somewhere near Bristol when she remembered how I had felt about her all those years ago and felt bad we had never got together but realised that she absolutely had no alternative but to find me again. So, without any plan, here she came. Now that's proper love. You can't fake that.

As I helped her into the hall, I felt seventeen again. I was a smitten idiot. Emma was a woman now, half-starved in filthy rags. My housemaid ushered her to the wet room and cleaned her up. My chef cooked some decent food and my fashion people sorted out some clothes. When she returned (I waited in the kitchen, left hand discretely in blazer pocket, right hand holding a goblet of Cabernet) Emma smelled, looked and felt perfect. She was ruddy and flushed, her superb genetics quickly mastering the ravages of her ordeal. Obviously the hair had changed since college, and age had lined her forehead but she still had that face, that snub nose, that yellow smudged tooth. The familiar enigmatic Emma smile was back on her face. I thought: Anthony! All the years wasted! That time poured away assessing every female who crossed my path. Looking for Emma. All those women: Penny and Toni and Alison and oh I can't remember; always judging them, always searching for their Emma-ness. Pale shadows, all. Emma was the ideal. She was always the one.

I invited Emma to sit and eat. As she attacked the breakfast, I sneakily stared. A bubble of excitement inside was jabbering that she was my woman. My woman. And it was no trouble to get her to change her hair back to the way I liked it.

That was last year. Now we're officially an item. Seven years, eighteen weeks and two days have elapsed since I, Anthony Graves, became a god.

Chapter 2

We walk arm in arm from Bankside to Borough Market. The people, hundreds of them, cheer us on.

London is getting there. The air is quantifiably cleaner, traffic has been significantly reduced, and inflated property prices are no longer an issue. The people who live here appreciate all the hard work I've put in for them. Four million human beings live in London. They are right behind me, all the time.

I love the city. All I need now is someone to share it with.

We pass my apartment. From my balcony I can see St Paul's Cathedral, the Millennium Bridge, Tower Bridge, even the London Eye if I squint upriver. These historical landmarks are clean and scrubbed after intensive maintenance. They gleam. I used to have to endure the sight of the Gherkin Building on the North Bank but I've had that eyesore demolished. The city is my responsibility. I have a duty of care. Thank god for me.

Mainly I love the Thames: that grey, tireless, timeless road. Pumping away century after century, the concealed currents, the power. In the absolute quiet of the city morning the only sound is the lap and slap of the freshening water. There's history in that river. When we hit high summer, I plan to take a dip with Emma. Once I've finished my swimming lessons and there is absolutely no chance of my being drowned.

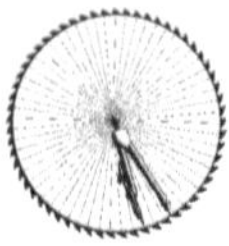

The police have blocked Southwark High Street and they salute as we pass. Their Land Rovers are washed and bright, the barriers clearly marked with hazard warnings. Officers salute as Emma and I walk by. I nod seriously and approvingly at their solid figures wrapped in those authoritative uniforms with their hi-vis jackets. I still treat the police with respect.

Southwark High Street cuts a gash through this geometric Grand Canyon. Instead of rock: hotels. Hilton, Jarvis, Holiday Inn.

From the windows, guests scream with good cheer. I wave at them, enjoying watching their pink heads and hands bob with pleasure. Flowers rain down on the freshly swept street. These folk have paid good money to travel here today and I want to give them something for their efforts.

At last, our rendezvous: Guy's Hospital.

My personal physician Doctor Conor and Head Nurse Margaret wait at the main entrance. Out of all my nurses, Margaret is my favourite. She's cheery and buxom and has lovely coffee-coloured skin. Originally, she was just an ordinary nurse but I liked the look of Margaret and put her in charge.

The hospital is quiet as we walk through the fresh spring afternoon air into reception. There are no longer any patients at Guy's; except obviously, me.

The members of staff in the hushed, spotless reception are lined up. They say 'Good afternoon, Anthony' as Emma and I enter. They have made a real effort. Good for them.

The floors are polished and the lobby smells of expensive soap. We've all come a long way since I was last in the hospital, back in the old days when the place was filthy and full of ill people. Ill people, fat people, poor people and nutters; shouting and wandering.

'Morning, all.'

They're lined up according to their jobs: doctors, nurses, receptionists, cleaners. I pass down the line and compliment them on their appearance. My philosophy is that if they can see I'm happy, they'll be happy. They'll go that extra mile.

'Good morning, Anthony,' they say again as I move on. They are as excited as me.

Now, despite the cleanliness and orderly lines, I have never been a fan of hospitals. I am uncomfortable. I am daunted.

Conor squeezes my shoulder. He has picked up on my unease. 'You'll be fine.'

I give Margaret a little peck on the cheek, and up we go in the lift.

Emma is still smiling. God, she looks wonderful.

'How are you feeling?' I ask.

'Whatever happens, I know you mean the best for me.'

'You're so brave.' I kiss her.

The room is a padded cell in the secure unit; where they stick the mental patients. That puts implications in my head I don't much care for.

'I just want to make sure nothing goes wrong,' says Conor. 'Like we talked about, our current psychological models suggest we are not removing your wonderful glamour but imprinting a new directive. We are, if you like, pressing the reset button. However, I still–'

'The operation will be a success,' I tell him. Conor is instantly happier.

Margaret leads me next door into the viewing room. There is a couch and a sink and cupboards full of hospital things like gloves and forceps and drip bags. Through a one-way mirror on a wall, we can see into the cell where Emma is standing; where Conor is trussing her up. Over my head, a strip light fizzes. I find this little technical hiccup oddly relaxing.

Conor checks that Emma is fastened then exits the padded room. He closes the door and locks my potential future wife inside. Emma mouths through the glass: *Love you.*

God, I hope this works.

Conor enters the viewing room, wheeling in a beeping ECG machine. I unbutton my shirt and sit back on the couch. Margaret sticks the monitoring pads to my chest.

I don't need to do any of this — the glamour incites not one physical ripple in my body — but Conor is taking every precaution.

Now, the downside with reversing the glamour, or re-imprinting or whatever Conor wants to call it, is that the effect can go all over the place. I might aim it at Emma but you never quite know who else might get caught up. Which would be bad. I have already checked there aren't any weapons in the room.

Conor nods at me. His grey hair and trendy little black half-moon spectacles reinforce his soothing, gentrified bearing. He flicks a switch next to a little microphone. When he speaks, he sounds just like a TV doctor. 'Ready, Emma?'

We hear his echo bounce around the cell. Emma nods, desperate to reassure me. She flexes the straps of the straitjacket, trying to make herself comfortable. She looks very sweet.

'Okey-dokey,' says Conor. 'Anthony. In your own time.'

Conor wanted to keep me in hospital overnight. I couldn't face that. I told him to get me back to my apartment.

There are only a few stitches and the sewing didn't really hurt. What got to me was how quickly the old fears came back. For a while I really lost my composure. I can only thank Conor for keeping me together enough to let them inject me.

I felt foolish being wheeled out of the hospital after all the palaver and ceremony we had going in. I had only sore knees and a few cuts to the head; nothing to write home about. Conor looked worse than me. In fact, he was a lot worse than me. He couldn't apologise enough. He was on his knees begging forgiveness. I think he would have done something to himself if I hadn't stopped him.

I remember how hopeful Emma looked in her cell; how she was willing the experiment to be a success. Before I glamoured her.

The push was like meeting an old friend; a bit 'Oh, I remember you…' Gone, I felt that hangover twinge, again not altogether unpleasant. But. Something happened. Understanding altered

Emma's face. She twitched. Her face morphed into an expression I hadn't witnessed for years. Disgust.

'What have you done to me?' Her voice crackled in the speakers. 'What have you done to all of us?'

There was a dreadful pause. Hideous. A pause which told me I couldn't deny the truth any longer. Just like the others, she was going to break down. 'Please,' I whispered. 'Emma.'

As she began to scream, I decided to glamour her again. Or rather: re-glamour her for a third time. No harm done. I readied myself. Before I could, Conor attacked me.

'Monster!' he screeched. 'Fucking monster!'

Conor dropped a fist and the top of my head exploded. My legs buckled and, as if in slow motion, I fell. For a second this was happening to someone else and I was just an observer. Then my knees crunched into the unyielding floor. Wires went everywhere and a cold, almost metallic pain forced its way up my legs.

I barely registered Conor as he jumped on top of me. I tried to remember all those martial arts lessons. I couldn't concentrate. Some distant part of me registered a thumping sound in Emma's cell.

Conor's big fingers scrabbled over my face, searching for my weeping eyes.

The thumping kept up. I tried slapping Conor's arms away. I needed space. I forgot about Emma, I just wanted saving. 'P– please…' I remember whimpering. Anywhere, anyone.

'Fucking… animal… bastard…' Conor hissed. He bared his teeth. I looked into his wet, raw mouth. He was too strong, too full of hate for anything I could do. He was going to bite my throat.

Margaret saved me. She sprang at Conor and knocked him over. She was wobbly herself, awkward and jerky, so I could tell her thoughts were blurry, but thank Christ she was still mine. Conor was forced to release his grip on my head and I rolled away. My knees were two burning circles. I bellowed in fear and agony.

Emma had dropped out of sight. Something red was smeared across the viewing glass.

Conor stood up. He was feverish; wild with anger. He looked around for a weapon. He picked up a metal stand; the ones they use for drips. As he raised it, Margaret went for him again.

Conor swung the stand and caught Margaret full in the face. She went over and hit the floor, mouth first. Her jaw shattered, spraying teeth. Her uniform rustled as she spasmed. Blood jetted in untidy spurts.

Ignoring her, Conor raised the stand again for me but I had been given my moment to think. As he slashed I glamoured him.

Immediately, he changed. He stopped in mid-stride, blinking as if just waking up. Conor looked at the metal stand like he had no idea how he had ended up holding it. We stared at each other. My knees were ingots of fire.

'What have I done?' he whispered.

I remembered Emma. I limped to the window. She lay prone on the cell floor, blood soaking into the padded tiles.

'Conor!' I yelled. 'You said she couldn't… she wouldn't… the whole point was she couldn't injure herself. You said!'

I could only feel the cold glass on my face as Conor unlocked the door and ran inside. I was left with the gently quivering Margaret on the floor.

My ears suddenly blocked up and I knew I was going to faint. I saw a chair to fall onto. *You're in charge,* I recall thinking. *You can't nod out.*

The next thing I knew I was on my back, frozen and caked in sweat, looking up at that defective, fizzing light. My knees were killing me. A new nurse was trying to stick a needle in my arm and I was fighting her off. I saw Conor shaking his head as if to clear something buzzing around inside. Anger overwhelmed me, brought me round. 'What did you do?' I snarled. 'Conor!'

He looked at me; face pale as death. 'If they want to,' he said, 'they find a way. I'm sorry, Anthony. This is my fault.'

Do you know what? He was right. It was his fault. Okay, maybe Conor had warned me but if he genuinely thought this might happen he should have been more forceful. He should have done something. This was his fault. His stupid fucking fault. And now Emma is dead and once again I am alone.

Chapter 3

Why am I writing? Why am I sitting with an open laptop at my imported walnut mahogany desk, staring at a mug full of pencils? A mug decorated with a golden crown? Why am I stuck trying to decide on a definitive font? I, who have never voluntarily written anything in my life. What's gotten into me?

Maybe I'm writing this to me. Perhaps I'm writing this to the person I once was: the Anthony Graves in a parallel universe where what happened to me didn't happen to him.

I often think of that Anthony; still commuting to his little job in the civil service. I wonder where he's going on holiday, what he is going to watch on telly tonight. I wonder how he's going to cope when he gets old. An Anthony who still goes to the Crown and Anchor after work. An Anthony who must by now surely have found a girlfriend. A girlfriend who will become a wife and, with Anthony's input, produce kids.

I hope you're happy, that Anthony. I really do. This story is for you. But this story isn't about you.

I can't bear to see people. Any people. I send them all away. I empty London. I worry what I will do to them if they stay.

On the second day, I head down to the basement. I shuffle thanks to the bruised kneecaps obtained at the Emma disaster. A couple of years ago I converted the underground car park into a firing range. I stock an extensive range of weapons and SAS Colonel Steve makes sure they're in working order. I'm now trained up in all sorts of guns and today I let rip with the XM8 assault rifle. As Colonel Steve is always telling me, to get used to a gun you have to fire a gun. The XM8 is a dream. I slip on the ear protectors, unfold the forearm bipod and slap in a magazine. Thanks to the long hours I've put in, I can now drill a hole the size of a fifty pence piece exactly where I want to from twenty metres. However, today I'm not going for quality; I just want to shoot things.

The rifle bucks in my hands in a thoroughly pleasant and movie-ish manner. The mannequins crumble under sustained fire. Head shot, torso, anywhere. The padded basement fills with smoke and the echoes of expended rounds. I leave the empty cartridges for someone else to clean up.

Does it make me feel better? For a while. Then not.

I take the XM8 assault rifle out onto the street and shoot up cars and the buildings that two days ago were filled with cheering people. I imagine snipers in windows, squads deploying across roads, fields of fire, cross-fire, blanket fire, cartridge cases flying out of guns to rattle on concrete and tarmac. The flat sound of my bullets echoes round the empty city. I cry and can't stop.

Clearly, I must accept the depression is not lifting.

I get so crazy I almost restart the campaign to communicate with the other Sirens. My fellows are probably nice men and women. We would probably get on very well over webcams. Despite undoubted initial language barrier concerns, we would end up able to coexist. But we wouldn't meet. We wouldn't do visits. I don't know who they are or even if they are still alive. The trouble is: any other Sirens would want to kill me, so it's complicated.

I endure a rough night. Maybe that's what the writing is for: these nights. I'm up and typing in the dark. The only light is the glow from the laptop. I have heard this is not good for the eyes. My knees have stiffened so now I walk like Frankenstein's monster. I can't cope with the loneliness.

Through this night, I think about Emma.

Emma was different. Part of the A Level art student crowd. She was… beyond fashion, beyond trend. She was a different species. She was terrible to behold.

I never asked her out. What would be the point? She was… who she was, and I was some fat little geek doing an NVQ in Management. I turned my head to another woman; another woman who said yes. For a while, until that didn't work out.

I don't regret not asking Emma out. I was seventeen. That's like asking a pet if it regrets not being married to its master. I never asked Emma out because the concept of me and her as a partnership was so patently ludicrous.

I see her on that padded floor.

These black moods are going to be the death of me. They're getting worse. I need someone. I have to find someone.

I walk out onto my balcony and stare out at the lightless smudge of London. I listen to the river and the quiet deserted streets. I am getting angry. I'll never bring them back. Four million people in this city and not one of them is my friend. I can get them to do anything except what I want. The one little shred of human behaviour I actually want. One person, that's all, that would be enough. I just want one person to honestly like me.

I know I'm honestly starting to hate them.

The laptop glows on the imported mahogany desk topped with the mug full of pencils and its decorative golden crown. What do I write? What do I want to write? What can I be arsed to see through to the end?

And then, for the second time in my life, something unbidden enters my head.

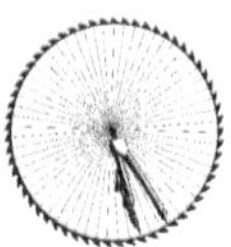

I stand on the Millennium Bridge and breathe in the fresh air. Clouds keep the light a dull grey and the silence absolute. I feel better. I've decided to let the people back in.

I'm thinking psychology. I'm going to do that which I vowed not to do. What the psychiatrists have warned is incredibly dangerous.

I'm going to look back. I'm going to sift through the mud of the past and see what I can dredge up. Or who. A person. Someone lurking there in my history. Just one. I will find them and then I'll be happy. I know I will.

I wait on the bridge as the population streams in from wherever it is it's been. I look at the people as they shuffle back to their homes and their jobs. Many are tired and dirty. Have they been sleeping in fields? It's good for me to try and see them as individuals.

Whatever, they are pleased to see me and wave as they walk back to their homes and offices. Many have never witnessed me in person before so it's a real treat for them. At twilight, the lights of Bankside are switched on. The people still come. We share a beautiful May evening. Welcome home, my Londoners!

Chapter 4

April 18th. 11:37 British Summer Time.

'Eighteen/Four' is its popular name. The American 'Four/Eighteen' has long been consigned to history's rubbish bin; or should that be garbage chute? I digress.

Scientists preferred 'The Moment', which sounds melodramatic until you realise they intended that term to rank alongside other significant terms. Terms like 'The Big Bang'. That melodrama was intentional.

I have often been asked to describe The Moment. I could never answer, even to satisfy myself. How to explain an occurrence that has no precedent, no points of reference?

Let's start with where I was.

I was at work. Twenty-two floors up in a government tower at the north end of the Tottenham Court Road. The tower provided a view overlooking the whole of London; from a distant Wembley Stadium to a distant London Eye. Not that I was looking out that crisp spring morning. I was at my computer terminal looking busy and enthusiastic. Busy online enthusiastically buying a DVD.

In my civil service office, photocopiers were photocopying, phones were ringing, the air conditioner was humming: a normal working day. I was staring at the screen, already bored of my upcoming purchase. I was just buying out of habit. DVDs were threatening to be as prehistoric as the dinosaurs. They said the future was streaming. How right they were.

As I clicked the item ('supersaver delivery!') into my virtual basket, something in my head switched on. A light blinked from red to green.

Okay, The Moment felt like someone slotted a new piece of hardware into my brain. The neural equivalent of a plastic board studded with gold tracing and black silicon that slid in and powered up. Plug and play.

At which point, my supervisor Christopher Samson enters the drama. The exact time is well documented: ten seconds in. Whatever innocence came with The Moment is lost here.

'Titanic' Samson was a patroller. Despite his pale, bald head, his skinny arms and protruding beer belly, Titanic was a lion; prone and patient in the long grass. He could sense 'not looking busy' at twenty paces. Just as I reeled in my swivel chair wondering what had happened to my brain, Titanic pounced. Titanic Rampant!

'Snowed under?' he asked. A crude rhetorical question; routinely employed. A question familiar to all Titanic Samson observers.

'Not really,' I replied. A mistake. 'Well, yes.'

I scrabbled with my mouse, trying to close the web-site. Titanic wore a sweaty white shirt and a tie from Next. He had a horrible little goatee beard, the type sported by rock fans and viewers of Robot Wars. I am told he liked maintaining classic cars. He had absolutely no sense of humour. The nickname 'Titanic' came from the movie. He was the dozy butler the toffs sent below decks to keep third class in line, while they escaped in the lifeboats. Never mind he was going to drown with the rest of us commoners. The name had grown so ingrained, colleagues struggled not to call him Titanic to his face.

'Are you ill?' His tone dared me to say yes. Actually I wasn't feeling great. My mind was tender and raw but he wouldn't care about that.

Titanic leaned over me. Another little tic: he had no idea of personal space. I could taste his breath. The air from his mouth reeked of chocolate.

'I can always find you something to do.'

He looked smug. I understood.

'Those dormant files need weeding…'

A lonely waste of time dreamed up as punishment. He had me.

'Sure thing, Chris,' I said. I tried to sound sincere. It wasn't worth winding him up; there were a million ways he could make life uncomfortable for me.

Thinking back, I realise we really irked Titanic, poor bastard. We irritated him because he honestly believed his job meant something. He wasn't bright and he found the work demanding. He was at the ceiling of his capability.

What he didn't need was a bunch of smirking lazy arses who breezed through tasks well below their competency and treated the whole place as a minor inconvenience in their packed social lives.

'If you're not too busy,' said Titanic. 'Oh, and just to let you know, this afternoon I thought I might take a look at the flexi-time stats.'

That last snide little comment used up any potential sympathy points. *No you didn't, you little shit. You just want to know how much time I owe. So I have to stay late and make it up.*

Irritation and frustration, work anger; the usual emotions anyone feels ten times a day at their place of employment. Nothing special. Only today, here on Eighteen/Four, there was something special. A slippery dislocation like I was on the edge of losing control. Something wild was inside that wanted out.

Titanic tapped at my PC, trying to work out what I had been up to. His sleeve brushed my face.

The new part of my mind, that raw nub, fizzed. I visualised words, worked them out. That little monologue you run inside your head. Things you'd never say aloud. Words like: 'Go.' 'Fuck.' And: 'Yourself.' I pictured myself slotting those words into a gun barrel and firing.

And then it happened. A fizz; a tingle; it blasted through a circular black space, a hole, right in the new part of my consciousness. Just a little blip of energy but from somewhere new; from some incredible reservoir of power. Bang. Gone.

I felt dizzy. A cracking headache was approaching. A tidal roar flushed my ears. Through foggy vision I watched Titanic stand up. He stared at me. I presumed at the time he was concerned I was going to faint. I rolled around in my swivel chair and put my head on the desk.

The sensation was total; something that coursed through every part of me. Not pain; I had been wrong about that. It was pleasure. Gentle readers, you may like to look away now but to put it crudely: I felt like I'd come my brains out. My forehead relished the desk's hard unyielding wood.

'Anthony?' asked Titanic. His voice bounced around like cannon fire.

'Chris,' I said. 'I'm sorry but I don't feel well and you're really annoying me. Please.' I couldn't even raise my head.

I heard Titanic turn and march away. Thank god. An intense shaking and nausea overwhelmed my senses; residual physical effects. What was wrong with me?

Eventually, the feeling dissipated. As the poets might say: I came to my senses. All that remained was a tremendous thirst and a tender new piece of software that hummed in my brain, awaiting further instructions. I already understood I had used a fraction of its power. That flicker I aimed at Titanic was Level One and it nearly killed me. There was way more where that came from. I lifted my head up. Coloured lights danced in my vision. Cold sweat blotted my work shirt. I remember (with some subsequent amusement) I vowed never to do that again.

I should have been shaking. I should have been scared shitless. I had just committed professional suicide. Much as I'd always been bored by this job, it was comfortable and now it was all over.

'Oops…' said my friend Toni from across the table. 'Bye-bye Anthony.'

After a lunch at the Crown and Anchor with Toni and Keano, where we deconstructed events and deduced I was going to get it big time and this was goodbye, I had completely forgotten all this stuff with my head. I was me again. We returned to the twenty-second floor to discover nothing horrible had happened: Titanic was nowhere to be seen and Anthony Graves was still a minor civil servant. Despite our worst predictions, all was right with the world.

We sneaked into the tea room for a quick coffee. This room was not an inspiring backdrop for the events of Eighteen/Four. Unaware of its place in future history, it contained little but a mug-stuffed sink and a peeling poster for a long finished fantasy football league. Despite this year's smoking ban the torn padded chairs still stank of fags. Not exactly epic.

Keano slumped over the sink, snuffling with giggles. He was a small guy of twenty-five, slim from exercise but burdened with terrible eyesight. He wore contact lenses that hurt after a few drinks, so most afternoons he was forced to replace them with his old ridiculous massive specs. He always regretted the lunchtime drink but that never stopped him going.

I feel uncomfortable when I remember Toni. Toni was what you might call my ex. At this point in time, she was overweight, black-haired and pale with bags under her eyes concealed by thick rings of dark eyeliner. She was sly and possessed an intelligent sense of humour that often tipped over into genuine malice. She was always being told she went too far. I liked that. I wanted to be in love with her. I worked very hard at it. Two years before, we had moved out of our parental homes to live together in a flat in Streatham. It lasted six months: the length of a tenancy agreement. When we ran out of money we abandoned the idea and came scurrying home. The problem was, Toni was a mate. We didn't even argue; we just got bored of living with each other. It was one thing to spend the day together but the nights and evenings as well; it was too much effort. We both wanted someone to fall in love with, I guess. It wasn't each other. Our coexistence was too mundane; too in the world. So we went back to just working together. It suited me. It was easier.

Toni and I were thirty this year.

'Get the bloody kettle on,' I ordered. Keano took one look at me and whatever he saw in my face caused the giggles to return.

The tea room door opened and in swooshed the clicking background sounds of the office. Phones rang, a woman coughed.

Keano stopped giggling. He didn't have to say, I knew who it was.

'Anthony?' said Titanic, an odd tone to his voice.

This was it. This was the time. Bye-bye job. I felt the tears start to burn my eyes.

'You all right, Chris?' Toni asked in that over-sincere jokey voice she did so well.

I turned to face Titanic.

His expression scared me. His little moustache quivered.

'Chris?' I asked. 'Look, I'm sorry about earlier. You just… it was just wrong time and wrong place. Sorry. I'm sorry.'

He held up a pair of scissors. 'For you, Anthony,' he said.

I remember I raised my hands; perhaps I intended to do something, I don't know.

Titanic put the scissors in his mouth and pushed.

'Oh shit!' Toni shrieked like she was stifling laughter.

Titanic coughed and prised the scissors out. Blood sprayed over the mugs in the sink and the poster and us. Titanic walked unsteadily towards me. He was blinking and making a strange strangled noise as if trying to clear the blockage. He swayed, holding the scissors up.

Keano was pressed up against the sink, Titanic's blood criss-crossing his face. 'Oh man,' he whispered. 'No.'

Titanic fell to his knees. He looked into my eyes and smiled. His white shirt was now crimson. A red puddle was spreading out beneath him. A South African temp girl opened the tea room door, swinging a ginger and mint teabag on a string. She stopped and looked.

Titanic gurgled and held up his arms as if he wanted me to embrace him. Apparently having trouble focussing, he concentrated on the scissors. He tilted his head up and bared his teeth; more blood.

'Don't…' said Toni, but nothing was going to stop this. She turned away.

Titanic gargled something unintelligible, opened his mouth again and rammed the scissors home.

At some point paramedics turned up and covered the body. That's all I remember. I sat in a fag-smelling chair, looking at the drying blood on my hands and shirt.

A young woman introduced herself as Kate. I gave her the standard Anthony Graves assessment: artificial tan, bleach blonde hair; the bossy fitness instructor look. Humourless and therefore a no. Poor Kate; she would never know what she was missing.

Kate led me into a seminar room and said she wanted to interview me. She claimed she was a sergeant with CID. I was so shocked I barely understood what she was on about. That she believed I might be a suspect.

Kate stated she was very interested in the relationship between Titanic and Anthony Graves. 'Why would he say those words?' she asked.

What words? I'd forgotten.

'He spoke to you,' she reminded me. That tilted mouth, the scissors. 'For you.'

'I don't know. Honestly, I don't.'

Kate made some notes on her tablet.

Keano had been taken to hospital in shock. Toni was asked to stay. I don't think the police suspected her of anything but I'm guessing she made some smartass comment which annoyed them and they were getting their own back.

'Your parents are here,' said Kate. 'Downstairs.'

'What? How did they know?'

'I imagine someone rang them.' Kate looked annoyed. Perhaps she didn't like to see a shapeless lazy man cry. Perhaps she just didn't like me. 'You can go home,' she said.

I was waiting at the lift when the paramedics wheeled Titanic's body out of the offices.

'You probably want to get a different lift, sir,' said one of the paramedics. I thought I detected sarcasm in the confident professional way he spoke. The fizz in my head grumbled. It wanted out. No way.

I mumbled a vague thanks and looked at the floor. We waited.

Gordon Rice walked out of the office as we waited. Just what I needed: the big boss. Gordon was a friendly fifty year old bloke with a taste for bad cardigans. He stared at the prone figure under the sheet. 'Christopher Samson.' Tears were close. 'That poor man…'

Gordon tried to take my hand. His was shaking. He was in such bad shape he seemed like he needed an ambulance himself. I felt uncomfortable with his grief and him touching me and the ambulance men staring and the body under the sheet and the lift not coming, that without thinking about it I pushed again. The power pulsed out from behind my eyes. I gasped. The other men flinched.

Immediately, the paramedic men were sincere and attentive. 'You okay, sir? I'm sorry–' said the paramedic.

'Anthony…' said Gordon. 'What can I do for you? What do you want from me?'

'Gordon,' I said. I had that ecstatic rush again. The lights dancing in my eyes. But not as bad as before. In fact, not bad at all. 'Please. I appreciate your concern. But I need space. Go. All of you; please leave me alone.' Rude perhaps, but I'd had a rough day and he did ask.

The lift door pinged and opened. Gordon got in the lift with the body and the ambulance men. Poor bastard.

Three minutes later, my own lift turned up. That power still rushed through me. I felt fantastic.

That didn't last. As I hit the ground floor, there they were. My mum and dad, standing in reception, lost in the wide lobby with its designer furniture, security gates and glass doors. They couldn't have looked any more out of place. Dad was wearing his work clothes: jeans, old trainers and a paint-streaked jumper. He chewed gum and fidgeted.

Mum was a rock. She wasn't going to let the building intimidate her. As I walked through the security turnstile, she looked at me. I had the horrible feeling she blamed me for what had happened. 'It's late. Come on,' she said.

The whole building had been sealed, just because of Chris. A bored constable lifted a crime scene tape for the Graves family to walk under. 'Watch yourselves out there,' he warned us.

I asked what he meant but the constable had already turned away to talk to his mate. Mum and dad were blank-faced, determined to hold in their emotions until they felt safe. They knew what was coming. We pushed our way through the revolving glass door and out of the building.

The twilight street was full of news teams. As soon as we walked onto the pavement they were on us. Traffic churned past in the Euston Road. London people were going home. Normality and the outside air hit me and I felt sick. Someone snapped on a harsh bright light. We blinked in its gaze.

'Did you see it?' one posh-voiced bloke kept asking. 'Did you witness the murder?'

'It wasn't a murder,' I replied. My voice was lost in the jostling crowd. They were climbing over each other to get to us. The whole situation was ridiculous; a clump of people tying us into a knot of wires and microphones.

'Look…' I remember hearing my dad's hesitant voice as he tried to push through. He sounded coarse and feeble. A microphone knocked me in the mouth and dad tried to shove the people away. He was losing his temper.

Mum remained stone-faced despite the jostling. She wasn't going to crack, not for anybody.

I realised it hadn't occurred to either of them to call a taxi. They were going for a bus stop. Suddenly, I was embarrassed by the pair of them. I snapped. I got another crack in the face and that was it.

I snarled: 'Get lost!'

From my head, along the track, through the dark tunnel and out.

The knot unravelled. Instantly. The reporters and camera people and sound people and passers-by and everyone. They just stopped what they were doing and walked away. Some of them ran.

Traffic was still crawling down the road, three crowded lanes disappearing beneath a flyover, a last gasp of April sun reflecting off their windscreens. The journalists swarmed over railings and dropped into the road. I saw a man slip and fall heavily, coins spilling from his coat pockets. He grabbed the door of a blue Land Cruiser and pulled himself up. The driver yelled abuse through his closed window. Cars braked and tooted as the people threaded their way towards whatever destination they were so determined to reach.

The three of us, the Graves family, stood alone outside the glass tower.

Mum and dad looked round as if this might be a joke and the punchline was about to swipe us in the side. The silence was palpable, a vacuum. Only the growling engines from the lines of cars disturbed the London evening.

I was breathless. A scary, wild feeling was growing in me. They had gone; every one.

I made them go away. Titanic. The paramedics, Gordon Rice, the journalists. And it was easy.

Chapter 5

What did I do that first night? I did what members of the Graves family always did, no matter what went on. I watched telly. We all watched telly.

Dad plonked himself down on the sofa and snapped open a can of Guinness. He seemed miffed. Annoyed that after a hard day's self-employed plumbing he'd had to come into London to pick up a naughty boy.

Mum was cold, considering a man had shoved a pair of scissors into his mouth in front of her beloved one and only. She dropped a plate of reheated fish cakes onto my lap as I watched the news. Perhaps she could sense I was not entirely the same son who had gone to work that morning.

Although Chris's suicide was the news headline, much more time was spent on what happened outside. Perhaps because the TV people had actual footage. Perhaps because it involved their own.

Three Graves' mouths stopped moving as we saw ourselves on the screen.

There was the Tower, there was the Euston Road, and there were the three of us.

The picture bobbles as the camera operator is shoved. It stabilises to home in on a distorted shuffling creature that focusses to become me. My features are dark against the light from the building behind. Mum and dad stand like waxwork dummies. An unflattering camera light illuminates my startled face.

'Did you witness the murder?' asks a voice.

'It wasn't a murder,' my screen self replies.

Dad says: 'Look…'

We move; I get a crack in the face from a camera and snarl 'Get lost' and suddenly the camera swirls away and we're looking at moving cars and red London buses.

Cutting back to the presenters, it's as if they are seeing the footage for the first time. The female one comes to her senses, looks at the autocue, adds a jolly lilt to her voice and informs us that some of the journalists have yet to reappear. They truly are lost.

At ten o'clock, the news on the other side showed the same pictures from a slightly different angle. There I was again, caught in the light. The expression didn't change, but I knew that they had captured the moment when I had mentally wished the reporters away. And the reporters had gone.

Dad asked me if I was all right.

I swallowed. Those reprocessed fishcakes repeated on me. They tasted of plastic. 'Yeah,' I said.

When I went to bed, I got scared. Just me and it: alone together. I could feel the psychic circuit board lodged inside. Humming and itching and ready for action.

I kept mentally scratching the itch, like it was a blister or a boil. Whenever I did, I felt a tingle.

The vision of Chris shoving the scissors into his mouth was too strong for sleep.

I thought about things.

What was the potential bad here? What were the consequences? Was I sick? Dreaming the whole thing? Was I simply psychotically deluded? Maybe there was no power; I just thought there was. Christ, maybe I was insane and the power was my mind attempting to make sense of some weird shit that happened today at work.

I decided to zap everyone in the whole world. Might as well. Better to be safe. I shifted and stared at the poster over my bed. Alice Cooper in all his daft finery. Toni had put that poster up when we were at school. Must have been fourteen. Days when we lounged on my bed listening to her terrible taste in music; as exhausted and self-absorbed as only teenagers can be. I hated Alice Cooper; which is why Toni put the poster up. That stupid monster face gurned at me in the dark.

Righty-ho. Everyone in the whole world. Consider yourself mine!

Bang, fizz, there it went.

Or did it? It didn't feel right. The shot hadn't fired.

My room was almost silent; only the Xbox humming on standby.

I screwed up my face and tried again. Push. Push push push. Go. Everyone in the world: be my slave! Now!

My head hummed. No rush of chemicals to the brain; no comedown. Just a headache from all that squeezing. I thought about Titanic, the scissors going in over and over again. I was ridiculously, childishly frightened. I let out a moan but not the power. That just sat in my head waiting for whatever trigger made it work. 'Okay!' I said out loud. 'Job done. I rule the world.' Only the impersonal, inhuman sound of the Xbox remained. The scissors. The spray of blood.

My ears roared and I remembered yet again: those scissors plunging, over and over. I was about to faint. Luckily, that sparked some sleepy need and I didn't wake up until–

I spent next morning sat around the house waiting for my slaves to turn up. Slaves or the police; one lot had to arrive. Mum and dad had already gone to work. I think they were glad to get away from me.

I watched daytime telly in my t-shirt and leggings, spooning cereal into my face. Anything to put off thinking.

At three o'clock, when there was real danger of mum and dad coming home, at which point I knew my courage would leave me, I opened the front door. I was still wearing my crappy t-shirt and not-quite-pyjama leggings.

Across the road, the Uddins were having some building work done. A parked red van read: CASEY – LOFT CONVERSIONS. Scaffolding webbed the detached house. I realised drilling and hammering had been going on and off all day.

The street was quiet now and the van sat on its own. Soon the school run mums and their cars would return to jam up the residents' parking spaces.

As I watched, some builder — perhaps even the great Casey himself — emerged from a hole in the roof and climbed onto the scaffolding. He was carrying a bucketful of broken masonry. Kind of guy I'd be scared of: forty-ish, all practical and ruddy faced; self-sufficient and no-nonsense. I doubt if he'd had an imaginative, self-reflective thought in his life. If I could get him, I could get anyone. He was wearing a hard hat and an untucked blue shirt to hide his beer belly. He clocked me looking at him and although he didn't actually sneer, his expression loomed clearly across the road at me: gay ponce. The usual.

He would do.

I tried to remember yesterday. Titanic. The reporters outside the tower. How had it happened? What had I done?

No, don't think. The builder was climbing in again when I pushed.

The power burst through me. No doubt about it.

The expression on the builder's face changed. Something was added. A certain look I am now far too familiar with.

'You!' I said. 'Stop!'

He did. The builder stood on the scaffold, absolutely rigid.

Okay, perhaps it was coincidence. It could just be that. But he wasn't moving; just looking at me.

What to do? A car rolled past, the driver oblivious to my predicament. Casey, if that's who he was, kept looking. Pigeons trilled their coos from overhead power lines.

I thought of something. I shouted up to him. Something so pointless and silly I laughed out loud.

Casey disappeared back into the house.

I crept back indoors. I sat in the front room, looked out of the window and waited. It hadn't worked. That was that. Load of old bollocks and thank god.

Two minutes later Casey ran out of Mrs Uddin's house, leaving the door wide open. He unlocked his van, got in and drove off at high speed.

I put the TV on. I hoped I'd never see him again.

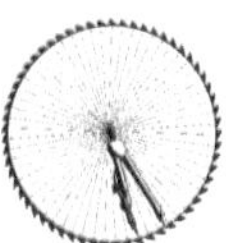

The hands of our mock classic carriage clock ticked round. Time moved so slowly it was physically painful and, although I looked as three forty-five became three fifty-five, I know for a fact it took longer than ten minutes. Cars were pulling into Selsey Road. A horn beeped. I heard the first shriek.

A red film seemed to creep over my eyes and I could hardly walk to the window. Coated in cold sweat, ears clogged and buzzing, I banged my head against the cold glass to fight off a sickness that threatened to overwhelm me. Oh for Christ's sake; enough with the fainting already.

Outside my garden wall, a chubby teenage mum with a buggy was staring. She looked disgusted. Disgusted, self-righteous and venomously amused.

She was looking at the builder.

He still wore his white hard hat. In my humble opinion, the hat worked well against the designer dress he had managed to squeeze into. I was impressed by how enthusiastically the builder had taken on board my suggestion.

He was waving at the returning mums as they brought their children home. Bright red lipstick gleamed on his face. An expensive handbag dangled from one wrist as he waved. He had changed from his practical worker's boots into an uncomfortable looking pair of black high heels.

The dress was green and fitted. He must have had help getting him into something that tight. I could imagine the shop assistant's shocked amusement. Difficult to nail those dress sizes. Those different body shapes.

A dark 4x4 crawled past; one smoked mirrored window lowering to reveal the driver: a woman with unfeasibly black hair speaking into a mobile phone. She held the phone up and snapped a picture of the builder. Her bracelets rattled. In the rear of that cavernous car, a solitary child looked puzzled and afraid.

Neighbours were out on the street; all of them I think. They too were taking their inevitable camera-phone snaps; looking around the street, presumably wondering whether this was a TV stunt. And finally, into Selsey Road Croydon, walked Mrs Uddin, the short Indian lady who had hired this man to convert her loft. She stopped and stared just like the rest.

Casey couldn't look at her. He wasn't enjoying this. In fact, the whole cross-dressing in public concept was profoundly shaming to this undoubtedly deeply macho, uptight and inevitably homophobic manual labourer. But he did it anyway because I'd asked him to.

I had to know. I slouched across the road. The neighbours didn't even look at me. I realised I cared about that. Why weren't they looking? Didn't they know what I'd done? His painted face stared at me. 'Go home,' I said.

Ignoring the stares, Casey walked to his van. He reached into his handbag, took out some keys and unlocked the driver's door.

'Hang on,' I said. Casey turned to look at me. The lipstick shone in the afternoon sun.

I felt sorry for him. But not sorry enough I didn't want him out of my sight so I didn't have to think about him anymore. Come on, he was a builder. You remember what they were like. It didn't kill him.

He just looked at me. No hate in his eyes, no malice. I had to know.

'Why did you do it?' I asked.

The builder's eyes were moist. 'Love,' he told me straight.

I sensed comedy. A dark, cosmic comedy. Laughter: but hysterical laughter if it was ever released out loud. Unhinged laughter.

The builder drove away. No one seemed to link me with him so I went inside, sat on the sofa and watched some snooker.

The world seemed the same. This was the same front room I had grown up in. The sideboards still held old nicknacks from the past: junk I'd made at school that mum had never been able to throw away. The sofa squeaked in the same way when I sat down on it.

The same pictures hung on the walls: me as a kid; the family sitting on a forgotten beach. The room even smelled like it always had.

Apparently, what was different was me.

Two days later, my manager Gordon Rice was stopped by immigration officials in Southampton. He was trying to board a ship to Bilbao. I had forgotten all about him.

The police charged him with murder. I don't think they knew what else to do. They just couldn't believe he was innocent. After all, why else would he up and get a ferry to Bilbao?

There was an underlying sigh of relief in the newsreader's tone. At last Titanic's death might make sense. A first clue to explain the unexplainable.

When they got in from work on the third night, mum and dad were different. They were tense. I mean, they had been tense ever since that first day but this was a new level of tense. This was tension upgraded. We ate in silence. Mum spooned out ice cream from a plastic tub. Dad drank his Guinness. More Guinness. His Irish Catholic roots were showing, I guess.

I had the feeling words had been spoken behind my back. They were going to tell me something. Finally, mum found the courage.

'The police talked to us today, Anthony.'

'Mm?' Inevitably, the ever bumbling Anthony Graves spoke through a mouthful of mash.

'About you. They say your boss; that Rice, he keeps talking about you.'

'They say you told him to go.' Dad brought his can up and drank, as if hiding his mouth so he could deny he spoke.

'To Spain?' I asked.

'Away,' said dad. He kept the can at his lips. 'What are you up to?'

I couldn't hold myself in any longer. I told them about the builder. I told them everything.

And when I'd done they said they didn't believe me. I don't blame them.

Dad looked old. Despite what he said, he looked scared. Mum was… just different. She wore a strange expression, reminiscent of the way she'd looked at me outside the tower.

Perhaps she was just concerned. After all, if your lonely slightly overweight un-ambitious son suddenly starts blabbing on about super powers, I guess any mother is going to think Columbine and start searching his bedroom for firearms.

'So: the police?'

'That's what they say.' Mum kept looking at me. 'They are going to ring you tomorrow.'

'Why don't they just come round? Why don't they just come round and talk to me?'

'Anthony. They want to know what happened with Mrs Uddin's builder. They say when they arrested him all he wanted to talk about was you. What did you do?'

I laughed. That big burly bloke in the street looking like the worst tranny in the world. 'Oh come on,' I said. 'It *was* funny.'

Dad stood up. He just wanted to get away.

Sadness overwhelmed me. Something had changed between us. This must be what it's like when your kid heads off for university. This kid you've raised from a baby; when you've had a certainty that is suddenly not certain at all. There's no going back.

Don't let this happen, I thought. I wanted to hold my dad and beg him to bring everything back just the way it had been. The Graves family might not have had the most exciting of existences, but it was our life and we had been comfortable. I wanted to tell dad I was sorry. Whatever I'd done… none of it was my fault. I could change it all back again. 'Look,' I said and felt my voice break in my throat. 'I won't use it on you. Ever. I promise.'

Dad made his decision. 'Don't be stupid,' he said. 'Don't be so bloody stupid. Load of old cobblers, the lot of it.'

And he walked out.

I looked at mum.

'Talk to the police,' she said.

I stood up and she flinched. She flinched away from me; her son.

He did believe. They both did. I knew it.

Chapter 6

The police rang the next day, just like mum said. A chief inspector. He was very polite. I forget his name.

A car was coming to pick me up. Two minutes. I said I could make my own way but the chief inspector insisted. They just wanted a statement. I wasn't going to be arrested or anything. The receiver hung limply against my ear.

I understood: this was a done deal. My stomach hurt. Stabbing pains. Happened to me a lot in those days. The nerves. Funny how nervous I could get then.

I felt the fear of the innocent; of those unfamiliar with authority suddenly forced into confrontation. I didn't know my rights; I wasn't going to cause any fuss. Like all innocents, I didn't believe it mattered to them whether it was fair or not; nothing you said would make any difference. I nearly told the chief inspector to get lost. I nearly zapped him over the phone. Would it work? Give it a go…

Mum came down the stairs. I thought she had gone to work. She looked at me. Twenty-nine years of everyday life kicked in and I said yes into the phone.

I thought about using the zap but then I realised I already had. Hadn't I sat in my room last night and got everyone in the world? So why wasn't the world obeying?

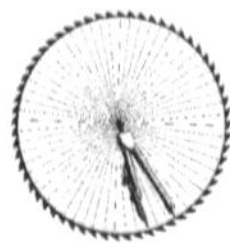

I thought they'd take me to Croydon Police Station but instead the two uniform guys drove me right into town, to Marylebone.

I had to convince myself that whatever was waiting for me couldn't be too bad. I hadn't actually murdered anybody. I was just as much a victim of Titanic's suicide as anybody else. This interview would be routine; one of dozens. What did the police know about that thing in my head?

We drove through the dull traffic-clogged streets of South London: Tooting and Clapham and Balham. Serious Bengali and African faces looked at me through the windows. I sensed a mix of empathy and sympathy. Was I a copper? A copper's pull? My experience of the police up until yesterday was nil.

We passed The Oval and up the long road to Elephant and Castle. The two policemen with me stayed quiet. What would they have been told and what would they believe? A radio jabbered.

Waterloo roundabout, then Bridge. Aldwych, Kingsway and west along the Euston Road.

London: huge, historical and fantastic. Only a suburbanite could feel so romantic about the centre of a city.

I thought about all the rich people and hustlers who lived here. Here in the middle of things. They never had to endure a bruising commute every day just for the pleasure of getting to work. They never had to leave anywhere in time for the last train. Never had to travel out, never had to live near a chicken shack or a kebab house.

I don't know why the policemen chose this route, but we just happened to do a drive-by of the tower where I worked and where this had all started. Maybe they thought this would shake me up. It did.

As we waited at the traffic lights at the north end of Tottenham Court Road, I saw they'd reopened the tower. Shirt-sleeved men and stylish city women smoked cigarettes outside the revolving doors. An early summer sun was poking through the clouds and you could see a fresh energy in the people. The long winter slouch was over.

Titanic's death was already part of the crowded, colourful tapestry making up the London legend. This city absorbed everything.

The police car shuffled through the lanes and eventually we took a left down posh Marylebone High Street. My mood turned accordingly. The buildings here were old, tall and serious. Thick stone, closed doors and blacked-out windows. Doctors? Lawyers? Embassies?

Someone at this police station was serious. I began to wonder if maybe they had scientists who knew things.

Why had they told mum and dad first? To make sure I would actually get in the car?

Had the chief inspector hoped I would do a runner, like Gordon Rice?

We pulled up next to a reinforced concrete slab of a building. I'd seen it before on the news. This was the police station where they took the terrorists.

Apart from the guys with me, there were no police outside. Just what looked like — yes, inevitably — a builder's van. I thought about yesterday and did a mental comedy gulp.

I may not have mentioned this before, but conflict situations are not ones in which this initial incarnation of Anthony Graves traditionally excelled. His first instinct in the face of officialdom was to do exactly what was asked of him. I have been told this stems from a strict upbringing but I don't think those psychiatrist types know what they're talking about. I never had a strict upbringing; we just didn't want trouble.

So I followed the two police officers inside. At last one of them spoke. He told me not to worry.

Now, I don't know about you but when a policeman escorting you to an interview concerning a suspicious death tells you not to worry, you're going to worry. That's probably true all over the world.

I worried. I worried a lot.

The station was teeming. It was full of people going about their business in an orderly fashion and they all looked at me. Clocked me, you might say. They seemed to be storing my face in their memory in case they had reason to see me again. So they could arrest me.

I saw a couple of painters in their white overalls doing up a reception area. They kept their eyes low, like they didn't want to attract attention.

A trio of uniformed policewomen were on their way out. They also looked at me like they were saving my image onto their brain hard-drives. The women were stocky and wore blonde ponytails under their black caps, like all WPCs seem to.

'This way,' said a voice. Familiar but one I had trouble placing. Another woman. The one from the other day. In uniform. Kate the Sergeant. 'Hi, Anthony, how are you?' She acted like she was pleased to see me.

'Fine.'

'Thanks for coming down.' She sounded very sincere. 'We're all waiting for you.'

'All?'

Kate smiled. 'Nothing to worry about. There will be four of us.'

'Four?'

'This is a unique case. Complicated. Do you have a problem with that, Anthony?'

'No,' I replied. 'What about a lawyer?'

'We're just taking a statement,' she said, a little too quickly. 'Of course, if you think you need one…'

'I'll manage,' I said.

Chief Inspector Whateverhisname smiled as Kate and I entered the office.

'Sit down, Anthony,' he said, utterly relaxed. A minion indicated a chair. Four coppers were beaming at me like I was their best friend and we were about to play a fun little game.

I tried to think of how best to act. How do you sound innocent? Were innocent people calm and relaxed in their innocence? If they were I was doomed. Were they petrified; gabbling out their insistence of innocence?

What did guilty people sound like?

Me. They sounded like me.

He was a big man, this chief inspector, like a rugby player. One of those blokes who's so big you wonder how a human being can be that large.

He was sweating. Not surprising; this little office was far too warm. Radiators blazed away. Five of us stuck in here and not enough room.

'Anthony,' he said. 'Anthony Graves.' He looked at me. They did know. They had to. They knew all about me and this thing in my head. Perhaps they even knew how to get it out. I realised I wasn't sure I wanted it out. The silence was painful. I had to break it.

'This… I'm sorry.' I coughed. Shit.

'Why do you say that, Anthony?' asked Kate.

To be honest, I was fed up with everyone using my name all the time. Especially Kate. It was like they were all using tricks they'd learned from seminars on people skills. Special police seminars on how to relax people and keep them calm. They'd obviously forgotten that I was a civil servant just like them; I'd been on those same bullshit courses too.

'Nothing,' I said back. 'Sorry.'

'We just want to talk to you,' said the chief inspector. They just couldn't keep still, these policemen. They were fidgeting all over the place.

Why did it need four cops, including the Chief and Kate, just to talk to me? The young policeman behind the Chief looked at his uniformed mate at the door. They shared a glance. It meant something.

'Anthony,' said the Chief. He had a plummy Oxbridge accent; something you wouldn't expect from a cop. I wondered if he was who he said he was. I wonder if he had been fast-tracked.

I sat down. Computers hummed around me. A DVD player and telly combination sat on a desk. What was that all about? Were they going to show me a film?

'Look, what do you want? If you think I've done something…' I tried to sound tough, but I think it was that Oxbridge accent more than anything that made me feel dumb. Coppers were supposed to have monotone estuary accents full of dull menace. This guy sounded like he was about to head off to Thailand on his gap year. I had the feeling he knew exactly what I was thinking.

'All right, Anthony,' he said. 'This is what it's about.'

'I haven't done anything.' I meant it. Although a vision of that builder in a dress wouldn't go away.

'Shut up,' said the Chief. Just like that. 'Now, you listen.' He looked round at Kate, as if expecting her to intervene. She kept her expression neutral, on me, all business.

The Chief looked back at me. 'I want to know why we've got your supervisor, Rice, in our cells. I want to know why he's telling me the reason he tried to leave the country on a P&O to Bilbao is because you told him to. I want to know why he keeps bursting into tears saying he's failed you. You.'

'He tried to kill himself, Anthony,' said Kate. 'He tried to smash his brains out in the cell.'

The Chief sat back, as placid and calm and unfathomable as a mountain lake. 'I want you to tell me why.'

I was… stunned. I couldn't… couldn't think, couldn't move. Rice? *Gordon?*

I hadn't told him to go to Spain. I hadn't told him anything. I hardly knew him, for Christ's sake.

Except, just except.

The Chief nodded at Kate. She took a breath. It was almost funny.

'Anthony Graves,' she started. 'You have the right…'

And I'd had enough. 'Bollocks to this,' I said.

The push came easily; it came in a flood. It gushed out. Much more powerful than before.

The Chief twitched. He sat back in his seat. 'Oh Christ,' he said.

The other cops, they just looked horrified. No: appalled.

'Anthony…' Kate said, the blood draining from her tanned face. 'I'm sorry. Sorry.'

'All right, all right. Let me out of here. Everybody; just let me go.'

The Chief started to cry. Fat tears were growing and dropping from his blue eyes. I couldn't stop looking at him.

'I'm so sorry, Anthony,' he said. 'Please… please… off you go.'

Even then, I still wasn't convinced they weren't playing a game. 'Really? You won't shoot me or anything?'

They looked like they didn't even understand the question.

This was no act. No one could pretend this well.

'So I'll go then,' I said. 'Open the door.'

The Chief stood up as if to follow me. 'Please, let me help you.' His posh voice was broken with emotion.

'Good idea, Chief Inspector,' I said. 'Escort me out.' I looked at their four anxious faces. Kate. Should I bring Kate along?

'Just close the door behind me,' I whispered.

I didn't need the chief inspector. They moved aside. The cops, uniform and plain-clothes. The admin staff, even the prisoners in their plastic handcuffs. Everyone shrank away, smiling in deference. Their eyes gleamed. They looked grateful. Somehow, I had them. That one push. I wasn't even in the same room; they weren't looking at me or anything but I got them anyway.

'Thank you, Chief Inspector,' I said as he unlocked the security door into the reception area. 'You can go now. Tell the others, you must all stay here and not talk to anyone.' He nodded seriously. The officers at the reception desk nodded also. I pointed at them: 'No one go anywhere,' I said in my best menacing tone. 'Or else.'

The chief inspector closed the door and left me there in reception. The people waiting there looked at me with devotion. I headed for the door.

As I walked out, one of the painters was bringing a couple of pots of paint in from his van. We stood in the doorway in front of each other.

'Sorry. Thanks,' I said as I stood aside. He walked past with his pots. What I was thanking him for I neither knew nor cared.

'Wanker,' he whispered.

'Thanks,' I said again.

'No worries mate,' he replied and walked into the police station. God knows what he found there. For some reason, that 'mate' brought a smile to my face.

I stood in Marylebone High Street and wondered what to do. Habit came to my rescue. It was lunchtime and at work lunchtime meant Oxford Street with its crowds of lunchtime shoppers.

Chapter 7

The world had not changed. London was too warm and Oxford Street swarmed with lunchtime shoppers getting in each other's way. I still had to walk everywhere. I was still just me.

Only: that electrical charge continued to hum in my brain. It wanted more. It always wanted more. What was I supposed to do? These oblivious shoppers brushed past me, hurrying in their chaotic, endless stream. I thought again about zapping the lot; getting it over with. Their bustle and energy seemed misplaced, it seemed ridiculous. This ants' nest of hurry and rush with no purpose except to buy rubbish and kill off their hours. I was sick of the whole world.

It just didn't happen. I didn't let the push win. I was just too frightened of what might come next; how much the world might change.

In the end I took the Northern Line to Tooting to see Toni. She was still on leave after Titanic's demise. At the very least, I would get a beer out of Toni. We did the text thing and met in our regular South London pub.

These days, The Bull is apparently a shrine, but back then it was not one of your modern London boutique public houses. Gentrification had glanced at The Bull and passed over with a discreet 'not today'. Back then it was old and carpeted. At half past two in the afternoon only the hardiest boozers were in attendance:

the impoverished, the bulbous-nosed, the all-dayers. A migraine spring sun latticed through filthy windows.

It took me two pints before I could tell Toni the whole story and even I didn't believe it. Her reaction was not exactly what I expected. Toni crinkled up her black painted lips and said, 'Show us.'

If there's one thing I knew from those six months flatting with Toni, it was that she was a determined sensualist. She believed firmly in black: hair, t-shirt, jeans and Doc Martins; all black. She also believed firmly in drinking alcohol. Toni believed she could tell the difference between lagers. The week off I had given her, thanks to Titanic's suicide, had brought the best out in her. The alcoholic side. Great, scary and fun. Just don't live with her.

'You believe me?' I asked. I finished my pint. Already I was hungover. 'Get off.'

'Proof is in the pudding, right?' Toni jabbed a beer mat for emphasis.

'What do you suggest, dear Antoinette?'

She waved in the vague general direction of the bar. 'Magda. Get her to fetch us drinks. Free drinks.'

I looked at the lovely Lithuanian blonde girl behind the counter. The delicate ring in her nose glinted. She was new and wary and hardly understood her way around the delicate, Jane Austen-esque nuances of a British pub. There seemed something wrong about this setup. It felt like one of those unfunny telly programmes where posh people prank members of the public. It felt like bullying. Tie that to a feeling that whatever was in my head was too wild and powerful to mess with. That letting it out always bounced back on me. Repercussion after repercussion and more repercussion. But Toni knew me better than anyone in the world. She was my friend, and I already suspected I was going to need friends.

The juke box was playing R&B garbage. I don't remember the song. I looked at Magda and tried to push without thinking; trying, if I could, to keep it *minimal*. Motes of dust flitted in the shafts of sunlight. Magda flinched and I knew I'd hit her. 'Two pints,' I shouted across to her. An old black man in a pork pie hat looked up. 'Please,' I added.

As Toni and I watched, Magda hurried. She put a pint glass under the plastic pump, filled it up and moved on to a second. Her hands were shaking so much she rattled the glass.

Toni just looked on. I don't think she believed, not really. Not even when the girl placed the glasses on our table. 'Is okay?' she asked. She was practically panting waiting for my answer.

'How much?' I replied.

She looked at me; lovely and terrified. 'I not understand…'

'Don't worry,' I said. I felt shitty. I'd done a really cheap thing. 'Go back to work. Please forget it. Be happy.'

She scuttled away back to the bar, suddenly smiling. She began to sing along with the R&B.

Toni just stared at me.

'What?' I said.

She picked up her glass and sipped. 'Fuck me,' she said. She couldn't look at me. Her hands shook.

'Toni, what is this?'

'*This* is something… special.'

'I don't know what to do.'

Toni swigged my remaining beer. 'You twat,' she said. 'You've just won the fucking lottery! Fourteen zillion to one and that.'

'You're pissed.'

Her face was red and looked even more wolfish than usual. 'You're the guy that got hit by lightning. Picked the numbers. Oh, they're gonna hate you.'

'Who?'

'How does it work? Is it hypnosis? Is it like…' she affected a TV hypnotist pose, 'Look into my eyes…' She waggled her fingers.

'I don't know. Sometimes it doesn't work. It comes out in little bits.' I couldn't tell her that a vast reservoir of the power seemed to be hanging out in my subconscious and so far I had only managed to open a tiny little window.

'Do strong-willed people resist? Like in what I said: hypnosis? Can they resist what you ask them if they wouldn't normally…'

That little wild shine in her eye dimmed, just for a moment. The implication was starting to hit home. I had the sudden feeling Toni was jealous. 'Does anyone say no?'

'I don't know,' I answered. 'It's not really like that. It's more like…'

'More like what?'

'Forget it.'

'Like what?'

'Like they fall in love with me…'

Toni didn't laugh. Instead, she calculated. 'My friend, we are gonna have some fun today. Let's go.'

Standing up, she caught her chair in the carpet. She stumbled. Again, she giggled. Magda burst into song again, loud and proud. The wrecks in the pub were staring; big grins across their faces. 'God be with you, girl!' shouted the black man in the pork pie hat.

'Toni,' I said. 'I don't think…'

'Don't you get it?' She stared at me. I didn't too much like the stare. Toni was scared and envious and drunk. 'You diddled a fucking police station into letting you walk out. They haven't even come looking for you. And all you can think of is to ring me up for a drink? This is fucking brilliant!' She shook her head. 'Come on.'

'Where?'

'Hammersmith.'

'Hammersmith?'

'Hammersmith. Don't you… look, Graves.' Toni reached for my arm then thought better of it. 'Open your eyes. You can have everything. Whatever you want.' She staggered to the door, opening it for me. The noise of the teatime traffic blared in. 'You are the very definition of the Nietzschean fucking uber super mensch!'

Halfway along the Piccadilly Line, a nodding, reeking drunk tramp in the seat opposite popped open his can of Stella. The smell of him and the lager caught in my already alcohol-fuelled nostrils. What was I doing sharing space with the likes of him in this reeking, sweaty carriage? I realised I could have just got in a cab and blitzed the driver into giving me a free ride. Why *didn't* I get a cab? Why didn't I just commandeer the nearest Porsche driver? Jesus, with a bit of forethought I could avoid the unpleasantness of London Underground for the rest of my life!

I looked at Toni, who was dozing in her seat. That was the kind of thought she would have. She would know how to use this thing.

The wreck drank greedily from his can. It was four-thirty in the afternoon.

I began to wonder how I would feel if this tramp had got this ability instead of me. What if I sat here and knew he had it? What would I do about it?

We motored through Earl's Court, out through the tunnel into the sunlight of Barons Court, then a quick shuffle to the steel and glass of Hammersmith Station.

I was feeling weary now. Three pints in the day had its inevitable effect. The nice lunchtime buzz replaced by a tight, thudding head. Toni shook me out of my doze.

'I just want to sleep,' I said.

She pulled me out of my seat. The mischief was in her. The tube train doors hissed open.

'Get up,' she said. 'We are going to have a laugh.'

Toni led me off the train, up the stairs, through the ticket barrier and out of the station. 'Think about that cop shop,' she said. 'They're probably still there now, busy covering up how they let you go. I can see them, working hard to get you off, not even wondering why. Not even knowing they're doing it.'

'What are we going to do?'

'Look,' she nearly swore at me. I could see her mouth shape the word but hold it in. 'Graves. Anthony. What are all Londoners obsessed with?'

Not a rhetorical question. I had to think. People were looking at us as we strode through the subway towards the river. 'Sex,' I said. 'Money.'

That made Toni laugh. 'You dumbass,' she said in her comedy American movie accent.

I stopped talking. She was making me feel stupid. I didn't much like it.

'We went to that party round here,' I said. 'That girl, what was her name? That posh one?'

Toni led me to the bridge, that beautiful Hammersmith Bridge. The River Thames spread out below us, lined by playing fields, rowing clubs and packed upmarket pubs. I looked upriver. There was a slight haze of smog but the surface was shining like silver in an afternoon 'should be at work' sunlight. A flat tourist boat on its way to Richmond tore a white line across the calm. On the playing fields, a team of private school kids were playing rugby. Despite the cars grinding across the bridge behind me, here was space. I felt a million miles from my grimy Croydon suburb. This was a brighter, better place.

'Which one?' asked Toni, pointing at the North Bank.

'Eh?'

'Fuck's sake!' she snapped. 'Last time here you couldn't shut up about it. Which house do you want?'

So that was what she meant. What all Londoners talk about. Property.

I squinted into the sun and pointed down the tow path, past the pubs. A line of terraced riverside houses, stupendously expensive, buttressed up with black railings and security cameras. So far out of my league, out of anyone's league, it was dumb even thinking about them. The idea that ordinary human beings actually lived in them, people who went to work or lived in a way that I would recognise, seemed ludicrous.

I started to see what Toni meant by fun. I pointed out a particularly prime slab of chichi property. Five storey terrace: all shining windows and freshly spruced white stone. A house that looked particularly tight and buttoned up. An Englishman's castle no doubt empty and paid for by laundered Russian money. Had to be five million and up. 'That one,' I said.

Toni clapped me on the shoulder. 'Location, location, location.'

I was leaning over a railing, peering into the huge front room. Like all posh people's places there didn't seem to be anything inside except wooden floorboards and incomprehensible paintings. The smattering of furniture within seemed like nothing but specks.

Toni was looking at a complex digital number pad bolted to the iron gate. I guess this was what they used as a door bell. There was no sign of life.

A fresh wind blew up from the river as we stood on the paved North Bank. Cyclists and walkers passed by and I knew they were regarding us with suspicion.

'Fuck knows,' said Toni as she stepped away from the number pad. She breathed heavily and I could see the alcohol was wearing off. She was going to have to go to the pub a few houses up in a few minutes and reinvigorate herself. That or go home, which a big part of me was increasingly thinking was a good idea.

Locks clicked from inside the house. I had a strange sense of disappointment. Time juddered to a brief halt. Something had kicked into motion events that were now beyond my ability to stop.

A troubled female oriental face peeked out round the door frame and scowled at us. 'What you want?' An upward, annoyed inflection on the *want.*

The housekeeper. They all had them. Indonesians or Koreans or whatever.

'Good afternoon, madam,' said Toni, brightly.

'You come to hang wallpaper?' she asked, maintaining her position behind the door. Ready to slam.

'No. We've come for the house,' Toni replied. She gestured with sweeping arms. Time I did my stuff. The housekeeper scowled and closed the door.

'Fucking bitch,' Toni snarled.

My natural instinct was fear and obedience. I didn't want to get into trouble. 'Let's go.'

Toni turned to me and I saw the drunken contempt on her face. 'You wimp,' she snarled. 'Fuck off.'

Toni pushed me. I staggered against the railings. A young professional couple of joggers in expensive gear sidestepped past, very deliberately not seeing either of us.

'That's ours,' said Toni, squinting at the house. She kept her voice calm but I felt the anger simmering underneath. 'Take it. Just fucking take it.'

'It's not even her house. Toni. Come on.'

'So? Do the lot of them. Do everyone. I would.'

I laughed and it was Toni's turn to back off. She… quailed.

I really fancied her right at that moment; scared and pale and black and drunk. I thought about zapping her but pushed the impulse away. I don't know if she realised. Perhaps she did and understood she had to go for broke. 'Or let's forget the whole thing. Go back to your little Croydon, with mummy and daddy. Never be able to afford a place, never be allowed to get nothing.'

That did it. She was daring me. I barely thought about what I was doing, but suddenly it burst out. I shovelled the energy. If I pushed that hard these days, it would take out half of London. I felt good, really good, like a boil had been lanced in my brain.

Beyond the black railings, the door clicked. The housekeeper was opening up. Then she was racing to the iron gate to operate the digital pad.

'Shall we?' I asked Toni.

Turned out the housekeeper's name was Mrs Mary Kim. She lived in a rented two bedroom flat in Greenford with her husband and her mother. She worked here in The Mariners — the name of this Hammersmith terrace — six days a week, beginning at five every morning.

The actual owners of the house were the Hargreaves: Peter and Amy. He was the European Corporate Executive Head of a Saudi bank and The Mariners was their London home.

Mrs Kim told me the Hargreaves had kids, two girls both in their teens, who lived in Hammersmith only in the school holidays. Toni and I looked into their bedrooms, up on the top floor. We found lots of photos of healthy, nut-brown haired girls at various ages, in smart school uniforms, posing on horses, on white beaches, in yellow lifejackets on the decks of yachts, holding monkeys in the jungles of Borneo. I asked Mrs Kim their names and she told me: Lydia and Emily.

Mm. I looked at Toni and she winked. She had a filthy mind.

Peter Hargreaves was currently in Dubai. Amy was a corporate solicitor and was at work somewhere in the city, Mrs Kim wasn't quite sure exactly where. Mrs Hargreaves was living in the house on her own at the moment.

I asked Mrs Kim if she had a mobile phone number for Mrs Hargreaves (I wasn't that comfortable calling her Amy). She phoned her boss straight away.

Very quickly, and presumably in a state of utter confusion and anger, Mrs Hargreaves announced she was on her way back to Hammersmith to sort us out. I was tempted to zap her over the phone but to be honest, I still wasn't certain the power would work over a Vodafone network. Before I realised I should try it anyway, Mrs Hargreaves had hung up.

She had some trouble getting a black cab through the choked early evening streets but Mrs Kim made us some tea while we waited. Toni found some beers in the fridge. By the time Mrs Hargreaves got to the house, my lovely ex-girlfriend was firmly asleep on the first floor living room sofa. I was looking over the balcony at the night lights on the Thames. The house had a great view. I couldn't believe I was going to steal the place and no comeback. I wasn't drinking. I wanted a clear head. Mrs Kim found me some Ibuprofen to cope with the hangover.

Mrs Hargreaves was an attractive, intelligent-looking woman of forty-six. I was so scared I got her as soon as she walked in. Mrs Hargreaves had one of those posh accents you don't think people have any more, that make *flat* sound like *flet*. She was wearing a smart Armani business suit, which she told me she'd bought in New York.

I asked her to phone Mr Hargreaves out in Dubai. Again, I was nervous about whether the power would travel all the way to Saudi Arabia over a phone network but I needn't have worried, everything went smoothly, I zapped him fine.

The change of ownership took some time but we were persistent. Between them, the couple sorted out the legal business of signing the house over to me. Mrs Hargreaves was very keen to make sure there were no hiccups. It was clear she was a high-flying finance operator because she knew her contracts. I was glad I didn't have to try and interpret all the legalese. Of course, I got everything.

Mrs Hargreaves told me the full transfer of the deeds for the house would take a couple of days but I wasn't worried. She was fine about moving out straight away and knew plenty of people she could stay with. The family had another large country house out in

Devon, so I hadn't even put them out in any real sense. She insisted I hold on to the furniture and all her personal belongings. I don't think she would have taken them if I'd tried. Actually if I'd tried, she would have.

As Mrs Hargreaves was leaving, Toni woke up.

'What about the kids?' she shouted at her.

Mrs Hargreaves turned on Toni, absolutely furious, until I explained that she was my best friend and whatever Toni wanted, I wanted.

'I'll have them brought down from school tonight,' Mrs Hargreaves told me. 'It might take a while. They're up in Buckinghamshire.'

'Yeah, fetch them down tonight,' Toni insisted. 'Little Lydia and Emily, isn't it?'

'That's right.'

'Hmm. You can go now.' Toni dropped her head back on the sofa again.

Mrs Hargreaves smiled. 'Thank you. I could probably get the girls here for ten.'

'That would be great,' I said. And she went.

I decided to keep Mrs Kim on. For the cooking and cleaning and whatever other domestic duties were required. Only I'd triple, no: quadruple, her money. She could have whatever she wanted. After all, I wouldn't be paying.

Chapter 8

Those weeks at The Mariners were the best fun in my life. I should go back there again; check the place out. Perhaps I'll rediscover that fun.

I know I won't. The memories would upset me. I've got a feeling I'm not too strong these days, and I can't afford not to be strong. I've got a city — a country, a continent — to run.

I remember now, on the first night in Hammersmith, we went out to a pub. Another pub but a million miles from the cramped, despairing South London boozer where we had started the afternoon. This was The Cricketers; one of the plushest watering holes on the bank of the river. We rang Keano and a few others. After a few hours' solid drinking, I invited everyone back to mine. They all came.

At some point in the night, the two Hargreaves girls turned up in a taxi. They were rather frightened, expecting to see their mum rather than a pack of drunks in their house. I'd forgotten all about the Hargreaves girls.

Lydia and Emily were fifteen and sixteen. They were privately educated, slim and haughty. Way out of my league. Only now I could have anyone I wanted.

Although… not that night, not with Lydia and Emily Hargreaves. Because when I blearily realised who they were, I was so ashamed I let them go. I was drunk but I made sure they got out of the house alive. I told them to get back in the taxi and go and find their mum.

I didn't even zap them. Toni was annoyed with me, but she knew not to push it. I managed to get drunk enough to forget all about mind powers; to be free again.

After that party fizzled out, we had another. A slightly more modest party because this power of mine, it doesn't actually do anything useful like make hangovers easier to endure.

One night we went clubbing. And not to Cinderella's in Croydon. To Inferno's (apostrophe deliberate) in London's Mayfair: the one where the celebs and the footballers go.

This was a memorable one. I learned something that night.

Actually, now it makes me laugh to remember, because Toni and Keano and I had some fun with the bouncers.

The club was a discreet-looking place from the outside. Its presence on the street was marked only by the lines of punters trying to get in. All very upmarket. Not for the likes of Toni, Keano and my humble self.

As we strode to the front of the queue — past the lines of dolled-up blondes and their property developer or mobile phone tycoon or investment broker menfolk — we were approached by the bouncers who politely but firmly told us to bugger off.

Toni and Keano were in good spirits; literally, after consuming half a bottle of vodka each in our free taxi ride. They smiled at me, knowing what was coming.

I looked at the bouncers: one white, one black, both huge. They glared with their best R&B take-no-shit polished LA gangsta stares. They wore the uniform: creaseless tuxedo, funny curly wired earpiece, shaved domed heads, sunglasses.

I felt like a conjurer about to perform his first trick. I even waggled my fingers.

'You two!' I yelled at the bouncers. The queue came alive. They were suddenly exuberant, looking forward to a good old piece of street theatre. They presumably imagined fun involving amusing, yet incredibly brutal, violence upon myself and my friends. Well, I'd give them theatre all right.

The two bouncers chose not to look at me despite my shout. I was beneath their notice. A familiar tactic.

All right then, I thought. No mercy. Toni and Keano looked at me expectantly. I gave those bouncers both barrels.

Only it didn't happen. I pushed again. Come on, power. Do your fucking stuff. The crowd watched me, wondering what the hell I was up to. They were bored of me.

'Come on, Graves,' said Toni.

The black giant at last made a gesture. 'Yeah, all right. You three. Fuck off now.' He couldn't have sounded less interested.

'Get them!' Toni commanded.

I couldn't. My sphincter was tightly clenched; blocked. 'Shut up,' I said. 'Let me think.'

'We should go,' said Keano. He turned away.

We were off the bouncers' radar now. They were too professional to come and sort us out. They didn't need to. We weren't any threat. We were less than insects to them. The mocking beautiful crowd was slowly shifting into the club. But not us. We were outside. The provincials. The nobodies.

Toni glared at me. Her drinking made her reckless. I remembered her when she was drunk. In that flat we rented. The picking away; the disappointment in her chosen partner; the need. 'Same old Graves,' she said.

Anger flared up; a vodka-fuelled burst of rage. Perhaps all the anger that had waited since that morning in April. I raised my fists and I saw Toni recoil. She was terrified. I felt the power build to bursting point and she knew it. Her time had come.

Only, only, I turned away and could almost see comic book sparks of energy as they blasted out from me. I looked at Toni and Keano and that power in my brain wanted them; it wanted them sooo badly because I knew them. I just wanted to gather them in and bathe them in the power. But no. God knows how but I forced myself to bend those lines of energy away. Into the crowd. That sneering crowd and those tosser bouncers.

The two giants reeled. The crowd in the line oohed like they were watching fireworks.

And when the bouncers' eyes met mine, they were wet and shining.

I turned to Toni and Keano, who gaped at me. They seemed to me to be fully aware of their near miss. I realised everyone was looking at me: them, the crowd, the bouncers, passers-by, drivers. I felt great. A bubble had burst. I felt good-humoured and relaxed and aware I needed to break the tension. I wanted to get this party started. And this power: I could aim it.

I said to the bouncers, the big black one; the big white one. 'Boys,' I said. 'I'm Anthony Graves. And I am here to change your lives. The time has come. No more violence, no more aggression. I want you to make love. To each other, in the street. Set an example,' at which point the laughter bubbled up. I managed to say: 'A love example,' before snorting up alcohol induced joyous tears.

I waved Toni and Keano to the club entrance. Tentatively, they obeyed.

The bouncers started undressing. They couldn't do it fast enough. As they got to grips with each other, my friends and I sauntered into Inferno's. You know what: we had a great night.

After a week, Keano told me he was leaving.

We were on the second floor balcony, stretched out on sun-loungers, eating eggs and freshly smoked kippers whilst watching the commuters stream across the bridge. Mrs Kim was a great cook.

Toni was still in bed with some bloke she'd picked up. Life was good. We were getting up later and later. We were wearing brand new, thick furry John Rocha robes; a result of yesterday's shopping spree. I say shopping. Money never changed hands.

I felt a little sting of anger when he told me. Keano was a really old friend. We had started at work on the same day and I thought the two of us had really hit it off. We liked the same books, when I bothered to read them. Keano wasn't a looker; too pale and quiet for that, but he was always up for a laugh. I thought he liked me. I didn't want him to go. My throat was dry.

The light wooden stairs creaked. Mrs Kim was bringing up more coffee. Keano was fiddling with his mobile phone. What was wrong with him? Wasn't he having the best time?

'Why?' I asked.

Keano looked up through his thick specs. His obvious sincerity made me uncomfortable. 'Okay, Ant. What it is: you scare me shitless.'

'Keano, I'd never do you. I promise.'

'Yeah, I know,' he said. 'Thing is. None of this feels right, you know? Okay, it's a laugh getting one over on the rich poshos but don't you see?'

'See what?'

Keano stood up. 'We haven't… earned what we've taken.'

'Bullshit,' I snapped, and he flinched. Yes. He was still scared. Good. At my side, Mrs Kim glared at Keano with something like hatred.

'Ant,' he said. 'It can't last. You can have anything, get people to do anything. There don't seem to be any limits. You're going to change. Look at Toni. She fucking scares me too. She's going over the edge, going nuts. Pretty soon you're going to lose patience with her…'

Now I really was angry. 'How many times can I say it? I'd never do her! Or you, or anyone I know!'

'You say that now. You mean it now. But it can't last.'

'Keano!' I don't know why I shouted. I still didn't understand what reaction that would provoke. Keano turned white. He tripped against the breakfast table and fell to the panelled floor. Mugs and the cafetière rolled around, ringing. Jesus, I hadn't meant to…

'You okay?'

'Ant, please…'

Mrs Kim reacted. 'I clear up.' She stabbed a finger at the prone Keano. 'You upset Anthony!'

'All right, Mrs Kim,' I said. I moved to help Keano. He shot up like he'd got an electric shock, scurrying towards the far wall.

'No!' he shrieked. 'I'm fine. I'm going to get changed and go. Sorry.'

His hands were shaking. But credit to him, he gave me one last try. 'Ant,' he said. His voice trembled but he was brave. He was a brave bloke, Keano. 'Think about the people you've controlled already. So many.'

That was true. Obviously, our occupation of The Mariners hadn't gone unnoticed. We'd had solicitors, the police, neighbours, bailiffs, the council, all coming round wondering just who the hell had walked in and convinced two of the most powerful people in London to give up their home. And they'd all walked away satisfied. I could see what Keano was getting at. But I'd told them straight off. We were all in this together. It was supposed to be fun. That was the whole point.

'Thing is,' he said. 'There's always going to be more. For every one you send away, you're going to get two back. And you're going to do them. I think, and I've been doing some checking, there are people you don't even know you've got and they're helping you stay safe. But… they're still going to keep coming and you're going to have to keep getting them.'

'Please, Keano,' I said. 'I don't… don't want you to go. You're my mate.'

He chewed his lip. A genuine bloke. He even still liked me. But, as he had admitted, he was scared shitless. Although now I think back on that confrontation, I think I saw something more than fear in his eyes. Keano was probably the best friend I ever had. I think ultimately, he pitied me.

Not that I realised anything of this at the time. I just looked at the floor, waiting for this whole scene to be over.

'You could stop this, you know,' said Keano.

'Stop it?' I laughed. I hadn't expected that. 'How can I do that?'

'If you can zap them, I guess you can unzap them. I think you'd have to.'

'Why?'

He was eyeing me warily. Perhaps he thought what he was telling me was going to make me angry. Angry enough to do something about it.

'There's no half-measures,' he said. 'I reckon that's how it's going to have to be with you. I think you'll have to get everybody.'

He stopped. 'Okay, Ant. If I can't… If we really are mates, please do me this favour.'

I knew what was coming. 'Okay…' I said.

'Let me go. Just, let me go now. Please. I'm… I'll beg you if you like.'

I looked out over the balcony down at the churning, shining summer water. I should have protested, should have kicked off a good old mates' argument. I think we could have sorted something out between us. He might have helped guide me on what the hell I was supposed to do. But I couldn't. I didn't. Getting to grips with my situation just wasn't in me.

'Yeah, okay,' was what I said instead. 'Go.'

'Thanks,' I heard him whisper, and he scuttled away.

Of course, the media got onto the fact that parts of London were turning strange. There were too many affected people out there now for my actions not to be noticed. There were two girls claiming that somebody had brainwashed their mum and dad into handing over a house. There was the unsettling and gory Euston Tower suicide; there was Gordon Rice the mild mannered manager in the cells having gone stark staring mad. Not mentioned by the media was the staff of armed Met coppers who had barricaded themselves into a maximum security police station in central London and were refusing to come out.

The trouble was nobody could piece any of these bizarre events together. What was the big picture? Because, of course, there had to be a *big picture*.

On the news and in the papers, they interviewed politicians who spoke about cover-ups and corruption. Somebody blamed terrorists. Muslims came on to deny everything and throw the blame back. Someone even dug out the suggestion that the water supply of London had been laced with a hallucinogenic drug. The stock market was down; there was tension and uncertainty in the money markets. Property prices kept rising but then again in London they always did. Apparently, even I couldn't affect that. The two bouncers caught shagging each other in a street outside a Mayfair nightclub made the local TV news. I saw them interviewed. They looked shell-shocked, unable to comprehend in any way what happened to them.

This was England, and the country wasn't right. Something was going on, it had to be. That or the world was crazy.

Toni and I watched it all on television and laughed our tits off.

Keano once said, and this was one of his famous quotes, that London was a city of ten million people, one million of whom were mad. Every nutjob with an opinion found some platform for their views. They were all on telly. And those that weren't on telly were on the radio, or in the papers or blogging. All the time. One paper described that summer as open season on common sense.

And only the two of us, well, three counting the departed Keano, had even the slightest idea as to the reason why. It was great.

Keano's exit did affect me. I was shocked that he'd been so harsh. I hadn't hurt anyone, not directly anyway, and I never intended to. It wasn't like I was killing people.

I could have been a lot worse. I could have anything I wanted, but I couldn't work out what I wanted. For now, living on the Thames, getting drunk and having top clothes for free would do.

In a rare moment of sober introspection, I realised what I liked best was being liked. At the moment there was no trouble with that. I was making friends left, right and centre. Real friends, not just the ones I was forced to zap. People looked at me in my smart new clothes like I was a success. I exuded confidence.

We invariably spent evenings in The Cricketers and I treated everyone who came in to free drinks. After a few days of not paying, we'd had so much beer that the brewery sent some inspectors over to work out where all the money was going. The landlord sent them over to my table to explain the situation. They went away happy enough. I told them to think of a reason and never come back. They didn't.

After that, depending on how Toni and I felt, we would be in The Cricketers, or off to town. One night, as we were bored of Inferno's, Toni phoned up a trendy radio station and got their top club guy to recommend the hottest clubs in London. I even saw Beyoncé playing a private gig in Camden. Got to say she still looked good. Yes, I slept with her.

A good time. I was living at a level I'd never thought possible. I didn't have to go to work and had plenty of company. I was a life coach's wet dream. How to make that change for the better? Develop the ability to make everybody you meet fall madly, unconditionally, in love with you.

Of course it couldn't last. And it didn't.

Because four weeks and three days after I moved in to The Mariners: my mum turned up.

Toni and I were discussing a holiday in Florida. I was on the phone to the States to a guy who we found on the internet, to book us up a massive villa.

I was sitting on the floor in the middle of the gigantic living room. The windows were open on the river. A t-shirted, knickerless Toni had got a couple of blokes in who were lounging all over her. She was stretched out on the sofa, looking up at the ceiling; spliff in mouth. She was telling me what to say to the American villa guy. *Make sure it's got a pool…*

In the background, some sci-fi DVD was playing away. No one watched it. I was by now well into the habit of drinking a bottle of red wine at lunchtime — hundred and fifty quid a bottle — and was working on bringing a second bottle into that habit.

I was beginning to think that, concerning Toni, maybe Keano had a point. I can't deny it. I was getting a little tired of Toni. If truth be told, I was simply getting tired. This new life of mine was nothing if not full on.

Then Mrs Kim came rushing in to tell me that someone was buzzing away at the little digital gate thing and it was an old woman and she was claiming to be my mother.

I fumbled the phone down; Florida forgotten. I froze. All that child stuff came back to me. That fear.

I hadn't even thought about my parents since going to the police station, ages ago.

They must have been sick with worry.

The Mariners was an absolute tip. Mrs Kim seemed to have lost the urge to clean after I told her she didn't need to bother. I couldn't let mum see this, she'd kill me.

I snapped at the blokes to get lost. Toni sat up, looking at me, trying to work out what I was going to do. She tamped out her spliff. 'I'd better go.'

'Don't,' I said. 'What am I going to say?'

She sat still, eyes wide open. She was caught between bolting and disobeying me.

'What can I possibly do?' she asked.

'I don't know…' I began picking up the scattered paper and cans and wine bottles and vodka bottles and ash trays and drugs.

Mum walked in. She was breathing heavily, always a bad sign. She hadn't dolled up to visit me; just in sweatshirt and jeans and trainers. She must have left the house in a hurry. I stopped in mid-tidy. She was looking around at the room, amazed.

'Mum…' I said.

And she turned her laser beam eyes on me. That old stare.

'You know Toni?' I said. Weak.

'Hello,' said Toni. Toni sat in her t-shirt, legs apart on the sofa, with no underwear. Great.

'I know the place is a mess, but I was just…' I tailed off, too beaten to attempt a lie, too ashamed.

Mum was just looking at me. Her expression was one of malign triumph. I'd never noticed before how thin her lips were.

'What?' I asked.

'You're not the only one,' she said.

'Only one what?'

'There are others.'

Chapter 9

She had a taxi waiting at the head of the bridge, back at the M4 flyover. A taxi she was paying for and no arguments about free rides. I left the stupefied Toni quiet on the sofa, legs apart, as I sloped off to get dressed. Girls were giggling somewhere in the house.

We walked to the bridge past the millionaires' mansions. What time was it? What *day* was it? My throat was tugging; red wine glued there like dried paint. My hangover was reminding me just how long it had been lurking inside; waiting for the right moment to strike. It was telling me I wasn't going to get away with this kind of behaviour any more.

Mum wasn't looking at me, wasn't speaking. I traipsed behind her, up the stone steps to the road. She wanted me to ask. I did.

'What did you mean I'm not the only one?'

'You'll find out.' Her anger was a real force, a physical object she was barely keeping contained.

'Where's Dad?'

'In church I imagine.'

Had I heard right? 'Church?'

'I suppose it's his way of coping. Some of us have lives to lead.'

'Where are we going? The police?'

'Home, Anthony. But yes, the police.'

She still couldn't look at me. It must be Sunday morning because my young, healthy, toned and moneyed Hammersmith neighbours were out jogging and cycling and rowing.

I watched these young professional bodies doing their thing and I realised I didn't want to go back to Croydon again. Ever.

I considered myself one of them. I didn't want to go back to Sunday mornings of men with bellies washing cars, then speeding off to B&Q and IKEA and garden centre after garden centre. Getting stuck in traffic on the Purley Way. Drive-in McDonald's to shut the kids up, then a resentful Sunday carvery in a heaving, crushing pub full of people just like you. For the rest of your life.

Never again. Not if I could help it.

'I don't want to go home,' I told her.

Mum stopped. I hadn't meant what I said to come out as an order.

At last she looked at me. Her eyes were hooded, and I could see she hadn't slept. She was like a new person, no longer the beige figure in the background of my childhood. I saw her as a sharp, calculating woman. One who wasn't too happy with me.

She thought about her words. 'There's someone I think you'll want to meet.'

We walked over the bridge towards the Apollo Theatre. The Hammersmith flyover was deserted. A stationary car was parked on the pavement. Inside, the smudge of a black face looked over the steering wheel. A minicab.

A fat man smoking a cigarette leaned against the car bonnet. He was wearing a shabby, creased suit and wore large, thick-rimmed spectacles. When he saw us he stood up straight.

'Anthony!' he called out.

The hangover was banging now. I wasn't in the mood. 'Who's this?'

I'd never acted like this in front of my mum. The man walked towards us, his smile never dropping.

'He's a journalist,' said mum. 'We need him.'

'Stan Bergman,' he held out his fat hand for me to shake. I did so. Like all fatties, he sweated. Not only did he sweat, he smirked. 'How you doing, Anthony? So you're the man, eh?'

'I called Mr Bergman the other day,' said mum. She clearly felt she was remaining admirably patient with me. 'He knows you're the one from the police station. I've told him what you can do.'

I got it. I knew what was coming.

Bergman said it. 'Care to give me a demo?'

How many times already had I heard that? I was so sick of having to prove myself.

Bergman pointed at a harmless old couple crossing the road under the flyover. 'How about them?' He looked in the mood for good sport.

'How about you, you fat fuck?' I said and zapped him. No mucking about; straight in, narrow and channelled. 'Why don't you stop smoking and lose some weight.'

'Jesus!' he yelped. He threw the fag away as if it had stung him. Bergman looked at me, all trace of that smirk gone. Replaced by pure and simple devotion. To me. 'Better?' I asked him.

'Oh yes,' he replied. His voice was soft and reverential. He pulled a packet of Marlboro Lights from his suit pocket and hurled it away. I don't think he even knew he was doing it.

'Right,' I snickered. 'I guess you're on my side now.'

Mum slapped me.

I reeled away from her. The crack of her palm echoed around the Sunday morning air. I was stunned. She'd never hit me. I put a hand to my cheek. She stared at me, defiant, ready for whatever I gave her back. I saw the driver flinch inside his cab. He would be wishing he was somewhere else; hoping he wasn't going to have to do anything. Except, I realised, I had got him too. My focus hadn't been as narrow as I thought. I had other things to think about.

Mum had lost her temper. I lost mine. Didn't she understand who I was?

I pointed a shaking hand at my mother. 'Don't think…' I told her, 'don't think I won't get you!'

She stood her ground. Her drab clothes, her drab jeans and t-shirt, her Croydon-ness, were barriers to the Anthony I was trying so hard to become. 'Come on, then. Do it to me. I dare you.'

You know I might have, I was that angry. But Bergman intervened. With a roar, he launched himself at mum. He fully intended to kill her. Mum screamed.

'No!' I yelled. 'Leave her!' I was so surprised I hardly knew what was happening.

Instantly, Bergman stopped in his tracks. He looked at me, puzzled.

'Never touch her again.'

Bergman nodded and walked back to the car. He looked light-headed, confused, even a little drunk.

'Listen, Anthony,' she said. 'And listen properly.' She clasped my arms, uncaring of what she was risking. 'They're calling them incidents. Abroad, America. They wouldn't tell me. These people, they just turned up at the house. Scientists. Police. When we get home, they're going to make out they're… that they're in control and know all about… you. They'll even say that they're here to help you. But don't trust them.'

She was comforting me. She was helping me. I understood. 'What about him? Bergman?'

She gestured towards the reporter. 'I phoned the Croydon Argus before I let them in. I didn't know what else to do. I told them to send someone; that I was the mother of the terrorist that had escaped the police station. I thought if people knew about you, then maybe they won't try and harm you. But look what you've done. What you've become.'

She let go. I felt the echo of her fingers on my arms.

'I didn't kill him did I?' I said. 'What I did to him makes it easier. Mr Bergman is on our side now, believe me.'

Mum looked at Bergman, who was leaning against the car again. He lowered his eyes, unable to meet my gaze.

'Anthony,' she said. She sounded sad. 'You *have* killed him. You know you have.'

That stung more than the slap. My throat convulsed and this time it wasn't the red wine. The whole situation, it didn't feel fair. Everything I did was wrong.

'If I'm such a monster,' I said, hoarse with shame and resentment, 'why are you helping me?'

She opened the cab door. 'Get in.'

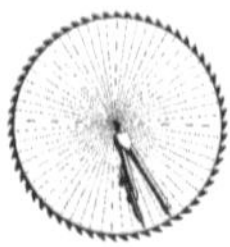

Not surprisingly, this long-delayed cab ride back to Croydon was conducted in as much silence as my journey in the police car, all those weeks ago.

I had gotten used to being in charge of situations.

'There are others,' mum had said. If another person had the power to zap, that was panic-inducing. More than one was petrifying.

The minicab motored through Putney into Wandsworth. Bergman sat up front, silent and calm, next to my new driver. The fact that he'd tried to murder my mum ten minutes earlier appeared to have slipped his mind.

Mum sat stony-faced beside me, watching my hangover bite deep. In silence she opened her handbag and fished out two Ibuprofen. 'I don't have any water,' she said.

Sunday morning didn't make any difference to the eternal South London traffic, such a contrast to serene Hammersmith. Still the same choked, shitty old place. The buildings hadn't toppled; the crowds weren't on the streets trying to catch a glimpse. London still stood. I hadn't impacted on the city at all. It was like I'd had a week's holiday and it was time to go home. The fun was over. Out the window I saw horribly familiar streets. Nothing streets with no identity. But I knew them. They were part of me. I was them. Would I always be them?

The truth was that I had changed. Ramshackle curry houses and pound shops and cheap supermarkets; their overflowing rubbish bins garlanding the pavements. South London seemed like one single drab high street that stretched on forever, an endless parade of dreary shops selling cheap crap no one wanted to buy. Wage slaves living in cramped Victorian houses full of strangers too close to each other. Even now, at half ten on a Sunday morning, the anonymous poor were clustered outside the Colliers Wood Sainsbury's, waiting for the place to open. They stared at the locked glass doors, in tracksuits and caps. A ragged army. Why? What did they need that was so important?

The dull ordinariness of most people's lives; it seemed a million years ago. Already, I was used to a brighter, better, richer style of living. Civilised neighbours and no noisy kids stinking of cheap skunk. No bins tipped into the road by drunks. No fly-tipping. No filth. Just smart-looking people, mature people in good clothes who worried about what they ate. Who went on holiday abroad several times a year, and not to Tenerife or Florida. Who sometimes even worked abroad and were married to exotic spouses who worked all hours in the City. People whose only knowledge of Great Britain was London, and suburbs were somewhere they passed on the way to airports. That was what I wanted, and now I had it. What the hell was I doing going back?

The minicab turned into my road and pulled up. The driver clicked the handbrake, making me wince, reminding me of teenage driving lessons.

Mum had the money in her hand. The fact she didn't need to pay but insisted made me feel worse.

I got out of the car. The familiar smell of… well, Croydon. Of suburbia. 4x4s and Land Cruisers and people carriers. The weight of thirty years of same old same old settling on me. A suffocating armour.

'Mum,' I asked. 'Tell me.'

'Remember this, Anthony,' she said. 'Whatever they say, they're afraid.'

'I don't understand.'

At last she turned and at last I saw. I don't know; was it something in her face? She too was a different person now. A plotter. A schemer. She was thinking in ways I'd never believed. My quiet, polite little mum. 'Keep this in your head,' she told me. 'They may mean you harm.'

They turned out to be three men in my house. My old house.

'Anthony,' said the first one and shook my hand. He didn't look like a copper. He looked like a lawyer on his weekend, all steel-framed specs, pressed jeans and Sunday jumper. 'Matthew Angler. I'm a psychologist. I'm a consultant for the Department of Health.

Thanks for coming. These are Paul and Bob. They're policemen. But don't worry, you're not in any trouble. In fact, quite the opposite.'

I didn't need Doctor Matthew Angler to tell me the other two were police. Plain clothes, but with that look. They couldn't keep their eyes still. I guessed they didn't believe in what I was supposed to be able to do. If they did, they probably wouldn't have agreed to come.

As I walked into the dining room, I saw they had set up an expensive laptop on the dinner table. 'I've got something to show you, Anthony,' said the psychologist.

'Who's this?' asked the larger policeman, Paul. 'He can't stay.'

He was talking about Bergman, who had strolled in with mum.

Doctor Angler was clearly irritated but controlled himself. 'Paul, you know what we said.'

Paul waved him away. 'Yeah yeah…' and he plonked himself heavily into a chair. If he thought he could have gotten away with it, he would have lit a cigarette. The other copper, a thin man also wearing glasses, just kept looking at me. He was pale, with bad thinning hair.

'Anthony,' said Angler. 'I want to say we understand that you are in some way capable of controlling our minds.'

I almost laughed. So, we open with Star Trek. How amusing after all this time for someone to come out and say it. Although, as I glanced round the room, it was clear I was the only one who found this funny.

'Look,' I replied. 'If it's about the house in Hammersmith, I never meant to hurt anybody. I was just…'

'As I say, we're not here to arrest you, Anthony,' said Angler, calm and measured. 'Judging from the extent of your… talent, I doubt we could.'

'You're right. And it wouldn't take any effort on my part. He's…' I pointed at Bergman, 'a reporter. I did him. On the way here. I just thought about it and now he'll do whatever I say. Won't you, Mr Bergman?'

Bergman nodded, that placid smile fixed in place. 'Oh yes, Anthony. Whatever you say.'

Everyone in the room, excepting Bergman and I, seemed to have an attack of the fidgets. Noses were rubbed, hands went to mouths, lips were licked. The copper who looked like he needed a fag shifted in his seat.

Bergman was just staring, at me. 'Wait outside,' I said. He went; like a lapdog.

The trio from officialdom watched Bergman leave. Whatever they thought, they managed to hide it well. Angler was the epitome of patience. He was making sure he kept eye contact with me.

'You see?' I said, very reasonably. 'I just wanted you to know.'

Angler gestured at mum. 'Perhaps Anthony would like a cup of tea?'

'If he does, he'll ask for one,' she replied.

The two policemen looked at each other. Paul might have been a thug but Bob was quiet and thoughtful; he was more than he seemed.

Angler nodded, remaining the most reasonable man in the world. 'Thing is, Anthony, we need your help.'

'I heard.' If truth be told I was getting impatient; having trouble concentrating on him. I was really thinking how small and poky this house seemed. Had I really grown up here? This little dining room with its flower wallpaper and glass cabinets seemed too cramped for that to be possible.

Angler was losing his relaxed charm. But he tried. 'That's very good, Anthony. Like I say, we're not here to do anything to you. All I can ask is that you choose not to use your talent on us.'

'Oh yeah?'

'Believe me when I say it would interfere with our ability to help you. We've got something to show you. About the others.'

Angler knew he'd got me, even a little. 'I think you'd better see this.' He indicated the laptop.

I looked at mum. She looked at me but I couldn't read her. Did she know what was coming?

'Anthony?' asked Angler, pulling a chair out for me. One of our cheap creaky wooden dining room chairs.

I looked at the laptop. A multicoloured screensaver whirled around. The policemen were tense. They were waiting. I suddenly imagined a series of red dots from sniper rifles trained on my body.

They could be hidden upstairs in the neighbours' houses. What would they do if I said no? Could I afford not to get them right now?

'Okay,' I said, and sat down at the dining table.

Chapter 10

Doctor Angler clicked on a website and the laptop hard drive rumbled into life. We all crowded round the compact screen.

'Not too close now,' I whispered. It was a joke but Angler instantly backed off.

'Mum said something about America.'

'That's right, Anthony,' said Angler. Did he have to keep saying my name? I guessed he had also been on those man-management courses. Had every official in the world been on them? And if they had, did that actually neutralise whatever effect they were supposed to create?

'Oklahoma,' said Bob the quiet policeman. 'A town called Anadarko. Thirty-two days ago.'

'Ring any bells?' asked Angler.

Was he talking to me? Thirty-two days? How long was that? Who thought in terms of thirty-two days?

The screen flickered and we were abruptly looking at a very flat, very American residential street. Nice widely spaced single storey houses; nondescript houses whose frontages revealed nothing of whoever lived inside. The scene was rendered in digital colour: the black tarmac, tan pavements, driveways that gleamed in the sun, bright blue sky.

The camera turned slowly, across the street. The picture was awful, real low-resolution.

'What is that?' I heard mum whisper.

We panned across to, what were they, cars? Big American cars. They were all piled up on top of each other outside one of the houses. Windscreens and bonnets reflected fierce sunlit glares. Stacked up and tangled up, like they'd all driven head first at each other at maximum speed. There must have been twenty, thirty cars. Some were burnt out. Some had shapes inside.

The camera moved in. The street looked hot and airless. A heat we simply didn't get in England. I could hear flies buzzing out of the laptop. The film-maker was cautious. Every now and then he dropped the camera to reveal a denim leg and a trainer shoe. Whoever he was, he was coughing.

In amongst those cars, in the road: people. On top of each other: a crushed mass of them. Bodies and blood. It looked like they too had smashed into each other.

'What's going on?' I asked.

Bob's voice sounded dry, like he didn't use it much. 'It's a housing project in Bridge Creek, just outside Anadarko. This is footage taken half an hour after… the event. Some sixteen year old kid on his way to school using his camera phone.'

I couldn't see the images on the screen too well; the camera kept shaking. I'm not sure I wanted to. 'What is… what's…' I couldn't form the words.

'One hundred and twenty dead.'

'One hundred and twenty?'

'There were more in the house. A lot more. And out of that, ninety-eight were women.'

'What were they doing?' asked mum.

Angler leaned forward and looked at me. 'We were rather hoping you could tell us.'

The camera was swinging now. It hit the ground with a thud. I realised the camera kid must have dropped to his knees.

'The local police took the kid in and the FBI sealed off the area. Stitched it up really tight. No news teams. Confiscated all the footage.' I wondered why it was suddenly Bob doing all the talking.

This was too much for me. FBI? *Sealed off the area?* What was this, a cop show? Not for the first time, I considered the possibility I was the butt of someone's practical joke. The whole experience was a big grift and I was the mark. 'What's that got to do with me?'

'The details are sketchy,' said Bob.' The whole town suffered a severe catastrophe. Date is April 18th, this year.'

'Ring any more bells?' asked Paul. Not altogether friendly enough for my liking.

Of course the date rang a bell. It was the date I–

Now I understood.

'Exactly,' said Angler. 'Bob, carry on.'

Bob coughed. Man, his throat was *really* dry. 'The first Bridge Creek PD reports came in when a patrol car was called to a disturbance in this street. Maple Street. Public disorder.'

'What did they find?' I asked.

'They never reported in,' said Bob. 'Last message was that they had reached the housing project. The two officers were later found among the dead inside the building. There were multiple lacerations and severe blood loss. They'd been torn apart, along with half the neighbourhood.'

'Who did it?'

'As far as anyone can make out, they did it to each other.'

'We don't know,' said Angler. 'We have to be careful about what we conjecture.'

'And the pileup at the house?'

Bob looked at Angler. No doubt who was the boss here. 'This is where it gets… strange. People in Bridge Street started attacking each other.' His voice was wavering; I think he'd been reading that report for too long.

'Mass murder,' said Angler. 'They were out on the streets. Some kind of… frenzy. Husbands, wives, kids, everything. Didn't matter. They just kept going.'

'What about the cars?' I asked. 'What was going on?'

'It's a baby,' said mum. 'It was a baby. Wasn't it?'

That stopped the conversation dead. So much information. Far too much.

'We think so,' said Angler, finally.

Had I heard right? I think I sniggered. 'You what?'

'I'm glad you find it funny my son,' said Paul from behind me.

'Sergeant…' Angler warned him.

Mum shoved me in the back. 'Anthony!'

Here they were again, getting at me. I felt like zapping the lot of them, mum included. Why did I always feel I was in the wrong?

'What do you mean: a baby?' I asked.

A few glances between Angler and the cops. However, it was mum who was on a roll. She walked away to look out at the back garden. It was still the same, a Sunday morning suburban English garden with lawn, hosepipe and untidy paving slabs. The same garden I'd been looking at all my life.

'What does a baby do?' she said to the glass. 'It sleeps. And when it wakes up, it's hungry. And when it can't get food… when it can't get food *now*, what does a baby do?'

'It screams out for attention,' said Angler. 'And it cries. And it rages.'

She turned to him. 'Was there a…' she started.

Bob played with the laptop. He clicked to full screen the still image of a small baby in a cot. 'LaVonn Sheridan. Age three months and twelve days. A little girl.'

I pictured the baby in that sprawling bungalow. Sat in her cot; getting along with her little baby life. In that heat. In that place.

'How do you know all this, Bob?' I asked.

He quailed a little. He believed; oh yes, Bob was a believer. 'I've been there. I work for Interpol. I arrived back from the crime scene two days ago. These images don't begin to reflect the extent of the destruction.'

It had come to her. It flicked into little baby LaVonn's mind, just as it flicked into mine. At exactly the same time. She wouldn't have had any control. I thought about what it felt like when I used the zap. I always focused on what I wanted, on particular people. Always that feeling that I had to rein it in; keep in control. But what if you couldn't? What if you didn't even know you had it? If what I did was pencil strokes, hers would have been vast, all-encompassing blocks of colour, just spreading and spreading.

'Interpol. I didn't think that was even real. And now you're here because you think: me.'

Bob and Doctor Angler had no answer. What could they possibly say?

'How did it — she — the baby — do it?' I asked, to get them off the hook.

'Do it?' asked Bob.

'Cause… that. This power. It's not mind reading, I don't know what it is. But, if the baby sent out the thing and it got into the others, why did they all go mad? I mean, nothing really happens to the people I get. They're still themselves.'

I may have wanted to believe what I was saying, but no one else in the room seemed to share that opinion. They were trying desperately to stay calm.

Bob consulted his notes. Mum kept looking out of the window. Of them all, only Paul the copper could look back at me. I guess he was too stupid not to.

Angler pretended the laptop was his focus. 'My guess, my inference,' said the good doctor. 'Is in interpretation. I would think that wires got crossed. That victims — recipients of the imprint — are implanted with a new directive: to serve. How they serve is possibly open to interpretation. Perhaps the mother understood the baby was hungry and ordered the others to bring food *right now*. They did their best to obey. Perhaps the mother became a kind of, I don't know, filter. Like a priest literalising the word of God. Perhaps the uninhibited force of LaVonn's imprinting was so strong and uncontrolled it caused an emotional breakdown. Somehow, this led the neighbours to go on the rampage. The murders might have been caused by unaffected people trying to confront those who were–'

'So why doesn't that happen with me?'

'I think in some cases it might, Anthony,' said Angler. 'Think about your supervisor, Mr Samson.'

'I try not to.'

'I am guessing with practice you are more able to control the force of your imprint. To focus and control it more efficiently.'

I thought about that night outside the club with Toni and Keano. The way I managed to shift the field of fire. Whatever Angler saw in my face, he didn't like. 'I may of course be completely wrong. We have so little data.'

'What happened?' asked mum. 'To the baby?'

Bob coughed and rubbed his nose. 'We're… we're not entirely… it died. She died.'

I couldn't get those images out of my head. The cars. The piles.

'What is this thing?' asked mum. She turned to me, accusing. 'What is this thing in his head?'

'Mum…'

'What about the doctors? There have to be drugs. Get it out of him.'

Angler eased his way between me in the chair and her at the window. 'That's what we're here for, Mrs Graves. We all want to help Anthony.'

The shitty cop, Paul, lost his patience. 'Fuck this,' he said. 'I don't believe a fucking word.' He stabbed a finger at me and Angler and mum in turn. 'What is this fucking fairy tale? Let's just arrest the time-wasting cunt.'

The guy was such a heavy, such a leg-breaker, that I almost zapped him there and then. I was getting used to threats, and I hadn't tolerated one for over a month now.

'Do it,' I told him.

I stepped forward and, unconsciously I think, Angler held a hand against my chest to stop me. It was enough. He rounded on the cop. 'Get out!'

'You'd better go,' I said to the dimwit policeman. 'You'd better go now.'

The policeman glared at me. In another time, another world, he would have had me down in the cells and not a word spoken. He would have enjoyed himself with me. But times had changed.

I laughed at him. 'Or,' I said, 'arrest me.' I held out my arms for the cuffs.

'Anthony, please…' whispered Angler. He kept his eye on Dumbo. 'Get out. Go now.'

PC Paul didn't want to, he really didn't. But he was a good boy. A good copper.

I decided to get him. Or maybe I shouldn't. After all, I promised. No; no, I should.

As Paul picked up his coat, gave me a contemptuous glance and stomped out, I squeezed. Only something went wrong. I don't know what but it didn't happen. Paul walked out of the room and the front door slammed. Angler watched the empty space for a few seconds. Perhaps he was reassuring himself Paul wasn't going to storm back in. He was shit-scared. Jesus. *He* was shit scared? What about me? The bloody thing hadn't worked. It still sat there whirring away in the skull but I hadn't been able to pull the trigger. Oh Christ. They must never find out, these people here. What would they do to me?

'Anthony,' said Angler, apparently oblivious, 'believe me when I tell you I'm sorry that just happened. He had orders. He shouldn't have…'

What to do? Panic was bearing down. I had to fight it.

'Don't worry,' I replied. 'He's not important. I know you're here to help. Doctor Angler? Bob?'

Angler smiled and some of the colour returned to his face. 'Yes, Anthony. That's right.'

I sat down. I was thinking about what mum had said. Could they find out what had gotten into me? Was there a way of getting me back to normal? Did I want them to? What if this thing had gone forever anyway? No. I understood: the power was still in me. I just needed to figure out why it hadn't worked. What had I done wrong? Perhaps I did need these guys after all.

Bob was hovering at the keyboard; sweating.

'What else have you got, Bob?' I asked. 'More, what do you call them?'

'Incidents.' Bob's fear was interfering with his thought processes. 'Incidents,' he said again.

'Incidents. Let's hear them, eh?' I willed myself to stay calm; stay casual. They must never know.

Bob took a deep breath. 'Outbreaks of strange behaviour. Across the world. All on or around the same date. Riots in India, some sort of armed uprising in the Philippines. An incomprehensible mass slaughter in central Africa. Most disturbing of all, an explosion in China.'

'Explosion?'

Bob licked his lips. 'Yesterday,' he said. 'A city called Changchun. Jilin Province. For a reason unknown to us, and without any explanation, the Chinese government in Beijing fired a missile into the heart of that city. Apparently, there was a disturbance at the main civic hall. Some kind of gathering.'

I looked past mum into the garden. I needed normal. In my head I named all the items I saw, all the familiar garden stuff: grass, paving, hosepipe, shed. This was too much. Way too much.

'What kind of missile?' I asked.

'A nuclear detonation,' said Angler.

'How– how many?' I needed a drink. Water. Diet Coke with lime. Vodka. Anything would do. So thirsty. I had joined Bob in the croaky voice thing. That's what shock and awe did, I guess.

'Twelve million.'

I stared out at the garden. This is Croydon, I told myself. This is my house and that out there is my garden. This is the world. This is how things are. How they should be.

But I wasn't convinced.

'And how is this connected…' mum tailed off. 'How is this connected to Anthony?'

'I don't honestly know,' said Angler. 'But I think we had better start finding out. And rather quickly.' He looked at me. 'What do you say?'

'They bombed their own city. Their people. They did that rather than…'

My throat was so dry, so tight I barely recognised my own voice. I had to relax. I'd had one misfire, that's all. Everything was going to be fine. I would just go with them until I got my mojo working and hope to god they never asked for a demonstration. I didn't know what else I had. 'What do you want?'

Chapter 11

I confess: this whole fuss over me? I loved it. Once I had gotten over the panic and fear and sickness and belief they would suss I might not be what they dreaded after all. I had never been so in demand.

Doctor Angler and Interpol Bob drove me to a small but chichi designer hotel halfway between the City and trendy Hoxton. I thought about trying a sneaky little zap but was too afraid of it not working again. That was a possibility I didn't want to face. I caught a glimpse of the room rate on a card in reception when they weren't looking and believe me, the hotel wasn't cheap. This was celebrity.

This hotel was an old factory that had gone bust or something. Designers had come in and done it all up. The décor was all brown and bright red patterns like the building had escaped from the seventies, but that was probably the idea. I was the only guest.

Doctor Angler personally took me up in the shiny lift to a corner suite. I had windows looking down onto Clerkenwell Road. Those windows had fancy shutters, the ceiling housed discreet lights and the bed was massive. A flat screen plasma television performed all sorts of digital tricks. I wouldn't have had the faintest idea or interest in how to design a room; never even thought about it. But now someone *had* bothered, I felt right at home. It was a room for people used to other people doing things for them.

As Doctor Angler helped me move my luggage in, I asked him: 'Who's paying for this? It's a bit steep.'

He laughed, dropping my shabby rucksack onto the giant bed.

'Oh, the top bodies, my friend.' He was so warm; I grew to believe he might even have genuinely liked me. 'Nothing but the best for Anthony Graves. You may not know it but you're probably the most talked about human being in government today. They all want to know who you are, and no expense spared. So don't worry: you can have anything you want.'

I thought about the penny-pinching and shabby little sandwiches they used to provide at my work and how often we were told to appreciate what we were given. How the deficit was cutting deep and budgets were being cut and times were hard. Well, they had enough budget for me now. For my own hotel. Funny that.

'I have to ask you something,' said Angler. 'Something very important.'

Again, panic. What? What did he want? I felt the urge to zap him but what if it didn't work and he knew it?

He picked up on my brain freeze and held out his hands.

'Please, Anthony. It's nothing bad, I swear.'

I nodded. I had to pretend. I had to go on as if I was god. There was no other way out.

'I am asking you to trust me,' he said. 'You have to trust me when I say I have a very good reason for you to keep me free of your influence.'

'Okay, Doctor Angler. Tell me.'

Angler had it all down pat, I'll give him that. He had the spiel. He even looked right: a genial, intelligent, professional man in a subtle, smart suit. 'When you use your power, the people you affect. Their judgement becomes… it becomes flawed. You have implanted in them an impulse that overrides their common sense. I believe, I sincerely believe, that in their desire to serve you, they don't always act in your best interest. And I am determined to act in your best interest. That's why I am here.'

'I don't understand.'

Doctor Angler gestured to the street. 'We are here to protect you. Myself, Bob, the others. You must understand that. You could get them; of course you could. You could get all of us. But I am asking you not to. It's in your interest and our interest for you to allow us our free will.'

'Really?'

'Really. It's difficult but you have to trust me.'

I walked to the window and looked out. I saw a simple scene: cars, vans and people. Although now I looked, there were quite a few well-built men down on the street. They didn't seem to have much reason to be there. 'Why should I trust you?' I asked.

Doctor Angler nodded. 'Of course. Well, for a start, we don't know about the other affected people. Perhaps they know about you. If what I believe to be true *is* true, then soon they will start looking for you. Now, we can detect people who have been... implanted. Easily. But not if we are ourselves implanted.'

'They're going to come looking for me? The others?'

'We are already seeing significant shifts in the movement of populations in other countries and continents. Movements we can't understand. An awful lot of violence. Unexplained but incredibly savage. North America. India. Ghana. As close as Southern France. Something is happening in the world. We're going to need you, Anthony. And sooner or later, I believe you are going to need us.'

This fancy suite made me imagine I was important. Hammersmith suddenly felt too far out of town. When this was over, when the juices were flowing again (for policeman Paul was surely a one-off), I would get myself a nice house in the City. Or maybe just keep the hotel. That would be the simpler option.

As Doctor Angler left, he asked me again not to get anybody. He was very polite. I said yes, because he so obviously needed my help and there's nothing like being wanted.

I ordered a pot of tea from room service and was slightly surprised when there was a knock on the door to announce its arrival. I thought about the couple in Hammersmith whose house I had taken. The Hargreaves would have been perfectly at ease with this hotel. God, I was provincial. I drank the tea and watched the men in the street act busy. I figured they were the police or the army or something. Guards. I had a big temptation to try and get them but Doctor Angler's words stayed with me.

As the hours passed, I felt much more relaxed. I watched the men outside and got to suss their routines: where they waited, which cars they used, when they changed shifts, that kind of thing. They were probably very good.

Okay, I admit it: I tried zapping them. Despite the promises, despite everything, I had to know. I looked at the men in the street and I pushed. Nothing. Not a dicky bird. It really was like when you install some new software and it sits there in your PC looking innocent and happy and eager to please but when you press that button, absolutely bloody nothing happens. Again and again and again. I was just stuck. Constipated! I needed to figure out why and fast. Either that or it was time to do a runner. And how long would Anthony Graves last doing a runner from these people?

At this point, I was impotent, compliant and docile enough for them to take me down.

I suppose they didn't want to nuke London. I was such an idiot, completely trusting. Now I'm a lot smarter. A lot more paranoid.

They could have put a bomb in the hotel; I'd never have found out. Gas me while I slept. An assassin with a silenced pistol in the lobby: nail me when I'm eating breakfast. A sniper in the building opposite, poison in my food; there were a million ways and I would never have known.

Why didn't they?

At first, I think they wanted to recruit me. They wanted me to be their superhero; the man to protect the United Kingdom from her enemies, from the other people like me. They thought they could control me. I suppose it was difficult for the authorities to believe that I really was going to change the world forever. It was difficult for *me*.

I was just what I seemed to be: an absolutely normal, dull, unimaginative man from Croydon. I think the authorities were waiting for a catch, something behind the façade, something planned. It was the randomness of the whole business that took them by surprise.

There is another explanation. You never know, perhaps they didn't bump me off because I hadn't done anything wrong. They just weren't prepared to murder an innocent man. I wonder why they didn't. They should have. I would have.

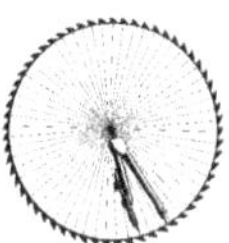

The food was terrific. I discovered I had a permanently reserved table in the swanky glass and chrome hotel restaurant and could order food day or night, whenever I wanted. And man, I ate.

Braised lamb, pollo diavolo, pear and vodka sorbet, fresh polenta, I had the works. And if I wanted a greasy bacon sandwich for breakfast, I got that too.

I went to bed, surprisingly exhausted. I didn't even have a glass of wine. Next morning, after months of abuse, my head felt clear. I'd forgotten what it was like to wake up without headaches and nausea and dry mouth. I figured now I knew about the baby and the nuke and the whole scary picture, I lost the appetite for drinking alcohol. Instead, I rang down and ordered the aforementioned bacon sandwich and a pot of tea. I felt a lot more relaxed than I had any right to be. I guess Anthony Graves was appreciating being pampered; being taken care of by someone else. Until I knew how to get the power back on, I was in danger.

I thought about the Chinese. To blow up a city to get their man. Who was he? Or she? I don't doubt that my Chinese counterpart had been someone like me, some ordinary sap who woke up one morning to find him- or herself completely different. A human being who accidentally found out that they could now get anybody to do exactly what they wanted. How had they discovered their new talent? Had they worked out what they wanted to do with it? And before they could get started: bang; blown up with the city.

I was concerned how quickly the Chinese authorities made their decision to press the button; what they were prepared to lose to prevent the spread. I had been pretty unpleasant last month. I mean, I hadn't actually harmed anybody, but I knew I had not been nice.

Just how dangerous did they think I was? Even if I told them the cupboard seemed to be bare, insisted even, that I just wanted a quiet life, would they believe me? Would they take the chance?

And the worst scenario, my biggest fear: what if this power was gone for good? Imagine the kind of revenge people would take when they realised what I'd done to them.

Next morning, I got a call from the hotel lobby. I had a guest. I went downstairs and there was Penny. She was wearing a short fashionable raincoat and she couldn't have looked less European if she tried.

Now I'm older and more cynical, I think Penny — Doctor Penny Dean, a Canadian psychiatrist — was summoned to London as much for how she looked as for what qualifications or experience she might possess. They were trying everything to keep me happy.

It was ironic that in order to stop me zapping, they gave me everything I wanted anyway. Lucky for them I was such an unimaginative dumbo. Anyone more creative would have tested the boundaries; demanded more than they could give. Me, I just wanted a nice place to live, an easy life and people to like me. I wanted people like Penny. She really was beautiful. Long, shiny dark hair. Smart fitted business clothes. Tiny, exquisite spectacles. Just my type. Yeah, I think they knew.

'I am honoured to meet you, Anthony,' she said. Her teeth were white and polished in that North American way. 'I am a psychiatrist and life coach. I want to help you develop your gift.'

When Doctor Angler and Penny first talked to me to prevent me zapping them (the subtext to the words: *help me come to terms with my gift*), I was shy and uncommunicative. We talked over my second breakfast; this one in the restaurant. The breakfast went into lunch. They talked more. Doctor Angler said they just wanted to find out what made me tick. Yeah right. Shrinks always had a hidden agenda. You just know.

At first, I didn't say anything at all. And because I wouldn't talk to them, Doctor Angler and Penny just talked to me.

Doctor Penny Dean, of course, was all business. She hadn't come all this way just to be mooned over by one overawed Croydonite.

When lunch went, an Estonian guy with a little goatee and a shaved head served us coffee and snacks. I was so stunned by Penny's appearance that I hardly noticed him.

'Where's Interpol Bob?' was the first question I asked. They sat back. They had made their breakthrough. Penny opened the lid of her laptop. I heard it power up.

'Abroad,' said Doctor Angler, as if I had been in conversation all the time. 'America.' He looked at Penny. 'The United States, I should say. We're not sure what's happening over there.'

'Like what?'

'Really, we don't know. Which is worrying. We may have less time than we hoped.'

Penny's laptop beeped.

'Okay, Anthony. These are the facts as we understand them,' said Penny. 'At one particular moment on the morning of April the 18th of this year, a number of human beings around the globe were simultaneously empowered with a strange ability. They manifested no previous symptoms nor had any prior knowledge of The Event. They did not know each other and no correlation has yet been found that links them. Nobody has yet identified the nature of this ability nor been able to quantify how or where it originated.'

I nodded, not sure of what to say. It was odd, hearing this fizz in my brain spelled out like a scientific report, but I suppose they'd all been very busy since that April morning

Doctor Angler looked across the table at me. 'They're calling it, this ability: *the glamour*.' He glanced at Penny. 'The American Surgeon General's office. They have to have their melodrama I suppose.'

'Makes it sound like a magic spell,' I said. 'You know, like in D&D.'

'D&D?' asked Doctor Angler. 'I'm not familiar.'

'Dungeons and Dragons,' said Penny. 'Isn't that right, Anthony?'

I gazed into my coffee cup. 'Whatever. Forget it.'

An awkward pause.

'Whatever you call it,' said Doctor Angler, 'the glamour is the telepathic ability to make another person, or even groups of people, become absolutely devoted to the person influencing them. Total voluntary subjugation. In simple terms, they fall in love with you, Anthony. Head over heels; absolutely without restraint. They would die for those who have influenced them. And so far the effect is one hundred per cent successful. With no relapse.'

This all seemed a bit heavy for a lunch meeting at a boutique hotel. We dwindled into one of our many silences.

'So far, twenty-eight definite subjects have been identified,' said Penny.

'Twenty-eight?' I replied. 'How bloody many are there?'

'No need to get excited, Anthony,' said Doctor Angler. 'Really there isn't. Yesterday we only had the baby, the bomb in China and you. That was yesterday. The others came in this morning.'

'How do you make twenty-eight?'

'Our best guess. But I think there will be more. A lot more.' Penny flashed me a look at her laptop screen. I saw a graph with lots of ragged lines. 'We are only detecting those who have voluntarily gone public; or societal events we cannot explain except by significant probability. We believe there to be many others who have yet to make that impact. If you break down the global population into density clusters, you'll find that ninety per cent of people in the world don't live in developed areas. They've never even made a phone call.'

'You're joking.'

'Yes, it sounds odd to us in the developed world,' Penny continued. 'But that is a fact. We in the technological countries are a minor percentage. We haven't heard anything from those in these less developed regions of the planet yet. However, I think we will. Given their sociological make-up, religions, lack of education and the like, they'll have even less restraining societal forces on them than those in the developed world.'

Doctor Angler interrupted. 'I have to say, Anthony, that Doctor Dean and I disagree here. I happen to believe that the more perceived "primitive" societies do in fact have greater elements of social integration and control than our more individualistic culture.

The fact they are so primitive technologically speaking means they are more interdependent. Tribal warfare is probably the–'

'I'm sorry, Doctor Angler,' I said. 'You're losing me.'

He shut up. He looked at Penny. I had the feeling I had upset him.

'So why?' I asked. 'Why me?'

Doctor Angler nodded. 'The ultimate question,' he said. 'We simply do not know.'

'How many will there be? In the end?'

Penny said: 'Based on current projections, statistical population density, spread and geopolitical estimations, we think the final number will be around two hundred.'

Two hundred. Jesus.

'I know that sounds a lot, Anthony,' said Doctor Angler. 'But you have to remember, there are over seven billion human beings alive on the planet. And over one third live in China.'

'Which got nuked.'

I could sense them waiting for me to reach a conclusion. Something obvious that all these brainboxes had sussed ages ago. I spoke slowly. 'So, most of them, these… glamourers like me…' — yeah, sounded good and technical — '…would be in China. Statistically speaking.'

I think I had it. Shit. I didn't want to think about it. 'Maybe they met up. Out there in Ching Chong province or wherever. Maybe a gang of them met each other.'

The pair nodded in unison.

'Indeed,' said Doctor Angler.

Day Two.

'Lucky?' I asked Penny. I didn't believe a word. 'Me?'

I hadn't glamoured anybody since I moved in to the hotel, and the urge was getting stronger. Especially when I lay in bed at night. The energy in my brain was wild and it needed release. But no matter how hard I squeezed, nothing came out. You get the metaphor. A part of my brain understood I was much more relaxed than I should be. A fuzzy remote alarm bell was ringing.

I was getting used to our little talks now. Used to and a little bored of. The good doctors, I realised, were getting round to asking for things like blood tests and anal probes. If I let them, they would scan my brain. They would put me to sleep; drug me. Good luck with that. I didn't trust them. They would… Ah.

'Doctor Angler? Penny?' I asked; all good humour and bonhomie. 'Are you drugging me?'

They did well; they both suppressed their instinct to blink. They couldn't have looked more innocent. I knew they were guilty. 'Don't lie to me now.'

A single bead of sweat appeared on Doctor Angler's forehead. I stared at him.

'Well done, Anthony,' said Penny. 'It's Prozac. Very mild.'

'Okay.'

'In your morning tea is all. It's a tiny dose. I promise. Honestly, we were concerned for your emotional state. The trauma of being one of the most unique human beings on the planet. Prozac is harmless. It does nothing but equalise the peaks and troughs of your emotions. It stops you making rash decisions you might later regret.'

'Without asking. Not very nice, is it?'

Penny kept her composure. Angler looked like he wanted to bolt and run right there. 'You're correct. You might not have agreed. Doctor Angler asked you right at the start of this to trust us; that you allow us the capacity to make decisions on your behalf we might not be able to make if you implant us.'

The power in my skull was fizzing nicely. Perhaps this was what I needed. 'Well, Penny. Nice speech. But maybe that's not exactly the whole story…'

'What if I told you this,' said Penny. 'What if I show you evidence? We know of at least two situations where the– where people like you have committed suicide. One in India and one in Chile. In both cases, the subjects were in hospital at the time. Both women; both in their late forties.'

'Reports.' Yes, this power — this glamour — was churning nicely. Building up. It all felt right again. The hunger was there; slightly dulled, yes — presumably the Prozac — but still quite happy to come out and take these two smug know-it-alls. This was what I had been waiting for to get things back to normal.

Penny rushed with the laptop. Her hands tapped away. Angler was sat back now; his face white. 'I have evidence. Look. Look at it if you want to.'

I was up and running, I knew it. Whatever they said, their time had come. I feigned a bit of interest in Penny's laptop and pushed.

And it didn't happen. The glamour screamed for release but I just couldn't; couldn't do it. I felt like screaming. Oh shit. But I kept it in. I made myself pull back. I couldn't give anything away to Angler and Penny. If they knew; if they had any inkling… What the fuck was wrong with me?

So I looked at the laptop and pretended.

'We in Europe could have had it a lot worse,' said Penny. We were round the same table, drinking more tea. All drinking from the same pot. Doctor Angler was back to his old self again; Penny still had her professional cool. The situation all round was a lot more relaxed.

I *say* relaxed. They were relaxed. It was me who was a raging, internal mess of panic and anger and frustration. What did I have to do? What would bring my glamour back?

'Let's say you were a poor Algerian stuck in a Parisian ghetto?' Penny was saying. 'How would you feel about this power then? What would you want to do with it? A sweatshop labourer in East Timor? A low-caste peasant in Southern India? A Tutsi in Rwanda with HIV, no education and a blood feud? You'd have scores to settle, wouldn't you?'

'I suppose so…'

'How about a Muslim fundamentalist in Syria? Stoked full of hate and ready to wage a jihad? Or a good old Christian boy in the back end of Texas?'

'I don't understand.'

Penny smiled. Her beauty, a television sense of beauty, still overwhelmed me. 'What I'm saying, Anthony, is that out of all the… people like you that have been reported, you appear to be the most stable.'

'The most normal?'

'What's normal?' she responded. 'Here and now. You tell me what's normal.'

I looked at her. How would she feel about me if she knew I was impotent? I thought about what would have happened if I'd never gotten the glamour *(if, in fact, Dear Other Anthony, I had stayed you)*. Penny would never have known I existed. I would have made no mark on her life.

I wanted to know about *her*. How had she gotten to being this fantastic looking important psychiatrist now charged with handling the type of person who got cities nuked? Where did she come from? Did she go to school, get bored in lessons, piss about? Had she had private tutors, gone travelling on a gap year? Out in Canada, had she always known what she wanted? Looking like she looked, how hard had it been for her? Had she leapfrogged over more able but uglier wannabe psychiatrist life coaches, perhaps without even knowing how favoured she was?

I thought all this. What I said was, 'You're saying I'm boring?'

She smiled. 'Anthony. You should think better of yourself. You're stronger than you know. Perhaps being boring has kept you sane. What do you think?'

'I am boring. I'm starting to realise just how boring. I've never been anywhere, never done anything. I always assumed I couldn't. I've wasted so much time.'

Penny touched my hand. 'Well, now you have your opportunity. To do some real good.'

Penny's face was truly unreadable. She kept her composure well. I could never tell what she was really thinking.

'Are you afraid of me, Penny?'

She sipped her healthy herbal fruit infusion. She thought about what I said. She looked at Doctor Angler who stayed impassive.

'I'd be stupid if I wasn't,' she said.

Chapter 12

Week Two. I was in love with Penny. She was all I thought about. Perhaps they planned this to happen. It didn't matter.

I discovered that the more we talked, the less I was listening to what she was saying. I was too busy concentrating on what type of skirt she was wearing, the lustre of her hair, her breasts. Not lust, you understand, this was love.

I was used now to playing at filling in the gaps in her life. What had she done before me? Was she married? Did she have to wake up at a prearranged time in the middle of the night to phone a boyfriend in Toronto? What did she do in the evening, when I was in my room? Was she required to attend heavy debriefing sessions or could she head out into town for a relaxing drink? What did her colleagues think of her courage, dealing day in, day out with a potential time bomb? Did she really like Doctor Angler? Did she really like me? On and on.

I'd been in love before but this was new. The unattainable Emma Raynor all those years ago, whom I'd never gotten over; Toni (yeah, so I thought), the others; I forget their names. They had been sketches; this was the painting. Penny was thirty-six and she had sharp, hooded green eyes which made her look sexily tired. Sometimes she smiled and I could see the little girl she had once been; out in those snowfields or whatever they have in Canada.

Obviously, Penny was more intelligent than me, which put us at a disadvantage. She was the first woman I'd met since getting this glamour that I didn't want to zap. For once, and impossible as it may sound, I wanted to earn her.

Day after day, we talked. Informal talks; very reliant on me agreeing not to leave the hotel. Not that I wanted to. I was even pleased that the glamour seemed to be blocked. Imagine how happy she would be when I eventually told her.

Very soon the only question on my mind was what Penny would say when I asked her to… well, to go out with me. Be my girlfriend. Oh, you know.

Nerves held me back. I went hot, I went cold. I dared and promised myself. I rehearsed and planned and berated my cowardice but I never had the guts.

What if she said no?

On the surface, where it didn't matter, she and Doctor Angler tried to get me to agree to the medical tests. I felt I was being amenable in most areas but for this I said no.

'Not a problem, Anthony,' said Doctor Angler. 'Nothing will happen. We'll wait for you.'

'I mean, I want to help you. You know that.'

'Of course.'

Penny smiled. 'You've already been incredibly helpful.'

'You've been studying this glamour, right?'

Angler's turn to smile. 'Believe me, Anthony, I don't do anything else.'

'So tell me. What do you know? How does it work? What are the rules?'

That stunned them. They looked at each other. Finally, Angler sighed and said: 'Where do you want to begin?'

Penny suggested I should be reintroduced to Gordon Rice. I agreed.

Doctor Angler arranged to have him brought to the hotel for a meeting. I don't think they really knew what else to do with him. He hadn't actually been charged with Titanic's messy death (and how long ago did that seem now?) and there was a limit to how long they could keep him in a cell when he hadn't done anything.

Thing was, there wasn't any legal precedent for being glamoured. The extent of his crime was that I asked him to go away and he had done his best to make that happen. The fact he had interpreted my suggestion ridiculously literally was amusing but hardly worthy of prison.

Doctor Angler explained that since his arrest, Gordon had been transferred to a psychiatric institution. Although never charged by the police, he never asked to be released and he never questioned why he was there. He was rational on every point except one. And that point was me.

I didn't know what to expect upon seeing him again. I had zapped him without knowing. Gordon Rice was my manager; I hardly knew him. For some reason, as I waited in my room, I was embarrassed.

I made an effort with my appearance: shirt and tie. I didn't know what he'd think of me. Maybe after a while, his extreme reaction would wear off. I could even tell him to forget about the whole going away thing. I mean, I had ruined his life and killed one of his staff. I guess I owed him an apology.

I left my room and walked round the spacious atrium to the fancy lift. Penny was waiting. 'Ready?'

I nodded. I was finding speaking to her more difficult the more we got to know each other. My love for her was stifling.

'Look,' she said, and I glanced down. Over a glass bannister, next to the stairs I could see into the lounge. I was used to Gordon Rice in the bland peeling scenery of a government office, not a gaudy boutique hotel. My ex-manager sat on a settee, incongruous in the luxury of these surroundings. He looked uncomfortable. I felt sorry for him. Three men in dark suits stood round him. They were talking. As I watched, Gordon put his hand to his mouth and coughed, before replying to one of the men. I couldn't catch his words, but the familiar buzz of his voice took me back to a warmer, simpler part of my life. He seemed absolutely normal.

'He doesn't know,' said Penny. 'That he's meeting you, I mean.'

'If my last order to him was to go away, I don't suppose he'd have come willingly.' I was catching on to all this psychology lark.

'Very good,' she said. 'So be careful. And remember, we don't want you using the glamour on the poor man again. God knows what that would set off.'

'Penny,' I said. I wanted to tell her the truth. I really did.

'Yes, Anthony?'

She really was beautiful. I was definitely in love. But would she still love me if I told her I couldn't… couldn't do the thing?

'Nothing,' I said. 'It can wait.'

She turned away and jabbed the lift button. I took the opportunity to look at her trim, weight-controlled figure. Yeah, she was pretty much everything I ever wanted.

As we waited, Penny studied me. 'Are you okay, Anthony?'

'Fine. Why?'

She nodded a few times, as if coming to a decision. 'It's just you sometimes seem uncomfortable. Physically. Like something isn't right. If so, please talk to me. I'd like to help you.'

My stomach growled. Just at the wrong time. Shit. I was giving myself away and didn't even know it. How was I supposed to conceal my impotence in front of two professionals trained to read body language? How long was I going to get away with this? Christ, I loved this woman. I was going to tell her. I knew I was.

'Nothing. Nothing wrong. Penny. Why? What… why does it look… what would I…'

The lift door pinged open. 'Another time,' said Penny. I was more than aware she was letting me off the hook.

When we hit the lobby, Penny walked out first. The three men turned and eyeballed me. I don't know what they'd been told. Or maybe it was Penny they were staring at.

These guards towered over Gordon. Compared to them, he looked like a tubby mole. He had gentle, moist eyes.

'Mr Rice,' said Penny. 'I have a surprise for you.'

Gordon saw me. He began what was to climax in a very loud, very drawn-out scream.

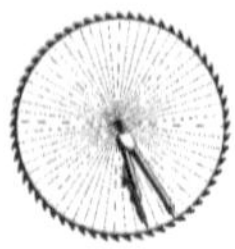

They got him calm in the end. Apparently, one of the guards was a doctor, and he was ready with a hypodermic.

Turns out that what everyone expected would happen did happen. Gordon Rice hadn't gone crazy: he just felt he'd absolutely failed in the one task I'd asked him to perform: to go away. And he was so devastated he couldn't hold on to his sanity.

Even the injection didn't calm him. Despite Penny's suggestion, I secretly tried to glamour him again. Again, a buttock-clenching failure. The pipe was still blocked.

Next, I tried to tell Gordon I didn't want him to go away any more and that he was all right just here. Unfortunately, instead of reducing his emotional crisis, Gordon continued to go nuts in a different way. In fact, Gordon was so grateful he fell to his knees, pressed his face into the floor and stretched out his arms like I was a statue in a church. Upon which he began loudly bellowing pleas for forgiveness. Until the drugs knocked him over and the men took him away.

Over dinner that evening, Doctor Angler, Penny and I discussed what we had learned.

Well, they spoke and I listened. Listened and tried not to look at Penny. I just couldn't help myself.

'For our own sake, Anthony, I really would like to do some tests,' said Doctor Angler as he tucked into his vegetarian risotto. 'Quite harmless. Just a scan. I suspect the imprint has caused permanent restructuring in your brain. Physical restructuring. It could be damaging in the long term. This really is quite some power you have there, Anthony.'

I felt sorry for Gordon. They told me he was going to be released and sent home, but to see a man act like that… I didn't think he would recover.

'I wish I'd never gotten this thing,' I said. I stared down at my specially prepared roasted pepper pizza. I was so sick of *specially prepared* everything. Why couldn't I have normal back?

Penny touched my wrist. She was genuinely concerned about me, I was sure. She had feelings for me, I was sure of that too. But what if I was wrong? What if I was just seeing what I wanted to see?

'Remember,' she said. 'You're still you. You're in control of the glamour. It doesn't control you.'

'There have been some developments,' said Doctor Angler. 'Around the world. The Chinese deny that Changchun was anything to do with people like you. They're claiming they were putting down a counter-revolt; a coup. Perhaps they really believe that.'

'But you don't?'

Doctor Angler scooped up his rice. 'It's possible. Perhaps the Sirens out there built themselves a little army.'

'Sirens?' That was a new one on me.

Penny nodded. 'A euphemism. For a new phenomenon in human biology. From Homer.'

I still looked blank. Yeah, unfortunately I hadn't studied the classics at Harvard. Why don't you two brainboxes make me feel really dumb?

'The Odyssey,' she went on, as if that explained anything. 'Sirens were supernatural creatures, women, who captivated passing sailors with their songs and enticed them to wreck their ships on the rocks.'

'Right. Who came up with that one?'

'I did actually,' said Doctor Angler. 'We had to define you somehow.'

'*To the sirens first shalt thou come, who bewitch all men,*' said Penny.

We both looked at her. She smiled. 'That's the quote.'

'There's more,' Doctor Angler continued. 'We think there's one in France. A woman.'

France.

'That's close,' I said. That was too bloody close. I had a real aversion to the idea that my life might get this complicated. That I might have to meet one of them. Another Siren. One who still knew how to make it work.

'We have a confirmed case in the United States. A man called Max Angstrom.'

'Mad Max.'

They both looked blank. Once again, I had said something really bloody stupid in front of the one person I was trying to impress.

'Right,' said Doctor Angler. 'Actually, he appears extremely sane. A sixty year old college professor. He's volunteered to allow the authorities to study him. At the moment, he's undergoing tests at a neurology hospital in Boston.'

'You're saying I'm not helping enough.'

'Not at all,' said Penny. 'You are an immense help, Anthony. Really.'

My radar perked up. I pushed my plate away. 'I don't know… there's so many of us. It doesn't seem real.'

'Many?' Penny replied. 'Statistically speaking, in terms of the population, the numbers don't even register. All that power in so few hands.'

'Anthony my friend,' said Angler. 'You'd better start believing, because we need you.'

'What for?'

For the first time, Angler looked like he'd overreached himself. He shot a glance at Penny, who looked away. She was thinking.

'We won't beat about the bush, Anthony,' Penny said. 'We're worried. Pretty soon this whole… situation is going to become public knowledge. And when that happens, well, what do you think is going to occur?'

'I don't know. I haven't thought.'

'You're handling your new ability with extreme maturity,' she continued. 'But what if we get someone who doesn't?'

'What if a Siren turns up who is utterly destructive?' said Doctor Angler. 'How are we supposed to stop them?'

Penny held my wrist again. Oh god, she felt beautiful. 'And there's something else. When people learn you can control someone's will just by wishing it, well, what do you think most people will think of you?'

She was right. Except of course, my glamour was the only glamour in the world that *didn't bloody work*.

'They will say I'm a monster, I guess.'

I must have spoken oddly because both Angler and Penny looked puzzled. Perhaps they already knew.

That was a step too far. Of course they didn't know. They didn't know because if they did, I had a sudden certainty; if they did, I would be dead.

All I wanted, right at this moment, was to down a bottle of wine, go back to bed and watch telly. I wanted someone else to sort out whatever it was I was supposed to do. I wanted Penny. I wanted her to take her clothes off. I wanted to kiss her. I so much wanted to kiss her. Most of all I wanted to tell her I was normal again and her to tell me she loved me.

'Oh man,' I said.

'I know, Anthony,' said Angler. 'I know.'

That evening, two weeks and a day after I had arrived, I made a decision.

At seven o'clock on a Friday evening, I went out. I walked past the guys sitting in the lobby and out of the hotel. A test. Did they or did they not know the truth?

I left the guards reaching for their cell phones and walked with measured steps away from the hotel. Every step, I expected someone to start firing; to feel that hot bullet between my shoulder blades.

I walked along the Clerkenwell Road towards Holborn. I started to pass normal people who didn't give me a second look. I wasn't anyone special here, on these early summer pavements. I sensed London ahead. Noisy, busy, unpredictable London. The city was life. The city wasn't about me.

After a mile or so, I couldn't think of anywhere to go. So I went to the pub. The Crown and Anchor up at Euston where I used to go after work with Toni and Keano and those other wage earners. God, I'd wandered out of that place barely able to walk on more occasions than I cared to remember. Weekdays from five o'clock that pub was heaving. Young and not-so-young Londoners drinking and yelling and laughing as yet another dull working day drew to its close. Perhaps like the old me they were thinking that this was only temporary. A bit of a laugh before what they were really going to do with their lives got going. And funny how that extended and extended until they realised that just maybe, in the end, this *was* what they were going to do with their lives. That was their Crown and Anchor.

I walked in and instinctively looked round for familiar faces. The roman numerals on the clock over the bar pointed out seven thirty-seven. No one from work was here.

I once came to this pub on a Sunday evening. I was in the area and fancied a pint. Maybe I was with someone and trying to impress; can't remember. However, the place was shut and looked small and lonely. Unrecognisable. The whole area seemed utterly transformed, empty and desolate. Deserted, like there had been an evacuation. For some reason that had made me feel sad.

Not tonight though. Tonight the Crown and Anchor was definitely open. A trio of little wall-mounted TVs were gleaming with the same football match. I smelled the familiar stale beer and toilet cleaner. Yeah. This was more like it. Stuff your designer hotels. This was my world.

The barman, the inevitable Eastern European, was looking at me as I walked up to him. He was puzzled, as if he recognised me. I took that to be a good sign of being in the right place.

I decided that for once I'd pay for a drink. It had been a while but I found a mouldy old fiver in my wallet. 'Pint of…'

He stopped me dead. 'It's you,' he said. 'You're the guy.' He was possessed by a compressed, concentrated enthusiasm. He was a bit scary.

'Am I?' Suddenly the old need flared up. The fizz. I wanted to get him. That unexpected flare was so refreshing. Perhaps I wasn't finished after all. Perhaps this was just what I needed.

'On the news,' he said. 'The guy who can do things.'

'That's me,' I told him, and pushed.

Again, the burn was there; the energy that wanted out. I could feel it building and building until inevitably it had to trigger — it had to come — it was so ready, so ripe. Nothing was going to stop it, yes yes yes!

Except, except. It just didn't happen. I just couldn't push that glamour over the top and out. Instead, the tidal wave hit some mental wall, rammed it and receded.

'Fuck!' I yelled. 'Fuck it!' I think I even punched the bar. 'What's the matter with me?'

Before I could react, the two muscular men whom I now realised had been following me since I left the hotel gripped my arms.

'Anthony,' said the one with the goatee beard (he looked army). 'If you don't mind, I think we had better go back to the hotel.'

As they pulled me away, I saw the smirk on the barman's face. Same old Anthony. Same old Anthony Graves.

Chapter 13

Doctor Angler poured me a Carlsberg from a bottle. He said: 'If it's a drink you want…'

As it happened, it was a drink I didn't want. The Doc looked like someone had gotten him out of bed in the middle of the night, although it was still only nine o'clock. His suit was askew; his hair stuck up in two places. Penny, of course, looked immaculate.

My two army friends had dropped me off in the hotel lobby. I noticed there was a new barman. In fact, now I thought about it, there was always a new barman. Every day: always suspiciously tough looking, always a bit too discreet. This barman sat shrouded in shadows, watching MTV, well away from me. The hotel, with its artsy décor, was stifling now; my experiment in going AWOL was instinct telling me to get away. They knew. They knew everything. Of course they did.

However, when Angler and Penny turned up, they had something else on their minds. They didn't even mention my little excursion. I don't know but I had a suspicion they had been expecting it. They probably thought I would try it ages ago. Good old Anthony: always last to the party.

'Mr Stan Bergman has been busy,' said Doctor Angler. 'You have been invited to appear on television, Anthony. Prime time.' He mentioned a chat show. A big one.

'Why didn't anyone bother telling me?'

'We didn't know,' said Penny. 'I promise we didn't.'

'This is something your mother has cooked up,' Angler snapped. 'We told her to trust us. But no. She's convinced we have to be up to something. That we mean harm. This is a big mistake.'

'Matt, I agree but there's nothing we can do about it,' said Penny.

Matt? I didn't like her and Angler being on first name terms. This was new. Not good.

'Knowledge about you would have gotten out eventually,' Angler continued. 'There's too much happened to keep quiet. Bergman apparently has connections. First I knew was an hour ago when the bloody Times rang my mobile. God knows how they got the number. Still, they don't know your location, so for the moment you're safe enough. But please: no more excursions.'

'Okay.' I was so relieved they hadn't clicked onto my failure in the Crown and Anchor, I would have agreed to anything.

'I think this chat show scenario may prove beneficial,' said Penny. 'A chance for our man here to shine.' She smiled at me. 'Anthony, how do you feel about becoming a celebrity?'

Me? I was stunned. Flabbergasted. Sideswiped. I had no idea mum had it in her.

'Smart lady, your mother,' said Angler. He looked pensive. 'I wonder just how smart.'

Penny gave the slightest shake of her head. Back off. 'She's just looking after her son, that's natural. After all, it's only logical for her to presume Anthony is in trouble.'

Angler looked at me. 'I don't know. Sometimes, I get the oddest feeling about her…'

We stared at each other. An over-hysterical laugh track to a reality TV show blared from the lobby television.

'What?' I asked. 'Have you spoken to her?'

He smiled. 'No. The only fact that matters, Anthony, is that you're now hooked into the public consciousness. In twenty-four hours every man, woman and child in Britain is going to know who you are and what you can do. You need to be ready. Unless of course you don't want to.' He tried not to make his voice sound hopeful.

I raised an arm for the hotel barman. Forget Angler pouring it out of a glass. I never did get to have that pint in the Crown and

Anchor. I was bloody well going to have it now. The barman hurried.

'I don't know how to go on telly,' I said. I sipped the cold, gorgeous liquid. It tasted good. 'What am I supposed to say?'

Angler and Penny sat back. I had given them what they wanted to hear. 'Don't worry,' said Angler. 'We'll handle everything.'

I had a thought. About someone I hadn't considered for a long time. 'What about my dad?' I couldn't remember the last time I'd seen him.

Again: the awkward pause. I realised they had been waiting for me to ask. Angler ran his hand through his sticky-up hair. 'He– he doesn't want you home, Anthony.'

'What?'

Penny held my hand again. That, I liked. 'We have been keeping a dialogue going with him. He has developed some kind of religious belief. Very strong.'

'Dad? Never.'

'It's true. He's driving your mother crazy. He's very vulnerable at present and I think some very unstable fundamentalist people have got their hooks into him.'

'Let me speak to him.'

'He doesn't want to see you. In fact, he's terrified that this is exactly what we are going to make happen. Now, we can't stop you but we believe it's in both your interests if you don't meet at the moment. I'm sorry.'

In my room, I lay on the bed and watched myself on the news. I didn't need to go on any chat show to become a celebrity. I was everywhere already. The guy who works miracles. The UK's answer to Spiderman. I switched the thing off and picked up the ring binder perched on my stomach.

Doctor Angler had given me a report. He ever-so-casually left the folder on my bed.

It was a folder with a picture of happily smiling multiracial medical staff on the front. Just the same kind of bland bullshit my department at work would issue with tiresome regularity. How long was it since I had read anything?

I looked at a whole bunch of statistics and diagrams I didn't understand. In the end, I just read the conclusions; the only parts that seemed to be in English.

Funny to see one's own story written down so mathematically. One's life dissected. A human being reduced to correlations and numbers. The report felt second-hand, like a biographer who hasn't been allowed access to his subject.

There were interviews, centred on the events at Marylebone Police Station. The Department of Health had performed extensive physiological tests on those affected: adrenalin, serotonin levels, that kind of thing. I gathered they were looking to see if the glamour caused a chemical change in the brain of the target. Apparently, it didn't.

They then speculated whether my 'victims' were suffering from mass delusion. That they got themselves glamoured because they believed in my power rather than there actually being any power. I got very confused trying to read the statistics and probabilities, all the time wondering how the hell they could prove that. As if anyone would agree that thanks to my mighty charisma they would now do whatever I wanted for the rest of their lives. I mostly skipped those pages.

The report noted that the subjects were happy to volunteer information to the authorities. The police chief, Kate the pretty sergeant, even the people from the reception area. They seemed undamaged by their experience. No breakdowns, no emotional traumas. To them, the idea that they had let me walk out of a maximum security building and then refused to leave themselves was perfectly natural. The only time they got upset was when they were informed that there might have been something wrong with their powers of decision making. In fact, they completely rejected the possibility.

The report writers were reluctant to go all sci-fi over the glamour. They grudgingly admitted they had submitted the subjects to what they called parapsychological tests, which looked like trying to pretend that tests for ESP and telepathy were proper science. The tone of embarrassment was palpable.

After thirty-six minutes' reading on my part, and despite all the mumbo jumbo, they never figured the glamour out. The closest they came to a definition was the conjecture that the victim received an impulse; a fundamental psychological imprint right in the central core of their mind like a computer virus that wired itself tight into the operating system of a machine. The glamour permeated emotional centres of the brain and rechannelled the way things were going to work from now on.

The report admitted that how this happened, by me just wanting it to, was beyond their comprehension. Still, they were confident enough to put 'as yet' after that statement. Mm.

I read over psychometric tests, IQ tests, detailed interviews. I guess I was going through this stage at the moment with Dr Angler and Penny. Similar to the sort of cosmetic questionnaires our HR department would occasionally send out depending on what theory of handling employees was trendy at the moment. I remembered that Toni and Keano always took the piss when filling them in. I had always given the things a go; too worried about possible comeback.

One interesting concept, which Angler and Penny obviously hadn't gotten round to yet, and which I hadn't talked about, was how I felt when I used the glamour. What did I get out of the experience? I'm guessing they never asked because they were too worried about getting a practical demonstration.

Finally, we got to the part about physical tests. They were serious; no matter how much whoever had written this report tried to sugarcoat them for me.

Medical tests. Blood and needles. Ugh.

Then off we were into the realms of the psychophysiological. EEG scans which would look for changes in the electrical potential of the brain (so the doctors said). MRI scans to look for anatomical changes. I guess they wanted to see whether whatever had slotted itself into my head that fateful April morning had altered my brain structure. And finally, my personal favourite, the PET scan. Positron Emission Tomography, involving injecting me with a glucose solution and a radioactive tracer. Apparently, this would allow them to look at the levels of neural activity in different areas when I performed different tasks.

I tossed the report aside. It hit the carpeted floor with a satisfying thump. Yeah, good luck with that. Like I was going to allow anyone to inject me with fucking radioactive whatever. I wasn't sick; in fact I'd never felt so well. Was I really going to spend month after month letting some white-coated government scientist stick thermometers up my backside until they figured out what the hell was causing this? Because after all the mumbo jumbo, they might actually find out that Anthony Graves, once so powerful, was just a sad little South London boy after all. A boy who had been on holiday for a while but was now back where he belonged.

I went back to the television. There were worries about Chinese fallout drifting in the wind. Everything had its consequences. That reminded me of what Keano said when he left. For every one I got and sent away, two would come back. There would always be somebody left to get me. I couldn't glamour them all, could I? In fact, until I got it going again, I couldn't glamour anybody. I had to get back in the game and quick. It was time for Anthony Graves to step up.

Angler had dropped the pretence and officially drafted in what he called bodyguards. There was one outside my door all the time. He must have been exceptionally brave, whoever he was. More likely they hadn't told him. Angler had the Clerkenwell Road sealed off. I was beginning to see just what kind of power he had. The cars and vans multiplied. There were an awful lot of men in raincoats out there.

I stayed in my room as often as I could. No more trips to the pub. I cut down on the tea. I actually liked the effects of the Prozac and I didn't dare stop taking it. I had to find a way to overcome through force of will the numbing effects of the drug. Was it an Incredible Hulk thing? Did I have to get angry to tap into the glamour? I don't think so. In fact, I mainly used it (so casually, oh so painfully casually back in Hammersmith) when I was in a good mood.

The telly kept flashing up this terrible picture of me from three years ago on holiday in Cornwall with mum and dad. I was gurning like a bumpkin. Even younger, I certainly wasn't an oil painting.

More recent footage was the familiar image of us leaving the tower in Euston Road, when the reporters wandered off. No: when I *ordered* them off. I studied my face on the screen. What was I doing there, at that exact moment? What wasn't I doing now?

There was no way I was going to keep fooling Angler and Penny. And just how was I supposed to go on television? They were bound to ask me to use the glamour; even if they had no idea what that would entail. They would crucify me when they found out I couldn't do it.

This bloody hotel was driving me mad. But all I had was their belief that I was voluntarily not using the glamour. What was mum playing at? I'd tried ringing her, but I think they'd manked the phones up and I couldn't get a signal. On the landline I got nothing but an answerphone.

I remembered what mum had told me about Bergman. That she'd brought him in to keep me safe. Was going on a TV chat show part of that plan? I had half a thought to go home and make her explain, to tell her I had messed up the power anyway, but the idea of Croydon was depressing. And also, did I really want to meet a new, evangelical dad? I missed him. I wished I was seven again and he was there to look after me. I would have liked nothing better than to let him know the glamour was gone.

I seemed to be on course for a place I didn't like the look of. A place from where there was no coming back.

As the hours and days in the room passed by, my thoughts spiralled into ever more conspiratorial theories. At what point would the authorities take me out? Did they have an actual moment; a trigger pulled when I did something; crossed some kind of threshold? What if not using the glamour was the only thing keeping me alive? The idea seemed ludicrous. But so did nuking a Chinese city.

If I was a good boy, would they let me have Penny? Would she be my reward? I didn't think so.

You see, I had sussed Penny. She didn't like Angler, not really, but she did like me. Penny was all I had to cling to. She couldn't come out and tell me her feelings; they were watching her, but she was clever. Penny was making herself clear in other ways. There were too many clues, too many eye-contacts and brushed knees for this not to be true. We were on the same wavelength. I couldn't explain it; I didn't even want to think of why or how, but it had happened. We both knew. As our meetings progressed, I had come to realise the two of us were playing a little game which would eventually see the oblivious doctor edged out. I liked Angler, he was a good guy I'm sure, but it wasn't him I was in love with.

Perhaps that's why I agreed to the interview. Ultimately, I trusted mum more than any of that lot. If she thought going on the telly was a good idea then I would do it.

It hit me. I was going on TV. After a lifetime of nothing, I was going to be somebody. Already I was recognised when I went out. I was out of patience with this whole setup. I felt like I'd been here months, sitting around, being prodded and poked by these psychology types. Tell the truth: I was bored. It was time for action. I needed to get on with my life. I needed Penny.

I made my move. Obviously, I left it until the night of the ill-fated television show. I had to. I'd bottled up all the desire for so long that I couldn't keep going. I'd rather get rejected. At least then I would know.

Besides, our little secrets game together — hints and nudges and smiles — was getting blatant. I ought to act, for Penny's sake. Those watching her had to be suspicious. We were practically advertising our giggling flirtation.

Unless I helped her out, she was going to get into trouble for falling in love with me.

Had I realised that this would be the last day of my old life, I might have handled the situation differently. As it was, inevitably, I cocked it right up.

Late that afternoon, she knocked on my hotel room door. I don't know whether she'd been sent, or genuinely wanted to talk. Anyway, she was there. She was there and I could hardly speak.

I was pulling a Paul Smith jacket on. One of those great pinstriped ones. Dark blue, with thin lines. Daringly, I went for a t-shirt underneath. I thought maybe it would make me look younger. I thought it looked cool. Penny disagreed.

With a seductive authority, she hauled open the wardrobe door and searched through my clothes. 'You have to wear a proper shirt for TV,' she said. Her Canadian accent was a dream.

I stepped forward. I hardly knew what I was doing. Just as I reached her she turned and whacked me in the mouth with a dark grey shirt. The hangar scraped my cheek. I stepped back.

'Anthony!' she screeched. 'Oh my… I'm sorry.' She put her free hand to her mouth. I could see she was trying not to laugh.

I prodded my smarting face. 'No, no… it's okay,' I blustered.

'Are you hurt?'

'It's nothing.' I felt the heat of humiliation spreading across my face. But I couldn't stop now. I couldn't lose the momentum. Penny looked puzzled as I reached forward and kissed her. I felt her breath on my lips.

I'd made a mistake. I'd been utterly, devastatingly wrong.

She flinched away, almost panicked. She dropped the shirt and stumbled against the wardrobe. The mirror she'd backed into wobbled.

'Anthony?' She was trembling.

I couldn't look at her. 'Sorry… sorry…' I mumbled. 'I thought… I got it all wrong…'

I wanted her out of the room. I wanted her so much. I was afraid of what I might do. I managed to say: 'You'd better… better go…'

'Anthony?' Her voice pierced me now.

Why couldn't it have been easy? Why couldn't I just have had her? Why couldn't she just want *me*? Taking command, as usual, Penny knelt to the minibar and poured me out a miniature bottle of Bells into a plastic cup.

'Drink that,' she said. I could hear that she was keeping heavy breathing under control. She was figuring out what to say, thinking on her feet. 'I understand what just happened. And I think the… feelings you've developed are only natural. I don't want you to think that you've done anything wrong at all. These feelings, emotions, always occur between a psychiatrist and her client. With this degree of intimacy, that's inevitable.'

I didn't want to listen. I didn't want my feelings to be rationalised; put in a box and understood. I was worth more than that. Something tickled inside my head. The easy way out. Only it didn't bloody work.

'Look at me, Anthony,' she said.

'I can't.'

'Please. Look at me. Let's talk about this.'

She made me take a mouthful of burning whiskey and sat me down. She was great and I didn't blame her in the least.

'No problem. Whatever.' I was going to cry, I was so ashamed.

'You look fine. You're going to be great.' She took a deep breath. 'Listen, Anthony. You could get people; a lot of people. You might be able to get everyone. But is that what you want?'

'How do you know what I want?'

'I have tremendous admiration for you, Anthony,' she told me. 'You're a good man; a moral man. But you are a man with the power to alter the world.'

Penny's eyes were narrow. She was thinking hard. It made her look amazingly sexy. I tried to concentrate.

'You're an intelligent and perceptive man, Anthony,' she said. (Mm? Really? I liked Penny even more!) 'I am sure you've realised that if you allow the glamour to control you; if you give in to it, you will be utterly unhappy and there will be no going back. Now, I'm sorry if you think… that you feel I've forced an emotional bond onto you. It's put us in an awkward position. I admire the fact you could have, well, *taken me* any time you wanted. It's a sign of your maturity that you didn't. For that, I thank you.'

Penny held my hand. She sat me on the bed. 'You want to be liked. Truly liked, even loved. Not because of the glamour but for who you are; for what you can achieve.'

'I love you, Penny.'

Penny nodded. 'I know, Anthony. I want you to hold it back. Even if it's just for tonight; hold it back. Give the people a chance to love you in the right way. Don't cheat. You don't need to cheat. You're better than that.'

I smiled and stroked her wonderful arm, feeling its warmth beneath that expensive silk.

'Okay,' I said.

'Promise me.'

'I promise.'

Little drops of moisture appeared in her eyes. She dabbed them with a tiny piece of tissue paper. She stood. You know what? I felt better. I felt better than I had felt in months; ever since this thing had happened to me.

And then Penny asked: 'Anthony. Okay. I'm going to level with you.'

I felt that euphoric mood burst. I couldn't breathe. 'What?'

Penny, for the first time since I met her, looked frightened. 'Matt — Doctor Angler — and I. We're wondering if everything's okay. With the glamour. We… think… somehow, you might be finding it, er, difficult. That there's a problem. I'm sure that's not the case but if it is, it's something we might be able to help you with.'

I looked at her.

'Don't say anything yet,' she continued. And why not; after all, she now had nothing to lose. 'Before you answer, let me share some of our thoughts with you. When you first got the power, using it was a shock. It kind of came on its own. You weren't in control. As time passed, when you were up in West London, it was fun and natural. You were having a good time; enjoying yourself. No harm done. Only now, here with us, something has happened. And it's good, Anthony, it's really good.'

'What's good?' I tried to keep my voice neutral.

'Remember those suicides? The two women? We believe those women took their own lives because they knew what the power made them capable of. They foresaw the inevitable consequence of gaining the glamour. They rejected it. Their intelligence and upbringing and conscience made them feel they had no choice but death. They were good people. What is blocking you, Anthony, is the real you. Thirty years of behaviour and learning. Your subconscious is telling you not to do bad things. You're a moral man, Anthony, but what is in you is not moral. You know that.'

I stayed stock still sat on the bed.

'It has gone, hasn't it?'

I nodded. 'Yes.'

We looked at each other. If she felt any satisfaction in finding out, she didn't show it.

'Do I have to go on television?' I asked.

She sat next to me on the bed and held my hand. 'Not if you don't want to.'

We kept looking at each other.

'Thank you for your honesty,' she said. 'I'll tell them to cancel. Right now.'

Penny stood and turned to open the hotel room door. She looked back at me and smiled. I glamoured her.

Chapter 14

Something broke in my head. Physically, the push had been minute. I had forced it out as if through a tiny hole but a great burning torrent of pain soaked into my brain nonetheless.

Penny fell against the door. I fell on the bed and yelled. This was burning, searing agony I'm talking about. I had finally unblocked but what was the cost? I screamed out loud. It was never going to subside, never. 'Make it stop!' I remember calling out. 'Please, make it stop!'

Penny saved me. I felt her lower me to the bed. She shushed me and stroked my head. 'My darling, my darling Anthony,' she said. 'It's okay, it will pass. I'm here. I'm yours.'

Slowly, far too slowly, the pain went away. I heard a knocking on the door. Penny said some words that made the knocking stop.

I blinked the tears away and could see her clearly again. She had a new look in her eyes; a gleam I'd not seen before. I liked that gleam, but it didn't come for free. There was sickness too, a guilty sickness. She had been right: the glamour was bad. I was a bad man.

This was my first really rotten trick. I'd been naughty before, but this was downright evil. If it had been within my power to reverse the process; to make it that I'd never glamoured Penny; I would not have glamoured her. And I would be long dead.

'What are you planning to do with me?' I said through a mouthful of ache. 'You. Doctor Angler. The Government. Everyone.'

She checked my pulse. 'You're fast,' she said. 'They don't tell us anything about each other's research, Anthony. A deliberate policy. They knew you would use your power on us to ask this question. We're strictly to gather information. To take notes.'

'Simple as that.'

'I have found things out. They're worried. They fear you. They don't love you like I do. They fear your might. I would expect they have made… contingencies. They're taking a risk on the television and they trusted me to stop you using your wonderful power. But we were reasonably sure you were blocked

I sat up. The pain was an echo now. Distant but enough to remind me. 'Listen, who's to say I'm not still blocked?'

'You seduced me,' she said.

'Yeah, and do you know how much that hurt? It was nothing like before. I hardly got it out and it almost killed me. I can't go through that again.'

Penny kissed me. 'Poor darling. I'm convinced it's you blocking yourself. The old Anthony learning to accept just who you are now. When the time is right, you will shine. I'm certain of it. They have seriously underestimated you. Don't worry.'

She was good. She was very good. I almost believed her.

'Do you think they will try to kill me?'

Penny looked at the door, as if someone were listening. 'They already have. At least twice now.'

I heard a new buzzing noise as my aching head filled up with the news. Fright threatened to knock me over again. I had to stay in control.

'What do you mean?'

Penny put her arms round my neck and kissed my face. 'Oh Anthony,' she said. 'Can you forgive me?'

I pushed her back. She didn't resist. 'What do you mean: twice?'

'Please. I didn't know.'

'Just tell me!' I felt like smacking her face. Giving her a good slap. I like to think it was a symbol of the good, mature Anthony that I didn't.

'Something Doctor Angler mentioned. He didn't want to tell me directly. I was supposed to be your confidant.'

'Penny! Fucking tell me!'

'On the way here, in the taxi, a few days ago he hinted that signed orders had been given. They were going to poison you; maybe shoot you. Somehow he stopped them; got the orders countermanded. The information; that knowledge frightened him. He is desperately afraid you will glamour him.'

'Why would he help me?'

Penny looked up. Her eyes were dark and moist and lovely. I could smell her Canadian body, her scent; feel her within those chic clothes. The pain was draining out of me now. I wanted her so much but I needed to think. To plan. 'Up,' I said, with unbelievable self-control. 'Get up.'

Penny obeyed.

'Tell me about Doctor Angler.'

'He believes we will need you against the other Sirens when they come. Doctor Angler believes the genesis of the Sirens means the end of the human race as it has historically functioned. He thinks the Sirens will become the queen ants of the planet; running their individual colonies. And he believes you are the key to our survival. You will be the one to stand against less… less malleable Sirens.'

'Why the hell would he think that?'

'The same reason you agreed to be here now. The psychological profiles suggest you are a very passive young man susceptible to authority. That you crave acceptance which we can use to overcome your desire to control.'

'What does that mean?'

'Anthony, what drives you is your wish to be loved. Properly loved by people who love you of their own free will.' She stood up. Doctor Penny started to unbutton her chic, expensive blouse. 'Like me. Like I love you, Anthony. Do you think you could love me back?'

I pulled Penny down onto the huge hotel bed and did my best.

Ten minutes late for the car, we emerged from the room. I told Penny to pretend I hadn't glamoured her and that I was still blocked. She was to act as if she was still my psychologist. If I was still blocked, I was going to need her. I wasn't convinced by all this waffle about subconscious and new self. I was still the same old Anthony. Same daft me.

'Psychiatrist,' she said, as we reached the lift.

'What?'

'Not psychologist.'

'Who cares? What's the difference?'

'Psychologist.'

'Good girl.'

I stood in the lift and looked at her magnificent face. A face that now belonged to me.

Glamouring Penny didn't feel as bad now. The pressure that had been building up in my head was released. I couldn't understand why I'd felt so worried, so tight. She was happy and I had what I wanted. Love is love, right? In fact, she looked happy for the first time since I'd met her.

'Penny? Do you think I should go on TV?'

'I don't know,' she said. 'What do you want to do?'

'There must be a plan. I can't believe they're just letting me do this. They must be out of their minds.'

The lift pinged. We were down. Penny pressed the button to keep the doors shut. 'I honestly don't know,' she said. 'They don't want to. They really don't like your mother's influence; the way she manipulated this situation. She has gone into hiding to avoid assassination. She is a remarkable woman; way ahead of the game and really on your side.'

Penny kept her finger on the button. 'Listen, Anthony. The speed at which this has all happened has thrown them. If there is a conspiracy against you — and I honestly don't know — I advise you not to fall into the trap that conspiracy theorists always fall into. They always believe the conspirators to be incapable of error. Reality doesn't work that way. Wires get crossed, communication is bad, no one works for a common goal; no one really understands what to do. The conspiracy might be real but the means of delivery, the infighting, the lack of clarity, misunderstandings and petty feuding will always make the plan go wrong.'

At last, she lifted her manicured finger from the button. The lift doors swung open. Drivers and guards tensed in the lobby.

Penny lowered her mouth to my ear. 'But. It won't take them long to realise the folly of letting you do this interview. I don't believe they will give you another chance.'

We got caught in the inevitable traffic at Regent's Park. The streets gleamed in the sun. We'd had a humid day and people were commuting home, coats over their shoulders. Three months ago I would have been one of them.

As the chauffeur manoeuvred, sudden, dramatic sunshine lit the car. The evening felt momentous, and not just because of the telly thing. It was the way the light, the unreality, the thing I'd done to Penny all worked into each other; a strange blend creating a powerful cocktail.

I expected to be taken to that doughnut-shaped Television Centre in Shepherd's Bush but was regretfully informed it wasn't there anymore. We were heading for some studios in West London. Television had apparently moved. How come nobody told me?

I glared at the neck of the uniformed chauffeur as we headed along the A4. Without warning, the sky darkened and the heavens opened. I almost glamoured that neck but something, a lingering fear of failure, held me back. Memory of that pain was too tender, too raw. I just couldn't.

We drove through a raised, dripping security barrier and stopped outside the studio. The rain hammered down and we dashed inside beneath a policeman's umbrella. I caused no one to stop and look at me. There were no crowds lining the streets; nobody cheering my name.

Yeah, well that was the last time that happened.

We were whisked through a reception, where lots of trendy, well-educated and thin people supped plastic mugs of herbal tea. They coolly watched Penny and me blink and stumble through the atrium. They were used to spotting the famous. Penny got a few admiring glances but I was ignored; confirmation I was not in that category.

A head-setted young trendy with a clipboard arrived to lead us up elevators, along corridors and through doors to a plush green room. Nondescript couches and sofas lay scattered around like a bunch of people had been interrupted and ordered to leave. Someone had stacked a trio of plastic coffee cups on one of the seats.

Doctor Angler, dressed in a smart suit, stood against the far wall. He was alone.

'Have some drinks,' said the trendy telly chap with his fashionable haircut. 'We'll come and get you.' He smiled and shut us in together.

I felt Penny's warmth next to me. I had the strangest desire to put my hand under her short skirt and run it up along her sheer black tights. I wanted to show Angler. I was having trouble breathing correctly. Hopefully the good doctor interpreted that as nerves.

'How are you feeling, Anthony?' he asked.

'How much should I say?' I asked him.

'I really don't think we're capable of dictating anything to you, Anthony.'

Damn right my friend, I thought. I felt like I had my life back; that I'd become active again. Yeah. Angler's face was red. I suspect he had done a lot of shouting down the phone to try to get this interview cancelled.

'Just remember,' he said in that tone he always used when trying to convince me to do something he knew I didn't want to do. Coat it in sugar and fire it off; that was Angler's style. 'It may not be in your interest to reveal too much. There's a lot of people going to be watching. God knows what kind of nut you might attract.'

He looked at me. His eyes were very kind. How old was he? Forty? Fifty? I didn't know anything about him. Did the destiny of the human race really hinge on this man's conviction that I was good? Had he actually saved my life twice over?

'You're going to hear every theory in the universe after tonight, Anthony,' he said. 'Theories about you Sirens. About the glamour. About why.'

'Right. Yes.'

He was cautious, clearly not sure of whether to risk asking me. 'I'd like to give you my theory first, for what it's worth. Penny knows.'

We both looked at her. She nodded; as unreadable as I could have hoped. Was Angler testing her out? Was there some way of telling, some mark?

'Yes,' said Penny. 'But I'm not sure Anthony really wants to hear your theory right now.'

'I do,' I said. 'Please.'

Angler preened himself. He was preparing a lecture. I thought about something Gordon Rice used to say in meetings. He'd look down his nose and mutter in a kindly uncle voice: 'Short version.' We all laughed. Every time.

'They're going to come at you from all sides. You'll hear talk about God, the supernatural, drugs, radiation, hoaxes; everything. But my theory boils down to pure Darwinism. There's a lot of wiring in the brain which we still don't understand. The real question is not why you and the others got this power, but why you all got it at exactly the same time. In every reported case the switch was thrown that same morning in April. I'd go even further and speculate that the glamour came to you and your… fellows at exactly the same time. To the second.'

He looked at me. Doctor Angler was hyped up, like he had waited a long time to tell me this. I realised he wanted me to say something.

'Why the same time then?'

'I don't know what set off the alarm clock,' he replied. 'I imagine we'll never find out. It might be some undetectable natural force; a certain alignment of the solar system. Radiation reaching us from some distant quasar. It might even be connected to the invention of the internet and the ability for instant global mass communication. My own view? Pure supposition, but I suggest the trigger was biological. The Sirens were created because evolution insisted upon it. In a way, your time is nigh.'

'What does that mean?' I asked.

He glanced at the room around us with its bland décor. 'Think about the human race. How we've conquered pretty much every aspect of this planet. There are, what, ten billion of us now? Ten billion people; taking up more and more space. Fighting among ourselves, using up available resources. All humanity, tearing off in ten billion different directions. Where do we go next?'

'I don't know…'

'We're not lucky monkeys wandering round deserts trying to figure out how anything happens any more. There's too many of us. We're too clever. Collectively, we're an entirely new type of human. What we lack is an organising principle. Something to bind us. Think about ants, or bees, and how they work for each other, for the communal good. A group mind which can flourish only by working together.'

Angler glanced at Penny. 'Aren't you going to disagree, Doctor Dean?'

She looked at him, a dreamy expression implying he'd just woken her up. 'Hmm?'

'You usually have some pretty strong views about my "extreme" theories. Not going to argue?'

Penny shook her head. 'Not today, Matt.'

He ran his hand through his hair. Penny had distracted him. I got it: he knew all right.

'In some ways I don't want to think about it,' he said. 'All notions of democracy, of individual freedom, independent emotion: all gone, subsumed by the new impulse. The impulse to serve you, Anthony. You and your kind. The evolutionary necessity of survival annihilating everything we in the western world consider vital for our lives. Freedom as a concept could be about to go the way of the appendix or the prehensile tail. The ancient Romans willingly elected dictators to lead them out of times of crisis. They were prepared to sacrifice individual sanctity for the good of the body politic. Basic fascism. It might not be fair or nice but since when was nature fair or nice? Such concepts only emerged when we became a society that believed it had conquered nature.'

I couldn't think of anything to say. Was he after reassurance? From me? I wondered if he felt that me zapping him was only a matter of time.

'Red in tooth and claw,' Doctor Angler chuckled. 'And that's the story.'

The television people were buzzing around, making motioning gestures and listening to their headsets and shouting. It felt like chaos.

'What's going to happen, Doctor Angler?'

He turned away. I thought he looked sad. 'Happen?' He chuckled again. 'You could be a saviour. Or a destroyer of worlds, Anthony,' he said. 'What do you want?'

The TV people were calling out now; desperate for me to get a move on.

'Show time I guess,' I said. I hoped I didn't sound as nervous as I felt.

Penny was still dreamy and beautiful. 'How are you feeling, Anthony?' she asked.

Doctor Angler's voice was soft; very cool. 'I'm thinking it was in your room,' he said. He was looking at Penny. 'When you glamoured her?'

I felt like I'd been caught with my willy out. I mumbled a sort of yes.

'Don't blame Anthony,' said Penny. 'What other choice did he have?'

Doctor Angler was a calm man. In fact, he was one of the most self-controlled men I had ever met. He looked natural in a suit. The casual jumper/jeans combos of our lunchtime hotel chats had been purely for my benefit.

But something funny was happening to Doctor Angler's expression. His facial muscles were moving in odd spasms. His left eyebrow flinched.

'Doctor… Matt?' I asked.

He began to laugh. I didn't like the sound much.

'Stop it,' said Penny. 'You're disturbing Anthony.'

Angler snorted a giggle and flopped into a chair. He held a hand over his face. His whole body was shaking. The telly people looked at him angrily.

'What's the matter?' I asked. Tell the truth, he *was* disturbing me. 'What's funny?'

Angler belched out a laugh. The sound rang round the quiet room. He managed to control himself.

'Nothing,' he sniggered. His eyes were watering. 'There's nothing funny at all.'

Chapter 15

People were moving out of the green room now. The show was about to begin. Without me working out how, Stan Bergman was by my side. 'Anthony!' he said. 'An honour to see you again. How are you?'

'Fine, Mr Bergman, fine.'

Bergman took a step back. He looked down at himself and gestured; clearly expecting me to say something. I hadn't seen the journalist for a few weeks and he had really shed the pounds. There was nothing of him. He looked like the thin twin brother of the man I'd met on Hammersmith Bridge. Cheek bones protruded awkwardly beneath his eyes. His skin was yellow and sallow. Despite that he was still wearing the same suit. It hung off him like a pair of pyjamas.

I sniffed. He was tottering; could barely stand. I had to ask. 'Been to the gym?'

'Sorry?'

'You look like you've lost a few pounds.'

Bergman smiled. His head resembled a skull. 'No, no, just natural. All thanks to you, Anthony. You remember?'

'What? No, Mr Bergman, I don't remember.'

'You told me to lose weight; called me a fat fuck. I haven't eaten since. I think I'm getting there.'

The floor beneath me suddenly seemed to turn to liquid. I felt shaky. Penny stopped me from falling.

'Really?' I asked.

Bergman kept smiling. 'Really.'

'If you'd like to follow me,' said a telly girl, muttering 'On our way' into her headset.

'Your mum's in the studio,' Bergman whispered. He looked at Angler and Penny with obvious suspicion. 'These people don't want her to see you.'

The telly girl tapped her watch. 'Please…'

'That's not true!' snapped Angler.

'Is it?' I asked Penny.

'I don't know.'

'I want to see her,' I told Angler.

Doctor Angler started to giggle again. His phone was ringing. I realised it had been ringing all evening. I just hadn't heard it until now. Whoever was calling was out of luck; Matthew wasn't answering any more.

The telly girl grabbed my arm. Bergman and Penny immediately pushed her away. She backed off with a: 'Jesus!'

'It's all right,' I said. 'Let's get this done.'

I'd lost all enthusiasm for this silly chat show. I had the horrible feeling that I was being played. A subsurface hysteria, the barely suppressed lunacy I was seeing in Doctor Angler, threatened to bubble over. I didn't want to come across as stupid. Somebody somewhere had a plan. Forces were at work but what could I do? I wasn't going to run away; they knew me too well for that.

We moved into the corridors again. The telly girl passed me on to the producer: Lucy. An older version of herself. Glamorous, rich, confident. Big white smile. 'Studio Six, Anthony,' said Lucy. 'We're all very excited. Half an hour to go.'

I have to say, Lucy didn't convince me she was excited by my presence. In fact, I would go as far as to say she looked confused. *Why the hell is this nondescript loser here?* would have been closer to the truth.

'Not long now,' she said. 'We're going to the dressing rooms. Dana can't wait to meet you.'

Dana.

Dana Mehtra, presenter and chat show host. Sexy, mumsy but one of us. A people person. Her chat show was a new vibrant concept still in its early days; evening and populist. Aimed at the whole family: late enough to flirt with mild controversy but early enough not to offend. Who would have thought I would be meeting her?

'Great lineup tonight,' said Lucy. 'We've got Sam Weller the new Bond villain, and Kristine Kenton-Booth, the sexy face of wildlife programmes. You'll be up first.'

Lucy hustled us into the back of the bright, noisy studio. Large wooden flats and cables dangled everywhere. Technicians in headsets rushed around. Despite myself, I was excited. A real TV studio. I could see the lights shining beyond the flats, even caught glimpses of the audience. It was hot and actually rather smelly: sweat.

Doctor Angler seemed bewildered by Lucy's attitude. He had been tagging along behind but he grabbed her arm and pulled her round. 'Do you know just who Dana is going to be interviewing?' he asked. The technicians shushed him. Angler ignored them. 'Do you have the faintest idea who Anthony Graves is?'

Lucy looked me up and down. What she saw sent a message that I was a clear third in the pecking order after the new Bond villain and the sexy face of wildlife.

'Some kind of mind reader, isn't it?' she replied. 'One of those hypnotist types. Drop your trousers in public, that sort of thing. Now, I need us all to get a move on.'

Angler stayed on her. He clearly felt like the last sane man on Earth. 'And the Chinese incident? Have you even been briefed?'

He was annoying Lucy; there was no doubt about that. 'Look, your government lot are out there on the studio floor. Talk to them instead of wasting my time.' Lucy pulled free and ushered us on.

I looked back to see Doctor Angler stand alone in the darkened corridor, hiccupping with giggles. He was definitely having trouble holding in his emotions.

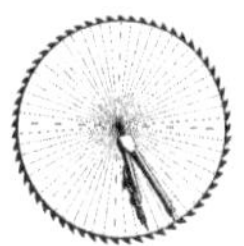

Lucy led me to a dressing room. She and Doctor Angler went away, still arguing. Penny and Bergman followed me in.

Dana was in the dressing room. The Dana. She was twice as beautiful as she looked on the telly (though, for me, not nearly as beautiful as Penny) and quickly put me at my ease. She was, you know: sincere. I think I was star-struck.

And yes, I don't like to name-drop but I was soon joined in the dressing room by first, the new Bond villain and second, the sexy face of wildlife. The wildlife lady, Kris Kenton-Booth was lovely and well-travelled. Sam was just funny. However, their confidence and charm just made me more nervous. They were so healthy and handsome and shiny they looked like a different species. Now I wanted a drink. After a few congratulations they tired of me completely and went off together to 'give me some time'. Another party to which I was not invited.

'Nervous?' Penny asked. I shook my head. She and Bergman were still with me. For some reason, that felt very comforting. I wondered if they'd let Penny sit on the telly couch next to me. I felt like showing her off.

'Anthony!' I heard mum shout. 'Where are you?'

'In here!' Bergman shouted. He opened the door and in she came.

Only she wasn't quite the mum I remembered. She was all dolled up, like she was going out for the night at the local working men's club. I was embarrassed. She looked tacky.

'There you are,' she said. Her tone was direct and serious. This was one woman who wasn't going to treat me as special. She glared at Penny then looked at me.

'You're putting on weight,' she said.

Bergman was grinning behind her. 'This life is agreeing with him,' he said.

'Go and eat something,' I told him. 'Have a meal. Now.'

Bergman nodded, relieved. 'Thanks, Anthony.' He sprinted away, as best he could; considering his condition.

Mum watched me. 'The woman too.'

I nodded to Penny. 'Wait outside.' She obeyed without a word.

Mum kept watching me. She was observing me. When she spoke there was a new remoteness to her voice. 'They told me to stay away but Bergman got me in. Your father has disappeared. If you see him, call someone.'

'Why?'

'They've got to him. Put strange ideas into his head. They swear blind they don't have anything to do with him and this church business, but I know they're lying.'

'What's all this about, Mum?' I asked. 'Why get me on television? I'm just going to look stupid. I don't know what to do.'

Despite the tacky clothes, mum shined with a new authority. 'Well you should,' she whispered. 'You've had long enough. You have to make yourself known. They have to know you.'

Someone began knocking on the door. 'Anthony Graves! Anthony Graves!'

Mum opened her mouth, as if considering giving me an instruction; then thought better of it. 'I'll wait for you,' she said. 'Show them.'

I looked at her. 'I can't,' I said. 'It's gone.'

As the door opened, mum's look at me was pitiless. 'If that's true, Anthony, you're dead.'

Dana said my name. The eternity of waiting, of anticipatory pain, was over. Penny squeezed my arm. A runner pushed me forward.

I walked out from the tacky wooden joists of backstage onto the warm, blinding pretence of a front room. People I couldn't see clapped my short walk.

Dana stood up as I blundered towards her. I stumbled as I realised she wanted to kiss my cheek. I was halfway to sitting down. I rose and we knocked heads. There was a lot of laughter.

'Relax,' Dana whispered.

We took our places. Cameramen watched us in silence from behind their machines. I heard voices from the gallery crackling out of earpieces.

'So, Anthony,' said Dana, as if we were old mates. 'What's this all about?'

I froze. I was too hot. How could I be both? 'Mm?'

'There are a lot of worried people out there, Anthony. In the audience, the viewers watching, everybody. What's your take on the world situation? The events in America with that poor baby. The fighting in Africa and the Middle East. The Chinese. A nuclear accident they're calling it. Are you really Superman?'

A reassuring laugh for the final stinger. Didn't exactly put me at my ease.

'Um,' I said. 'I don't really know… you know…'

Dana leaned forward in her Dana chair. 'Come on, Anthony. People need reassurance. Can you really read minds?'

'Read minds?' What idea did they have? 'No. Of course not.' Is what I tried to say. What came out (in many frequent rewatches) was: 'Mmnghffrot'.

Dana leaned back again. She got the applause she had been after.

The interview went on; interview a polite term for her pristine questions and my bumbling, stuttering incoherence back. What I didn't realise was that I wasn't going to get off again, not for the whole show. As the first guest, I was expected to stick the whole half hour out. That threw me completely. I guess I was supposed to sit in awe as greater magnitudes of celebrity were introduced.

The wildlife girl came on, full of enthusiasm and fizz for her recent trek amongst the penguins with new, high-definition lenses. She never mentioned my name nor even looked at me.

In fact, until the Bond villain actor arrived, I felt that when the programme was over, that would be the end of any interest in me at all. Quite obviously no one believed I could do what I was supposed to be able to do. Perhaps that was why I'd been brought on to television: to demonstrate to the people of Britain that I was just as ordinary as them. I felt deflated. Like once again I'd let people down.

Fine. What did it matter? I could just sit the whole programme out. I couldn't see anyone; the bloody lights were so bright. Just stay quiet and wait for the show to finish.

And then he said it. The actor. Sam Weller.

Up close, what had always appeared naturalistic on screen now seemed false and theatrical. I could see the ruddy flush of his make-up. How old his waxy skin really looked. His voice was overly loud and he forced his mouth around consonants that clicked so much he could have been a crab. 'I feel humble,' he was booming. 'All that audience out there. I feel a connection with them, I really do. I'm a lucky guy to get the part. The villain. And of course, the franchise is so huge, so long-lasting, that I owe it to the public not to let them down.'

He turned to me, mischief in his eyes.

My friend, I thought. I really wouldn't. Don't.

He did.

'How about you, Anthony?' he barked. 'Do you feel you owe your audience something?'

Dana intervened. 'Now now, Sam. You know what you were told…'

Sam patted my knee. 'Oh come on. It's just a bit of fun.' He turned to the audience and raised his arms. 'You want to see Tony in action, don't you?'

The cheer spoke for itself.

This was an actor I'd respected my whole life. I'd seen him in a hundred roles from cops to comedy. And I realised that only now was I seeing the man behind the act. He was full of contempt, of self-love and self-interest. He wanted me to fail; I saw it in his gleaming, insincere eyes. They all did. The future of wildlife giggled stupidly. Well fuck them.

A flicker of doubt appeared across Dana's stupid people-person face. I felt the glamour charging up inside me, wild for release. I couldn't help smiling.

I asked Sam Weller, 'Why don't you tell your audience what you really think of them?' And without thinking about it, I pushed.

I thought at least one person would laugh. After all, it was a joke, right?

But no, all I got was silence. Absolute silence. The faces in the audience just stared at me. The future of wildlife just stared at me. Dana just stared. As for me, that explosion had gone off in my head again. I moaned; I reeled. I could see nothing but white sparks. Only the fact I understood I was still on television stopped me from falling to the floor.

The only person who displayed any animation was Sam Weller himself. He chuckled, like he'd just shared a great anecdote rather than the five minute stream of hate and filth and bile that had issued forth from his mouth. The white fire was clearing from my vision; the cotton wool leaking out of my ears. I caught the end of it. He was looking at me. He was after approval; some sign that he'd been a good boy.

Still nothing from the studio audience. No movement; no noise. I realised they were stunned, all of them.

No, not stunned. They were scared.

'Jesus Christ,' said Dana. 'What did you do to him?' She looked like she was going to throw up or faint or something. I heard the gallery director screaming into her earpiece. Were we still on the air?

'I won't do it again,' I said. 'I can't…' But no one heard me.

There was movement from beyond the cameras. I caught a glimpse of Doctor Angler, picking his way across cables. This galvanised the studio audience into action. They were muttering to themselves. Perhaps they didn't believe what they'd just witnessed. But the language, what Sam had called them was so extreme, so post-watershed that it had to be real. Not comprehending his career was over, Sam beamed at his public.

Somewhere from the rear of the studio, I heard a woman scream. A real from-the-heart terrified shriek. There was a thump as someone attempted to get out of his or her seat.

'S– Stay calm…' said Dana. She sounded unsure of herself, as if she hadn't quite heard the instructions. No one listened. The thumping multiplied and I could see bodies moving beyond the lights.

Someone shouted, 'Open the doors!'

Angler stumbled onto the set past a camera. 'Anthony!' he yelled. 'Let's get you out of here! End this farce!'

Suddenly, everybody seemed to be moving. Dana shouted at Angler: 'We're still on air, you moron! Get off the set!'

Doctor Angler ignored her timely advice and reached me. 'You really did it, Anthony. No one's going to forget you.'

'Get out!' screamed Dana.

'I didn't mean it, Doctor Angler,' I said. 'How did I know he'd say those things?'

'The idiot,' Angler snarled at the smiling Sam. 'God knows what he's done. Come on, before they burn you at the stake. And for Christ's sake, Anthony, please don't do it again.'

I half stood; weak with pain from the push. Dana shoved me back down. 'Did– did you do this to him?' she asked, nodding at Sam Weller. She was frightened and angry.

Getting away seemed a great idea. I had a talent all right. A talent for buggering everything up. I just wanted to get back to my hotel room. I clutched Angler's arm. 'I can't push any more,' I told him. 'It hurts. Help me.'

'Of course,' said Doctor Angler. 'Of course I will.'

Another figure strode onto the set. He was wearing a baggy raincoat and jeans and was so out of context that for a moment I couldn't place him. Unshaven, white-faced and gaunt and, without doubt, Mr Colin Graves.

'Dad?' I asked. The presenter, Doctor Angler and the Bond villain stopped talking and looked.

Dad walked forward. He shuffled as if he were asleep. Television crew people rushed to block him getting on the stage. My face burned. Would you believe it? I was embarrassed. Even here, even on television my family could arrive to show me up.

'Let him come,' said the host. She tried to regain her composure; to return to some semblance of an organised chat show. At that point, I couldn't even remember her name.

Dad stepped into the light. He looked terrible. His unwashed clothes stank. Purple bags swelled around his eyes. 'Anthony,' he said, as if there was nothing else for him to say.

'What are you doing?' I asked. My whisper was horrified; minimal.

'This is your father, Anthony?' asked the host.

Dad just stood. He looked dazed; like he didn't know where he was. After an age, he took a step forward. He smelled of weeks of sweat. 'Jesus, Dad…' I said in disgust.

'Mr Graves, welcome. Sit down.' The presenter, Dana (that was it), was smooth and professional; like this happened all the time. Perhaps she was sensing the most important programme in television history. Dad came towards me.

'Anthony!' shouted Angler. 'Get out!' And he shoved me. I tripped over a piece of something… cable, floor, person. I don't know. Everyone suddenly seemed to be shouting like Doctor Angler had given them permission. As I fell I clutched at Angler; grabbed him and accidentally knocked his legs away. He sprawled across the sofa. I landed on my right wrist and a spongy twist of pain spasmed up my arm.

I smelled cheap tobacco and rain. Dad's coat. He hoisted me up; strong hands. Strong workman's hands.

'Son,' he said.

'Hi Dad,' I said back. I tried to smile but I'd run out of humour. He took a step back. He put his right hand into his pocket. In turn, my right hand was doubling its pain measure.

'My son,' he repeated and I didn't like what I saw in his expression.

'Dad? I've knackered my wrist…'

Angler launched himself at us. As he did so, dad put his left arm around me and pressed something cold but incredibly fiery into me. A thick injection of pain burst up through my abdomen. Dad's weight was hauled off me. I saw him lash out at Angler with a shiny and dripping hand.

Then I fell. The pain pushed up my body like a catheter. I was looking at the sections of carpet draped over the chipboard set floor. Somewhere, liquid leaked out of my body.

Save me, I thought, incapable of speaking the words out loud. *Don't let me die. Somebody save me.* To the whole studio. To anyone. Metal clamps seemed to fit themselves round my head and squeeze. The visual world was swimming and growing dim. All I could do was think, *Don't let me die. Don't let them nuke me. Do whatever. Save me.*

Chapter 16

Dad was one of those people who always had a deal going. Not just his decorating but doing little odd jobs, sometimes very odd: like the time he used the car to transport a dead body from the hospital to a funeral home. The funeral director was a friend of his, and the funeral van had broken down and there was a lot of flu around and they couldn't get the drivers. Dad wasn't qualified to drive an ambulance or hearse so he made this deal that he would transport the body in the back of his Volvo Estate. He covered the dead person up in black bin liners so no one would see.

I remember when he came home and told us he'd done it. I was still at school. He opened up the back of the car and I looked in awe at the empty space and the torn plastic. The car smelled of disinfectant; that hospital smell. I was really impressed. It was funny and horrible at the same time and I liked that. All the time, a little part of me wondered if I was going to get my first look at an actual dead body. Of course now, from Titanic on, I've seen more than my fair share.

I feel bad about my dad. To this day I've never worked out just exactly what happened. Did he get religion like they claimed? I don't want to believe I could make him hate me that much. I think about my situation now and I know that if he lived in my present world, he would have been happy. He would have everything he ever wanted.

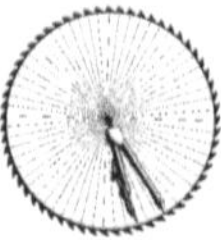

I put Penny in charge of finding out the truth about dad. Mum knew a fair amount. Together they brought the church people to my hospital bed. There were two of them, both black, a man and a woman. They were bigwigs in one of those evangelical fundamentalist churches; you know, where everyone sings a lot. They stood at the end of my bed surrounded by my new guards and advisors. Heads bowed, both cried softly like they were prisoners of war brought before a primitive king. They were waiting for judgement. They were waiting for wrath.

Mum was convinced these people were part of some government plot to brainwash dad into sticking me with a knife, but not me. Dad wasn't an idiot and these two definitely were. They looked so thick and so pitiable that I just waved them away. I think they were killed. There is so much I don't know about that time; what people were doing in my name. The lack of control I had then, now frightens me.

I understood that I wasn't going to be able to stick my head in the sand and play dumb any more. I actually would have liked the conspiracy theory to be true. At least in that version dad would have been coerced into doing what he did. But I wasn't in the mood for illusions. I knew who I was and what people thought of me.

My mild, even-tempered, hard-headed, down-to-earth practical old man had made up his mind that I was the spawn of Satan, and God had ordered him to expunge me from the face of the planet.

They tore dad apart in there, in that TV studio. But not before he killed Doctor Angler.

The doctor fought to take the knife off him. I never figured out why. He had nothing to gain from keeping me alive. I can't believe he got himself stabbed because he liked me.

Only one explanation seems right. Doctor Angler actually believed what he said about the Sirens being the new inheritors of the human race. He believed we were the inevitable next step; that evolution had decided to organise the species around a new guiding principle. He believed it was his duty to convince others that survival for the human race was more important than freedom. If he had lived, I'm starting to think that Angler might have been the first man to volunteer for the glamour.

My instinctive, panicked mental cry for help in the studio saved my life. Dad had stabbed me twice in the abdomen and punctured one lung. He missed my heart by two and a quarter centimetres. I'm told the blood loss was tremendous.

Only prompt action saved me. The newly glamoured studio audience worked frantically to keep me alive. The weeping TV crew apparently lamented my injuries with almost biblical fervour. That it could happen on their programme! I heard that Lucy the producer hung herself with an electrical cable… so it wasn't all bad (ha ha).

Many doctors were present — after all, I was a medical curiosity — and they kept me alive until the ambulance arrived. I was rushed to Guy's and St. Thomas' and hauled into immediate surgery.

Doctor Angler was left to bleed to death on the studio floor. I wish I had been awake just a little longer and spared a thought for someone to save him.

Dad? Well there was no putting him back together. Not that anyone there would have wanted to. There were stories about members of the studio audience disappearing down the Portobello Road with my father's head held aloft like a trophy but I've never found anyone who could corroborate that. I never found the head, either.

Crucially, mum escaped my push. I don't know if she planned it. I can't believe even she could think that far ahead. She said she was unceremoniously escorted off the premises and was arguing with security in the street when dad stabbed me. The first she knew about it was when the fire alarm started clanging away. The guards rushed straight back inside.

She traced me to the hospital and somehow managed to force her way into the operating theatre, where I was busy having emergency surgery and a blood transfusion. She told me she was convinced the government would try and kill me whilst I was unconscious. Again, I don't know.

Mum organised. She ordered the members of the audience who took me to the hospital to be my bodyguards. For a while I had thirty well-dressed middle-class men and women patrolling the eighth floor. They challenged anybody who dared to come up there, ready to pounce on anyone who even started to seem hostile. Mum didn't want anybody coming in. I don't know if she grieved for dad. She certainly didn't show it if she did.

When I watch footage of the episode, all eyes are on Weller. I'm this little toad-resembling bloke who looks like he wandered onto Dana's sofa by mistake and hasn't yet been told to bugger off. Dad turns up and all hell breaks loose. I can't even see the moment I glamoured them all. I am too busy sinking to the studio floor, blood spraying from my wounds.

Twenty-seven point two million UK subjects and an innumerable amount around the world watched Sam Weller telling them exactly just where they were placed in his estimation. I got all of them. That's what it took for the dam to burst; for whatever mental blocks my mind had built to crumble. I had to be stabbed near to death by my own father on TV. I had to get rid of my conscience and let the survival instinct take over. I have never been blocked again.

From what I can gather, those who didn't see the programme thought it was a con. Everyone outside London thought I was a London problem; just another faddish waste of time designed to annoy provincials. London people reacted in the way London people always react: they grumbled and got on with it. To them, I was just another irritation to add to the list that interfered with their journey to work. Quite literally. The most concrete manifestation of reaction to me was that the tube drivers went on strike. I still don't understand why.

When the footage was repeated and my followers organised another live interview, I bagged another ten million. I was beginning to be influential.

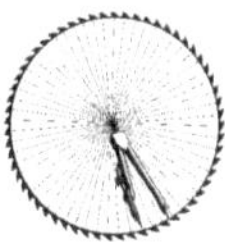

Can't say I'm a big fan of hospitals. Bad things happen in them. Certainly, three months in bed stuck with drips and needles wasn't going to turn me on to these establishments. Not being able to go to the toilet; nurses shoving all sorts of painful apparatus up your backside, it makes a man irritable. It gets to him, despite his knowing the sterling work being performed on his behalf by the best doctors and nursing staff available to mankind. Or at least to the Westminster NHS Hospital Trust.

In fact, I was getting hacked off with quite a few aspects of my life. Once upon a time I would have simply laid there and accepted the discomfort and the pain. Not anymore.

I suppose that some clever types out there will see all sorts of symbolic doodah about my recovery. You know: death and rebirth. I won't deny the experience changed me but to be honest I think I was heading that way in any case. You could also argue, if you wanted, that I just changed the world to fit me.

Chapter 17

With a glucose drip up my nose, a burning pain in my stomach where the knife had done its work and a nervous system pumped full of the best drugs doctors could stuff inside, no wonder I figured my visitors were hallucinations.

Somehow they had convinced mum to let them in to see me. They were, in their own words, a deputation from a much larger group gathered in the rainy streets of Southwark and Lambeth.

The man who led them was red-faced, tubby and very sweaty. He was in his fifties and all Brylcreem and vests. His florid round face was hidden behind the thick black frames of NHS glasses. He was flanked by a couple of girls. Not nice attractive girls, you understand; no, these were colourless, shapeless types in flowery print dresses. Girls who barely seemed to fill their own physical space. I just knew they were god-botherers. A whole family of them.

'Mr Graves,' said the man and bowed. Already I didn't like his stuffy fawning. He held out a sweaty hand.

I shrugged as best I could. 'I'm hardly in a position to shake hands. What do you want?' I looked at mum, who seemed to be finding this whole situation funny.

'Kevin Charles,' he said. 'Lay Preacher of St Luke's in Harrow. Baptist Minister and spreader of God's holy word.'

Mention of religion frightened me. Was this something to do with dad? Had they come to finish what he started?

'Mum? What's this all about?'

'Don't worry,' she replied. 'Mr Charles has a request.'

'Yes, yes I do,' said Charles. Madness was in him I could tell. It lived quite happily inside his sweaty body. The politer they were the more you could spot it. I still failed to understand how people like this could have got to such a laid-back, lazy figure like my dad.

'These are my girls,' he continued. 'Ruth. Sarah.'

He waved a dismissive hand at 'his girls'. They looked at the floor. They looked like they'd never spoken a word in their lives. My head was full of flashing lights. I was inches away from drug-induced sleep. Why couldn't they just go away?

'Just get on with it,' I snapped.

Charles gave a polite chuckle then motored on. He was used to having his way. 'Ever since your revelation, my brethren and I have prayed.'

'Didn't you see me on television?'

'I have never allowed my family to be corrupted in such a manner. I am very strict on this matter.' Charles's smile never faltered.

So they missed it. Good for you, I nearly said, but I saw mum and she wasn't amused.

'You want me to spare you, is that it?' I said. 'Okay, don't worry. I–'

'Oh no,' said Charles. 'Not that at all. My congregation voted to watch your broadcast; many times since. You struck at the heart. You shine a much needed light.' And with a complete lack of self-consciousness, he knelt at my bedside. He nodded at his daughters to follow suit. Even in my addled half wakefulness, I could see they were both terrified. Poor Ruth and Sarah.

'We want you to take us,' he said. 'We want you to enter our unworthy souls into your rapture.'

With that, he bent his head and began to mouth a silent prayer. He was so close I could smell the mints on his breath.

'You're joking,' I whispered.

'No,' said mum. 'There's hundreds outside. They think you're… I don't know who they think you are… but they want you to put them under your spell.'

This was crazy. I mean, I don't know about you but if I was them and I'd just found out there was this guy who could make you fall in love with him just by thinking about it, I'd be halfway to a remote Pacific atoll by now.

'I don't get it,' I asked. 'Why?'

'Because these are the end of days,' said Charles. 'Release us from the burdens of this terrible world. Touch us. Free us.'

I looked once again at the girls. Despite their downturned faces and meek-as-milk manner, I could see they weren't quite as wholehearted in this rapture as their father. Poor little Sarah with her frizzy ginger curls; she looked like she was about to scream. Perhaps she was.

'What good will that do?' I asked.

'We are lost, cast adrift, bobbing like icebergs in a cruel and cold ocean. You have been sent to make us all whole. Make us all one. Touch us with the white heat of your all-encompassing love so we may serve God through his earthly vassal.'

'You mean you *want* to lose your free will?'

'Oh yes,' said Charles and the relief and ecstasy in his voice were palpable. 'We will give ourselves up to your Word and rejoice. Within you.'

Mum snickered. 'They've seen what you can do, Anthony. They've seen the interview at the studio. Those that were torn by strife, you have brought them peace. Isn't that right, Mr Charles?'

Charles was crying. He was actually shedding tears. 'Yes. Oh please. I've waited all my life to serve.'

So that was it. He just wanted out. No more decisions, no more worries, no more wondering what it was all about. He wanted to give up responsibility for his life and let me do the sorting for him. To get that, he would give up his self, his being. As he might have put it, he wanted to give me his soul.

'What about your kids?' I asked. 'They don't look too…'

'They will do my bidding, won't you girls?'

I looked at them kneeling there. They wanted to run, to say no. We could all of us in that room see it. But Ruth and Sarah, well, they just had too much of their father in them. They just weren't wired to stand up to him, even here at what they knew would be the end for them.

'Yes father,' said Ruth.

'Yes father,' said Sarah. Both were crying. Sniffling in that irritating, snotty way that kind of girl always did.

I was tired. I just wanted to get them out. With the drugs and everything, I can barely remember what happened.

'Please, Anthony,' said Charles. 'Lord.' He closed his eyes tight, like he was expecting a blow. His clasped hands shuddered with tension.

'Have you ever considered the possibility that I might be a false idol?' I asked him.

Charles smiled with well-practised, absolute certainty. 'Never.'

Well, it would have been rude not to. I glamoured them and they all lived happily ever after.

Five months in hospital is a long time. For anyone. Let alone the new Messiah. No, I'm only joking. At least I think I am. Let's face it, that Mr Charles talk would go to anyone's head.

Once I was out of intensive care and it didn't look like I was going to die and I didn't keep slipping in and out of consciousness and not being able to breathe, hospital became intensely boring. I still felt enough pain that I couldn't actually be discharged but I was too restless to bear the convalescence. Also, I'd been admitted in late April, so I'd missed the whole summer. Once I was well enough to look out over the concrete tangle that was Guy's Hospital, the skies were full of rain again. The air was as grey as the car park.

Penny of course stayed by my side. She was lovely, loyal and totally adoring. In fact, one Tuesday morning I married her. I lay in my hospital bed; got the hospital chaplain to say the words and we were man and wife. Who would have thought it?

Only, after a week I sent Penny away. She was getting on my nerves. She just wasn't the woman she used to be. There was no physical stuff, obviously, not in my condition. She got on my nerves, agreeing with me all the time. I started looking at other women. I started thinking about Toni. I missed her. Probably, I started thinking about Emma too. The lovely Emma. The Venus who, in any sane universe, would never be mine.

So I told Penny to go. I sat up in bed and told her to her face it was nothing personal, but I think she took it badly. She took it personally. I have never seen her again but I'm sure she is fine. There were rumours that she drowned herself in a bathtub near Heathrow but no one confirmed that to me one way or the other. Wherever you are, Penny, I'm sure you are better off without me.

I told mum to keep all but the most necessary staff away. My room was becoming increasingly crowded and all those tearful, loving, bovine faces were driving me nuts.

She informed me that the government had emptied the hospital of all the normal patients. The other floors had been cleared. She didn't like that much and was looking into the situation. She was convinced we were being set up as a target.

Mum was becoming a proper manager. She was determined to keep me safe.

On increasing occasions I hobbled to the window, drips hanging from my arms, to look down to a sea of people obscuring the tarmac car park. They filled the streets, thousands of them. There were people carriers and camper vans and tents where they slept. Despite mum's disapproval, every now and then I opened the window, shouted down to the sound of their roaring approval and glamoured the lot. You know: just in case some assassin types had sneaked in among them.

To the crowd, I was the answer to unhappiness. I offered freedom from thinking, from making decisions, from wondering whether their lives meant anything. With me, they knew. It didn't really matter whether I was talented or good-looking or did anything. I was just someone they could give themselves up to. Someone who would *deal* with them. I still can't understand why. I was better than god; if only because I was actually here.

This brought me round to a different set of questions. Questions about the ability itself. Oh, I don't mean how it worked or where it came from. More like: how far could it go? I mean, I hadn't met a single person who had resisted the glamour, nor had I encountered one for whom it had worn off.

I tried a few experiments. In-between the physiotherapy sessions and the endless fucking checks by every doctor under the sun. I was prone to headaches and of course my physical condition was pretty wretched, so I got tired easily. Therefore, I limited my attempts.

The first experiment proved more successful than I'd anticipated. I got a webcam set up and posted a video where I ordered anyone watching to gather up the scaffolders of the world and get them online on a certain day; at a certain time. On the day, at that time, I looked into the webcam and ordered all scaffolders to be gay. Yes, that subhuman, angry pond life of the building trade. I asked them to become screamingly, flamboyantly camp homosexuals.

I did laugh when the first reports of riots on building sites started coming in. Because of course, none of their mates were gay: the builders, the plumbers, the electricians. They were all still hyper-tense testosterone-filled cavemen on eighteen pints a night and a startling loyalty to zero tolerance. Most enjoyable.

The news reported a wave of (rather funny) violence from Glasgow to Cornwall. It seemed there wasn't a scaffolder in the UK who wasn't a raging woofter. I felt I did the country a service. I still do; you agree?

When I thought about what I had done to the scaffolders, my range frightened me. How far did my influence stretch? I hadn't had to meet, see or know anything about those people and they hadn't had to know anything about me. They just had to be there; even if they were just watching a screen. I tried radio and that worked just as well (though it took my guys an age to find even one unaffected person to test it out on. Mr Bennett, his name was; a blind pensioner).

Next question: was there a limit to the glamour? I wished Doctor Angler had been alive. He would have proved really useful. Had I got every scaffolder in the world? Did I have a quota or a certain number of times I could use it? What would happen when, god forbid, I died? Would they all go back to normal? What if I got blocked again? What if, after a year or a month or even tomorrow, it just faded away? That was a nasty thought.

My sleeping problems started round about then. I managed to get all worked up about whether the glamour would fail when I was unconscious. I should have sussed that after five months in hospital and half that time in a coma, that question had answered itself.

And of course, there was the question that plagues me to this day: if I glamoured someone, could I unglamour them? And would they really be unglamoured or just re-glamoured?

Stupidly, without thinking it through, I experimented. I had this pretty little black nurse who brought my breakfast. One morning, I ordered her not to be under my influence any more.

Luckily, when mum came in for my briefing, she managed to pull the nurse off before she actually strangled me with the tubes. I still remember the sheer hate in the girl's eyes as she came at me. Later, I was told that my people threw her off the hospital roof.

That taught me. No more experiments.

Of course by now I was big news. Despite my best efforts, there was a large proportion of people I hadn't glamoured. Now they knew about me, I guessed they kept themselves well away from possible contamination (not a nice word, but one I heard rather too often). The calm that had been hanging in there for the last few months was dissipating. I was awake and active again. I couldn't be passed off as a joke.

At first, I enjoyed the endless television discussion programs about me and the other Sirens. Mainly me, as information about other countries was ominously scarce. Air travel had been restricted and most airports closed to civilians. It appeared that after my first appearance, half the country tried to make a run for it, flooding the railways, docks and airports with refugees. Society was crumbling; they could feel it, and all because of me. Mum's fears weren't so groundless after all. Nobody knew for sure who had been glamoured so nobody trusted anyone. Executive orders were contradicted as my people struggled against their people. An RAF airstrike on the hospital was averted at the last minute by one of my wing commanders giving me the radio frequency for the Tornado jets so I could glamour the pilots. To lighten the mood, I ordered them to turn round and bomb the airfield they had taken off from. That'll larn 'em!

Still, we all knew: something was going to get through eventually. My army guys arrived to seal off the building with barbed wire and patrols but I discovered through my generals that units of unaffected soldiers were being stockpiled in secret locations. These men were denied any kind of electronic communications to avoid (that word again) contamination. Luckily, my generals managed to infiltrate their generals and my side was very confident.

They were scared. But they were coming. And they only had to kill me once.

I was staring down through the November rain, at the tents and the people and the trucks in the distance when suddenly the grey light was washed with orange colour, right at the blocked road entrance. I never saw the car.

Before I could define what the growing flower of flame meant; the boom hit the windows. Glass shattered over me and I thought my ear drums had been punctured.

The men driving the car had all been industrial executives at a chemical plant in Solihull in the Midlands. They had been on a plane returning from a conference in Saudi Arabia on the night of the broadcast. They had put the car bomb together themselves at their various houses, using ingredients from the workplace. When interviewed, the wives claimed ignorance but you could see they were lying. We never found out whether they were in their right minds or this was the first recorded example of another Siren trying to get me. Although the bomb caused terrible damage, and killed twenty-eight of my followers in that car park, I was, for once, unhurt. So it wasn't all bad.

No, it was the unseen sniper who fired into my room and put a bullet into the brain of one of my lung specialists that convinced us it was time to get away. We never found the assassin or where he was positioned, although mum was convinced it was from a helicopter. So I had to glamour all the helicopter pilots too. Nothing fancy, just compel them never to step into their machines ever again. However, mum had had enough. That night, with just a few doctors and nurses helping me, we used a secret underground escape tunnel to get out of the hospital, into a waiting limousine and back to my house in Hammersmith. After months and months, I was free again.

Chapter 18

I was surprised mum took me back to the Mariners. Surely the authorities knew I'd been there before. However, as the doctor and nurses eased me out of the ambulance back onto that windy embankment, I could see she had a plan. She knew exactly what she was doing.

For a start, the area was quieter than when I left it. Fair enough, at four o'clock in the morning you don't expect trumpets, but there was no life anywhere. Not on the bridge, the road or any of the houses.

The doctor, a Nigerian man whose name I forget but who was very big in tissue damage, supervised my exit from the car. Walking was hard. I was all Frankenstein stiff-legs but it was nice to be outside again. I looked through the fine rain and saw the pub I'd taken over.

The Mariners was a black block, solid and dark. Doctor Nigerian led me across the slippery paving stones to the old gate. Funny how I felt I was coming home. Croydon was out of me forever.

As mum fiddled with the electronic lock, the feeling increased that I was being led into something prearranged. She wanted me to see something.

As the door opened, I heard something bump about in one of the upper floors. Then the smell hit me. The whole house stank. There was something rotten in here.

'Whatever it is, Mum,' I said, 'I don't think I'm ready.'

'Tough,' she said and pressed the light switch. She twisted the dimmer and brought up the scenery of the huge reception room in all its glory.

The place, my lovely Mariners, was trashed. The expensive parquet floorboards were now laced with grindings and scratches. A smashed and buckled mountain bike lay prone in the middle of the room; someone had used it as a bludgeon. Great chunks were hacked out of the walls. There were pizza boxes, there were beer cans, there were spilled-out rolls of blood-soaked cotton wool. There were little glass phials.

'Oh my,' said the doctor.

'What does it mean?' I asked.

There was a bumping from the top of the wide stairs at the end of the room. A landing light clicked on. A thin shape dropped into view. 'Shit,' said my friend Toni.

'You need to know what you have started, Anthony,' said mum. She sounded imperious again.

Toni was naked apart from a ballooning pair of boxer shorts, which emphasized how scrawny she was looking. She looked bad in that landing light; yellow and lined. Her breasts: delightful plump dumplings I had always slathered over, were deflated sacks. Purple pouches under her eyes made her appear even more wasted. And I could smell her from down here: sweat, booze and fried food.

'Anthony,' she said in a dry, cracked voice. 'Mate.'

'Bring Anthony up,' mum ordered the doctor. She glared at Toni.

'Wait… wait…' Toni hopped about. She hopped about on spindly limbs, resembling some horrible frog. I felt sorry for her. Mum had dropped her right in it. 'I know it looks bad, but I can… you know, I can tell you…'

Mum started climbing the stairs. Toni backed away. She was manic now. Hyper. 'Please, listen. It's not my fault. I've got to tell you…'

The doctor and his nurse moved me to the stairs. 'Toni,' I said. 'What have you done?'

They lifted me up onto the steps. 'One at a time,' said a nurse.

I felt even more like some shuffling monster.

Mum marched right past Toni. My friend cringed away; not able to look at me. The ruin continued up here. More wall gouging and what looked like a fountain of blood sprayed across the antique pictures that lined the hall. Bedroom doors hung off hinges. Discarded syringes revealed what had gone on.

At the top of the stairs, the nurses led me past Toni. She still couldn't look at me. Her skin was crawling with sores and needle tracks. She had disintegrated, barely the same human being I had once known.

There was more movement now and a groggy girl staggered out from one of the rooms. She was dressed in a stained t-shirt and her blonde hair hung in filthy knots. 'Toni?' she asked in a thick Eastern European accent. 'What is happening?'

Mum was breathing heavily. She stood in front of the girl. 'Get out,' she ordered.

The girl giggled and mum slapped her. The giggling stopped. Contest over. The girl scurried out of sight.

'Oh Jesus,' Toni said and bounded in front of me. 'Anthony, you've got to believe me. I couldn't help it. It just happened. Got all out of control. You know, like things do.'

Mum pointed into one of the rooms. I remembered it as being the viewing room I'd been eating pizza in when she had come and got me all those months ago. The rotten smell was very strong. I didn't want to go in there.

'I swear,' Toni begged. 'It's not me. I'm not an addict.'

'Anthony, I want you to look,' said mum and I couldn't disobey. The nurses released their grip and I staggered forward. I already knew what I was going to see.

There wasn't much moonlight but the river still kept a little shine from its glow. Enough to bounce into the room and let me see what had been left here.

I don't know how long the boy had been dead but his skin was dry. There was an ugly black stain on the floorboards underneath his body. The rest of the room was the same mess of bottles, needles, torn clothing and filth that festered throughout the house. He was face up, arms over his head like he was stretching, reaching for the river.

Mum pushed me into the room. I nearly fell. 'Do you understand now?' she asked. I didn't like her voice any more. It wasn't my mum. Toni was crying in the hall behind me.

'This is you,' she continued. 'This is what you do. So no more playing. No more comfort zones. Pull the cotton wool out of your head and understand.'

She turned away. 'Toni. Come in here, please.'

'No,' she sobbed.

'It's all right,' mum insisted. 'Come on in.'

I could hardly breathe, the stench was so tangible. The air was thick, clammy. My imagination must have been in overdrive, what with the lack of sleep and my own beneficial drugs, but I was certain that everything in here, all the ruined furniture and garbage, was covered in a film of oily gleaming liquid. A goo that had leaked out of the body and coated the room.

'Open the window, Toni,' mum said. 'It's okay.'

Toni could hardly stand. She crawled in past me, head bowed. 'Yes,' she said. 'Whatever you say. Anthony, you know. We're mates. Aren't we? I couldn't… you know, he just came in. He was in this state before he got here. I didn't know about the drugs, I swear…'

'Toni, the window,' said mum.

She did her submissive frog walk to the large panelled windows that looked over the river. The first rays of a winter sun were touching the water. Mum and I watched her struggle to work out how to get the things open. She wet herself. At last, the liquid streaming down her legs, she managed. The air smelled good. Too good for Toni. She threw up.

Shaking, she looked at me. The fear, the obedience, in her expression was more than I could stand.

'You know what to do now,' said mum. 'Don't you, Anthony.'

'Oh God, no!' Toni folded up. She dropped to her knees, not even realising she had done so. The crunch as she hit was painful. She didn't even notice. Instead, she lay on the floor and held up her tracked arms to me. 'Please don't. We're mates. I helped you. Please, Anthony. Just don't.'

She looked up and her mouth was wide, her ruined teeth large and ugly, the lip ring crusted with blood. She didn't seem human.

'Tidy up,' I said. 'Tidy up and go.'

'Anthony!'

'Mum, leave it.'

Toni howled. She couldn't believe what she had just heard me say. I couldn't believe it either.

'Anthony, do it!' mum bellowed.

'Toni,' I muttered. 'Go. Put some clothes on. Clean yourself up. Sort it out. Or I will do it for you.'

Toni was weeping. She looked up with black mascara lines inching down her cheeks. 'I will,' she whispered. 'Thank you. Thank you.' She stayed kneeling and sobbing.

'Get up and go, Toni,' I said, 'because I really, really want to get you. And if I ever see you again I will. Go!'

Unable to look at me, unable to stop the violent shakes twitching her skinny body, Toni did what she was told.

Mum left me alone. She was afraid I would glamour her. And believe me I was tempted.

As I slept and morning brightened the Thames-side day, people came to clean the house. I don't know what they did with the boy's body. Mum probably had it thrown in the river to drift away.

As I lay in a new bed, I was annoyed that I had been so willing a dupe; that I was so easy to manipulate. My own mother.

I knew why she was staying away. Along with the others, she feared me.

However, despite appearances to the contrary, I wasn't stupid. I knew it was her scheming that had kept me alive. And she was my mother. That had to mean something.

I spent days locked in my bedroom. I threw the television out. You don't want to know how sick I was of seeing my own face. Bad enough that I could hardly move and that my injuries kept me trapped stiff and rigid in my own body. I felt mummified, a pharaoh buried alive while the servants built my own spectacular pyramid, sealing me in, layer upon layer.

I couldn't get Toni out of my head. She had been such a good friend. I kept seeing that spidery frame scuttling in the moonlight, begging me to spare her. How could that be the same woman I'd shared an office with for three years? I had destroyed her.

Mum must have known all the time what Toni was degenerating into. She had kept tabs on the situation here, her little network of spies and informants keeping watch. Not doing anything about her, not helping her, no. Keeping the pot simmering, ready for when I would come out and be forced to deal with the situation.

There was no dodging the moral of the story. I had blown my chance to make her happy. There was no arguing with the contrast between the messed-up, free-minded Toni and the serenity I could provide. Perhaps Mr Charles was not as beyond belief as I thought.

Maybe the glamour was like an injection. There was fear, there was dread; but after a small, insignificant sting, you were cured. Let's face it: most people spent their days waiting for someone to tell them what to do. All I did was give them a purpose. I was a man who would look after them. A man they could look up to.

Mum waited me out. On the third day, I emerged from my room looking for her. I'd had just about enough of feeling sorry for myself. I was ready for a scrap. As I walked through the suddenly empty house, I wondered if even now I was entering another one of her little moral experiments.

She was standing in that same room, overlooking the river. The trash was gone and the scrubbed floorboards gleamed. Instead of that ripe stench, the air smelled of polish.

Mum was wearing a little business number. Not unlike the kind of thing Penny would wear. Penny? What the hell had I done with Penny?

'Feeling better?' she asked. There didn't seem to be any fear in her. She knew exactly what she was doing. What I was doing.

I crumbled. I had spent three days building up the courage to shout at her but now… there was no way. 'Mum? You've changed.' That was all I could manage. Feeble.

Her reaction surprised me. She looked tender again, like someone who cared. She looked ancient.

I just looked at her. I was aware that through the window, outside the river still flowed, the birds still flew. But there was still no traffic on Hammersmith Bridge and all the houses were empty. Mum stood silhouetted in grey London light.

'I just want to be like everybody else,' I said. 'I don't want a war.' I sat down on a freshly cleaned sofa.

The tender mum was gone. New mum was back, looming over me. 'Then you might as well throw yourself out of that window now,' she said. Her voice was cold. 'Because they know the situation even if you don't.'

I couldn't look at her. Yes, that was one way. Do the world a favour, Anthony, and top yourself. It's what everyone wants. A little bit of me even looked forward to the idea. No more thinking, no more fear, just the deep, dense water from that river closing over my head. Yeah, the peace would be nice.

'All the old things, they're gone,' she said. She sat down and stroked my head. It had been ages since she had done that; probably not since I was a little boy. Her fingers felt bony, like being stroked by the medieval cartoon of Death. 'You have created a new world, Anthony. But you have enemies. You're in a war. No more half measures. No friends, no equals, no compromises. There must be you and everyone else beneath you. It's that or nothing. You take everything or you die.'

She knew the situation; she knew much better than her dozy son. She knew.

As she stroked, I thought. What would be so wrong about taking it all over? After all, who had I been before? Nobody, that's who. Not all these other people: like the lawyers at the Mariners, with their bewildering arcane careers, indifferent in their wealth and full, rich lives. Why should they continue to get everything? Why shouldn't I have a bit for myself? After all, it was me who got the glamour, not them. And who was to say I wasn't given it for a reason. What would they have done with it?

I could be in control. I could do what I wanted. I could do what I wanted all the time. No one would give me any shit. What had I been thinking, worrying whether I should use it or not? Why had I wasted so much time letting them plot and scheme against me? Everyone in the world envied me and here I was moping about, feeling sorry for myself.

'Time is against us, Anthony,' said mum. 'We have to get started.'

I turned over, looked up at her and smiled. I felt stronger already. Better than ever. As ever, mum sussed what I was thinking. She smiled back.

I walked to the window and looked out at the world. The glamour howled for release. I would never be blocked again. Get them all, it told me. That was the glamour's job. What it was put in my head for. Get the bullies, the bastards, the entrepreneurs, the property developers, all the girls and boys with their perfect lives who don't even see you. Get the rich wolves and the poor sheep. The cold thin ones; the dumb fat ones sitting on their dumpy arses watching TV on disability benefit. Let's get the nasty racist grannies, the car-loving selfish suburban men in their fifties; the smug, intolerant mothers, the dole-merchants, the petty managers, the go-getters, the stay-at-home teenage mums, the idle pampered gap year students, the financial officers, the council officials, the artists, the musicians, the football fans, the builders, the Spanish tanned OAPs. Let's just get them all because I am what they deserve.

So I turned to my mum, with her cold smiling scared face, and I told her: 'Okay.' I told mum: 'I'll start.'

Interlude

Chapter 19

I'm taking a holiday. I've chatted to Conor and he thinks that's a wonderful idea.

I'm getting a boat and I'm going to sail it down the Thames. The expedition takes me round the south-east heel of Kent to the Sussex coast. There's a beach there called West Wittering, which I love. It's just a long stretch of unspoiled sand and gentle water where I used to go as a kid. I can't wait to see the castle I've had built on it. They showed me a video of how the project is shaping up and believe me: that is one impressive building.

Writing about dad and the knife is what brought about this sudden decision. I winced as I typed up those memories. I had to lift up my new baggy writer's shirt and take a look at the scar. I couldn't help myself.

The scar is now a pale pink slash rather than an angry red one, but it's still there.

I could do with a holiday, I really could. It's been a while. Memories of dad, and wishing Penny was still here, and that business with Emma which is staying with me, and so on, are all thoughts I could do with getting out of my head before I decide on my next step.

The problem of Emma, or rather, the problem of loneliness, is foremost in my mind. This autobiography (which I guess this writing stuff is, although that puts me in mind of something a football manager would go in for) has opened up way too much memory. I'd forgotten the world had been such a random place, full of so many people. I look back and wonder how I could have been satisfied with so little.

Writing is bad for me. Of that I am convinced. It makes me broody and bad-tempered. I find myself becoming preoccupied with my past and I'm not sure that's healthy. I've got a country to run.

Ultimately, my main worry about writing is that, like every project I start, I probably won't finish.

The basic downside is that it's such a solitary occupation. I'm lonely enough already. And it's boring. My Covent Garden movie is miles easier: you don't have to write it. There's a whole army of people who will do it for you. Even when I'm not there somebody's moving it along. With writing it's just you and the keyboard. Hard work.

I did think about getting some famous author or other to take down dictation and transcribe this thing for me but would they be my real words? I have to think about the other Anthony. The man I'm writing this for. He's still stuck there in that parallel universe with no power, being a nobody. I owe that Anthony the truth.

Somehow, I have to finish, so I've reached a compromise. I'll take the boat down to Wittering for a holiday, but I'll also put the story so far on a memory stick and continue writing down there. I could take a laptop, but I find the keys too small.

Oh yes, I am no longer afraid of the water. During the three months I've been writing, I've also been taking those diving and swimming lessons I'd promised myself. They are a reward after all my hard efforts grappling with the muse.

Swimming's great. I'm really getting into it. No, seriously. Swimming's great and diving's even better. I do my swimming at the pools in Buckingham Palace (who knew?).

All the parts I used to hate about swimming, I now love. There's a weightlessness; a freedom. The flippers make that easier. I can turn right over now, do somersaults, there's no stopping me. I love the weight of water. I love bouncing on the diving board and the drop as you head down. Each jump is different. Each jump is special. And now I wonder: what was all the fear and fuss about?

At the start, I used to panic. At every new stage, I panicked. I even panicked when we first went into the Thames, despite knowing the environmental guys had declared the water safe and my instructor allowed me in. The river is such a muscular mass, deep and solid. But after you've sussed the secret of diving, you find you want the water to be deep. The deeper the better.

Lose the concept that water is trying to kill you. It can kill you, but only if you let it. Water is a tool, like everything else. If you don't know how to use it you're going to hurt yourself, but once you understand its potential, you can do anything.

The boat I've got to take me to Wittering is one of those big power jobbies. My guys scoured the marinas of the UK to find one, eventually tracking the bugger down in Hull. The boat itself is called a Skater 40, which means it has a forty foot hull. This puppy has twin Sterling 1100/1300 HP engines and can hit over 160mph in open water.

Chris the owner is going to let me have a go at driving. Obviously I'm not going to let him let me do anything dangerous, but you have to have a go.

Chris was a power racer and a successful property developer, back in the old days. I didn't realise there were no professional racers. Chris tells me he once represented Britain in the Olympics. That's impressive. So many lives, all going on at the same time as mine, all different. I'm still surprised.

Chris has got that dark brown face and fluffy sun-bleached hair that goes with this kind of thing. The kind of face you expect to see wearing mirrored sunglasses and brightly coloured lipstick sun protector like skiers and cricketers wear. It's a look that's growing on me. I might do myself up like that and look cool.

Conor and the others are taking the train, which is how I used to travel to Wittering before. I want them to get into that nostalgic seaside vibe.

This will be the first time I've ever seen my holiday palace from the sea. I wonder if they've got the sail-in dock sorted out. I plan just to drift right inside. How cool is that?

On the first morning of my holiday, I'm up early. I do the usual stuff with breakfast but I inform Conor I'm not going to be running today. Staying alive on the power boat should be enough exercise for me. You know, I believe I am nervous. I remember nervous.

I head down to the Millennium Dock where Chris is waiting for me. A crowd has gathered; those who know I'm going away for a while. They're here to cheer me off. I couldn't stop them coming.

Well I could but I don't, if you know what I mean.

The day is warm and sunny, as if I'd made it that way. Of course I haven't and a little chop on the river reminds me that I'm not actually god.

Chris's assistant Mark hands me my helmet. The boat bobs like a tethered animal and I'm worried that perhaps I've taken on more than I can handle. After all, I've only been swimming properly a few weeks now.

My mum would have said this trip was good for me. That I could do with the air and the exhilaration. Real exhilaration, not that stuff from the past that my writing has been dredging up. New activities, that's what I need.

The Skater 40 dips and rolls as I step aboard. Chris and Mark squeeze me into the passenger seat. We're all wearing great looking red power boat tracksuits with patches. Already I can feel how powerful this machine is and we're only just idling. This is going to get scary.

'No worries,' says Chris in that public school bray of his; not sure I like that. Reminds me too much of arrogant bosses and the kind of people I had to serve when I was a part-time waiter at the restaurant. You see, I haven't even mentioned I worked in the restaurant, have I? This writing malarkey: it's more difficult than it seems; the more you write, the more you leave out, the more you realise is left to write.

Chris revs the engine. The water roars and churns. Bloody cool; this boat is going to shift some. I strap myself in. The panels and displays make it more like a cockpit than a bridge. I wave at the people on the jetty, taking in my apartment block, the Tate Modern, the Millennium Wheel, the Millennium Bridge, Tower Bridge, London. And it's mine. Fucking great.

'Be ready,' says Chris. 'This is one fast puppy.'

'Yeah all right,' I tell him. 'Enough jargon. This is England.'

Mark thumps the hull and shoves us off and we're floating. Already the power potential is immense. Actually, the sensation is rather brilliant.

'Well?' he asks.

I feel good, perched on top of all this water.

'Okay,' I say. 'Let's see what this puppy can do.'

And off we go.

Skater 40 lives up to expectations. We blast down the Thames at a rather astounding speed. I was expecting heart-stopping thumps as we accelerated but the ride is surprisingly smooth. Despite that, I'm gripping the plastic hull like I'm going to leave finger marks in it.

Chris turns his helmeted head to me and shouts. 'When we're out to sea, I'll increase the speed of the boat! A bit more!'

I can still barely hear him; the roaring engine is making my teeth shudder.

More? The wind's almost taking my head off as it is. Still, there's a buzz. No doubt about it. I know I am going to have to learn to drive this boat.

We head east and London slips away. I haven't been out of the city for years. We pass endless blocks of luxury apartments that line the bank of the Thames, then a lot more that aren't luxury. I've hardly ever been as far east as this. And with good reason if the whole lot is this dreary. I can't name the bridges or anything. I'm a Central London boy at heart; a boy with an aversion to place names like Mudchute, Isle of Dogs, Wapping. Grays and Dagenham. When I come back I doubt I'll let them stay standing.

It's difficult to tell when and at what point we actually leave London. There are now huge metal domes full of gas and oil instead of apartments. I suppose I will have to keep them if I wish to maintain my current standard of living. For the first time I wonder who keeps me and my city stocked up. Are fuels and gasses and materials and things still being imported?

I suppose they must be. I don't think most people's lives are any different from what they were five years ago. I wonder whether I should be keeping an eye on this kind of thing. I already know I won't be bothered. I have someone else, my people, to sort out all those boring practicalities.

We finally reach some countryside. The English coastal landscape. A few boats are tethered. Sun shines on the water and flat land. I don't see any human beings. There aren't that many left round here I suppose. Those that made it through have probably moved somewhere a lot nicer.

Chris takes the Skater 40 a bit steadier now; he doesn't want to use up the fuel. The Thames widens and then there we are. I can see ahead. Open sea. Fantastic. The wind has pummelled my face into numb submission but I can still feel that sun underneath, warming us up. The boat leaps as if in anticipation and with a nod, Chris properly guns the engine.

I scream as the g-force flattens me back into the seat. The noise is tremendous. That line of steel grey sea through the windscreen races towards us. This is fantastic. This is living.

My holiday has commenced.

The palace is coming on fine. I say palace, but really it's just the old Chichester Marina done up a bit. All right: done up a lot. You can see the high pointing towers from miles out. It's more tasteful than it sounds.

And yes, the sail-in dock is ready. A huge decorated metal arch over the harbour entrance points the way inside. The management have even laid on a little reception for me. The construction staff lines the jetty and I feel suitably daft as Chris cuts the engine to a purr and we drift into this big fancy hangar. Horns blare out a fanfare. A bit much, really. I sense that discomfort I always get when I feel that unseen hands, events managers and the like, have been working tremendously hard to make it seem spontaneous.

As Chris docks the Skater 40, the staff applauds. I stand up and give them a wave. These poor people have been building this thing for two years and I haven't visited them once.

The summer palace (as I think I shall call it) is built to my exact specifications. Despite the architect's original misgivings, the building resembles a villa on Lake Maggiore I once saw in a magazine photograph. Only to a much larger scale, of course. I don't know how they managed to make the palace look so nice and still build in protection from the UK weather, but they have done a grand job.

I spend lunch with the management team but before they start getting too technical with me, I explain that I'm on holiday and haven't come to mess them about. What I'm after is a bit of peace and the chance to get on with my memoirs. They nod and promise that they will do what is best. In fact, this might be the ideal time to let the workforce take a little holiday of their own; their first in two years. Not my doing; apparently they insist on staying and working even when they have the opportunity to go.

By the evening, I get what I came for. I drive a courtesy jeep a few miles down to West Wittering beach and watch the sun set. The wide sandy beach keeps the water shallow and gentle. The waves really do lap, just like they're supposed to.

There's always a breeze but you can tell summer is almost here. There's something about the sun dipping and colouring the water red and yellow and orange that I will never tire of.

Sitting on a sand dune, I'm reminded of how I used to come here as a kid. The nostalgia is almost physically painful. I have so many memories of this beach. This beach, I remind myself, *this actual one here*. Anthony then and Anthony now. We are separated only by Time and that one fraction of history. Me on my own living in this strange, altered world. Him with cousins and aunties and mum and dad. Windbreaks and paddling. Sand castles and football. When could a day last so long?

I miss my dad. He was a good swimmer and always played with me. I wish he was here now.

I think I'm tiring of this holiday already. But a plan is forming.

The writing appears to be working on me. My sluggish brain feels exercised for the first time in its five-year paralysis. That's what I'll go back to. Maybe this time I'll even finish. I will finish. Maybe then I'll know what I've got to do in the future. The writing. Yeah.

Chapter 20

The management set up this huge office for me at the palace to write in. It was this gigantic room equipped with up-to-the-minute PC, huge mahogany desk, reams of bright pristine printing paper and a wall of shelves stuffed with books. A fantastic dream of a writer's room, only I couldn't think of a dicky bird. To write anything felt like I would, I don't know, make the place dirty. Like pouring soot on the carpet.

I just kept going out on the veranda to stare across the expanse of Chichester Harbour. Without any boats but mine, the sparkling waves were free to fold and unfold in a whispering, eternal relentlessness. I found their persistence and unhurried effort incredibly relaxing. What I did not find, however, was the inspiration to crack on with the work.

After that, and many a deep frustrated sigh, I would watch a DVD or play with my iPod through the five speaker surround sound system. Anything to avoid actually sitting down and writing, which seemed odd as I clearly could recall walking into the room bursting with ideas, determined to get right down to business. I could just never get going.

After two weeks of half-hearted attempts that always ended in failure, I quite accidentally found the solution.

I noticed when I drove back from the beach there was this cramped little cottage; a real traditional place with roses growing up the side, thatched roof and old stone walls. The building was nothing fancy; nothing like my palace, but for some reason I can't explain, I kept seeing its image in my mind. I kept defaulting to a mental picture of the cottage. It came most especially when I tried to write.

So a couple of mornings back, I drove down in the jeep and took a look inside.

Of course, no one lives here now. It was obviously an old person's cottage at one time; the interior is pretty basic. There's a nice big fireplace, some solid-looking furniture and those old-fashioned metal-lined, diamond-shaped windows.

I brushed off the protestations of the palace management and their alternatives. Their suggestions were always for bigger, fancier; and that didn't feel right. So I decamped. Me and a little laptop. And here I sit.

The writing power has come back. I am tapping away again. I realise those frustrating hours in the big office weren't wasted after all. I needed the time. The brain was working away without my knowledge, under the surface. I just needed time and the right place to make sense of the memories.

As I sit here in my cottage, in my peace, I can feel the past coming into focus. That world has long gone. It has vanished, as remote as the Silurian age, banished along with the dinosaurs. When I've gone and future archaeologists come and dig out the fossils of my time, will they call this the Anthony Age?

The cities still stand; the roads still carry traffic; the people still rush about getting on with their stuff. Those archaeologists wouldn't be able to see any difference; that anything happened at all. But it did.

I happened.

Book Two

THE EARTH UNDER ANTHONY

Chapter 21

How could it only be a year? If not for the national television coverage, the spontaneous street parties, the warehouses full of gifts and the horse-drawn parade through swarming crowds to the open-air festival in a specially rebuilt Soho, I might have forgotten the anniversary entirely.

I let myself off: after five months in hospital no wonder it all blurred by.

April the Eighteenth was sunny. Sunnier than the last one anyway. On this Eighteenth, an army of quirkily named event-planning companies, under the safe hands of Danny Boyle, ensured Central London was transformed. A visual feast to celebrate the day boring, passive, mild Anthony Graves became Glamorous.

My anniversary was the biggest outdoor party in history. Everything I ever mentioned I liked, from liquorice to James Bond films to Call of Duty was beamed in IMAX onto gigantic screens stretched across huge buildings, etched in lasers. As every new topic was introduced, the million strong crowd roared its approval. Sound systems blasted every word I had ever publicly uttered up into the ether; set to the music of my favourite playlists. Swarms of extras dressed as me dangled from buildings in interesting geometric patterns. Leicester Square was a throbbing mass of worship. I felt silly, smiled and waved a lot as my car pulled me through the streamers and bunting. The spectacle, the waste, the sheer indulgence was shocking. I never realised until then just how deeply embedded it was, this thing I'd put into them. I could do anything to these people and they would love me for it.

On the main stage in Leicester Square, I watched Coldplay, Muse, even Oasis. The greats. I sang along with my millions. I was in tears. When Chris of Coldplay dedicated 'Yellow' to me, I made sure I thanked him personally. My people and I communed as one. I felt the love. Although I did send everyone away at half eleven because I was so drunk.

You know what anniversaries are like. A person gets to thinking about his life. The mistakes he has made and the losses he has suffered. He reviews his time.

The day after, mum and I walked through Piccadilly. The tidying up had taken place overnight so the roads and pavements were clean and litter free. Twelve months down the line and London already smelled better. I enjoyed the peace. The fact sunk in that all the panic, all the dread — the noise and violence — were over. I doubt the city had ever been that quiet, not since the Romans first decided to build a handful of huts on a flat bit of marshland next to a river.

Despite the massive job of improving London, I had been fair. It was long understood the capital was overpopulated. The city needed thinning out. So I made a balanced decision. You people who bailed during the days of panic, good luck to you. Wherever you ended up, that's where you stay. The loyal ones who remained with me as I lay in hospital: take your pick of where to live and be happy.

Mum and I sat down under Eros. She told one of our people to fetch a coffee. If memory serves, I had a penchant for skinny lattes. Piccadilly Circus was now paved. The builders had worked quickly to be ready for the anniversary. I had long banned cars from Oxford Circus to the river and now Central London seemed to shine with a new form of light. On this new morning, as mum and I sat, the stone cherub with his slinky bow and arrow looked rather smug as he watched over the city.

'Do you ever think about dad?' I asked. 'Silly question.'

Mum patted my hand. 'You know I do.'

'Yep.' Still the Graves unease separated us. We were still incapable of normal, relaxed conversation. 'He would have liked this.'

'Yes, Anthony.'

I still didn't understand mum. After her initial enthusiasm for the business suit, she had returned to the old leggings and cheap blouse combination of old. She still wore the same old suburban mum hair, even the cheap off-the-shelf specs with big thick lenses. I would have expected a woman in her position to, well, to make herself look better. Isn't that what women were supposed to crave? I didn't dare ask her to glam up for her new job of being a parent to the new Emperor of Britain.

Me, I'd had the full monty. My teeth were capped and whitened. My hair was styled and I had my own manicurist. I had a woman who sorted my clothes and shoes. Now I was out of hospital, dieticians and personal trainers replaced doctors and physiotherapists. For the first time in my life, I was losing my plumpness. My every material need was taken care of by the top professionals in the country. But mum, she just kept working. Why? What stopped her relaxing and enjoying her new life?

Perhaps it was shock. After all, she had gone from watching television to running the country. Send anyone a bit funny.

'We should go on holiday,' I said. 'Somewhere sunny.'

'Abroad? I don't think so.' She didn't even look at me. Instead, she tapped a number into her phone. 'It's not safe yet.'

'Safe?'

I looked out across the developing plaza. There were a couple of hundred people rushing about trying not to look at me. A couple of small Japanese girls plucked up courage to stroll by. They both wore padded pink raincoats. 'Hi Anthony!' Their voices were shrill with excitement. They waved and giggled.

I smiled and waved back. *Safe?* What did that mean?

A year ago I was sitting in my office in my department on the twenty-second floor thinking about buying something pointless on the internet. And now I ran London. I ruled Great Britain and countless numbers in other countries.

Mum put the phone back into her handbag. She sniffed; her way of saying 'job done'.

'Important?' I asked.

'Not really.'

'Mum?'

'Yes?'

'Don't you worry that one day I will have to get you?'

She touched my hand. The most maternal gesture I could remember she ever made.

'I'm your mother,' she said. 'You got me a long time ago.'

I looked across the peaceful roundabout to the sinuous streets of Soho. 'We should move house,' I said. 'Somewhere central. Somewhere bigger.'

Mum smiled, strained. 'Whatever you say, Anthony.'

I think mum sensed I was getting restless so she suggested I take a tour of the realm. Nothing fancy, just five coaches. She got someone from the Tourist Board to book me into all the best hotels up and down the country. I realised there were so many places I'd never been. Liverpool, Scarborough, Bristol, Stoke (although to be honest we missed that one out. There are some things you can choose not to experience without feeling bad).

When I got bored of being driven, we went by train. I liked that more as the scenery was better. Obviously with mum in charge, the trains all ran on time.

Everywhere I visited, the people there laid on all sorts of goodies for me. Which was nice. They were all determined to impress with their own regional uniqueness. That helped as I quickly struggled to remember what town I was in. Unless you live there, what's the difference between Winchester and Whitby?

Still, I got to see the sights you're supposed to see when you're doing these things. I saw Edinburgh Castle, Shakespeare's house in Stratford, Heartbeat country in the Derbyshire Dales, Last of the Summer Wine Country in Yorkshire, Blackpool Tower, Brighton Pier, the Grimsby docks, the Humber Bridge, the Robin Hood Experience in Sherwood Forest, Alton Towers, Tintagel, the

Glyndebourne Opera, the ferry across the Mersey, the fog on the Tyne, Carmarthen Castle and Legoland.

My favourite part of the tour, apart from the many drunken parties laid on by my admiring provincial fans, has to be the visit to the Manchester United football ground at Old Trafford. I've never been much of a football fan, which I suppose was one of several factors that separated me out from my fellow Englishmen back in the old days.

When my train pulled into Manchester I sensed straight away that this was going to be something special. The platform was mobbed. I was used to crowds but this was a different magnitude. It was like the whole city had come out to see me; all waving plastic flags. The red cross on white background: St. George. Now the flag of Anthony Graves (I never dared rename it the Saint Anthony flag; despite the pressure groups).

As we slowed and rolled to a stop, the crowd surged forward and began thumping on the windows. Drunk, I waved back. I swear two died of heart failure as they were squashed against the unbreakable plastic. I could hear the screaming even in the compartment.

My SAS guy Major Pete shoved his way out of the door as soon as it hissed open. He held a pistol up ready to disperse them but as soon as I followed him out the mob drew back to clear a path for me. All the noise stopped as one. Thousands of people suddenly went quiet. The heat was tremendous. I wondered how long they had been waiting.

Major Pete hustled me and my entourage through the station concourse. This was a bit more than a few banners and meeting the local Lions Club. This was the arrival of God.

I transferred to a nice open-top black limo and we drove slowly through the crowd to the massive glass and steel edifice that was the most famous soccer stadium in the world. Yes, I thought, this is sufficiently big. For the first time in a while, I was impressed.

I thought the station noise had been wild, but as we approached Old Trafford I heard a sound so extraordinary I wondered how many people in the world had ever experienced such a phenomenon: the sound of your own name being roared over and over again by an unbelievable number of voices. The car emerged from the mass into a fenced-off roadway to an underground car park. I felt like I had been at the bottom of a huge pile of bodies. I could breathe again.

'Sixty-eight thousand,' said mum, reading a text. 'God knows how many more outside.'

She handed me a can of lager. I needed it.

Yeah, the day at Old Trafford. Not an experience I'm ever going to forget. The driver parked the limo at one of those temporary umbilical tunnels. They really wanted to put on a show. A smart black woman wearing a huge, linked gold chain approached the limo as I got out. She shook my hand. 'I'm Jocelyn. Mayor of Manchester,' she said.

'No, Jocelyn,' I replied. 'I'm the Mayor of Manchester.'

I looked at her. She nodded.

'Joke,' I said. Jocelyn laughed heartily.

We walked through the tunnel into the stadium. Coloured lights swirled across a huge black backdrop. Camera operators listened to their headsets and switched on their UHD 4k cameras.

The stage was huge, like a band was going to play. But unlike any of the handful of festivals I'd seen on telly, this one had no music at all.

I waited in the tunnel as Mayor Jocelyn took the stage. Looking overjoyed, pure rapture in her expression, she raised her arms. 'Manchester welcomes Anthony!' I was startled, expecting a bit more of a build-up; a bit more showbiz. Mum gestured me forward.

I walked on-stage. A wall of noise hit me, like nothing I'd ever experienced. 'Anthony!'

Writing just doesn't do those three syllables justice. You could have heard my name on Mars.

As I said, I didn't get back home until the end of June. I had missed last summer altogether, what with being stabbed by my father, so I was determined to spend this one in the capital; in London and actually living in the centre. I had been dreaming of that since I first got the glamour. No, I had been dreaming of that since I was born.

My city. I couldn't wait.

I started by moving into a big house overlooking Green Park. A big five-storey job right in the heart of Mayfair. The property belonged to some South African corporate bank bastard but he was more than happy to give it to me. He was a big chap, was Rodney Witters. Handsome, extroverted and confident: a rugger player with a dark tan and thick golden hair. Rodney played a lot of sport and he shook my hand when he opened the door for me.

But something was not right with Rodney. Maybe I've got a thing about South Africans — maybe it's the accent, maybe it's their superior bullying chumminess, maybe their seeming genetic alphaness — but I sensed he was somehow not quite in the game. He was charming all right and was very proud and happy to give up his house to me. No one else seemed to sense anything wrong about him so I suggested he might like to try sleeping rough on the streets and while he was at it see how many knife fights he could get into. For the rest of his life. Rodney smiled, thanked me for what I had done to him and walked out the front door.

I often think about Rodney. I have some idea now; I wish I had had it then.

No matter. Finally, thirty-one years after I was born, I got the summer I had always dreamed of. London was mine.

And what harm had I done? The country was cleaning up its act. All the people I had encountered on my travels were not upset to have me in charge. In fact, they appeared only too pleased to have someone to look up to. Without me, I'll bet Manchester hadn't been half such a jolly place.

They still went to school, to work, watched telly and finally to bed. I wasn't going to change any of that. Most of them would never see me, would never even get close. Next day, I went on television and asked all the South Africans in the country to do the same as Rodney. Naughty perhaps but it did make me laugh.

All that hot summer, the streets were full of people going about their business. There were no fights (I guess the South Africans all killed each other), no drunkenness, no riots caused by the heat, poverty and racial hatred. Crime dropped to zero. Whenever I wanted I could get a group of people together and we would have a party or make a little movie or drive a car round the city. No one said anything.

I know you're supposed to get bored of too much of having a good time but that never happened to me. I could have messed about like that forever. I presume it was because I had always been such a dull bloke, that the party-going Anthony who had hibernated deep inside had a lot of energy to expend. He just wanted some fun.

At the end of July I got to sail down the Thames in a luxury yacht. And every time we reached a bridge, fireworks blasted out from the banks across the water. They turned the sky purple with smoke. I remember looking across at my friends for the night — all beautiful, all thoroughly enjoying themselves — and I knew at that moment there was an upper limit. I really actually couldn't be happier. That was the best night of my life.

On the seventh of September, I was eating breakfast in the lobby of Claridge's with mum. Mum was living there now and they did a mean full English breakfast. She said it kept her close to what still needed doing. It was another beautiful morning in London. As I looked up, a man strolled in. He had one of those creased faces that remind you of kindly grandads in movies. You couldn't help liking him. I assumed he was one of mum's flunkies come to tell me something. Funnily enough, mum thought he was one of mine.

'Anthony!' the man said in a warm, American accent.

'Hello?'

He held out his hand to shake. 'I'm Max Angstrom. And I'm a Siren, just like you.'

Chapter 22

Max Angstrom was amused. In one of our subsequent chats, he confirmed he had been most tickled by my reaction to his arrival. As I stared at him across the hotel breakfast table, a poached egg slowly slid from my mouth. It crept down my chin and, opting to avoid the plate/table possibility, dropped as a congealed blob in my lap, like the sorry remains of some startling blowjob. Outwardly, Max merely observed; a warm smile his only expression. His amusement was all inside; the stark hollow comedy that comes from relishing another's humiliation. Schadenfreude. He was too nice a guy to show it.

There was no such ambiguity with mum. She looked, and was, decidedly unamused. I watched her face drain of colour at a startling pace. I had to look away. Panic was too close.

Max Angstrom had tufts of grey hair. Small but undoubtedly expensive glasses dangled from an efficient silver chain at his neck. He sported bright blue jeans and a padded body-warmer worn only by steam engine enthusiasts and people who build fighting robots. Oh, and Americans in Europe.

My next impulse was to worry about mum. Unglamoured mum. For safety (mine) I loaded a push. It had been a while. The fire still burned. I had to get her before Max Angstrom did.

She saw it coming. There was terror in her eyes but Ma Graves retained enough composure to shake her head. Hold back. Please hold back.

Somehow, I did. I shoved that disappointed spark back into its box. I hoped to Christ she had a plan. Two million fucking guards in this city and this guy just walks through them all. What if Max had a knife? A gun? In one second everything would be his.

'Kill him…' said mum. It was almost a question. For a moment, I wondered who she meant.

Finally the guards understood. They stopped being waiters and produced their guns.

Max's smile nearly dropped. 'Anthony. Please. I'm unarmed. Hear me out.'

He stared at me with his kindly eyes; willing me to understand. Something about him; I don't know; it appealed to me. He had a look I hadn't seen for a long time. Independence.

'Coffee?' I murmured through egg mushed lips. I waved the guards back.

Mum stood up so quickly her chair crashed over. She kept her breathing under control. 'Will you excuse me?'

Aware of her anger, I mumbled something. She had never asked my permission before.

'Mrs G–' Max began but mum was already moving.

We watched her walk to the glass restaurant doors. 'Back in a minute,' she said. Gone.

Uncomfortable at having to be on my own with Max, I tried to smile. The glazed egg on my chin was sticky. I looked down at the mess in my crotch. 'Oh god,' I said aloud.

'Not quite,' said Max. He was a happy soul, looming over me like some benign… I don't know what. I couldn't think.

I remembered Angler and Penny telling me… how long ago? They were already ghosts from a different age. A different Anthony.

'Max Angstrom!' I said, too loudly. 'You're the American one.'

Max placed his hands on his heart. 'That's right, Anthony. I guess I am the 'American one'. The last American one.'

'You had others? What happened? I mean, sorry, if you don't want to tell me…'

'It's okay,' said Max. 'Let's face it; I guess you and me can say pretty much whatever we want these days, no? Seeing as how you're the European one. Pleased to meet you, Anthony Graves.' He held out a hand and I shook it before I even knew what I was doing.

I laughed. I was scared shitless but I couldn't help myself. He was just so bloody likeable. I had been so long without company. Without someone who genuinely seemed to like me. A dangerous thought. Where the hell was mum when I needed her? What was I supposed to say?

I lamely settled on: 'I've never been to America.' The guards glared at him as if they dared him to not take me seriously. Max thought about my statement; probably trying to frame a reply that made it sound not utterly inane.

'Well I've never been to Europe,' he replied. 'Come over some time.'

'I would love to.'

Yeah, right.

Yeah.

I drank my cold coffee.

'What… I mean, why?' I asked. 'Sorry.'

'It's okay. Take your time.'

'I mean. Why did you come here?'

Max looked at me straight. 'I'm a Siren, Anthony. We both are. There aren't many of us left. If we don't work together fast, there won't be *any* of us left.'

'But I mean, Jesus… On your own.'

'Mind if I sit down? I'm rather hungry.'

'Of course. Do what you want. Sorry.'

Max waited as a chair was pulled back for him. He sat politely and thanked the lackey. He then looked at the remains of breakfast with an expectant chuckle and started on the toast.

'I don't know about you, Anthony,' he said, 'but over there, in the States, I have everything. Everything and everyone. They love me. I want for nothing. But you know…' He looked up. At last, I saw the fear in his eyes. He knew exactly what he risked by coming here. 'I'm lonely.'

I decided Max was okay. Except I was waiting for the moment when the gloves came off and he tried to kill me like all the others. Because really of course, I didn't trust this bastard, not one inch.

Why didn't he? I mean: why didn't he try and kill me? In fact, why didn't I listen to mum and kill him back?

There, straight off, the big question. I'm not sure even now I know the answer.

As he tucked into my breakfast, Max told me how the US Navy transported him across the Atlantic in his own personal, top secret, type totally unknown to the rest of their NATO allies, stealth submarine.

The USS California surfaced off the west coast of Ireland three weeks ago. Max was rowed ashore by sailors; drove a previously hired car to Belfast, then caught the ferry to Liverpool before driving another previously hired car to London. During this process he learned exactly how efficient my people's attempts at securing my well-being actually were. Crap.

'Super-secret stealth submarine?' I asked. 'That's, er… well, a bit, you know, disturbing.'

'It's yours, Anthony,' he said. 'If you want it.'

I made some kind of vague gesture he seemed to interpret as a 'yes'.

'If I might borrow a cell phone?'

I looked at a waiter/bodyguard, who provided.

Max phoned the commander of the vessel and told him to sail into Belfast and surrender the vessel to the port authorities. After which he put the phone on the table and carried on eating. 'A gesture of goodwill,' he said. 'Enjoy your new submarine.'

'Why didn't you just ring me?' I asked. I chose not to add: 'instead of frightening me to death by turning up unannounced'.

'I didn't believe you would buy it,' he said. 'We have to trust and someone needed to make the first move. We need to be friends, Anthony. We really need to get on. The alternative is permanent isolation, and I don't know about you but I don't think I can take that for the rest of my life.'

Thinking back now, I still don't get Max. He had pretty much the entire arsenal of the greatest power in the world at his disposal, so why didn't he finish me when he had the chance? Was it possible he just was exactly who he said he was? Was he really just a nice guy who thought we Sirens could actually co-exist?

Max Angstrom was a lovely sweet man who pissed me off because he was completely correct. How the hell were we supposed to survive without trusting and meeting and all that shit? How come he managed to be more mature and smart than I would ever manage? He was so mature and smart he had to be hiding something. I just couldn't think of a way to figure it out.

Mum never came back. Instead, she rang me up. At the table. I asked Max to excuse me and rushed into the lobby. 'Where are you?' I was practically gibbering down the phone. Part of the answer was that she was in a car; I could hear that much. 'Where are you going?'

'I'm not going to tell you.'

'You can't leave me with him!'

'Anthony.'

'Mum!'

'Anthony! Shut up! Listen to me. I need you to listen.'

I took a deep breath, forced myself to calm down and do as she asked. 'Okay,' I said.

'I can never meet Max Angstrom again,' she said.

'What? Why?'

'You know why.'

'But–'

'I will leave a contact number,' she said, all business. 'It won't be me who answers in case he has your phone. I can still help. I can still advise. You have to speak to me whenever you can but never, never in the same room as him. That cannot happen. You understand?'

I stared at the phone. I looked through the glass restaurant doors at the American at the table. 'You didn't even pack any bags,' I said.

'Ring me when you're alone.' The phone went dead.

That was that. Just me, then. I was going to have to deal with Max Angstrom.

Shit.

Chapter 23

I showed him the sights of London. It was what he said he would like. I declared the day a holiday and went on television to order everyone to go home. I wanted London clear and uncluttered for the tour.

That sunny afternoon, we travelled in an open-top red bus past Buckingham Palace, the Tower of London and all that. Tate Modern, past what would become my apartment block. Max was wide-eyed and enthusiastic throughout. He was a born tourist: genuinely wowed by being here. And thanks to Max, I could see London for the first time; how it looked clean and sorted like I wanted. It was a memorable afternoon, one I look back on wistfully. Just myself, Max and my six-strong team of bodyguards with automatic weapons ready to bring him down the moment I gave the order.

'How many of us are there? Sirens, I mean.'

Max had been waiting for the question. He produced a small, well-used notebook from his padded body-warmer. 'There are some advantages to having access to the most sophisticated and paranoid satellite surveillance system in the world. I've got people looking out for any incidents. As far as we know, at last count we can accurately confirm there are ninety-eight Sirens currently active on Planet Earth.'

He looked at me with his kindly eyes.

Ninety-eight. 'Is that all?'

'All? I'm amazed we still have that many. At least fifty of us are dead. Probably more.'

'Dead.' That felt horribly final.

'Sometimes the authorities worked out the implications in time. That their time had passed. Most others were suicides. Some, like baby LaVonn, were tragic accidents. They weren't mentally or physically capable of survival once they had… changed. Two were the victims of their own followers by mistake, God knows how. The rest? Probably rivalry. Sirens and other Sirens. But mainly the authorities. The keepers of the old world.'

Dead? I was still hanging on that word. That horribly final word. I still suffered the recurrent nightmare of dad and his knife and that hot TV studio. I had lived under the shadow of death since that bloody day in April when this awful power came to me. When I became that other horrible cold metallic word; the word Max used so freely: Siren.

The tour terminated on Waterloo Bridge. Max and I got off the bus and walked to look at the river. The last people were gone. London was still; the only movement the water, the wind and the birds. Even a Siren could do nothing about them.

If Max was awed by the weight of old world history spread out in front of him, he didn't show it. Instead, he looked at the Thames.

My Thames with its deep, aged Thames water. Wrinkles around his eyes creased, enhancing that kindly grandad look.

'You can't blame them,' he said. 'Their world was ending. The bright ones understood that. Even in the States. I had people try to kill me too, Anthony. But unlike you they didn't put me on national television. That was a dumb move on their part. A move that ended up keeping you alive.'

I wanted to tell him that the chat show had pretty much been the death of me. That it had been mum's idea; but again, some little brain-lodged nut of common sense stopped me. She was right. She had to stay free of influence and Max must never be allowed to know it.

He smiled. 'Anthony. I meant what I said about feeling lonely. I believe you're lonely too. I want you to trust me. We need each other. We have to learn to share this world.'

He touched my hand. No, not like that. In, you know, in that sincere American way. Max certainly was an emotional type. As if he–

'You tried before!' I said. 'You tried with someone else.'

'Yes.' Max looked into the water again. 'There was a girl. She was the third American Siren; after the baby in Anadarko and myself. Very young. Paula Rodriguez, the fifteen year old daughter of Mexican illegal immigrants. She had been working as a waitress down in some hellhole in Miami.' He winced at the memory. 'When I reached her, she had torn the city to pieces. The entire population was heading north; all on foot. Unimprinted refugees. Until they reached me and I got them. Rodriguez hadn't figured it out. Hadn't figured out how to reach out. Would I have done the same in her position? Given her intelligence and experience? I suppose so. I found out her identity very quickly. I flew down in a news helicopter. Didn't want to look threatening. I thought I could help her. We met.'

'When was this?' I asked. Already he seemed to be talking in a tone that implied ancient history.

'Let me see. Must have been August last year. Damn hot down there.'

August. I was just coming out of my coma.

'So what happened?'

'She was enjoying herself, having a whale of a time. She was on her own, driving round the streets in a pickup truck, draped in guns and clothes and jewellery. She told me she liked to smash in the front of all the designer stores and burn the clothes. Versace, Dolce & Gabbana, Armani, all of them. I don't know, maybe it was political. Probably just revenge. She torched Palm Beach and all those mansions. Imprinted the owners and made them stay inside to burn.'

'So what happened? With you, I mean.'

Max smiled. 'She tried to kill me. So I got her first.'

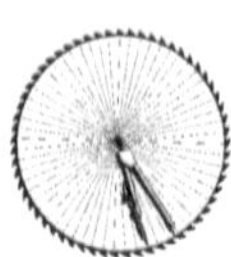

There were other stories. I felt dull and stupid for never having thought about what had happened in the outside world. I had been too wrapped up in my own misery. Or unconscious, which I suppose let me off the hook a bit.

The days passed. Max stayed in my new house in Mayfair that I took over for the occasion. He lived simply and despite being under twenty-four-hour surveillance was not plotting any invasion that I could uncover. I started to believe him. Why would he lie?

I spoke to mum a lot, like she wanted. She was hiding out in a basement bunker somewhere. Wouldn't tell me where. I think it was military as somehow they were monitoring communications in the United States to see if there was any reaction to Max's absence. I don't know if there was as she never told me. To be honest, I didn't want to know.

I don't think mum was very comfortable in her bunker. It must have been frightening for her, knowing there were two of us now who could put the zap on her. We never spoke about it but neither mum nor I were entirely convinced that this isolation plan of hers actually would stop Max if he put his mind to it. I didn't like the idea but I was increasingly warming to the thought of, just for safety, glamouring her. She knew it too and worked hard to keep me from doing so. For all I knew, maybe Max had already got her and she was now working for him and all this bunker thing was part of some arcane scheme to get me out of the way. Lucky for her, I couldn't work out how this would help him and more importantly, I just didn't have it in me to disobey my mother. Not yet anyway.

Mum made me put Max through the wringer. Every possible method of keeping him watched was employed. I think she would have got me to strap him to a chair and beat the truth out of him if I would have agreed. I didn't.

Of course, she kept telling me to kill him. In fact, that's what she spent most of our conversations telling me. It was only the direct threat of me glamouring her there and then over the phone that shut her up. She didn't get it. Didn't see that I was willing Max to be a good guy; to be for real. The truth was I needed Max just as much as he said he needed me. I needed a friend so badly I was willing to risk it turning out wrong.

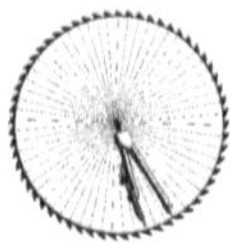

Max and I stayed in and listened to classical music over the eighty grand in-house stereo with Technics audio hard drive in the basement. The system with the hidden speakers in the walls. This place was tops. He taught me about his favourite composers and which recordings of their works were the best.

Max was as keen to talk as me. He said he was pleased to have found an equal to communicate with, even if the equality was only due to our single shared randomly selected ability. In every other respect he had been there, done that. Everything I had not. And of that I was glad.

This was different to my time with Penny and Doctor Angler. Max was like me, members of a very select club.

One day, Max talked about how he had given himself up to his government for testing. At least we had that in common. He made me feel less stupid for doing it myself.

He revealed he was initially shocked and horrified when he realised he had brainwashed his family and neighbours in Boston; how much they suddenly worshipped him. He said that the first idea that something was amiss was when his students in a lecture he was giving on Japanese Kaizen theory sat still, stayed awake and listened.

Unlike me, at first he sought medical advice. That seems so obvious now. When he watched the news reports of the disaster in Oklahoma, he checked into hospital. He was frightened. Two days later, the FBI came for him.

There was all the usual talk of men in black suits and mirrored shades hustling him around secret rooms and talking about bio-weapons and security ops and cool USA security services behaviour.

Max realised two things. The first was that he was not ill. The second was that this new power of his could actually come in handy for when inevitably his government would try and kill him. So he went on the offensive and got them first. He planned the whole thing out. Unlike me with all the panic and last minute bodge, he took his country over using stealth, increment by increment. They only got one decent go at him — his words — a bungled hospital bombing that left him buried under a pile of rubble. He sustained a few bruises but nothing more. After that, it was more planning and eventually control of the north-eastern seaboard. He now had command of the most sophisticated military hardware in the world.

'I realised then I had a responsibility,' he said. 'I don't mean a mission from the Lord or anything like that. A responsibility to a world that was now irreversibly different. Instead of ten billion or whatever people, there were now only ninety-eight. The rest had been relegated. There now existed a new order of humanity.'

His words made me realise how lucky I had been. Astronomically lucky. Why me? And why had no one, no other Siren, come for me?

'Probability,' he said. 'The UK might be a major economic power but mathematically it's tiny. A fifth the size of Texas. Technologically advanced, but in terms of population spread, a minor mark on the globe. Cluster statistics dictate that the number of Sirens in Europe will be minimal. You are a very rare creature, Anthony.'

He sat back on the sofa. God, he was cool. So calm and relaxed all the time. I wondered what he had been through in his time at the Boston Hospital, but I didn't dare ask.

'But there are others apart from me. In Europe.'

'Indeed.' He was as unruffled as ever. 'The old Soviet Union has three, we think. Two men, one last located near the Polish border and another out East heading into Asia with a sizeable but impoverished following. There's also a woman we've tracked in Chechnya embroiled in fierce fighting. I haven't been there. I'm not too crazy about going there either. They're aware of each other's existence and working on destroying one another. Each one tried to enlist me and the US onto their side. I don't think we can do anything but wait and see who comes out on top. I don't think they'll do anything but neutralise each other; at least for some years. However, there's a woman in France called Felice Beata.'

'I got told about her. You know what she's like?'

'I was going to ask you. I've been trying to communicate but so far: zip.'

'You think she's, you know, crazy too?'

'Who knows? I would have thought the odds of cracking up were probably higher than not cracking up. What do you think?'

I had to be honest. 'I haven't really thought about it.'
He nodded. 'Perhaps that's what kept you sane.'

In the old days, Max had been active in some Green movement they had over in the USA. You know: all for everyone stopping using cars and planes except them. I think now the Sirens were here he was actually pretty pleased. In fact, he hit me with his pet why-did-it-happen theory: that this was some last-chance gesture by Mother Earth to stop the planet being choked to death by its human inhabitants. Not a million miles from Doctor Angler's ideas just a bit more hippy-dippy. I just nodded.

Max had also defined a relationship with the people we had taken over; ie. everyone who wasn't us.

'In my view,' he said in his best liberal teacher tones, 'we Sirens have been granted a great responsibility. We didn't ask for it, nor were we elected. We were just chosen. There doesn't seem to be any way to reverse our effects on those we touch, so I guess we're here to stay. We are to be the caretakers of the Earth. Managers, if you like. In fact, I tried to coin the term 'Earth Managers' instead of Sirens but the authorities weren't having it. There are millions of people here and we must guide and care for them. You and I, Anthony: we have to lead them well.'

Again, I just nodded. Max was sincere, and believe me I was grateful for everything he was telling me. But he had his cracks too. Here he was, talking all fancy about caring and guiding; this man who admitted to killing a fifteen year old girl because he decreed it necessary.

One day, I took Max on a Thames trip aboard my favourite luxury yacht. We sat in deckchairs on the top deck; enjoying the sun on an unseasonably beautiful October afternoon. Up in Berkshire, where the river narrowed, I ordered the captain to turn off the engines and let us drift our inevitable way back to London. Mind you, he was under strict orders not to let the vessel drift too far downriver. I didn't want to end up in the dreaded cultureless hinterlands of Essex. Not this Earth Manager.

'I was wondering, Max,' I said.

'Mm?'

'I don't mean anything by it but were you thinking of going home at any point? I mean, what are your plans?'

Max thought for a moment. His favourite tipple was some godawful carrot-based fruit smoothie and he used this opportunity to reach for the glass and suck up a whole load through a straw. Me, I was on a strict G and T regimen.

'Anthony,' said Max. 'I've come here in good faith to ask for your help.'

'Me? What can I do? You look like you're all sorted out.'

He smiled. 'We're on our own here. There may be millions of people all around us every day but we are no longer the same species. Pretty soon, we're going to forget that they're people at all. You've probably already started thinking that way. I know I have. Unless we have real, unaffected colleagues to remind us, we're going to forget that we're human.'

'Perhaps we aren't,' I wondered. I could picture myself as mum probably saw me. A neutral eye. 'Perhaps that doesn't matter anymore.'

'Being human always matters,' said Max, but I was starting to understand he liked talking like he was in a movie.

'What do you want me to do?' I asked.

Max produced his notebook. This was another part he liked: sorting stuff out. 'I think we should pay Madame Felice Beata a visit. A trip to la belle France. Why don't you come with me?'

Chapter 24

Of course, we began with no. I told Max Angstrom there was no way I personally would ever be leaving my country to visit another Siren in theirs. He looked at me; that sad old gentle grandad look on his face. 'That's fine, Anthony,' he said.

'Sorry.' I was always apologising to Max.

'Just remember: if we don't go looking for them, they'll eventually come looking for us.'

We started with phone calls and emails. Government numbers and addresses. Nothing came back. Phones did not connect. Emails bounced.

Europe was silent. There was no digital traffic, no mobile phones, no nothing. The continent was quiet. They had the network coverage but no one was using it. There was nothing to listen to. Nothing to watch.

Max and I travelled to a top secret NATO headquarters in Scotland. We agreed this should be a joint venture. Despite mum's protests, I allowed Max to bring some of his specialists in. As the serious, crew-cutted blue uniforms arrived in my country, I made sure they worked under close supervision; I'm not that stupid.

Satellite pictures revealed a Europe that seemed unremarkable. Max and I sat in comfortable dark padded seats in imposing high-security briefing rooms and watched dull black and white footage of French, Dutch, Belgian, Spanish, Andorran, Luxembourgian, Portuguese, Italian and German countryside. There were no riots; no armies. The people of Western Europe were going about their daily lives; albeit at the level of an ancient pre-digital age around, let's say, 1990. The people in Europe seemed fine with that. They still lived in their houses and drove their cars. They just didn't seem to talk to anyone out of their own earshot.

I suggested sending spies but Max believed that would create the wrong tone. We weren't going to war with this woman.

'Also,' he said. 'France is a big country. Where do we send the spies?'

The advisors recommended we send spy planes to fly over and take pictures. Unfortunately, the first time we tried, a squadron of rather efficient jet fighters scrambled from a German base and flew straight up to home in on what we thought was our hi-tech secret undetectable aircraft.

'How did that happen?' I asked Max.

He was untroubled by the question; almost seemed to be expecting it. 'The glamour is no respecter of boundaries. It rewrote the rules and introduced a new era of openness that I for one find refreshing. North America had large numbers of diplomats, ambassadors and, I'm afraid to say, covert agents operating in Europe. Agents who knew many secrets and would rush to give them up to their new masters. I'm sure you probably identified the foreign agents working here as soon as you could. Standard practice. I know I did.'

I sucked my diet Coke up the straw from its bottle. 'Yeah, 'course,' I muttered.

Max and I spent days with advisors working out how to contact this Felice Beata. At last, we gave in to the fact it simply could not be done. I flew back to London, to leave Max to it. I wanted to speak to mum. I needed to see her without him. She wouldn't do a face-to-face but agreed on an internet conference.

I called the conference on my river boat and my people — the army, navy, air force, politicians, doctors, philosophers, spin doctors and spiritual healers — insisted I tell Max to call the whole thing off. They didn't want anything bad to happen to me.

I expected mum to try and talk me out of the whole France deal but she didn't. Max had been in Britain for six weeks now and something about him had captivated her. It wasn't the glamour, I was certain of that. She saw a change in me. I was less needy. Max was relieving the pressure on her. On the screen, I could see mum looked healthy and alert. This was new. I hadn't seen it before but I had worn her out. Without any experience, she had been forced to restructure a country. She was exhausted.

I didn't know what to think. Already I was tired of being the main man. Initiative had never been my strong point and having everyone in the country love me and bow to my every whim had, understandably, softened my resolve.

Max's influence boosted my mood. I didn't feel alone and he didn't seem dangerous. We might even have some fun over in France. Felice Beata: sounded exotic. Maybe even sexy. You never knew…

I don't know whether it was our attempts to communicate but a week later, Max rang from the NATO place to inform me something new had happened. I was up to Scotland again.

New satellite pictures were coming back. Our air force satellite guys showed us black and white photos of large-scale building works. From Denmark to Spain, massive earth-moving operations were underway. The Intel people told us it was impossible to determine what they were constructing. What they could tell us was that immense labour forces were moving out of the cities and being gathered and housed in gigantic work camps in the countryside. Europe was being rearranged. Quickly.

At this point, to ensure total clarity, I reiterated the fact I would not be going.

My chair creaked as I sat back. I'd done enough looking at satellite photos of mainland Europe. 'I just want you to be clear on that, Max.'

Max's benevolent smile never slipped. 'You have made yourself very clear, Anthony. I get it. You don't have to go.'

'Good.'

Good, I thought. I don't have to go. Max can handle it.

But. What if Max couldn't handle it? What if he went to Europe and found this Felice Beata who seemed to be doing such a marvellous, efficient job of sorting her countries? What if they got to making plans? Would this include plans for me? Without his vast resources, without Max on my side, I was going to be very vulnerable.

I had already learned this about Max Angstrom. For all his gentle, sensible talk, he liked risks. He had turned up in London on his own and unless he had an army of Yanks in more submarines waiting underneath the Atlantic for secret orders, he had more bravery than sense. I wouldn't have done that. There was a thrill-seeker in him; a quality conspicuously absent in myself.

As the two most powerful nations in the world waited for Max and me to make up our minds, I yet again made that return flight to London. The city made me feel safe.

That very afternoon, as I was unpacking in my Mayfair apartment, I got a call from mum. She had a request. She wanted to meet that evening, at the Ritz. We made the arrangements together.

When I reached the hotel, it was encased in a ring of barbed wire. All electronic equipment was banned and anyone entering was thoroughly searched (bar myself, obviously. It was hardly in my interest to bring a laptop, tablet or phone anywhere near). We closed off and emptied all the buildings within a mile radius of Piccadilly, just in case anyone had any public address equipment that could conceivably be heard from inside. Just when I thought we had covered everything, mum even put sharpshooters on the roof in case of helicopters or parachutes. She was as safe from Max's possible influence as was humanly possible. The big question was: why would she bother?

When I arrived and got through security, mum had not yet arrived. I was ushered to my table by the smiling *maître d.* She had, however, filled the restaurant with actors selected to add character and glitz. Tuxedos and tiaras. The actors made a lot of fuss and noise as they vied to impress me with their anecdotes. A band in white suits played muted show tunes. A sun-bronzed lounge singer with dyed black hair and a white tux — a singer I vaguely recognised — was singing to the music. He waved at me as I sat down. I felt a bit silly in my Force Awakens t-shirt and shorts. I shooed the actors away.

The lobster arrived; a dish I once thought scary and exotic, but Max had taught me to relish. I was about to crack some claws when mum walked in.

The noise stopped. The actors smiled nervously and looked to me to take the lead. She had dressed up. She was wearing a simple white summer dress that suited her tan well. There were also new gold highlights in her hair.

Before reaching me, mum gestured to the band. They stopped playing instantly. The singer skipped down and jogged to mum. He looked like a shop dummy as he kissed her cheek. The singer smiled at me and his impeccably capped teeth shone white. At last, I remembered him.

'Sammy Krystle!' I said in surprise.

Mum smiled, demure. Embarrassed. Sammy Krystle held out a hand. 'Anthony,' he said; his accent a suspect transatlantic mush as he split an infinitive. 'An honour to finally meet you.'

I shook his hand and looked at mum for an explanation.

Sammy Krystle had always been one of her little secrets. He was a singer, in that Neil Diamond seventies crooner type way. Mum had told me the story so often I think it was chiselled on my heart. Sammy Krystle, real name Isaac Wasibiak, the New Jersey American who had come over in the Sixties and made his name as part of the beat craze. Sammy Krystle was old-school: a Las Vegas wannabe who had never risen above the chicken-in-a-basket Bournemouth to Blackpool ballroom circuit. I thought he had died ages ago. Mum clearly knew otherwise. How long had she been searching for him?

'Anthony, I want you to free Sammy from your influence,' said mum.

Up to this point, Sammy himself had been staring at us like he was about to burst out laughing. With these words, however, he became very serious.

'Mrs G.? I think not. I mean, it could be dangerous.' Sammy looked at me with concern. 'For Anthony.'

Mum nodded. She didn't look far off tears. I was about to say something when I realised all the actors were watching us.

'Get out,' I snapped. I didn't want them seeing her like this. As fast as they could, they bolted for the exits. Plates and cutlery rattled. The jazz band trooped into the kitchen.

'This is… new,' I said.

Mum clutched Sammy Krystle's hand. 'I've really thought about this, Anthony. I need someone else. Someone for me. You have Max. I can't go on on my own anymore.'

'We're in love,' said Sammy.

'Maybe we'd better think about this,' I said. 'You know how dangerous–'

'I know what it is! I want him clear.'

Sammy and I looked at each other. I wish I could say we looked supportive.

'What about dad?' I asked.

I knew before I said it I had made a mistake. Mum changed.

For a second, just a brief second, I saw the woman I think she really was. Behind that Cleopatra make-up, her eyes burned, her jaw tightened and she hissed a breath.

My mother loathed me. She hated me.

But. She was still scared enough to master her emotions and keep this real person hidden.

I felt sick. I didn't want to know that woman. I couldn't be without the mum who had sorted my life. I couldn't be on my own.

'I'll do it,' I said.

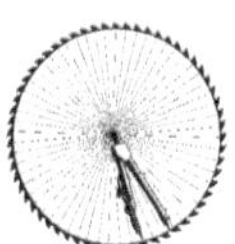

I was presented with a fait accompli. As usual, mum had already thought the operation out in minute detail. I didn't go far into her possible emotional reasons for wanting me to unglamour a fading lounge singer. Graves *mere et fils* didn't exactly have a history of sharing emotions and neither of us were about to start now. I never wanted that hidden snake woman to come out again, ever.

She had prepared a special room in her new house in St James's. Architects and builders reinforced what had once been a panic room for a Russian billionaire. Inside that room, which was rubberised floor-to-ceiling, she had placed a specially made piece of furniture, which looked like a cross between a dentist's chair and a psychiatrist's couch. Sammy Krystle was to be restrained here until such time he was deemed sane enough to be released. He would be watched twenty-four hours a day for a week. He would also be given daily psychotherapy to integrate him into mum's life, all to help him cope with the trauma of being released from my influence.

The idea of voluntarily releasing Sammy Krystle brought back a lot of unpleasant memories. Why do it? What was so wrong with him as he was?

I rang Max and even though I knew I shouldn't, I told him about Sammy. I didn't tell mum; she would have killed me. Max wasn't convinced by mum's plan but agreed to stay away. His theory was she maybe needed to 'get back in touch' with the woman she used to be. To return, at least symbolically, to a less complicated time in her life; something from her childhood. She needed a hero to dedicate herself to. A fantasy figure; strong, confident and dependable.

That was Max's theory.

We went through the rigmarole. Sammy lay strapped smiling on his couch. Mum and I and the medical staff were in the kitchen, watching him on a camera monitor. All sharp objects had been removed from the room. I had the only gun; an easy-to-use automatic pistol just in case collateral re-imprinting gave anyone any funny ideas.

Mum was biting her manicured nails; watching the monitor. The doctors busied themselves around us. Digital beeps announced his heart rate. In the room, Sammy Krystle smiled at the camera. 'Hello England!' he crooned to the ceiling. He looked incongruous and foolish. We were silent.

I left the kitchen and walked to the top of the stairs. Anyone who wanted to get me would have to run up and I had a clear line of sight on them. I sat on the top step and studied two laptop monitors: one of mum and the medical team in the kitchen and one of the panic room where Sammy Krystle was lying back and crooning 'My Heart Belongs to Daddy'.

I pushed. I heard a few cries from the kitchen which frightened the life out of me but they quickly died down.

Sammy sat strapped to the couch. His head was drooped; the singing stopped. Five minutes passed. He didn't move.

Later that evening, after many, many hours, I shouted down orders for two previously selected expendable nurses to go in and unstrap him. I watched them on the screen. I admit: I was waiting for disaster.

The nurses stepped away from the couch. Sammy thanked them and stood up. He looked dazed but still calm. He stretched and bent before humming a little tune. Mum paced nervously in the kitchen. The doctors were consulting their readouts.

I waited for the lunacy; the anger; the violence. I waited for screaming and shouting. Instead, he smiled at the camera. 'Anthony,' he said. 'Your mother is something else.'

The fact was: Sammy Krystle was a player. He had been one all his life. I think that's what stopped him having an overwhelming urge to kill both me and himself. He was also very vain and very stupid. He was like a dumb, friendly dog who thought no further than wanting someone to tickle his tummy and tell him what a good boy he was.

Mum didn't want me to see him in case it sparked something off but I had had enough of all that. I was the boss here; not her. I gathered a ring of bodyguards round me and walked downstairs. I gave the order to let him out.

The apparently free-minded Sammy Krystle was terrified when he saw me but he held it in like a true pro and flashed his bright teeth. 'Thank you, Anthony,' he said. I was so surprised I even shook his hand. To this day I cannot fathom whether I truly freed this man. My one and only success and I never figured out why. It seems to me his stupidity kept him sane.

I suggested to mum that we hold a concert. Let Sammy do his stuff now he was himself again. How about Wembley? Or the Albert Hall? I knew I could fill them. Wiser heads prevailed and we settled on Ronnie Scott's Jazz Club in Soho.

Invited celebrity guests made up the audience but mum had pride of place. I got her a table at the front and told the chef to surprise us.

I tailored up at Savile Row and we looked suitably rat-packed come the night. I liked the sharp grey suit and natty trilby; it was a style I thought I could warm to.

It was nice to be able to do something for mum after all her hard work. The lights were low and warm and orange. The chat was a nice murmur. Okay, it wasn't the Sands but there was a certain 1960s beat movie feel.

The compere performed the introductions and on came Sammy Krystle. He was beaming and leathery and resplendent. Even better, the guy could actually sing. He was more Tony Bennett than Tom Jones but I was impressed. Good set of lungs. And you knew the songs, all the old easy listening favourites. I think what was nicest was knowing he was free of my influence. He was singing because he wanted to and he was good at it. There was a certain flavour to his singing that I realised I hadn't heard for a while. Something genuine. Even my snipers, dark shadows in the wings, ready for anything Sammy might suddenly decide to do, were apparently smiling along to the music.

I don't quite know how long Sammy was going before I felt mum shake next to me.

She was crying, really crying. She had upgraded her dress once again, this time to a black fifties cocktail number and a string of pearls. Her hair was tied back, the way I'd seen it in photos of her as a teenager. The tears were silver trails on her cheeks, glinting in the stage lights. She didn't seem to realise she was shaking so much.

Well, I mean the guy was good but he wasn't that good. What was all this about? I think now, she was reacting to something outside of me. A genuinely selfish emotion. I didn't mind at all. It felt good not to be the centre of attention. Mum and Sammy Krystle: the last two free people in Britain.

'I'll leave you to it,' I told her. 'It's your night. Enjoy it.'

I sneaked away. Sammy's voice followed me into the lobby.

I don't suppose any son or daughter copes well with seeing their parents weep. I was filling up. Outside, my car purred into life. 'Primrose Hill,' I said. It seemed as good a time as any.

I got out of the car and walked across the grass. The city lights twinkled below in the dark; the electric blanket of a million occupied houses. There was a chill breeze in the humid summer air. A wind that felt clean.

'Hi, Anthony,' said Max.

'All right?' I said.

Max held up a bottle of Chianti and a couple of glasses. 'Nice suit.'

I waved at the guards and they melted into the night.

'Great to see you again,' said Max. 'Glad you invited me.'

Dark pencils of tree trunks were shadows in the park. I wondered how long they had sat here. Fifty years? A hundred? What changes had they been witness to?

Time seemed a heavy, weighty object; some relentless, slow-moving dinosaur that ground its way forward with people clinging to its reptilian hide, trying not to fall off, inevitably failing. All people, even me. Yes, eventually even me.

I looked down across London and understood how this could be a beautiful world.

‘Here’s to us,’ said Max. He handed me a glass and tipped some Chianti into it. ‘The inheritors.’

Now I recall that evening sat in the park with Max, nostalgia is threatening to get me all blubby. I am as sure as I can be that he was genuine. We were proper friends; grown-ups, equals, sharing a bottle of wine and a summer’s evening together. Something, some feeling that was there that night, has gone from me now. I can remember it, it sits there almost in my heart, but I can’t, can’t… get it back. Something I felt that night; now long lost.

‘I’ve missed you, Anthony,’ said Max.

‘Me too.’ I did. I really did. Man, that Chianti was good. He had real class, that Max Angstrom. ‘What’s so important?’

‘At nine o’clock this morning, we had a telephone call. One of the public numbers. A message,’ he said. ‘From Felice Beata.’

‘No way.’

Max sipped his wine. ‘Oh it’s completely genuine. We are invited.’

Chapter 25

I will be honest: the leaving of London was not a concept I readily embraced.

Unfortunately, I seemed unable to communicate my perfectly reasonable doubts to Max. He was fully, enthusiastically, committed; immersed in planning and preparation. His room in our Scottish Castle was crammed with maps and schedules. The Angstrom was enjoying himself.

My misgivings were not lessened by not being convinced he didn't have a massive navy sitting off the coast of Ireland waiting for me to drop my guard, despite mum trying to convince me that our guys were being honest when they told me the radar sweeps and SONAR beeps revealed nothing. I tried to explain to her about stealth technology but she wouldn't have it. It went against every grain in her body but, concerning my secret stealth navy paranoia, she trusted Max.

The entourage decamped to what was formerly Her Majesty's Naval Base, Portsmouth. It was still a Naval Base and it was still in Portsmouth; it just wasn't Her Majesty's any more.

Sorry Pompeiians, but I didn't get much of a look at your fine city although I'm sure deep down you'll agree I wasn't missing anything. What I did get was a lot of meetings in impressive hi-tech bunkers; endowed with giant monitor screens, top class personnel and excellent coffee machines. My chaps and I spent many hours consulting digital maps and computer readouts. The chairs were great. I kept falling asleep in them.

I couldn't get used to the saluting, so I told all the sailors to stop. Max talked about our 'insertion' into France. I liked such tough sounding jargon so much I insisted we keep using it; which annoyed mum when she found out. She didn't like me being so flippant. Clearly, she didn't realise I was covering the fact I was bloody terrified. The helpless inefficiency of our silly security measures was driving a wedge between us. I could hear the frustration in her voice. I was desperate for her to tell me not to go. She wanted to; she would have done anything to get me away from Max; even though she liked him and felt he was good for me.

I realise now, Max saw himself as this great statesman; a uniter of worlds. My role was to agree and tell him how brilliant he was. I don't believe he meant me any harm at all.

The day before D-Day I cancelled the mission. I told Max there was no way on Earth I was going to put myself in any form of potential danger. I made it clear there was nothing he could say to dissuade me. To reinforce my stubborn determination, I made sure I told him in the operations room with all my toughest people present.

Max's answer was horribly good. He looked around at the assembled generals, admirals and tough guys. The subterranean air was pungent with the smell of angry men. My people couldn't wait for that one little order that would get this annoying beardy liberal out of their master's hair once and for all. This didn't seem to faze Max.

'I believe you have to go, Anthony,' he said. 'For your sake. If the worst case scenario pans out and this woman is as crazy as Christmas, do you really want a stranger twenty miles across your English Channel? We may be the first unaffected humans she has encountered for over a year. If she meets you and knows you're okay, we have at least reduced the fear factor. For your safety alone we're going to have to try and make friends. Which is your own argument, no?'

Shit. Touché. A pause. Graves, stuck for words. Thank god my SAS bodyguard Major Pete came to my rescue.

'Why don't we just remove her?' he asked. 'Suicide squad? Blanket bomb the area? Better still: someone pretends to be Anthony, rocks up with a tactical nuke strapped to his back. I'll do it.'

I tried not to smile. I liked it when Major Pete said these things. They sent a pleasant shiver down my spine.

Max almost got angry. Almost, but not quite. 'Look,' he said. 'The whole point is that we create working relationships. It's that or the end of us. Siren against Siren in a bitter, calamitous dogfight. Okay, you might kill Felice Beata. But what message does that send to the other Sirens? Is that what you really want? Besides, I've been there. Killing our own? You wouldn't like it, Anthony. Never again.'

Major Pete gave Max his icy look. 'As long as Anthony wins that dogfight.'

'Thank you for your contribution,' said Max. 'But–'

'I could always break your neck,' said Major Pete.

Max turned white.

'It's okay, Major Pete,' I said. 'He's on our side.'

Major Pete nodded. End of conversation. I felt embarrassed for alarming Max, so I gave in to what he wanted. 'Okay,' I said. 'I'll go.'

Pride and a stubborn refusal to admit I was an idiot did the rest.

As my people made the insertion plans, Max and I broke for lunch. In the empty cafeteria, Max said:

'Thank you, Anthony.'

I spooned up my baked beans. I realised he had been rattled after all.

'No problem,' I said.

'Listen, I want to ask a favour.'

'Well.' I was uneasy. 'You can ask.'

'Anthony. Since I came to Britain, I have done everything you required of me to prove I can be trusted. But this is the thing: I would like personal protection. One man. He'll be under your orders; your major's too if you prefer. I won't even allow him to be armed.'

'You didn't need anyone when you came to me.'

Max was squirming. His forehead was dotted with perspiration. He didn't like having to request things from me. That was why he waited until we were alone. He didn't want me being advised.

'That's true, Anthony. However, I was almost certain you would be receptive to my visit. All my research pointed to you being one of the good guys.'

Really? Sometimes I wondered.

'It's one person, Anthony,' said Max. 'Someone to look out for me.'

I finished my beans, wishing to Christ mum was here to tell him that, no, he could not have his 'man'.

'Max, I will think about it,' I said.

I've told you about Major Pete, right? Old Etonian, SAS, veteran of some of the worst hellholes the British Army could throw him into. Big chap, deceptive dark floppy fringe and walrus moustache. Muscle and dagger tattoos. Oh, he always seemed very calm and charming in his tasteful grey pinstripe suit but something about Major Pete said: I kill people.

Major Pete became my bodyguard after he finished top in a long and dangerous audition process; a kind of X Factor for violent soldiers. I needed someone properly badass in charge of Priority Number One: my safety. Via phone, mum arranged for a full-on extraction team squad thing to wait off the coast; ready to scramble and pull me out if anything scary happened. I relaxed an inch. Whatever mum was up to in her hidey-hole, my safety appeared to be her primary concern.

Major Pete would be the only team member carrying a weapon in France. He would remain by my side at all times. There would be five of us in the helicopter.

Ah yes, the helicopter. I had forgotten I had ordered all helicopter pilots never to fly again. So I had to go round, find one and order him back in the air. It was more of a chore than it looks on paper, honestly.

The navy bods promised me all sorts of up-to-date personal tracking devices, mobile phone emergency frequencies and bleepers. No one was surprised when I wholeheartedly agreed to all such cautionary suggestions.

Field Marshal Pete (yes, I promoted him) summoned an interpreter from London. Her name was Alison Locke and she worked for MI6. When she was presented to me I realised that, much as I admired Field Marshal Pete's efficiency, I was going to have to work on his aesthetics.

I didn't much take to Alison Locke. She was short and squat with bad curly brown hair and little round specs. I wanted to change up for a better one but Max reminded me we didn't have time.

On the other hand, there was Max's bodyguard.

Did he know? I still ask myself: did he bloody know?

I was totally unprepared. Yes, they told me the American bodyguard had arrived; that 'Channon' was in the building. Yes, Field Marshal Pete informed me, Channon was being searched and tested and vetted and security checked. Even Max agreed that I should not be in the presence of Channon until the actual mission. We agreed he would sit with me when we set up a sneaky camera in a secure room so I could at least see what this bodyguard looked like.

I was expecting a testosterone-pumped musclebound cold-eyed killer the size of the Incredible Hulk. What I saw was the most beautiful woman in the world. My people opened the secure room door and in came a dark-haired, dark-skinned, thoroughly American supermodel, toned to perfection. Channon must have been what, thirty? Dressed in a simple grey business suit, she had the calm demeanour of a yoga master and the grace of a Bolshoi ballerina.

Forget Toni, forget Penny, forget… well, actually I'd forgotten the others anyway. Channon was the real deal. It was frightening but appallingly exciting. A woman, under someone else's influence, who wasn't mine. Jesus, I could hardly look at her. If this was what she did to me on a 1080HD smart screen, what was meeting her in person going to be like?

Max was impassive. ‘I trust Channon doesn’t seem too threatening?’

An attempt at humour? He couldn’t know. He must never know. Thank Christ I hadn’t said anything to mum.

‘I think she’ll do,’ I told him.

It had taken just a moment. Just a woman walking into a room.

I went to bed that night in my underground Portsmouth silo outwardly the same Anthony Graves as I always had been. Only something was different; something was changed. I had received an imprint in my mind in the form of Channon. Sneakily, without Max knowing, I ordered footage of her ‘interview’ downloaded into my laptop. I lay in bed and stared. This beautiful woman, her exotic skin matched against the grey suit, perfectly rendered in high definition television as she moved gracefully about a small room. Even when exhaustion meant I had to switch the laptop off, the images danced and swam inside my head. She was like a catchy jingle I couldn’t fight off or resist. Channon.

My rational brain understood this was insane. This was one woman I definitely could not, under any circumstances, make mine. Next morning, I understood I was going to have to sort this out. I couldn’t go to France with the song of Channon playing in my mind. How could anyone work efficiently with that kind of noise going on inside? How could I survive? And that was the important thing. Whatever happened in France, my feelings, my devotion to Channon would get me killed. I resolved, over my bacon and eggs, to fight that imprint. Channon could wait; I was strong enough.

I made myself busy. I started paying attention to briefings.

‘According to the invitation,’ said Max, addressing our fellow joint operation officers in the darkened control room, ‘Felice Beata is currently residing in a small country village called Autoire, in the Dordogne, or at least near it.’

He looked around, his face illuminated by the glow from the monitors.

'We are to be Felice's special guests.' Max nodded at a technical officer and a website flashed onto the big central screen. 'And here it is. Autoire.'

I was looking at pictures of a pleasant medieval-looking village and a dull rundown of its best countryside walks.

'Any thoughts? Anthony?'

I had been thinking about Channon again. Fuck. I had to concentrate. What did Max just ask?

'Er.' I pointed vaguely at the screen. 'I see the er– local Tourist Board website tells us this 800 year old village is one of the most beautiful in the Central South-East Quercy Region if not the whole of France.'

'Right?' Max looked at me expectantly. As did everyone else.

'So.' I felt my cheeks burn. Ah. I had something. A proper thought. I was getting the hang of this briefing malarkey. 'So what you're saying is,' I said, 'apart from confirming that the area is rural and unspoilt by mass tourism, no one knows anything.'

'We know where we're going,' Max replied. 'That's something.'

'Great.'

We all looked at each other — Max, the navy chaps, the army chaps — all waiting for someone to say something. I realised that person was supposed to be me and I was meant to call this craziness off. 'Right. Gentlemen,' I tried to sound sufficiently CIA. 'Shall we?'

An LPH — Landing Platform Helicopter ship — had been dispatched to moor off the coast of France. Three other identical LPHs were also dispatched, following the exact same pattern. If Felice wanted to hit us, she wouldn't know which one to aim at. We hoped.

Assuming the LPH wasn't attacked, our boat would then set off and rendezvous with it. Again six other identical boats would do the same thing. Stealth was the key. No frills, no marching bands. Once aboard the LPH, Alison Locke, Major Pete, myself, Max and Chan– Max and his bodyguard, would transfer to a Lynx helicopter and toddle over to Autoire; the pretty, sun-kissed not-spoiled-by-mass-tourism village. Up until the moment we landed, the Lynx would be broadcasting friendship signals in the hope the French Air Force wouldn't down us with surface-to-air missiles.

A naval limo drove us from our secret base to the dock. The land was flat and sodden, with clouds obscuring the sea. The weather was awful. England was saying goodbye.

Not many people's first trip abroad utilises a Royal Navy P2000-class patrol boat as their favoured mode of transport. Major Pete, as I still called him despite his recent promotion (Field Marshall being too boring to keep writing); he felt this was exactly what we needed. The boat looked compact, grey and very deadly.

I was painfully aware that Channon would already be on board; to be kept well away from me. I hadn't looked at that footage of her again but my bloody mind wouldn't leave me alone. It kept figuring out scenarios in which she and I would– well, you know, make a success of it. I wondered how I would cope with meeting her in person.

Our P2000 sat solid and remarkably tall in its dock. I didn't like the look of the ladder thing (what would one call it: a gangplank?) with what to me seemed rather flimsy bannister chains. Still, I couldn't look weedy. I would have to scale manfully. Uniformed chaps lined the deck at attention. Major Pete stood near the gangplank and barked out orders. He looked great in his all-weather military gear and I wished I could present as that capable. Alison Locke stood by him, dressed in a terrible blue kagoule and a pair of nondescript jeans. You have probably already guessed, I was only really thinking about one member of our team.

Max emerged from a car, consulting his notebook. He grunted a good morning; blinking in the rain. The air smelled of burning oil.

My mobile phone rang. Mum. A video call. It had to be serious, so I sneaked away. Her on-screen face was tiny and washed-out in the harsh subterranean light of wherever she was hiding. I was grateful she couldn't see me.

For a hopeful second, I thought she was going to tell me she had worked out a way to forget the whole thing.

'He may do something stupid,' she said instead. My first reaction was to shush her but the wind was buzzing so no one else could hear.

'Max?'

'Be ready. If it comes to– if you need… well, don't wait for him.'

I wanted to protest, to say something but she had that look. She knew I understood. Did she know about Channon?

'Okay, let's do this!' shouted Major Pete. He thumped Alison Locke on the back and she walked obediently onto the forbidding ladder.

'I have to go,' I said to mum.

'Call it off!' she ordered but too late; I had already ended the call, pretending I hadn't heard. The phone went into my thick coat.

I sniffed, trying to look unconcerned and cool as I climbed awkwardly up the gangplank.

'Anthony on deck!' screamed a petty seaman, or whatever. The assembled crew threw up a collective salute. I looked around the bobbing deck, convinced someone was laughing. The rain bounced off stern faces.

HMS Bugle bounced hard in the water as the storm threatened to become biblical. With our lifejackets and Gore-Tex anoraks, Max and I were dressed as neutrally as our image-makers could contrive.

I looked back at my country: a series of concrete jetties and nondescript warehouses. Dour and ugly and wet. My kingdom.

Finally I was going to see something different. That realisation helped hold back the terror. A little. A previously dormant, previously unknown part of my brain was excited by the concept of the rest of the world.

The engines thumped into life. I felt the unleashed energy under my feet. The huge, malignant potential of this warship thudded through my body. This is what it was like to run everything. This was power. I was beginning to understand just what I, as a Siren, could potentially do and what little I had so far actually done.

The captain marched up to me and saluted. 'Ready sir?' he asked. He was a smart bearded man in his early fifties; the best the Royal Navy had.

'Me? Oh yes.'

Max squeezed my shoulder. 'Here we go,' he said. The captain gave the thumbs-up and the boat lurched.

It was as if someone yanked my feet away. I fell over. Immediately, hands pulled me up. I looked around. Sailors hurried about their business. Still no one was obviously laughing but I wasn't fully convinced.

There was a roar of foaming, churning water and we were turning and tearing away from that harbour faster than I believed any boat could travel. This wasn't like I had imagined. This was no cruise. There was no distance between you and the motors, no first class lounge and comfy seats. Here, you were part of the process.

We shot across the grey sea, carving through the carpet of waves. Ahead I could still only see mist and clouds. There was nothing.

I was abroad!

What happened next was that Anthony Graves, ruler of the UK, its land and people, got very, very seasick. My entire experience of crossing the channel in one of the deadliest, coolest boats afloat was of hurling my guts into a steel bucket and wishing I was dead.

The navy guys were great; gave me all sorts of tips for dealing with *mal de mer*, but none of it helped. The journey seemed to last my entire life. I don't understand how I managed to fall so much in love with boats since. I guess we all improve with experience.

Of course, fate decreed this was the moment I would experience my first actual contact with Channon. Inevitable.

There I was, sat in the small galley, sweat plastered over my green face, wrapped up in a blanket. My head pounded along with the boat's leaps and buckles, just as she walked in

'Rest easy, Mr Graves.' Channon spoke with a voice like honey. 'Max has instructed me that no matter what the circumstances I am not to harm you nor allow you to be harmed. I swear now to uphold his orders to the letter.'

I lifted my head up from the bowl. Drool hung from my lips.

I knew from her file she was special ops. She was a black belt in something oriental. She could fly a 747 and hit a man-size target at eight hundred metres. Channon looked at me with wide, unbelievably gorgeous eyes. Apart from a tiny scar across her unblemished forehead, you would never have known she was anything but a movie star. Her full chosen name was Chyna Channon. Yep: only in America.

'Thanks. Great,' I retched. Despite the nausea, I managed to wonder how long her promise would hold if it really came down to it. A thought I found ridiculously sexually exciting. 'And please: it's Anthony.'

Max beamed from the doorway. He was proud of his little pet. 'I hope that puts your mind at rest, Anthony.'

Fuck you, Max. You know. You know only too bloody well, is what I thought.

I was captivated and I knew it. I wanted Channon. But. She was a beautiful, dangerous woman completely out of my control. She was Max's and nothing I could do would alter that. I had to be cunning. I knew I should get Channon off the boat but… I just didn't want to. If mum knew, she would have killed me. It was precisely that danger that made Channon so alluring. I may have been puking my guts up into a steaming bowl but Chyna Channon was giving me the hardest erection I'd had in years. I know what you're going to say, but let me tell you right here and now: love is the word.

Let's digress for a second. I accept, dear reader, you may think from past experience that my appreciation of women is somewhat shallow. That is for history to decide. All I knew at that moment was that I had found my best chance of a soul mate. She lit up my life and filled me with joy. I knew from that first time I saw her on the screen; Channon was the filter through which the world would come at me. And she would kill me at a moment's notice. Only, only, and this was the really insane part, what if I could win her? What if I could earn her? What if it really was possible to steal a woman from another Siren?

She turned and went away. She smiled at Max on the way. I understood I wasn't going to be able to sleep with Channon. Not yet. So instead, that night on the boat, I slept with Alison Locke.

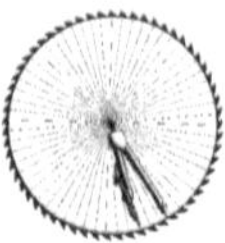

The further we went from Britain, the more the weather improved. We entered the Bay of Biscay and the whole rocking vomiting part of the journey eased up. Only now I was too warm and thinking continuously of this new woman in my life.

Max managed to drag me away from the toilet to watch our approach to the LPH. Channon moved with effortless grace in her stylish fatigues; always close to Max, always watching. She was continually watching me. Every time I caught her eye, I blushed and looked at my feet. Was there a spark? A something between us? Forget her, I warned myself over and over. Get her out of your head!

The LPH ship seemed tiny; a toy buffeted by the muscular waves. Three helicopters sat on its flat deck, like beetles. And I was going to have to take off from there. Oh god.

I kept thinking that at some point, someone was going to call the whole thing off. There had been a mistake; continuing was too dangerous. There were capable men and women here; why wasn't someone saying the obvious?

We crawled off one boat and onto another, escorted by my sailors. In my case: practically carried. One of the helicopters emitted a high-pitched wheeze and the rotors slowly began to move. Green and red lights began to flash on its casing. A gaggle of people swarmed round the machine, checking, preparing.

Next, it was my turn for the checks. Doctors attached sticky pad sensors and comms equipment under my suit. The noise was tremendous. Eventually, they crammed my head into a helmet and I was helped into the helicopter. I wasn't certain I could cope with all the rocking around. I needed some space, some stillness to give me the chance to think.

The cockpit winked its million digital computer lights, rattling in the vibration. A giant in a massive helmet and pair of shades appeared and shook my hand. This was my pilot: Flight Lieutenant Jason Hammond. Everyone agreed he was most reliable.

The side door slammed shut. Something squeezed my stomach and suddenly I was in the air, veering away from the boat. I looked around for help only to see Max grabbing webbing straps, with Channon next to him holding him still. Next to me Alison was being sick into a paper bag. I felt an increment better at the sight of her. For once, I wasn't the worst. The stench was bad especially mixed with the stink of engine fumes. The noise, however, was insane. Major Pete gave me a smiling thumbs-up from his seat opposite mine. He looked like he was loving every minute. He looked like Action Man. I glared at him, queasy and grey-faced. The noise and the vibration and the rattling threatened to shake my brain out of my head.

Twenty minutes later we were high up and flying over a dead calm sea. The Lynx stopped trying to throw me out and began flying straight and level. This was more like it. We passed over great sandy beaches to towns and woods beyond. For the first time, I started to enjoy the ride.

'Where are all the people?' asked Max.

Chapter 26

I must have dropped off. As someone shook me awake, my head was vibrating against the helicopter in time with its beating rotors. Not nice. I realised Major Pete was tapping me on the shoulder and pointing to the side of his helmet. Listen.

'Are we there yet?'

'We have company.'

The pilot Hammond's voice crackled in my ear. 'Two birds coming up on our right.'

I looked out of the little side window. Two black specks flashed by into the bright blue sky, their vapour trails straddling our flight path. A huge roar rocked the helicopter which gave an unpleasant, serious lurch. I had one thought: how did I, right now, end up in this situation? What was I thinking? My stupid bloody superpower was pointless here.

Did I really shout: 'Save your master!' I believe I did.

Distant French commands babbled in my headset, cutting into my panic. The jets whooshed by again and the Lynx wobbled. Engines even louder than ours rattled the cabin.

'That was close,' said Major Pete. He looked at Max. 'This is a big mistake.'

'We'll see,' Max replied. I gave him points for sheer nerve. He had balls.

'So we should get out of here,' I offered. 'Back to the boat?'

'I don't understand what they're asking,' came Hammond's voice. He seemed entirely unworried by this situation.

A brand new voice cut into the conversation. 'Don't worry, Anthony, I'll deal with this.' Alison Locke. She seemed pleased she finally had something to do. Already I could barely remember our night on the boat. She had been far too awestruck to do much except lie rigid and penitent until I told her what I wanted, which I'm sure you agree isn't much fun. I kept thinking of Channon. I'm always thinking of Channon unless you hear otherwise.

'Thank you,' I told her.

Alison unplugged herself from her comms and headed for the cockpit. I heard her talk in French back to the babbling voices. Two or three exchanges of incomprehensible dialogue later, she said to her expectant audience: 'Anthony. We have been invited to accompany the aeroplanes.'

A silence and I realised everyone was waiting for me to agree. Believe me, I didn't want to. If I had my way, I'd order our guys to fight our way past two super-advanced fighter jets then get the hell out of France and back to safety.

Maybe Max knew me so well he could read my mind. In any case, he placed a careful hand on my flight suit arm.

'We no longer have any choice,' said Max. He nodded; a *you know I'm right* nod. 'Anthony.'

He looked so fucking pleased I could have punched him.

We followed the jets towards a distant mountain range. When I looked out of the window down at the land, I finally saw the mechanics of Felice Beata's 'reconstruction'.

The land had been torn up. The earth was scarred, like a First World War battleground. Up ahead, a thick horizontal wall of smoke blocked the view. White ash flung itself against the window glass as we headed into it. The smell was pungent, somehow solid. People were marching across the hilly landscape. There were thousands of them, in long orderly lines. They looked like army ants. No wonder the land back to the coast was deserted. Here and there I spotted blue and camouflage uniforms, but these people were not being herded. They raised their arms and waved as we passed over them. Men, women and children: all running.

We dropped even lower, almost to tree height.

The running populace were dropping into earthen trenches and filing along to whatever place they were trying to reach. Miles of barbed wire had been twisted into arcane shapes along the way. Ornate sculptures stood up like mile posts: crosses carved and built from concrete, wood and stone; gigantic symbols of Felice Beata's new age.

No one in the helicopter said anything. The scale of the operation was almost beyond comprehension. How timid were my efforts to reshape London! How I lacked imagination!

The marching crowds no longer looked up at us. The trenches went on for miles and still there were more and more people. We must have flown over them for a good half an hour. I started to worry how much fuel we had.

The smoke was channelling up now, becoming thicker but narrowing into funnels and we could see again. At last, the marching army had hit a choke point. They were slowing, then bunching, then waiting. From what I could see from above, the people were chatting, singing, holding hands.

The smoke neatened into plumes, clearing the sky. From horizon to horizon the trenches led like the strands of a web towards a gigantic whitewashed citadel. The smoke was pouring out of crude, clumsily built brick chimneys. Finally, I understood their function. These were incinerators.

We both sat back; away from the window. 'My God,' said Max. I guess he couldn't look any more either.

The two French jets banked and veered off on a wild left. Our Lynx seemed to turn over as Lieutenant Hammond tried to follow. 'New course,' said Alison.

I was thinking about the citadels and their chimneys. 'That wasn't…' I stammered. 'They weren't doing that.'

'She wanted to show us,' said Max. 'She wanted us to see.'

Cold sweat soaked through my flight suit. 'Get us out of here,' I moaned.

'Anthony…' Max tried to think of a way to tell me no without getting himself thrown out of the Lynx.

Surprisingly, Major Pete backed him up. 'The jets will shoot us down in ten seconds, Anthony. But we could try landing.'

'No!' On that subject I was very firm.

'Why?' came Alison's voice over the intercom. 'What kind of person…'

It took me a second but I realised she too was talking about the factory. Max looked at me, as if only fellow Sirens could understand.

I had done some pretty mean things but that was just to stay alive against those out to get me. I didn't want to… I never would… I couldn't…

Major Pete seemed to pick up on my thoughts. 'I'm not having this. We're endangering Anthony,' he said. 'We should use the smoke to break away. It's worth the risk.'

I nodded, full of enthusiasm for that excellent idea.

Extremely quickly, Hammond's voice crackled in my helmet speakers. 'Sir, I'd just like to point out, they can easily engage a missile lock on this vehicle.' Again, he sounded unconcerned.

Major Pete was thinking. 'Hammond, the smoke should confuse the lock.'

'Possible,' said Hammond. 'But I can't guarantee anything. I won't risk Anthony's life if I'm not sure.'

I tried to stand up but the suit and the straps wouldn't let me. 'Oh no, my friend,' I snapped at Hammond. I was babbling. 'Risk it! Do everything I tell you! Jesus Christ, I shouldn't even be here! I work… I'm supposed to work in an office… I go for drinks with my friends and watch football! I don't even like football but this shouldn't have… this wasn't supposed to be like this. I didn't ask it to. We have to get out of here. Do it. Do it!'

Without hesitation, the engines roared louder and the Lynx peeled away. We all fell over each other again.

I saw the vapour trails curl back on themselves. 'They're onto us,' said Alison.

Max unsnapped his buckles and grabbed my shoulders. Instantly, Major Pete was on him. Then Channon was on *him*. Our respective bodyguards fought. There was no room, no space for anyone to do anything.

'Stop this foolishness!' Max yelled.

Somehow it worked. Major Pete and Channon froze, tangled together. They looked at Max, panting.

He lifted the visor to reveal his kindly, worn face. 'Anthony. We have to go on,' he said. 'We have to reason with this woman. Or we'll be next.'

'Ready to arm missiles on your order, Anthony,' Hammond said. 'Whatever good it will do us.'

I didn't care. I just wanted to get out and back home. I couldn't breathe, I couldn't think.

'What can I do?' I moaned. I was very aware that Channon had released herself from Major Pete and was looking at me, face hidden behind helmet and sunglasses. Suddenly, she seemed very close.

A red light began to flash on the cockpit dashboard. Something started beeping in my ear. The Lynx dived and headed for smoke. My stomach lurched.

'They're arming…' warned Hammond.

'Arm ours,' said Major Pete.

'Wait!' I fell back into my seat. From being freezing cold I was now boiling hot. But my brain was clearing. I had one thought. I didn't want to be shot down. Not here, not now. 'Tell them…' I said. 'Do what they say.'

Alison yelled something in French and the helicopter engine settled down to its old placid roar. At last, I overbalanced and hit the metal deck. Through the window I saw the two black specks grow into silver arrows then shriek past, once again rattling us.

'Shit,' hissed Major Pete. 'That was close.'

I lay on the floor, looking up at the helicopter's webbed roof.

'Follow them,' I ordered Hammond. 'Do what they want.'

'Sir!'

Max placed a reassuring arm on my shoulder. 'I will of course help you as best I can, Anthony,' said Max.

I sat up and hauled myself back into my seat. 'Oh fuck off.'

After a significant sulk, I looked out of the window again.

We were now moving in the opposite direction to the crowds. The smoke was more like fog. What particles made up those clouds?

I felt sick. I wanted to go home. An afternoon sun shone through the grainy mist. Get me clear, I thought. Get me air.

Another hour of flying and we dropped down into the Autoire Valley. The mountainous countryside was sane again. I chose not to look out of the window. Instead I concentrated on muttering and weeping in the vain hope that someone next to me would see sense and do something incredibly clever to get me back to London.

After a flurry of messages between Alison and the French pilots, we finally landed, a lifetime since we had departed from safe, rainy England.

The shame kicked in. I hadn't exactly covered myself in glory up there. Obviously, only Max was really *compos* enough to be judgmental but he was enough. The engine wound down. I was aware that people were running across a grass park towards us but I was too numb and ashamed to think of anything to do about it.

'Here we go,' said Major Pete. He was anxious and I wish I had listened to his original suggestion of dropping a few bombs by way of hello before lying down on the sacrificial table and handing over the knife.

Max unbuckled himself and shoved the door open. 'Get me out of this goddamned machine.'

Somehow, that cranky old man talk managed to console me. For all his superior, aggravating calm, Max was on my side. He knew what he was doing. When I climbed out, I offered my hand. 'I'm really sorry.'

There was a shine in his eyes; unbelievably, it was amusement. 'Damn that was close.' He winked and I laughed. 'You and me, Anthony, we'll get this fixed. Just believe.'

The people approaching us were out of breath but smiling as they stumbled up the green hill to the helicopter. I snapped the catches on my helmet and yanked it off. I was practically fainting in the heat and I stunk like a dead fox. Some impression. 'Round Two,' Max whispered.

Far from the trigger-happy loonies I was expecting, our welcoming committee was in fact composed of six very attractive and, possibly artificial, teenagers. They were three boys and three girls with shiny French faces and perfect, capped teeth. Their bodies were works of art: balanced, tanned, sports honed. The boys wore fitted short-sleeved shirts, ties and white slacks. The girls were outfitted in sleek summer t-shirts and shorts. Six specimens of perfection; just the type to intimidate Anthony with their confidence and enthusiasm and health and beauty.

A tall blonde girl with the widest smile imaginable curtseyed. 'Welcome, Anthony Graves and Max Angstrom.' Her Business English was too precise to reassure. Her head bobbed as she attempted to work out which of us was which. 'Welcome to France.'

Max held out a hand. 'Hi, I'm Max.' They shook. The gestures were practised, movie-like. 'Please,' said the leading French boy. 'Accompany us for refreshments. Her Reverend Mother Felice wishes only for you to have a happy stay with us.'

Max nodded and set off after them. I followed, chinking and jangling with the straps and metal clips hanging off my flight suit, the reek of panic hanging in the air like musk.

We walked to a larger group of happy French boys and girls standing by some white limousines at the edge of the field. These children of paradise pecked at our cheeks. '*Bonjour*… welcome…' All that.

I was wondering: when does the happy-clappy welcome bit dovetail with the marching-into-death-camps bit? When was I to get the nasty surprise?

Immediately, was the answer. The group suddenly broke off into a circle, held hands and closed their eyes. The lead boy spoke in English. 'Lord, we give thanks for the safe deliverance of your prophets from across the water.'

Us dirty, stinky prophets from across the water looked at each other.

The lead uber-girl raised her head. 'Would you like to join our prayers? To say some words to us?'

I couldn't hold back any more. 'Actually,' I said, 'it's been a long ride in a very shaky helicopter. I don't know about anyone else but I'm going to be much more able to concentrate if, you know…'

'I don't understand.'

'I could really do with a wee. I'm absolutely busting.' I looked at Max and my crew. 'Anyone else?'

Chapter 27

The beautiful, insanely religious children drove a now relieved Max and me into the village. It was a bright sunny afternoon but it took me a while to appreciate that Autoire lived up to its idyllic internet claims. I was otherwise occupied worrying about being separated from my guards, who were in a less ornate minibus behind us. After a while I understood that, short of starting a fight, we didn't have much choice. We had, after all, volunteered.

Our Mercedes limousine travelled along narrow cobbled streets past old rural houses and shops shining in the unblinking sunlight. Tricoloured bunting and pungent flowers dressed the scenery.

We parked in an empty, perfectly neat village square. The minibus containing Channon and Major Pete (oh, and Alison) pulled up behind us. No other motor vehicles were present. An ornate, overflowing stone fountain sprayed a rainbow haze across the cobbles; the cascading water overloud in the silence.

I sat in the car, sustained by the air-con and scared enough to be holding Max's hand. I liked it here in the dark and the cool. I didn't want to get out.

Alas, a door opened. 'Please disembark now,' said one of the smiling kids.

The hot light was a barrier; an omen; some metaphor or other. Frying pans; fires, call it what you will. I think I even said: 'No,' but only Max heard me. He shoved me in the back and I obeyed. The summer air was thick with the scent of flowers and freshly mown grass. My London had never seemed further away.

The children led us up a small hill towards the centre of the village. The houses grew tight on either side. Their ancient shutters were boarded and closed. I realised there were no road signs in Autoire. Beyond the buildings, heavily wooded mountains surrounded the village, hemming us in. They were dotted with distant grey stone chateaus or abbeys or whatever, poking through the trees… Oh, look at the website. I wasn't in the mood for sightseeing. All I recall is that we were marshalled inevitably and inexorably towards an incredibly old stone church at the top of the hill; tower, steeple, rusty old bell, the works.

More pod-like youngsters lined the way for us. All were physically perfect, multiracial, well-dressed and smiling. They had Christian written all over them. Dangerous.

Major Pete and Channon had picked up on the vibe. They were looking around as if scouring for snipers. Good. Alison Locke was clearly terrified as she sweated unattractively in the sun. Yep, I definitely needed a better-looking interpreter.

A portly grey-haired priest waited for us at the door. His serenity reminded me of Max; the kind of man you wanted as your grandad. He wore a purple robe and a gold chain. He displayed no outward signs of madness.

Using carefully prepared English, he said: 'Hello Anthony. Hello Max. My name is Father Stephen. I am advisor to Mother Felice and I welcome you to her realm. She appreciates the enormity of your gesture of trust to visit her in person. We welcome you in the name of peace and harmony to begin a long friendship.'

He looked at us, waiting for a reply. He looked like he could wait for days.

'Thank you, Father Stephen. I am Max,' said Max, at last. 'And this is Anthony.'

'I am Anthony,' I said.

'Yes,' he said.

'Sorry, I mean–'

Father Stephen turned and spoke some French to our lead boy.

'We have actually got our own interpreter,' I said, trying to be helpful. I indicated the nervous Alison.

'*Ah bon.*' Father Stephen spoke to her.

'He… he's asking if we need refreshment,' said Alison.

I began to speak, the usual tongue-tied garbage, when Max talked over me.

'Thank him, Alison, and tell him we will do as he asks.'

Alison spoke. Father Stephen held up his hands to indicate he understood. He then gestured theatrically to the doors of the church. Teenagers were strewing the paved path with bright flowers. 'Shall we?' He seemed pleased by his use of an English idiom. 'And Anthony, Mother Felice has arranged a very pleasant surprise for you.'

Max looked at me. I looked at him. I wanted to say no.

'Yes,' said Max.

Father Stephen turned away, then as if it was an afterthought, turned back. 'Ah. With respect.'

'Yes?' asked Max.

Father Stephen gestured to our team. 'I am afraid only those chosen can enter. I regret.'

'You what?'

'Your companions. They must remain here.'

No way, I thought. No fucking way. I looked at Major Pete and he looked about ready to start laying in. Channon shook her head. Very negative.

'We have no weapons in Autoire,' said Father Stephen. 'We are dedicated to peace.'

Before I could get going, before I could tell him there was no way I was entering that church without protection, Max intervened.

'Father Stephen,' he said, 'I promise you no one is here to cause any discord between us.'

'Nevertheless,' said the good Father. 'They cannot enter.'

We looked at each other. The perfect children smiled. I wanted guidance from Max but I didn't like what I might hear. His kind, calculating face was horribly calm.

'I cannot speak for Anthony,' he said. 'But for me, we cannot survive without trust. I will go.' He even took a theatrical step forward.

Everyone was looking at me. I thought about the pistol Major Pete had strapped to his side. I thought about his knives and grenades and the other shit I hoped to Christ he had on him.

'All right,' I said. 'All right then.'

We followed. I trudged up the squidgy path sure I was heading to my doom. We reached the studded, wooden, open door and I caught a glimpse of dark and shiny things inside. People were singing. We went in.

I was expecting Hieronymus Bosch; what I got was TripAdvisor. You could say I was disappointed. The interior was just like any old church interior (as visited by Anthony Graves upon the occasions of four marriages, three baptisms and one funeral). The church was normal. There was nothing remotely unhinged within. My expectant images of hooded inquisitors with racks, flaming crosses and *autos-da-fé* were apparently mistaken. I wanted to go home and start again. I didn't know what I wanted. I just followed Max and Father Stephen.

I felt the concept of age. There was that. The musty tapestries and cracked stonework had a weight. I assumed this was a tourist gimmick: keep the place looking authentic and whatnot. Max seemed suitably awed. I guess in America everything was still new enough that such centuries of history would be daunting.

Tucked discretely in a corner, smaller, younger kids were singing in Latin. The atmosphere was of calm, contemplative reflection. I couldn't fit this with the smoke and the trenches and the millions of people dancing to their deaths. It was like some delirious, insane drug trip.

'Mother Felice has long been looking forward to your visit,' Alison smoothly translated Father Stephen's words. 'She has visibly shown interest towards your messages of friendship.'

'Great!' I said. My words rang round the empty space. Someone coughed. Father Stephen stopped and looked at me, clearly thinking I had more to say. I didn't. I hoped no one could see my red face in the gloom.

'Where is the Holy Mother?' asked Max, sparing me. Father Stephen nodded and we moved again.

As we approached the altar, I realised we were being stared at. Nuns, a whole line of them in the full black-and-white nun regalia, studying us with stares so serious I felt the urge to laugh. You know: that hysterical laughter.

I guess, in my mind, I'd built Felice Beata up. I expected to confront a crusading, beautiful young firebrand whose innocent face would shine with murderous but sexy religious fervour. Me and my bad thoughts.

And yes, there was a woman in white standing at the altar. She was wearing one of those nun's three-corner hats. She looked medieval. My prediction as to Felice Beata's description had not been far off. She clearly fancied herself some kind of mother superior. And a very beautiful mother superior too: dark eyes, perfect lips, cheekbones. Very French. I tried not to think what was going on beneath the habit. I didn't want to appear crude. We might get along very well after all.

'Mother Felice,' said Father Stephen. He bowed.

The white nun lowered her eyes and stepped away to reveal an old woman in a chair. A woman wearing a simple black peasant dress and headscarf. A woman with swollen legs and an open mouth containing fragments of teeth. She must have been ninety years old. She muttered something; barely a whisper. The beautiful mother superior returned to her side, knelt down and listened.

'Anthony. Please. Approach,' said Father Stephen. 'Kneel.' Aware that Max had not been asked, I did so.

The old woman's quivering hands reached for my face. She smiled. I smelled sewage. She looked at me with the dull eyes of the truly, irretrievably senile.

'Please,' said Father Steven.

'Yes?' I asked. Surely he didn't expect me to…

He did expect me to. Containing my disgust, aware that my life might depend on this, I lowered my head.

Long fingered nails grasped my skull. A slobbery warm breath whispered to me. Her cracked voice said:

La Dieu merci, qu'ay désirée,
Où toute rien se renouvelle,
Et est du sec au vert temps née.

Felice Beata, for it was indeed she, tilted my face up and kissed my cheeks, giving me a gust of rotten molars as she did so.

'Thank you,' I mumbled and reverse-shuffled on my knees back to Alison. I kept smiling.

'What did she say?' I whispered.

'It's a poem,' she said. '*Ditié de Jehanne d'Arc.*' And then:

Thanks be to God, the lovely season called Spring,
which I have longed for and in which every creature is renewed,
has brought greenness out of barren winter.

'Right.'

Felice grinned; her eyes cloudy.

'Praise be to God,' said Father Stephen. He was crying. He clamped his hands together and sunk to his knees. 'Let us be thankful for His new reign upon the Earth. For the Angels have come down from high to create a new Paradise. All praise to almighty God.'

'Indeed,' I said. The cold stone was very hard on the knees. I wondered when I might safely stand up.

Seats were eventually produced and we spent a very long time just sitting and looking at each other. Water and wine were served, which we drank. All the while, Felice just smiled at me. I kept looking at the white nun; the nurse nun. God she was beautiful. Maybe that was why she had been picked.

As the silence and the gloom pressed us into our seats, my mind kept returning to the smoking chimneys. This fragile old grandmother was responsible. Her skin was incredibly dark (sun or pigment, I couldn't tell) and so seamed and lined it could have been carved from wood. Felice Beata didn't look like she had an evil bone in her body.

After an age, Max looked at me. I rolled my eyes, I couldn't help it. How long was this going to go on?

He stood up. 'Mother Felice,' he said. 'Would you like to accompany us for a walk around your lovely village?' His tone was even but I could tell he was nervous.

'Mother Felice does not leave the Church,' said Father Stephen. 'She remains in God's house so they may easier converse. You understand.'

'With respect then,' Max continued. 'Might we talk here? There are matters to discuss.' Alison translated, with just an ever so slight tremor in her voice.

Father Stephen looked puzzled. 'It is not for me to grant or deny the wishes of the Angels. You do me great honour but I am so far beneath you. If I have presumed…' And as the translation trickled out, Father Stephen dropped to his stomach and stretched out at our feet. The others in the Church did the same, except Mother Felice of course, who just smiled.

'I guess here will be fine,' said Max, clearly embarrassed. 'But Madame, we must talk.'

The white nurse whispered in her ear once more. Felice coughed. She raised her hand and with one bony, fragile finger, she beckoned me.

Perhaps the intensity with which she smiled at me had knocked some of the fluff out of her brain. Perhaps she had something important to tell me. I bent forward to listen.

Felice clutched my head and cackled. She was delighted to have me here. This could be something really important; a proper breakthrough.

Again, she kissed me on both cheeks. 'Julio,' she said. '*Mon fils.*'

Her physical presence was so insubstantial; it was as if she were already a ghost. Just dust and sack cloth. I looked in her eyes and I went cold. Those ancient eyes glowed with incomprehension and stupidity. I didn't need the translation. She thought I was her son. Oh Christ.

As I backed away, I knew one thing. One thing maybe even Max hadn't realised. I knew that whatever else she was, Felice Beata was death.

Chapter 28

'I am interested to hear her… the Mother's story,' said Max.

We were still there. We were still sat in that bloody church; still watching the bloody woman cackle and dribble. I didn't know how much longer I was going to be able to take this.

'Touched by the Divine Hand,' said Father Stephen. He seemed most satisfied. 'Ah, that I should live to witness such days.' He looked lovingly at his gibbering mistress. 'I cannot tell you of the great ecstasy I feel now the three of you are finally together. Truly, we live in the weightiest of times.'

Nuns brought in food. I ate. I was ravenous so I was too busy eating at first to listen. I tuned back in. Max was politely listening but his eyes looked suspiciously heavy.

'Indeed, that fateful day,' said Father Stephen. The wine, as they say, had loosened his tongue. He had forgotten he wasn't supposed to speak good English.

'You will forgive me that despite myself,' he continued, 'I was sceptical. Obviously, Mother Felice had been a faithful parishioner for so many decades.'

'This church?' asked Max. 'In Autoire?'

'Oh no, M'sieu. Far south. I had a parish in Marseille. Very different. Very… I don't know… urbane? Urban? You see, like the Lord Jesus Christ himself, Mother Felice was not from, er, the background of the privileged. Scholars are only now establishing that she may have been a refugee from the Civil War in Spain. A

Republican perhaps, who came north to escape the Nationalist terror. She herself does not recall. The grace of God touches those who are the most, like the baby, you know?'

'Innocent?' said Max.

'*Oui.* Yes. The child. I learn Mother Felice is known as a woman who is greatly religious. Who believe all things of the Bible. The miracles and the ghosts. A great chanter of prayer; a very intense believer. This I believe comes from her upbringing. To my shame, in Marseille I do not think of her as a… a right in the head? I helped put her in the home. She is one for the superstition, the mystery and I in my pride was not fond of such beliefs. My calling then was for the mundane; the practical: food banks and keeping the books balanced. Blind to the true spiritual magnificence of the Lord. I was misguided, of course. This was before the disease of age came to her. One night, Mother Felice calls me from her home and tells me that God has spoken to her. Has given her a great gift. She is upset, does not understand. She tells me there is an accident, a great thing. She lives in a house with many of them. The house for the old, you know?'

'An old people's home?' I helpfully suggested.

'Something happen to the old people,' said Father Stephen. 'Mother Felice tells me they were loud. Always making the noise. She tells me God comes to her one night and tells her to make them, her others, she make them to sleep. The Mother was bothered about so much noise in the night; they are so loud, so she had prayed God to make them all quiet. And God answered her prayer. The nurses, they put them all to sleep. The nurses then put themselves to sleep. With the drugs, no? The people sleep and no one can wake them.'

'A coma?'

Father Stephen shrugged. 'I do not know, Anthony. Mother Felice; she is afraid. Afraid the police will not see that God put them to sleep.'

Father Stephen looked at me. He seemed determined that Max and I comprehend, would confirm the truth of this new craziness.

'I was not happy with her. Before God enlightened me, I thought Mother Felice was, you know, suffer the dementia of the old. I could not understand so I take the Mother in my car and went and found them all. You see, still I did not believe. In the lounge, the sleeping ones sat all around like they were watching the TV. The smell was beyond measure. Mother Felice, she sat in her chair among them as if she had forgotten all about me. She talks to them as if they were still awake. She ask if I will bring her coffee and a bible. I recall saying I thought she needed a doctor. Then from her chair, she did it. I heard her song and her spirit enter me. I was reborn. And now, yes! I understand the purpose. The Holy Mother is a vessel. An empty vessel. I knew at the moment she was Divine. She is the physical embodiment of the Holy Spirit here on Earth.'

The rest of the story was escalation. Father Stephen had gone to his bosses and harangued them into deifying Felice Beata. She was an uber-saint, come to do God's work. They were quite sceptical. Fortunately for him, he brought Felice along with him. She probably had no idea that her life was about to take a turn for the better.

Together they reversed opinions at the local Cathedral. They started at the top and worked their way down: Cardinals, Priests, congregation. I think they might have got to the Pope had they had the chance. Perhaps they did.

Father Stephen smiled at the memory. The memory of a challenge met and overcome. 'Of course there was debate,' he said. 'Huge debate. The Church and the government. Much debate until all are blessed and there is no more debate; only certainty. The news began to arrive of the others. The tragedy in America, the bomb in China, the revolution in Odessa and finally the man in England on the TV. You: Anthony.

'In France, the matter was decided early. Government and clergy agreed. Holy Mother Felice was Love itself. The vessel of the Lord, forgive the translation. A new Joan of Arc. I could not understand the Earthly words, but in my head I knew the meaning of her sweet music. I understood everything! And I would tell the world!

'Well, of course I wept. All my life I had waited for God to bless his flock directly. Through the Holy Mother, I comprehend we had become corrupt and decadent. I had done my best to check the injustice. I deliberately chose the poorest to work amongst, but they would not help themselves. They would not rise up. There was no longer the will, you understand? Humanity was lost. I even began to question my own faith. How could he watch idly by and let this disease continue to propagate itself? Would He let us just blow each other up and that's the end of the matter?

'In His mercy, no. The Lord delivered us. The time had come to clear the ground. To bring forth a new and terrible sword of fire that would sweep across the land. He sent the Prophets. He sent you.'

Max was itching to ask a question. He sensed a break in the monologue and leaped in. 'How did you do it? I mean, how did the Holy Mother spread the word across the whole continent? And we didn't hear a thing?'

Father Stephen seemed pleased to have been asked. 'Ah, it was not easy,' he said. 'We could hardly interfere with your own great work. I knew I had to find a way quickly. So I prayed, and yes, God answered. One Sunday, in an ordinary service at St. Peter's in Rome, the Holy Mother was revealed to the world. Millions watched and listened and followed. A simple ceremony, where she spoke to the world in her sweet voice. God's voice. That afternoon, she was officially proclaimed as the Holy figurehead for all the people of the world.'

He sat back and reminisced. 'Ah, a blessed day indeed.'

'What Sunday?' I asked. 'I don't remember anything about that.'

Father Stephen smiled serenely; as if to say: tough shit.

'That very afternoon,' he smiled, 'the Holy Mother ordered us to switch off the machines: the networks, the telephones, the televisions, radios. Everything. All the machines that had poisoned the world. We have great influence. Armies of apostles travelled the continent, bringing Her word to the people.'

'How?' asked Max, without being able to help himself. 'I mean, our understanding is that for the… for the word of God to imprint itself, the object must have direct contact with the subject.'

'Another time eh, Max?' I was uncomfortable.

Father Stephen clutched my hand. His eyes shone with wine and glamour. From her chair, Felice giggled and slowly clapped her bony hands.

'Anthony! Max! You look anguished! But are you also not God's chosen? The vessels of the divine! I have tried to interpret the wishes of the Lord through the Holy Mother. I have set up the mechanism to clear the ground for His arrival on Earth. And the Lord has answered. From the Arctic wastes of Norway to the sunburned savages of Africa, from Belgium to Croatia to Poland to Greece, I have worked to secure the Rapture. Our people work tirelessly to build and bring themselves closer to God. To make the land clean for his Angels.'

Father Stephen wept, still clutching my hand. 'I dare to hope you trust your humble servant has completed his burden.'

Sniffing, he pushed back his chair and stood. The tears were gone; the smile was back.

'We wish for your stay to be a happy one. To help tie the bonds between us. The Holy Mother believes at first you will find our work difficult to comprehend. She knows God's purpose is not easy to understand. The journey to enlightenment may be long.'

I looked at this genocidal maniac and his drooling crone. I wondered: how the fuck do you know what this demented bitch thinks? It's all about you. All of it.

'Beds have been prepared in the village,' said Father Stephen. 'Sleep well. I will see you in the morning. The Holy Mother wishes you to be content, Anthony. She wishes you spend the rest of the evening in the company of your friend.'

'My friend?'

'Your old friend. You will see.'

I nodded wisely.

Old friend? Oh Jesus god, what fresh hell was before me now?

The interminable meeting ended. I don't recall how Max extricated us but somehow, at some point, we walked on cramped legs out of the church. Major Pete, Alison and Channon were still outside waiting. They hadn't been done away with.

The sun was lower now; the cooler air a relief after that closeted, dusty tomb. Bees were buzzing around the sumptuous bouquets hanging in their baskets. Shadows stretched across the cobbles from the tall, leaning houses. Evening intensified the colours of the flowers. They were bright blues and purples, richer than anything I had seen in England. Nature was at work here, indifferent and unchanged. Life; blessed life was out here; away from that church and life's opposite.

I felt the weight of the glamour fizzing inside, which just made me more scared. There was no one here to use it on.

Father Stephen hopped from foot to foot with excitement and mortal terror. He was in awe of us. We were powerful, but it was Felice Beata's glamour in him, not ours. We weren't his voice of God. He led us down the hill to the square.

'The Holy Mother is a shining beacon is she not?' he beamed, with his ever-present, smiling, not-as-dumb-as-he-seemed English.

Every so often a smiling, industrious teen would pass by with a cheerful '*Bonsoir*'. Presumably, they were up to God's work. I wanted to go home. I felt at any minute they would drop the façade and come charging in on us. All I could think was how the hell was I going to get away?

Old friend?

Father Stephen led us to the only open café in the square; a rustic, homely looking hotel. Through the window I saw, illuminated by lovely candles, tables full of French goodies. The acolytes within were already pouring the wine.

'So what happens now?' Max asked.

'This is the finest *auberge* in the village,' said Father Stephen. 'Rooms are prepared. The restaurant is at your disposal. Let us eat. Then you can sleep and we will talk more tomorrow. I am told the rooms are most comfortable.'

Despite myself, I was becoming amused by the way he spoke; like a character out of a bad thriller. I liked that about him. Perhaps I would employ one of mine to talk like him back home.

It could have been so easy. It could have been so fucking easy. It could have been some perfectly well-adjusted suburban French woman happy to step up to running a continent in the same sensible way she had run her household. We could have been friends; her,

Max and me. We could have got along. But no. Fate, that cosmic arbiter of probability, decreed otherwise. It would only have taken a modicum of thought to select the most suitable people and give them the glamour. Take the choice out of probability's hands. But there was no thought. No thought at all. No thought.

Chapter 29

She was in the lobby of the auberge; waiting at the door to the restaurant. She was wearing a nun's habit. The face was familiar but for a moment I couldn't place it. A face that was awfully, awfully familiar.

'So you finally got here,' said Toni. 'Welcome to France.'

'Anthony Graves,' said Father Stephen. 'Mother Felice blesses you. For she has found you this child.'

She looked better. She looked unbelievably better. Among these children of paradise, she looked human. I felt my groin stir in a way I hadn't felt since… well, a long time. Father Stephen beamed a great big bright smile and touched her lightly on the shoulder.

Toni walked to me and kissed my cheeks. She was still plump; plumper than the others; far less perfect. She looked radiant in her nun's hat. She looked beautiful.

I thought about that half-dead desolate skanky creature who had scuttled from my Hammersmith house all that time ago. How long? Probably not long at all. 'Oh my god,' I said which, given the circumstances, was probably not the most tactful of responses.

'It's so good to see you again,' she said. Her face was starting to fill with very un-Toni tears. 'Anthony.'

'Anthony?' asked Max. I heard a dark note in his voice I hadn't heard before. I ignored him.

'The Holy Mother said you would come. You look terrific.'

Toni was so sincere, and the habit of her so ingrained, I couldn't help but wait for the gag, the punchline, the sarcastic comment. It never came. That old Toni was gone.

'Please?' asked Father Stephen. He indicated the restaurant and its riches.

Toni bowed and stepped back. 'I have been allowed to keep you company,' she said. 'If you like.'

I wanted to see that look of mischief in her eye but there was nothing but sincere happiness. A burning, passionate happiness. My newly awoken stiffy shrivelled.

Max touched my arm. 'We should eat.'

They gave us a table by the window; discreet space. Toni was very demure in her stiff, starched gown. She refused the wine and the waiters quickly learned to leave us alone.

Max watched, worried, from the other side of the restaurant. He sat with Channon (my Channon, whom I swear was giving me the occasional smile when she could). Alison and Major Pete pretended to study menus and regarded Toni with outright hostility.

My old girlfriend and me; we chatted about the old London days. It just made me realise how much I missed her. She was still the same Toni, only nicer and happier, which of course didn't make her like the same Toni at all.

'You remember that time when it first happened?' I asked. 'When I was off work, when I took you to the pub? That barmaid? She didn't know what hit her.'

I wondered what kind of reaction that would get. Would she even remember? Thankfully, she laughed. 'Yeah. That was good. Although…'

'What?'

'I don't know. I was different then.'

'They were the best. Those weeks.'

'Before it all went wrong.' Toni looked down at her food. She looked… she looked young again. Something strange started to happen to my sinuses. I felt a sting that spread up from behind my nose and into my eyes. Indeed, I was crying.

I got it. I understood. This woman here, this slave to that doddering old woman, was mine. She should have been mine all along. If only we could have made it work when we lived together. If only I hadn't been a stupid, lazy prick who couldn't be arsed. Maybe I wouldn't have been stuck in that office on that day at just the wrong time. And the glamour would have missed me. It would have missed, and Toni and I'd have had a proper life. Nothing special; nothing out of the ordinary. Just a life.

'Oh god, I'm sorry,' I said.

'It's all right Ant.' She reached for my face and brushed the tears aside. 'Don't cry. It's for the best.'

I held her hands against my face. I couldn't stop the tears. All those years of anguish, of pain and unhappiness, I understood at last that Toni could take it from me. I wanted to lose myself in her. Lose myself in her hands. I pressed her fingers into my face. I didn't want Max to see. I didn't want anyone to see. We could have made it work. Why didn't we? All those years, instead of being selfish, why hadn't we just worked out how to share?

'I really fucked you up, didn't I?' I said.

'Ant. It's fine,' she whispered. 'It's all meant. Really. There is a plan. Sit up. Listen.'

Gently, Toni removed her fingers from my face. She stroked my cheek. Her eyes were bright and, yes, also moist with tears.

'When you let me go,' she said, 'I was a mess. You were so kind to… you know, give me another chance.'

'I knew you would sort yourself out.' I sniffed.

'It was God's plan. It seems like a different person. I wanted to die. Instead, I hitched a lift with a lorry driver. A Ukrainian. He dropped me off in Calais. I had no money so he– I don't mind now; that was part of the plan too. I was lost. Lost and wandering.'

She nodded at the *maître d* who came between us and began to clear the table. Max looked worried. I had forgotten he would be listening. Channon was tense.

Channon. What a twat I'd been; thinking I was in love with her. Thinking I was in love. I'd been 'in love' with every woman who ever gave me a hard-on.

'Everything changed, Ant,' said Toni. 'The police and the soldiers were in the streets. They were looking out for people using technology. They marshalled us into the churches. Of course, we didn't want to. How were we supposed to know? Silly now: the guns, the shouting. I guessed what they were up to and, well, after what happened in London, I tried to get away but they were shooting people. Idiots. They got me inside; of course. Some little chapel in the port. And through the speakers, she spoke. Mother Felice spoke to me. The whole country; no no, the whole continent was transformed by the word of God. The same word that was given to you. You were right to spare me.'

She was gabbling now; lost in her own mad world. Or rather: Father Stephen's mad world.

'This planet is poisoned. There was no going back. So God intervened; like in the old days. He told us it was time to start again; to clear the ground. We are all to ascend, Anthony. To Heaven! Isn't that the most incredible thing?'

She looked at me; so certain I was sharing in this rapture; this ecstasy.

'They were asking for help,' she said. 'People were going round asking for information about Britain, and you. I told them I knew you. That I could help work with you; end your doubts. I knew you would have doubts.'

I looked at her. This girl I had lived with. This girl who I probably loved and should, in a saner world, have spent my life with. As happy as a human could ever be. It was so wrong; so fucked.

'You do have doubts, don't you, Ant,' said Toni. 'About what needs to be done.'

'Toni,' I said. 'I don't care. I don't care about any of that.'

'What?'

'I don't care what she, the Holy Mother, does. I'll do anything you want. If– it sounds stupid… if I can have you.'

Fuck knows why I said it. It must have been the heat of the moment. It was the heat of the moment. I meant it. Deep down, I didn't give a shit what that crazy woman did to anyone, I just wanted my girl back.

Toni looked at me, puzzled. On the way to angry.

'Toni, listen…' I tried.

'Are you mental?' Toni hissed. 'What do you mean, have me?'

'I don't know. Be with you. All the time.'

She scraped the chair back. 'I told Father Stephen you would be a cock about it,' she said. 'You can never have me. You know that. I am hers. And they might trust you but I don't. I know you've come here to stop us in our great work.'

'What? No!'

Max coughed. We both looked up. They had all been listening to everything.

'May I join you?' he asked.

Max brought a wooden chair to the small table. He ordered a strong black coffee. We took a breath as we waited for it to arrive. Unhurried and relaxed, Max thanked the *maître d*, who bowed and walked away. Max stirred the tiny cup and took a sip. Finally, he was ready.

'I understand your fervour,' he said to Toni. 'Believe me I really do. I think Anthony is very much in love with you. You must forgive him.'

'Max,' I hissed. I could have killed him. Except I understood he was probably saving my life. Toni glared. She was a whisker away from storming out.

I was shocked by my own behaviour. What had I said? What had I been thinking? Because of me, the rollercoaster was about to come off the rails. Maybe it really was god's plan, because I understood we were about to head into some uncharted territory from which there would be no return. I should have told Max to stay out. I really should. But I didn't have the strength. I never had the strength.

Max was wearing his best Max smile; all compromise and 'let's work this'. He sipped that bloody coffee of his.

He took a deep breath. 'I'm not trying to change anyone's mind. Believe me when I say we mean no harm.' He looked at Toni. 'And we certainly do not mean to interfere with the Holy Mother's intentions. We want to work with you; to build a better world. It's a matter of interpretation. May I continue?'

Something of the old Toni was in her face as she looked back at him. 'Go on,' she muttered. I was tired now. Very tired and my head was spinning.

'Can't we do this in the morning, Max?' I asked. Or, I thought to myself, when I'm back in London and able to think. He ignored me.

'The Christian Church teaches love, does it not?' he said. 'It preaches a fellowship with all humanity. Unconditional love.'

I think she believed we were testing her faith. We were beginning to irritate her. Bless her though, she kept trying. She ignored Max as best she could and spoke only to me.

'Anthony, if you could see the serenity, the joy, on the people's faces. One year ago, when the first furnaces were built, the people, they threw themselves at the gates to offer themselves. I was one of them! Christian, Muslim, Atheist, Jew. Humanity united at last. Many were crushed before even entering the stadiums. You couldn't stop us now if you wanted to.' She held up her hands to heaven. 'We are at the end of Times! There is no doubt left in the world. Not now. We must purge the land. This is our glorious task!'

She stared at us, triumphant. Max was shaken. He didn't know what to do. Perhaps for the first time he understood that his actions could put us in real danger.

'We… should talk about this in the morning,' he said. 'When everyone's a little calmer.'

'No, we should talk about it now!' She was really going.

'We aren't your enemy,' he said. 'Believe me.'

'Toni,' I said.

She stood up; chair clattering to the floor. She was angry; after years of experience I knew that anger. Part of me welcomed it. 'You know what, Anthony. You never had a fucking clue. Even before you were blessed, you were just a little selfish child. Maybe the Lord gave you the Gift because he thought he could change you. Some fucking chance. You know what? I'm glad you sent me away. God knew. Here, I am the real me. At last. All I had to do was get away from you.'

She was shaking. She looked at me and the tears flowed; real emotional tears. I raised my hands, for what I don't remember.

'Don't touch me!' Her shriek probably woke up the whole village. I could feel tears returning. This girl. My girl; gone. Another fucking part of Anthony Graves's life well and truly fucked by the Gift; the stupid fucking glamour.

Toni got herself under control. She wiped her face with her nun's sleeve. I remembered that red flush on her fleshy neck. She was scared and furious.

'Listen,' tried Max. 'Please. I don't want to cause a rift between us. We have to be reasonable. The human race is our responsibility. We are their guardians. We are all God's chosen.'

'What are you saying?' asked Toni. I prayed to god he wouldn't answer.

It was coming; as inevitable and unstoppable as a train wreck. Fuck.

Max Angstrom in full flow: trying to do the right thing. Fuck fuck fuck.

'Max, leave it,' I said.

'I don't understand,' said Toni. 'You also are Divine. Surely you know our purpose is ordained. The human race is diseased, unclean. We must prepare and sanctify the Earth for His coming. God is calling the sinners home. You have been chosen as the shepherds. Who are you to say we are wrong? To cast doubt upon our great Mother?'

'This foolishness must stop!' Max said. His voice was louder than I had ever heard it. 'This cannot be what Felice Beata wants. You cannot exterminate the human race.'

Toni turned from me to him. Her face was purple with anger. She was under control but it was coming. After all those nights in Streatham with her, I knew it was coming.

'Oh Jesus,' I said. 'Max. Just shut up. Please.'

Toni slapped me. Right across the chops; just as she had done all those years ago in our Streatham flat when she walked out. I fell back into my chair; raging with injustice. 'It wasn't me!' I said; my voice full of childish injured pride.

'Fuck off,' Toni snapped. 'Who's he, your new mummy? You will never stop us.'

Toni marched to the door. She looked back; seemingly unable to believe we could be so stupid. 'The Holy Mother offered you the world. And now you're dead.'

Before Toni could move, Major Pete was across the room. She flinched but it was too late. He got an arm around her throat and dragged her away from the door. Her flailing arm dragged a tablecloth and a pile of crockery over. The noise was relentless. Outside, the little street was dark and empty. 'Close the shutters! Door!' he hissed.

Channon moved across the room and closed the restaurant door before anyone else had even understood the situation.

Without thinking, I got up and ran into a couple of tables before noisily getting to the window. I caught a glimpse of a dark empty street outside and yanked the chain to pull the shutters in.

Toni was making a strange squeaking noise. She was back-kicking Major Pete as he forced her to the floor, arm locked round her neck. She twisted to look at me. Her eyes bulged with hatred and spittle bubbled in her mouth. Major Pete forced her face to the floor. 'Tablecloth!' he hissed.

I made a move to stop him. I really did; yes, I was almost very brave. A strong hand dragged me back. It was years since anyone had touched me like that. Channon. I flinched, part cowardice, part revulsion. I couldn't believe I had ever thought I might have feelings for her. She was a creature like Toni; someone else's. In that instant, I wanted her dead; I wanted them all dead.

Channon threw a checked cloth at Major Pete. It was stained with wine and solidified gravy. Somehow, he wrapped it round Toni's head. She still kicked and bucked but he held on; pressing her to the floor.

I heard a voice in French. The *maître d* ran into the doorway. Someone blurred past me. Channon again. She drove a steak knife into the man's throat. I looked away. I closed my eyes and listened to two people die.

When I opened my eyes again, the first person I saw was Max. He was staring at this mess, this ruin, in absolute shock.

'Oh my God,' said Alison Locke. I thought she was rather calm under the circumstances. I saw Channon calmly wiping a knife; a pool of blood moving across the floor.

Toni was still; her head wrapped in the gravy stained tea towel. Major Pete looked at me; sweat streaming down his red face.

'What have you done?' My voice cracked in several places as I asked this question.

Major Pete looked genuinely puzzled. 'I don't understand.'

Max was making a funny sighing noise; like he had forgotten how to make words happen. I'm not surprised; all his hard work undone in the course of a few bloody minutes. I didn't want to think about Toni.

'We don't have time,' said Channon. 'They will have cameras. We have to get out of here.'

'How?' I asked. 'How the fuck are we going to get out of here?'

Major Pete was back to business. 'Anthony. We have to get Anthony to a landing point. I can call in the chopper.'

'We have to assume they'll discover us sooner rather than later,' said Channon. I had never heard her speak so much. 'We need a way to get past them.'

'How's that going to happen?' I screeched. 'There's fucking thousands of them.'

'I don't know,' said Major Pete. 'But we can't allow you to come to any harm.'

'People,' said Channon, 'we have to move.' She kept looking out of the restaurant door onto the street.

'Max?' I asked and turned to him.

He was still sat in his chair, looking at the carnage. His eyes were wide open and he was muttering. Perhaps he was even trying to find a way to save the situation.

'Max,' I said, 'we have to go.'

He looked at me. 'It could have worked,' he said. 'We could have found a way.'

'Max…'

Clarity returned to him. 'We have one chance,' he said. 'We have to get to Felice and kill her.'

That shut us up. 'You're kidding,' I said.

He was different now. A different Max. I guess this was the man who killed a fifteen year old girl in Florida. A man who wanted to live.

'Anthony, we'll never have another chance. We kill her and this all stops.'

'Bollocks!' I shouted, way too loud.

Max stood up, angry. 'Then what do you suggest?'

We stopped; all of us. Something had happened. The lines were being drawn. Alison and Major Pete suddenly became very calm. They walked between Max and myself; shielding me. Across the room, Channon did the same for Max.

'Anthony, leave him,' said Major Pete. 'We are not going to fight our way through a hundred fanatics in the hope that one of us gets her.'

'Fuck you!' snapped Channon. 'You got us into this shit. You put Max in danger.'

They glared at each other across the ruined restaurant. Oh god. It just got better and better.

'What else do you suggest, Anthony?' asked Max.

'We don't have to do anything,' I told them. 'We just tell them the truth. That Major Pete killed Toni on his own. That's what happened isn't it?'

'Anthony,' said Max. 'You really want to do nothing?'

'Max, that's all I ever want to do.'

'Think about the probabilities. Do you really want to put us at that woman's mercy?'

'Why not? You did, you fucking idiot!'

'I've got an idea,' said Alison Locke.

'We're not going to get away anyway,' said Max. He was back to his reasonable old self. 'You think they're just going to let us walk to a hill, get in a helicopter and fly five hundred miles home?'

I opened my shirt and pushed the little button thing taped to my waist. A tiny green light began to flash. 'SOS,' I said. 'Help is on its way.'

Channon laughed. 'You think that's going to save you? We don't have time, Max. One way or the other, we have to leave.'

'Anthony,' said Max. 'Even if we do get away, what then? Are you just going to ignore what's going on? What happens when she comes for you? For both of us.'

'Max, no.'

'You have to stop hiding, Anthony.'

'I've got an idea.' She said it quietly. Meek little Alison Locke. I was impressed.

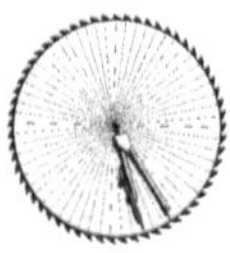

'What?' I asked. 'What did you say?'

'I don't know but…'

'I am not in the mood, Alison. Just tell us!'

Alison took a deep breath. 'It's probably stupid but I look a bit like Anthony. I could wear his clothes. Maybe that will send them off the wrong way.' She didn't look too happy about this prospect but I knew she would do it for me.

I didn't like the way that Major Pete and Channon were looking at each other; not hating this plan.

'Hang on,' I said. 'Hang on. You're right. That's stupid.'

'Why?' asked Major Pete.

'How many reasons do you need?'

'Well?' asked Channon.

'Well, for a start: whose clothes do I wear?'

I looked at Alison. She blushed. She didn't want to tell me; she really didn't. She looked at the dead bundle on the floor. 'Hers,' she said.

To my eternal shame, no one had a better idea.

The night was a livid, very non-English blue. Candles flickered in the houses as we ran in the warm, soupy, outside evening air. Very idyllic.

I led the way, Major Pete walked by my side; a black smudge keeping a respectful distance.

There were beautiful people in the cobbled streets, some in robes, some in white suits and some in overcoats. I don't know if they were guards or what they were. They certainly didn't spare me a second glance, hooded and gowned as a plump nun. I didn't know whether to be insulted. I smelled of Toni. What a humiliating way to make an escape; creeping out dressed in your dead girlfriend's clothes. It shouldn't have worked; it was a ridiculous, stupid plan but I guess when it came to plan-making, most Sirens' plans seemed to be as bumbling and inept and ultimately incompetent as this one.

The beautiful people bowed to Alison though, who, sans spectacles, was stumbling meekly behind with Max and Channon shielding her from scrutiny. I hoped Alison's impersonation of me was way out (it looked to me like a parody of a rather stupid dog), but, I suspected not.

I stayed calm by mentally cursing Max. I blamed him, of course. How could he read the situation so wrong? He should have known. Why the fuck didn't he know? Why couldn't he have waited? We hadn't even managed one day. I was now seriously worried about Channon. I confess, I was thinking how to get her as far away from me as I could. Max was pretty stuck on his 'kill Felice' plan. Pure suicide but how would that affect my chances? I didn't want either of them near me.

Major Pete would get me out. Of course he would.

No one in the village appeared to know what had happened. They didn't use phones or radios and maybe Channon was wrong about the cameras. A few heads looked out of cottages but they didn't seem alarmed. Quite the opposite; the smudges behind the glass looked totally blissed out. Perhaps I would really be able to wake up tomorrow in my own bed; safe and far away from the crazy.

The houses gave way to open land and a road lined with high bushes and a few sodium lights that stopped just a few yards beyond. We trotted out of the village and into full dark. A few stars blinked in the warm, cloudless sky. The distant hills rose even darker around us. Our luck, for once, appeared to be holding. I heard the rattle of a helicopter.

'I hope that's ours,' said Major Pete. 'We should head for higher ground. They'll home in on your signal Anthony.' From somewhere, he produced a pistol. He cocked it with a snap.

As if the sound was a signal, the church bell in the village began to ring. Single notes one after the other, loud and clear across the summer night.

'Oh shit,' said Alison. She was trembling. I don't blame her.

At first, I couldn't place the noise. Something above the bells.

'What is that?' I asked.

'Voices,' said Max. 'They're coming.'

Voices they were. Lots of them. All those calm beautiful people we had passed; all those benign faces that had looked out from their windows, I guess they had been given new orders. I heard chants; voices on loudspeakers leading the congregation, egging them on. The responses from the throng did not mean us good will.

'Where's that fucking helicopter!' I shrieked, picked up my skirts and ran towards the nearest hill.

When my panic subsided enough to re-engage rational thought, I looked back. What appeared to be a thousand dark shiny pretty French teenagers were streaming out of the village after us. We were halfway up a hill and the village lights looked lovely in the dark.

A little bitty part of my brain wondered why they carried no weapons. I can only guess that those that lived in this Disney Autoire were at such an advanced point in their grand extermination scheme they didn't think anyone was left to challenge them.

Max was bloody fit. Like all Americans, there was something larger and sturdier about him than appeared to reside inside Europeans. A bulky nun's habit didn't help. Very quickly, I was the one trailing and this meadow was very large. Every step was sending spasms of sloth-borne cramp into my knees. Where was this bastard helicopter? Why did it have to be uphill?

'Stop screeching!' Max yelled. I hadn't realised I was. My lungs hurt too much.

I stumbled and Major Pete hauled me up. We had lost our momentum. 'Keep going!' he snapped and I was too frightened to disobey.

Right out of the dark, one of the strong village boys leaped onto me. His flailing arm smacked me right in the nose. Major Pete chopped him down. The thump of his impact was nothing like a film. The boy hit the ground and Major Pete stamped on his jaw. The shattering sound made me feel sick. Major Pete followed up with a boot to the back of the head. Oh Christ, I don't want to remember that ever again.

'So close!' I yelled. 'How can that be?'

'Keep running!' bellowed Major Pete. 'Keep going!'

I ran. Although my guts were on fire and this stupid costume weighed a ton and I hadn't a drop of oxygen in me, I ran. Fear, you see. Just plain old fear the like I had never experienced.

Even then, Major Pete overtook me. How high was this hill? I saw clumped buildings and a flattened section at the top. An engine noise grew and a sleek helicopter buffeted me in its wake as it flashed overhead, almost at touching distance. The lights of the Lynx twinkled in the black night. As if emergency braking, the chopper halted, jerked its front end up, settled and lowered itself onto the grass, bouncing on its rubber tyres. It sat about two hundred yards away. Two hundred yards! How the hell was I going to get there?

'Just run!' Major Pete ordered. I was aware that Channon was somewhere beside me. I hoped to god she was going to look after me. She had to. I mean, I was Anthony Graves. I wasn't going to die here. How could I?

French voices were huffing and puffing all around and that chopper just did not grow any bigger. A pulse thumped in my head and bright electric sparks flashed across my eyes. The rotors whined.

Suddenly, bodies poured into the space between me and the machine. I couldn't help it; I stopped; I had to.

'Fucking… Jesus… Christ…' I heaved out. 'Save me!'

The dark bodies ran down the hill. Someone shoved me over and I screamed. Major Pete. 'Stay down!' he ordered. I knelt panting into the grass. He knelt next to me, pistol raised; looking through the crowd at the helicopter, trying to figure a way through. No one could see anything. It was chaos: a maelstrom of charging, directionless bodies.

A gun flashed. A beat later, the sound of the shot rang round the hill. Channon. Somehow she had a weapon too. Somehow she'd had one all the time. A man howled.

The bodies crashed into us. Major Pete fired a couple of times but then he was gone. A knee clonked me right in the forehead and I went over into the dirt. My head was on fire and I didn't know up from down. Someone trod on me. A hand grabbed the back of my neck and began to pull. I resisted and screamed 'Not me! Not me!'

I heard Alison shout something. The hand released amid a babble of French voices.

I think I heard her yell: '*Je suis* Anthony! *Je suis* Anthony Graves! Death to Felice Beata!' but then her yelling became her screaming.

I crawled forward as the massed bodies passed over me. I touched a body lying still on the grass; one of Major Pete's targets perhaps, and forced myself onto my knees. I could hear the deafening clatter of the helicopter again. Get on that and this is all over, I thought.

'Wait,' I croaked. 'Wait for me!' Unbelievably, Alison's screeches and gurgles got louder, even over the sound of the engine and the beating rotors.

Despite the robes, despite my panic overbalancing me, I reached my feet and saw the helicopter. The side door was open and Channon and Flight Lieutenant Hammond were hauling in what appeared to be a supine, lifeless Max. My fellow siren disappeared into the dark safety of my helicopter. I ran, not listening to the sounds of the mob tearing a human body apart behind me. A co-pilot kept the helicopter steady as they worked.

I was so hoarse and frightened and breathless, I couldn't speak. Channon looked up. I must have been fifty yards away. She pointed the gun at me. I threw myself to the ground. Her pistol spat twice. Something hot and horribly close ripped through my nun's skirt.

'No! Fucking no!' I screamed, although I don't know if my words were actually articulated. I bit down on muddy grass.

I was on my knees and so close when I heard Channon shout: 'Take off! Go now!'

I looked up to see Hammond shake his head. 'We're not leaving Anthony!'

Good on you mate, I thought, I'm nearly there. Just hang on.

Channon raised her gun and shot Hammond in the throat. She unbuckled him as the blood sprayed and pushed his body out of the helicopter. She then shot the co-pilot as he tried to get out of his seatbelt.

I screamed. I was up and running. 'It's me! It's me!' I yelled. 'Don't shoot!'

Channon looked out of the open hatch and I know she recognised me. I may have given her the benefit of the doubt before but not now. She knew exactly who I was as she grabbed the door handle. She smiled as she pulled the door shut. My Channon. My bloody traitorous Channon.

I ran into the side of the Lynx and banged on its metal side. The engine wind fluffed up my skirt. 'Let me in! Let me in!' I howled.

The engines howled with increased vigour and the helicopter began to lift.

'Jesus Christ! You can't leave me!'

I thought about holding onto the undercarriage but even in my utter desolation and panic, I remembered enough movies to know that in such a situation, eventually everyone falls off.

The downdraft blasted me over onto the ground again, right into the massed crowd of beautiful religious people determined to rip me apart. The noise and the heat were overwhelming. As hands clawed at me, I stared up into that night sky. The helicopter broke free, dipped with a sharp buzz of its engine and then flew away over the hills.

Chapter 30

Trouble starts when people are certain. When people imbued with certainty try to do what they know is right, trouble starts. When people think they know best.

Take for example my fall from the helicopter. Felice's French zombies had me in their hands. They literally had me drop in their laps. But what happened?

The guy who I landed on probably thought he knew best. He probably thought he was right; that he had done the hard work. There I was, hitting the grass really heavily and him rolling on top of me. Captured. Sunk. Job done.

However, the girl who then smashed him on the head to get to me was equally convinced that she knew best. She absolutely knew it.

So when this first guy is screaming and shouting for his assailant to back off, this only leads to more confusion and a whole mass of bundling bodies who all think they know how to handle this situation better than anyone else. They're all leaders; they all think this other guy is me.

Without wanting it to happen, doing everything they could to prevent it, these ever so certain people fucked up. They allowed me to get away.

There was nothing conscious about my escape. If there had, I would have failed. I'm good at instinct, especially 'saving myself' instinct. I did what Anthony Graves always did: I stayed quiet and waited for everyone else to mess up. The dark helped. So did the ripped and stained and bloodied remnants of Toni's nun's habit. With the helicopter lights gone we were all just dark smudges lost in a sultry summer night.

I realised in the dark I looked like everyone else so I hauled the torn cloth over my head. The noise was tremendous. More bodies were piling in, turning the landing field into one great big scrum. There was no order here, no control; just men and women screaming. I added a few '*Ici! Ici!*'s to seed more confusion.

At last, I was out of the mass. Without running I sloped off to some nearby dark trees.

I don't know how long I ran through that thick wood but at last I stopped. Terror had given way to exhaustion. I crawled up the trunk of a thick, leafy tree, feeling the knobs and bumps until I found a thick enough branch which enabled me to hide under its heavy summer leaves. There was no light at all. I held on like an anguished monkey as the branch dipped and rose with my weight. Finally, after an eternity, it settled.

As I held on and shivered, too scared even to moan, I realised this is what it must feel like for normal people when they knew I was about to glamour them. I didn't much care for the sensation. It must have been eleven in the evening. When morning came, what was I going to do?

They were going to catch me; no doubt. They had to. That inevitability was too much to bear. Only the transparent barrier of time separated me from being returned to that church. I threw up. The chunks of last night's meal bounced noisily off the leaves. I used my sleeve to wipe it up so it wouldn't fall to the ground. The smell was, well, the least of my worries.

I felt at my chest for the electronic gizmos strapped there. Were they still working? Could I allow myself to hope for rescue? All seemed to be gone, ripped away with half of Toni's habit.

Torch beams lanced through the thick blackness. Voices shouted. They were now organised.

Wave after wave of footsteps moved at pace below me. They wouldn't tire, no more than my own people would if I had commanded them to hunt. I remembered how the mob had ripped my dad apart. I imagined Alison Locke. I thought too much about the upcoming pain and my helplessness and their determination and knowing it would only stop when I was dead. I didn't want to die and I didn't want to suffer.

I stayed awake and aware through every second of that terrible night. Occasional beams of light would cross the tree but I think my pursuers credited me with more courage and resilience than they should have, for they appeared to believe I had got much further away. I heard ominous helicopter sounds. I heard gunshots and screams. Presumably, to be safe, they were shooting any lone people they stumbled across in the woods. I would have.

I realised I could see again. A pink sun was brightening the air. Another beautiful day and undoubtedly my last. Birds were singing their morning routine. It was a lovely day in the countryside. I must have been half asleep. I was imagining what today might have been like had I never got the glamour: travelling on the Underground, work at the office, chatting to Toni and Keano, staring at a computer screen, being bored, going for a pint and wishing I hadn't as I travelled the Underground home again.

As much as at any other point in my life, I hated the glamour. I hated it so much.

I couldn't stay in the tree. My body was telling me to climb down; to end this pain. My rationality refused.

Where the hell was I going to go?

A French helicopter buzzed over. Through the leaves, I watched it rise then bank left. A man with binoculars sat in the side door, scanning the woods.

I didn't want to be caught. I never wanted to be caught. My limbs were so stiff I could hardly move but I made myself climb out of the tree.

Wandering around lost in the woods was a hopeless idea. I was already faint with heat and exhaustion. They were going to pick me up if I just started walking around in circles.

When I got rid of the habit, I found one of the GPS devices. It was a little miniature satnav the size of a coin hanging round my neck. I had been wearing the thing all night and not known.

Now, this was not your ordinary satnav, no. This was a top of the range SAS issue micro-tablet thingy. I remember Major Pete had put it round my neck in the helicopter and somehow the village kids had missed tearing it painfully off my head. I kissed its little plastic casing.

A tiny screen displayed a virtual map of this hill, this wood. Turning the device around made all the pretty tiny digital numbers change. An orange arrow was blinking on and off, pointing west.

An arrow. And some figures: 8.5. That wouldn't be kilometres would it?

A high wooded hill grew in front of me, just where the orange arrow was pointing. I wish I knew what the hell that meant. Did I fall asleep in the digital direction gizmo meeting? Was I being told to travel 8.5k in a westerly direction thereupon to be rescued by my loyal army? I don't know. What else was I going to do?

I walked for hours, constantly consulting the GPS tablet, panicking every time I misjudged the distances or heard a noise in the foliage. There wasn't a soul about. I threw the remnants of my Toni disguise, along with all the useless dangling wires, into the trees. I was in my pants and I stank.

The sun was a giant burning yellow eye staring mercilessly down and I soon developed a nice pink sheen across my chest and shoulders. The hill went up and up.

I didn't see anyone, which was good. However, I was very hungry and thirsty, which was bad. There were plenty of streams and puddles but I couldn't make myself drink from them. The water was just lying there on the ground and I kept imagining thin wriggly French tapeworms growing in my stomach if I tried it. I wondered how long it would be before I no longer cared.

The forest was endless. The terrain kept dipping up and down so I couldn't see where the orange arrow was leading me. By midday the French helicopters came back. I had to hide again. Don't get any ideas: it wasn't in the least bit romantic.

Look, I'm not going to go into detail about what it's like to wander through woods. Long, arduous and physically demoralising. None of it stays in my mind anyway. Suffice to say I was a wreck when somehow I stumbled out of the trees and saw a road at the far end of a meadow full of high wheat. By now I was half-dead with heat exhaustion. The distant tarmac shimmered in the sun. No cars. No people. I started to understand that whatever embargo Felice had issued about not using phones and computers was working to my advantage.

I followed the orange arrow and pushed through the inevitably sharper-than-it-needed-to-be wheat. A slender wire fence divided the meadow from the road. The sun didn't blink. I crawled over the wire into a dusty drainage ditch just wide enough to walk at a crouch. I could see this would be the main road in or out of Autoire. I didn't question whether my people would really think it was a great place for a rescue.

Following the highway down the hill for a mind-numbing number of hours, treading over large, dusty white stones, I saw a long-abandoned café. It was complete with old tyres, wrecked Mobil sign and a banging swing door. Behind the café, birds sat peacefully at the top of two telegraph poles and watched me.

According to the GPS I was at the rendezvous. The café had to be my destination. My imagination was screening home movies of what would happen when god's children inevitably picked me up but I had no choice. I had to check the place out. Where were the jeeps? The crack extraction squad mum had promised?

I darted across the road and hid behind a big metal bin at the back of the café. I was certain the French would be waiting for me. Perhaps hiding behind those dusty counters, in the trees, maybe up in the hills where a lone, camouflaged scout watched me with his binoculars…

No. No more panic. Wherever I was, my pursuers had moved on. A pristine metal road sign indicated that Autoire was a mere six kilometres over the next hill. Presumably they were thinking that someone sensible would have got a lot further away from the village. After all my crazy walking, I was still in spitting distance of Looney Village.

The wavy summer air buzzed with the noise from spectral but unseen helicopters. The birds on the poles outside began to squawk. My pursuers were still out there.

So, what had the orange arrow led me here to find? I looked at the dial again. 0.1km. No mistake.

My first priority was water. I climbed through an open window at the café and had a rummage. I found some dusty plastic bottles of Evian in an old fridge, cracked them open and guzzled the warm liquid down. I also found some souvenir football t-shirts in clear packets hanging in the foyer. I couldn't decide whether a Lyon shirt or a French national team one would be better, then my head cleared and I wondered just what I thought I was doing. I ripped the first packet, grabbed whatever shirt was inside the polythene and pulled it on. The harsh, cheap cotton scraped my burned skin. This was a long way from the handcrafted silk I was used to wearing.

I heard an engine. Faint but getting closer. Sounded like a lorry. Rescue? About time. Of course, mum would have a crack team hidden in the vicinity for this very situation. She wouldn't have told me officially so I wouldn't give it away. The arrow was a rendezvous point where they would pick me up. The approaching lorry might even be that rescue.

I snatched up some dusty bars of chocolate and stuffed them into an Autoire Valley souvenir shoulder bag that looked like it would split as soon as anything heavy was put inside it. I climbed out of the window and into the road. There was no wind; only sun and a rippling heat haze across the dry fields. The lorry growled. I still couldn't see it. The wide dusty road stretched into the distance.

Despite the confusion, I was no longer panicked. Eventually, someone would come and sort me out. All I had to do was wait.

The invisible lorry clattered and rattled on its imaginary road. I couldn't tell whether it was getting closer or not. The hills were amplifying the sound. There was no other sound; only birds at the back of the café. I realised I was probably being a bit silly standing in the middle of an open highway, so I walked round the back of the café.

The stench made me turn my head. The telephone poles with the roosting birds were stuck into concrete bases and smeared by a cloud of insects. Each pole had a dead body nailed to it.

I don't think I was even shocked. I didn't care one way or the other. I was burned out. Forget it. Move on.

'Mmgh!' (or thereabouts) came a muffled voice. I froze.

For a second I wasn't sure I'd heard it.

'Arr… tee…' Someone was trying to form words.

One of the figures was moving. A man: face black with bruises and blood under a carpet of insects. The birds had worked at the man but I recognised Major Pete. A GPS device just the same as mine hung congealed in gore on his ripped chest. My dial read: 0k. The orange arrow had disappeared.

'Oh shit,' I said. I needed to pee very badly.

The second pole displayed what was left of Alison Locke; still wearing my clothes. She wasn't moving and the insects were all over her, in her mouth, eyes, everywhere. It was clear by the way her body had been dented she wasn't going to move ever again.

Major Pete spat out a thick globule of dark blood. It ran down his smashed chin. Still, he was determined. It took him a few goes but I understood him in the end.

'Anthony,' he said. 'I can… help you. Get me down.' More blood.

We looked at each other for a while; he looked very thirsty. I was fighting my instinct to do what he said; waiting for reason to prevail. Thank god it did. 'Your legs are broken,' I said. 'You'll have to stay there.'

Major Pete nodded. I could almost hear the dry creak of his neck as he tried to move. One eye looked really bad, a bruised swollen hood filled with blood and dotted with little holes which I imagine were peck marks. I could barely hear him.

'I'm sorry,' he said. 'You must get away. West.'

'Best? Vest?'

'West.'

'I get you. Are you in pain?' Stupid question. 'I mean; is there anything I can do?'

'Just get away. Don't let them find you.'

'What about the rescue?' was all I could think of in reply. I stared at him, squirming. 'What about the extraction team?'

'I don't know.'

'Well you should know! Where are the commandos? The air strikes? The nukes? What happened?'

'I'm sorry…'

Honestly, I could have slapped his face. 'Fuck sorry!' I yelled. 'Why don't you know? *Why don't you just know?*'

Major Pete winced; pain or shame I don't know. 'Should have… Something must have… must have…' his battered head dropped. He was on the verge of passing out or dying. 'I am yours,' I think he muttered. But I could be wrong.

An engine roared. Close. Much too close. I had forgotten the lorry! I sprinted across the concrete yard and into the woods.

When I was sure I could not possibly be under surveillance, I stopped and dropped into a dip in the ground. The sun was making me sleepy. My body was telling me to stop. It needed rest if it was to get me out of here. No help was coming. I had to find a way out and that was only going to happen if I made it happen. The little depression was dusty but pretty good at hiding me, I thought. Just a few judicious branches and no one would ever find me. Unless they had dogs. But I hadn't heard dogs; just a lorry and those birds at the concrete poles.

I couldn't entirely sleep. I kept sipping the bottled water. A million scattered plans fought in my head. I had to find a single thread, a path. When I woke up some hours later, with a chill in the air and a rosy evening tint to the light, my subconscious had boiled it down to the only possible solution.

Walk, it told me. Trudge to the coast and get a boat back to England. It will, so my subconscious informed me, be a frightening journey, which will involve exhausting hikes over harsh terrain, a threat of starvation and the constant danger of detection. Overall, a bloody lousy solution.

It was motivation enough.

West, Major Pete had said. Easy to say. Let's start with: which side does the sun go down? I felt I should know this. The dehydration, fatigue and fear were wiping me out. I would never be able to drag myself to the coast. I weighed too much; didn't have the strength. I told myself that didn't matter; eventually, I would find the right direction. I just wanted out of this bloody wood.

So, apart from the fact I was starving, knackered, filthy and couldn't speak French, I was fine. As long as no one saw me, asked me anything or worked out who I was, I was fine. As long as no one got me, I was home and dry.

Chapter 31

Despite that, when I began my route march through the countryside, I was certain I would quickly be got by somebody; rescue or capture. Surely, in the end, someone was going to turn up and claim me.

I held on to that dream for a couple of days. I prayed for release from this dull wooded nothing. I wept continually.

When the reality became so apparent even I could no longer ignore it, a new and much more practical Anthony emerged. He was needed and he was bidden. I don't know where he had been hiding. He was reluctant and grumpy, but he arrived, rolled up his sleeves and got on with the job.

The forest and the mountains stretched on for miles. Miles and more miles. I have heard that those who are keen on long walks suggest that one's senses are heightened during the experience. That the time passes quickly as one's bodily rhythms slow and synchronise with the pace of the natural world around them. Eventually, they are infused with a lovely sensation of fulfilment that transcends Time. Bollocks. I trudged every step in fear and boredom. I lived through every agonising second.

And what was I seeing? What was my in-flight movie? Oh yes, the one where I'm captured and strung up by a bunch of singing, smiling lunatics. Having nails hammered into my hands and feet. Scorching in the sun. Birds jabbing my eyes and swarms of black insects crawling over my face and mouth and eyes and a pain so great that no matter how much it hurts I still can't scream. That movie. I had cultivated fear and dread throughout my safe suburban life. I knew they would come in handy one day.

I was still being pursued. Felice's people still looked for me. It seemed sometimes the whole French Army had been mobilised. There were cars, patrols, helicopters. There were civilian mobs armed with nets and binoculars. There were checkpoints and searches and shootings. I passed a dozen or more corpses in those woods. Their murderers painted white crosses on their bodies and left them to rot. Shot down for looking wrong in the wrong place at the wrong time.

How could they know they were dealing with Anthony Graves and his true god-given talent? Not the glamour, oh no. The further I walked and hid and dodged and scavenged, the more I understood this talent; born from a lifetime of hesitancy and cowardice. My real talent was for keeping my head down and making myself so small no one noticed when I sneaked by. The talent for keeping going when you're out of food and your shoes fall off your feet and you stink and your legs burn with exhaustion and the whole world is after you. The talent for staying alive.

Father Stephen was not my mum. As ever, she was right: keeping her free of the glamour made the difference. Felice didn't have a general with a clear head.

Father Stephen lacked mum's planning, her organisation, but most of all her free will. He was distracted by his devotion to his mystical muse, no matter how insane. Every action he made was filtered through that senile old woman's mind. No wonder the search was so disorganised.

Finding me was not a priority. Father Stephen was a man with a mission and as I came down from the wooded mountain into the bright cereal fields and vineyards of the Dordogne I saw just how forceful and frightening that mission was.

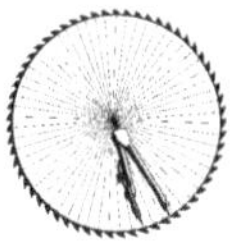

I don't remember the details of leaving the forest, nor do I wish to. It's not like anything changed. It was still just sun, trees, hunger and being very, very tired. All I know for sure is many nights had passed.

The search for me appeared to be abandoned. They must have known they were never going to find me unless I walked up and announced myself. I suppose they banked on me starving to death in the country. They probably preferred that. What could I do here to harm them?

I found more clothes. I stripped them from bodies. There were plenty of abandoned vehicles on the roads to provide water and scraps of food. The countryside was empty, silent but for the birds, squirrels, foxes and once even a gigantic pig. It emerged from the undergrowth, snorted at me and buggered off back in again. So much for respecting the monarch of Great Britain.

I hadn't spoken aloud for at least a week. All I had was the blind compulsion to keep going, to keep walking. I could have been heading for the coast; I could have been heading anywhere. All I could see were the stalks of untended wheat. My world had been reduced to ground, crop and sky.

The wheat suddenly parted and I was on a country road. Burrs from the crops draped me in irritating, scratchy webs. My feet were a mass of blisters and I was dying for a drink.

I emerged from the field and there they were, marching on the dusty road, singing. I suppose I had heard them but the noise didn't register. They stared at me but didn't stop, just kept marching on. I thought about plunging back into the safety of the corn but I had lost the will. I needed people. So I sat down and watched them go by.

The hymn the acolytes were singing sounded so beautiful. The evening sky was a rich sensual painting of purple and red clouds and I was so dizzy and full of pollen, the sound cut through that warm, ripe autumn air. If this was the end of me, so be it.

They were marching in a column. God's soldiers on the joyful road to extinction. There were twenty of them, utterly exhausted but deliriously happy. They followed a smart looking woman in a suit, holding up a long wooden banner with an ornate white and purple Christian flag on the end. Gold letters were stitched on the flag but I couldn't read them. Could have been the town they came from, could have been Latin; could have been anything.

'*Le Rapture!*' they would chant, at which point all as one raised their arms to the sky in a bizarre Mexican wave. They were men, women and children dressed in rags and as starved as me.

It must have been the heat, or hubris, or just something else to do but I lay back and shrieked with laughter. They were so stupid, dancing toward the chimneys to burn; all on the idiot behalf of some stupid, senile old witch.

I stopped laughing when a little girl in a pretty yellow dress dropped out of the column and held out her arms to me. '*Alle!*' she said. She looked so happy. '*Le Rapture!*' and she pointed at the sky. Her wide, innocent smile scared me into sanity. The others were looking at me expectantly; like maybe I wanted to come along and party like there was no tomorrow.

'No,' I yelled. 'No!' And I was back in the wheat and tearing away from them as fast as I could.

The next column I joined. Only for a while, I told myself. I wouldn't stay for long. Get my bearings and go. Perhaps I was that lonely I wanted to forget myself for a while.

This time I sang and danced along with them. I even pointed up at the sky and cried 'Rapture!' as often as they did. It was the most fun I'd had in ages. It also helped me to get through some rather stark looking checkpoints without trouble. Three times on the road I passed serious camouflaged men in shiny 4x4 jeeps; rifles prominently displayed. These men, these soldiers, had crucifixes attached to their blue berets. I'm sure they were all deeply religious. I kept my head down and walked past. None of them gave me a second look.

We marched and sang for days. More and more joined us all the time. I have never felt so physically tired. When some dropped, others equally tired would somehow muster the energy to hoist them up and drag them along. At first I worried that if I sneaked off I would be chased. Then I got so exhausted I stopped worrying about anything. We slept on the move. We trudged along the roads, just continuing, brains empty except for the single impulse required of us.

One evening we reached the top of a hill and saw smoke plumes. I should have been more wary. My little group was now several hundred strong. A big cheer went up and we all collapsed onto the road. Food appeared from somewhere and got shared around. I was so far gone that at first I refused the fruit and bread kindly strangers thrust into my cracked and bleeding hands. My throat was so thick and swollen I didn't think I could force anything down.

Nutrition brought me out of my white noise reverie. My vision cleared and I realised just where I had ended up. How long had I been walking? Shit, I'd had plenty of chances to escape. There was only so long I would get away with gurning and grinning like an idiot any time anybody tried to talk to me. It was early morning and the gathered pilgrims were asleep. Time to go.

However, when I looked, I could see only fields of baked mud that stretched into the distance. If I tried to make a run for it, I would be in full view. Already, the keener members of my party were hoisting themselves up to get themselves quicker to what was ahead. The movement was infectious and soon the entire army would be back on the move. Only my innate cowardice stopped me cutting and running right then. If I went now, I would have no chance.

The people around me stood up. An old woman smiled and offered me a hand up. She said something kind in French. I wanted to smash her head into the tarmac. Instead, I got to my feet and walked. We were a tributary, feeding into the river of thousands of pilgrims. By now, the soldiers were everywhere, marshalling the crowd. Their job seemed to be more about keeping the queues orderly rather than dealing with any trouble. There wasn't any trouble.

Slowly, through a disturbing smoky haze, the plain white death factory chimneys materialised. Four of them: placidly smoking. As the hours passed, the building reared up, shimmering in the heat haze like a gigantic living Battersea Power Station. It was all brickwork, concrete and pipes. The chimneys were gigantic; like the legs of a vast upturned table.

The sweating, bustling crowd let out a great roar of excitement. They had been travelling a long time. Beside me, Anton punched the air with delight. I had just started to get to know Anton. He was English, an expat, and had been a successful lawyer before moving out to 'live the dream' of converting an old barn in the Dordogne. Since Felice, he lived a new dream.

Anton's fine clothes were now like mine: rags. With his expensive tan, fleshy muscle-toned body and strong alpha male bone structure, he couldn't have looked less spiritual. Yet here he was, weeping and praising the Lord who was about to receive him. 'Tom!' he cried out to me (to my assumed name). 'At last! At last!'

'Oh yea, brother!' I yelled. How had I managed to get myself into this? How was I going to get away?

At last, we stopped moving. I was terrified; convinced I was going to go running straight into the fire before I could even think of a decent plan.

Luckily, there were so many people trying to get into the factory that the crowd stalled. The queue was miles long; patiently marshalled by the blue berets. This might have been the first time the French had willingly queued for anything.

The soldiers walked by and made up-and-down gestures with their white gloved hands. We had to wait for the furnace. No, they didn't know how long. We had to wait or we would crush each other to death before we got to the incinerators, and that wouldn't do.

The air was getting thick with the smoke. It started to smell; the stench of burned fat. Particles I didn't want to think about weaved their arcane trails across the shanty town that had built up around the dusty white walls. Closer, less than a mile away, the jerry-built cavernous building looked like a cement factory. There was one purpose here and no frills attached. I tried to judge the speed of the queue and the distance to the gate. I needed darkness.

The soldiers walked by and made patting shapes with their hands. People nodded and sat. I lay down with the others, straining to breathe in that choking air. I wondered why Father Stephen insisted that burning was the method of choice. Why not just shoot these people, or poison, or better still, get them to hang themselves? What had made Felice Beata and all those nice church leaders decide that burning your population one by one was what god intended?

The long hot day crawled by. There was no let-up; no opportunity to get away, just waiting in the road for death. We moved twice, a deeply frightening couple of minutes as the crowd surged forward only to pause again a few hundred yards ahead. As evening turned the smoke black, I still hadn't figured a way out. The guards ordered us up yet again and we were moving forwards, extremely slowly, but inexorably. The longer I waited, the harder it was going to be to get away. I had a horrible feeling I had already passed the point of no return. Shit, shit.

I needed a distraction. I needed something. All around were brown fields caked in soot. I couldn't just run. Surely I couldn't, not through all these people. But soon I would have no choice.

What would the guards do if I made a run for it? I thought again of the thousand times I could have slipped away. I thought of what madness had made me join these nuts at all.

At around midnight, we were ordered up again. The rest gaps were getting shorter. The factory was lit by strings of electronic lights all hazed up by the fumes. We would sit still for half an hour or so, then bodies ahead would stand and walk a few metres. Then we would sit down again. We were picking up pace. I could hear a low mechanical rumble from the death factory. Trapped among the heated, hysterical bodies of the faithful, I found what food I could and stuffed my face. My companions didn't notice. They weren't bothering to eat. What was the point?

Uplifting French spirituals and hymns rang around in the darkness. Thousands of people jostled and pushed and sang of the wonder and joy of the Lord as they waited for their turn. I found I was becoming angry. Tears ran down my face but they were hot with frustration. I wanted to smash their happy, singing, smiling faces to pulp. No wonder Felice wanted them dead.

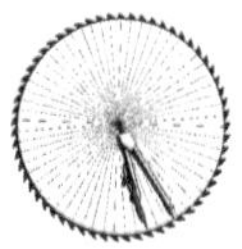

The sun lit the sky pink, then yellow, then bright blue. Another beautiful morning in the French countryside. Luckily, no one recognised my agonised, choked, panicked weeping for what it was. They thought I was impatient at having to wait to get into the oven.

I was right outside. The mechanical rumble was now a roar: a vast industrial operation a couple of hundred yards away. Smoke streamed from the concrete chimneys. The furnaces had been working non-stop. How many had gone in the night? How many before us? How many before me? I couldn't tell how far from the gates I was.

I was sick of the stench of burned hair, of breathing in human fat. The sun was blurred, as if smeared with molten grease. At the wall, crudely welded metal scaffolding framed an entrance which was nothing more than a carved hole. It was a funnel. People filed inside; along a gauntlet of priests in black who blessed and showered the entrants with sprinkles of water. The congregation went in one at a time; slow. Even at this current snail's pace, I calculated by midday I would be one of them.

As the followers sang and rejoiced and shuffled forwards, I finally managed to summon up the courage to act. Soon I would have no choice.

During the hours that we had been snarled up in front of the factory, I had occasionally spotted some dusty looking men and women. They carried shovels and picks and seemed to have a purpose other than suicide. It didn't take me long to figure out their role. Someone had to keep those ovens clean. As to how they had been selected for their duties, I had no idea.

As I closed in on the factory, I noticed these dusty white people walked to and fro inside a roped-off pathway the guards kept clear. The path stretched out from the factory wall, across a field for about a hundred metres, where it disappeared into the mass of people on their way in. These workers had their own private gateway in and out of the factory.

At one point during that long painful morning, three empty lorries came slowly from behind us, guards parting the followers like waves. The vehicles climbed off the road and onto the roped path; heading towards the factory wall, escorted by the workers covered in white dust. This close, the air was red soup with all the crap suspended in it and the engines were hellishly loud after my weeks of country living. My fellow pilgrims didn't seem to see the convoy at all. I realised I hadn't heard an engine since getting out of the forest.

I pushed my way towards the ropes as best I could without making it too obvious. The crush here was intense. As I went, Anton shouted 'Wrong way…' and pointed back to the queue like I had made an honest mistake. I waved, smiled and soon lost sight of him.

Through the mass, I saw the lorries inch forward. Even in their protected zone, the number of people crammed here meant there was always someone falling over the rope into the path. The dusty workers and guards escorted the trucks, keeping the path clear. By now, I was at the ropes, trying not to draw attention to myself but also not wanting to lose sight of the vehicles. I bumped into a soldier who barked an order at me in French — presumably 'fuck off out of the way' — and I obeyed, only to get back to the rope again as soon as he turned his head. Ahead, at the end of the path, I saw the entrance to the factory: two wooden gates coated in lethal looking metal wire. Shut.

The lorries revved, the gate opened and the first one trundled through.

This had to be it. Now or never and all that crap. In the midst of a crush of happy clappers and the guards, I made my move. I waited for one of the workers, one carrying a shovel, to come close enough. Then I scanned my immediate colleagues to find someone weak and feeble. There; an exhausted sun-burned mother carrying a hungry toddler on her shoulders. I waited for her to take a step forward, momentarily off-balance, then ducked down and shoved. The crowd parted as she tumbled over the rope and into the worker. The toddler hit the ground hard. People were so crushed they began tripping over each other. Guards immediately swarmed to sort the mess; to keep the lines moving. I kept my eye on the worker with the spade as he struggled under the weight of the unfortunate woman. Just as he tried to steady himself, I stamped on his hand and seized the spade. He fell back with a cry just as another body piled on top of him.

I walked slowly over the exhausted prone pilgrims as they picked themselves up. I was so angry, so intensely fearful that I wanted to yell out and start swinging the spade. A few well-aimed cracks on their pious heads would have calmed me down. Of course, if I did give in to temptation, I would be dead. I just had to keep going until I reached the side gate. The lorries were almost through.

I ignored the temptation, the very sore temptation to bolt away from the factory. Maybe it would have worked; maybe no one would have paid the blindest bit of attention to me scuttling away. But what if they did? Just at the wrong moment, as I bundled over yet another praying child, my feet stamped jarringly into a rut ground out by heavy wheels. 'Shit!' I hissed.

The soldiers helping the fallen looked up. I stood holding my spade; the child spluttering at my feet. I couldn't have been more obvious. French words came in my direction. Mirrored sunglasses stared my way.

I had to stay calm; I just had to. No choice, I told myself. There is no choice. The child started to cry. A mother's hands grabbed my shoulders; she cursed me in French. I shrugged her off. The last lorry was going through the gate, along with a couple of dusty workers. Voices shouting behind me, I put the spade over my shoulder and started to walk as if I hadn't heard a thing. I kept my eye on the back of that last lorry and walked straight into the cloud of ash blowing up in its wake. To survive, to live, I had to get inside the death factory.

Chapter 32

Johnny was a good bloke. I learned a lot from Johnny. He gave me a scarf to wrap around my face so I didn't have to breathe in the dead people.

I never found out Johnny's real name. Johnny didn't speak English and in my opinion even his French left something to be desired. I never understood him but we became very adept in the international language of mime. Johnny was always laughing and he was always smoking. A horrible Gallic fag was permanently hanging from his droopy lower lip. Out of all the French people I met, Johnny was the most French. He may not have been the brightest button in the box but I liked him.

We spent the first day shovelling white ash onto the trucks. Sounds easy but when I factored in the heat, the death, the backbreaking endless fucking labour, the insects, the more death, the sticky layer of grease that covered everything and the even more death, all in all the job wasn't as attractive as I first might have made it sound. Within the first hour my hands were a blistered, leaking mess and within two the flies had discovered that fact.

That was when Johnny rescued me. He emerged from the white dust, spat some gibberish and handed me a pair of thick, padded gloves. They were agony to put on but at least they stopped the spade sliding out of my hands. By midday my entire body was numb and I had fainted twice.

There were some fifteen of us shovellers and we kept to ourselves. If I tried to make eye contact they looked away. Their faces were masks of blandness, just like mine.

As the day of monotony and exhaustion became evening, as the work went on, I lost track of existence, let alone time. There was only the endless shovelling. White hot ash periodically poured down from metal chutes and we pitched it into piles. The heat melted the ground beneath our feet. To cool the ash piles down, we would spray them with fire hoses. The smell was beyond imagining. I tried to ignore the occasional solid shape still intact in the white mounds and after a while I didn't need to pretend. I was too tired.

Our work took place in the middle of the streams of people heading up the ramps into the ovens. The pilgrims ignored us; they were too busy gazing with longing up at those great concrete chimneys, eager for their chance for salvation in the sky.

Once in the furnace lines they never made a sound. They waited at a metal door until it slid open and then they walked in, fifty at a time. The fires inside whooshed and half an hour later the next lot of ash came pouring down the chutes.

Even fifty at a time was too slow. There were so many people, no wonder the queue had built up outside. We couldn't shovel fast enough. Why they didn't use bulldozers I'll never figure out. It was probably religion. I wondered how long before the whole country, maybe the continent, was empty and I could stop shovelling.

How long was I inside that factory? I honestly don't know. I soon forgot about escape. I kept thinking at any moment I was going to pitch forward into the ash and die; heart stretched past breaking. I kept shovelling.

One morning the trucks returned and Johnny and I and the others shovelled ash onto them and climbed aboard. They drove us away, out of that hell.

Somewhere in Central France there is a quarry. Don't ask me where because to this day I do not know. All I know is that this quarry, and probably many others across Europe, is full of the kind of dust you don't want to be making swimming pools out of.

I didn't care. When our truck bounced its way down the dirt trail I was beyond feeling anything but pain. Johnny held on to me as the driver negotiated the steep slope. If he hadn't held on to me I would have fallen out. Precisely what I needed to do, you might have thought, but I wouldn't have lasted the night.

There were caravans in the quarry. This is where we shovellers were meant to stay. We were needed so we had to rest. The authorities, Felice's authorities, didn't want us to suffer unduly. Far from feeling they had been spared; my colleagues were upset that being a shoveller delayed their own personal rapture. They couldn't wait to climb into the ovens. They were sacrificing themselves by staying alive and weren't happy about that fact.

My physical condition after the labour at the camp was not good. Apart from anything else, the dehydration was shocking. The stink I could live with, even the blisters, but I needed water. I can't believe I survived. Some didn't.

There were three guards at the quarry: two soldiers and a monsignor dressed in black and purple robes. The latter chap made us kneel in the cold mud and spent rather a long time exhorting us to carry on with what we were doing because God demanded it. I noticed one of the gang did not so much kneel as topple over and stop breathing. He was ignored.

The guards handed the rest of us bowls of hot soup, which we ate as we knelt. It was a thick, flavoursome vegetarian soup; I forget the recipe. I hope I never taste it again. Yes, the monsignor went on: God understood we were upset about being denied our rapture, but promised our turn would come. He told us we were favoured among the Angels. Despite my poor French, I figured out this 'being favoured' was apparently the reason we had been driven back here and why we hadn't been allowed to walk into the furnace when our shift was over which, of course, would be what we all wanted.

I'd like to know who told this monsignor all this but I smiled and nodded. I tried to look like an idiot. To this day, I don't know how in god's name the gang got chosen.

Still, so far so good. I was safe for at least a while. The trouble was that although these guards were keeping me alive, they were also watching over me.

We were to spend the night in the caravans, then oversee the disposal of the ash in the morning. Apparently our minister had to bless the ash. No, it didn't make any sense to me either. The whole idea felt like baptism in reverse; at the wrong end. We all know the lord moves in mysterious ways. He likes a laugh. Look at what he did to me.

Looking over the edge of that quarry full of dust, being told it was god's work to keep topping it up, I started to laugh. I couldn't help myself. They were going to kill me and I didn't care. Anything, anything at all to get out of this madness. I fell back on the ground, barely able to move, swallowing dust, laughing like a drain as the tears rolled out of my eyes.

The guards had to carry me into the caravan. I screamed and yelled all the way. Again, I presume I was saved because no one could speak English. Sometimes it's much easier when no one understands.

Not surprisingly, my co-workers chose not to spend the night with a raving Englishman. My fine colleagues weren't bothered about staying alive. They believed Felice's crap. They hated being away from the factory so they dumped me in the worst caravan and buggered off to pray. Which suited me fine.

Except Johnny. Johnny stayed with me. Maybe he was too simple to understand. Maybe.

That gap-toothed smiling idiot was treated as much like a leper as me. He was tough though. He looked like he could shovel all day and all night. He tucked me into one of those little wooden beds like I was a baby. He even put cold flannels on my forehead to calm me down. I loved him then more than I ever loved anyone. I clutched at him with my bleeding, pus-dribbling hands and told him so.

Once it was dark, I came to my senses. The world was quiet again, taking a rest from the insanity. I was in a bed for the first night for weeks and sleep wanted me. I was too tired even to be afraid. Yeah, sleep would have been just the ticket. Shame the pain in my joints and muscles kept me awake. I call that cruel.

Inside this simply furnished, uncomfortable caravan (but heaven after the camp), I saw a cheap printed calendar. It was pinned to a corkboard on a wall, illuminated by the moon's light. One of the dates, I didn't know how far away it was, had a crudely drawn circle around it. Little drawings of birds and smiles gave me an idea of what it signified. Clearly, the shovel gangs were not permanent fixtures. The authorities reckoned we had a sell-by date. That was the day on which we would have done enough to earn our reward; that, on a more practical level, we probably wouldn't last much beyond anyway. It could be a month away; it could be tomorrow.

I must have dozed off, because a torch beam shining through the caravan window woke me up. I was in one of those halfway points, stuck in a hideous choking dream. Very slowly, I realised that the odd plastic face looming over me was no longer from my nightmare but a guard looking in the caravan window. He rapped on the glass, nodded and went away.

'Yeah, thanks,' I whispered. I lay rigid as I felt a strange shifting under my skin. The intolerable work had been too much; neglect was taking its toll on a physique that had recently spent five months in a hospital bed. Something physical and important inside me was broken. Oh Christ. If I couldn't get out of bed in the morning, what would they do to me?

Somewhere in the gloom, Johnny was muttering. Jabbering to some imaginary friend. Why couldn't he shut up? How could I bribe him to get me out of here? I tried the glamour on him but nothing visible happened to his hulking shape. Fucking fool. Despite the dehydration, I sweated cold water. I had to stop myself shaking. And why didn't that idiot just shut up?

Only when I thought about it, Johnny was actually talking quite sensibly. For him: very sensibly. And someone was talking back.

A mangled voice was talking back to him. An electronic voice. Johnny was speaking into a mobile phone.

I lay back, trying not to let my breathing give me away. I had been so fucking stupid.

I thought, insanely, of Rodney the South African. The man whose house I had taken over in London. I knew there was something wrong with him. I'd known it instinctively, even if I couldn't define what it was. Now I understood: he wasn't one of mine. And Johnny wasn't Felice's.

Toni had come to France and got herself glamoured. But she wasn't French. Of course she wasn't. What if they had sent her back to me? She would have been Felice's creature in my country and I would never have known. Although, maybe I would. She was a smart, intelligent character but she had a fatal flaw. She would be devoted to her Siren. She would have been discovered.

So, what if she wasn't smart or intelligent? What if she was Johnny? What if instead of coming here myself to find out what the fuck Felice was up to, I sent a spy. Someone clever enough not to get caught but dumb enough to avoid suspicion.

No one was supposed to have a phone. It didn't take much to imagine what the penalty for being caught with one might be. Besides, there was no coverage; no networks. I knew that from our briefings back in England.

Which meant although normal phones didn't work here; this one was special. Johnny's special phone. My next thought was even more frightening. I hadn't sent Johnny here; I was pretty bloody certain Max hadn't, so who was talking to him?

Johnny looked round. I kept my eyes shut and controlled my breathing. My ribs ground with pain. I was going to get that phone off him. Now. Because if I didn't I wouldn't make it through tomorrow alive.

The caravan was nice and dark. It was one of those old seventies things with rickety wooden cupboards. I tried to visualise the furniture. What was in here to get in my way? In my agony, I hadn't paid much attention to the décor; just that date on the calendar.

I heard a little beep as Johnny switched the phone off. The only sound was our mutual breathing in the dark. A rustle as he hid it wherever he had been hiding it.

I didn't want to do this. I really didn't.

Slowly, ever so slowly, I reached down to the floor with my swollen hands, feeling for something to use on Johnny. He was bustling about onto a bunk, trying to keep the noise down for my benefit. I heard him sigh as he laid back. The caravan creaked and rocked. Johnny muttered something that might have been '*bon nuit*'. I felt something brush against my left hand. Clothing, probably my own. We were so confined here we could have been in a submarine.

I waited for him to fall asleep. My body burned with pain and frustration. Why couldn't he just sleep? For Christ's sake he had to be as exhausted as me. How long?

My throat closed up, almost gagging me. I had to switch my imagination off. I needed to be here in the now and nothing else.

I made myself visualise the caravan. Something. Anything. Sharp and quiet, that would be best. Johnny was stronger than me so I would have to be quick. I couldn't allow him even one blow.

Just as I thought I was going to have to get up, my fingers closed around a metal tool. A trowel or something else. My scattering mind went off searching for a better word. What did it matter? Shit, I wasn't up for this. I couldn't do it. Johnny was just a baby. He had saved my life. Maybe he was such a sad specimen that he genuinely didn't have a clue what was going on. Why couldn't we help each other escape? Why couldn't we work together? Because he was glamoured and he wasn't mine. I thought again of Channon's treachery. That bitch. That cow.

I ran my fingers along the blade. Blunt but with a sharp end, like god himself had left it there for me. It didn't seem nearly sharp enough. I wasn't going to do this, was I? I wasn't capable.

The handle had a rubber coating for an easier grip. My hand hurt so much I could barely hold it to my chest. I made sure I didn't scrape it and alert him.

'Johnny?' I asked in the dark.

Straight away, I heard him sit up. He had never been asleep.

'I need… I think I'm in trouble here,' I said.

'Eh?' came a voice in the dark. A voice full of compassion and pity.

He didn't understand. My French had gone. How could I get him over?

'M'aidez!' was all I could think to say.

The caravan thumped as he got to his feet. He scuttled across to me. His foul breath washed over my face. I could see his eyes gleam in the light.

Johnny asked me something. It might have been 'Where does it hurt?'. With my free hand I pointed at my face. He leaned forward.

With that same free hand I gently touched his hair then grabbed hold.

'Antoine?' He looked at me.

I steadied his head and with the other hand I pushed the trowel into his neck as hard as I could. Something tore and blood pumped all over my wrist. Johnny coughed and tried to stand. I kept hold of his hair and used all my weight to keep him still. He wriggled like crazy but I just pushed the trowel in harder. Tears were blurring my vision and I recall I just kept telling him how sorry I was. He kicked and fought but the initial wound was enough. The blood cascaded out of him and over me.

I held Johnny for a long time. He died in the end.

I had passed out with the pain. Outside, birds were singing a dawn chorus. His blood in my mouth woke me up. Johnny was lying on top of me. I was caked in sticky, congealing liquid. Every part of me hurt.

I held Johnny and wept. I couldn't stop myself. The poor sod. What had he done?

But really, I was crying for me. For all the terrible things I had done since getting the glamour. Since becoming a Siren. I hated myself.

But I was still here. I still lived and he didn't.

I rolled Johnny over and slid him to the floor of the caravan. The mobile phone was everything to me now. As soon as anyone opened the door I was finished. There was no way I could escape. I tried not to think about the thousand ways my plan could fail: low battery, password, signal; network. What if mum was out, or had changed her number? Would she listen to her voicemail?

I told myself not to think as I rummaged through Johnny's pockets. The blood and the sweat and the heat and the general rottenness of everything conspired to make this simple act as difficult as possible.

But I found it. An old phone: one of those brick-like monstrosities. I knew I could freak out, do what I wanted after, but until I made that call I had to stay rational.

Squinting at the device, I realised that finally one part of this wasn't going to be difficult. Johnny hadn't even turned the phone off. He had obviously planned more calls in the night.

Now I had a keypad in my hand I remembered the number. I even remembered the UK international dialling code. Be in, I willed. Just be there. If she wasn't, I would dial 999 and every other fucking number I could remember until the battery ran out.

I bet she wouldn't pick up. No one ever did; not an unknown number. It would be voicemail. She would be asleep.

I looked at the crude digital readout. It was displaying a number; an international non-UK number. Johnny's boss. The other Siren. I stared at it for a second then dialled a different number. Mum picked up.

'Anthony?'

'Mum,' I said, crying. 'I don't know where I am but you're going to have to fix on this signal. Find a way. Because you need to come and get me right now. I'm in a caravan in a quarry about ten miles from one of the death factories. Come and get me now. I don't care how. Find a way because if you don't get here before dawn I'm dead. I killed a man; got his blood on me. I'll stay on the phone as long as you need me to.'

The first rays of red sun were poking through the thin caravan curtains. I was hot and exhausted and something rattled inside my body.

'Just get here, Mum. Just get here.'

Chapter 33

I suppose I owe a lot to the medical profession. They always seem to be saving my life. Then again, isn't that what they're for?

As for my escape from that rotten little caravan in France, I simply have no memory; no recollection at all. All I have is the sound of Johnny trying to breathe, the slippery blood and his hot head in my hands. After that, I have to trust what I was told.

I have a black dream about flying and some odd noises which I can't place. Perhaps they are shots. And then I'm back in a bland English medical room, lying in bed surrounded by the doctor squad. Yes, once again I am hooked up to bags of glucose and blood and my insides hurt like a bastard.

I see mum and Max and a new army guy who is Major Pete's replacement. I christen him Colonel Steve. I have no idea what his real name is but the fate of his predecessor does nothing to dampen his enthusiasm for protecting me. Colonel Steve is the hero responsible for airlifting me out.

Those days passed in a familiar blur of tests and boredom. Being the world's most operated upon patient had long lost its novelty.

I was waiting for an explanation but none came. Max was by my bed a lot. He was, as you can imagine, very apologetic.

'I ordered Channon to turn back,' he said. 'But I was too late. By the time I came round, we were in the English Channel landing on an aircraft carrier. Thank God you're safe. I don't know what I would have done if I had been responsible for…'

He looked down at me, with those warm, moist grandpa eyes of his. He held my hand and stroked my hair. 'It was horrible. I am so sorry.'

'Don't worry about it, Max,' I said. 'Don't worry.'

It seems mum was mobilising NATO to launch an all-out assault on mainland Europe. Which was nice. My phone call saved her the trouble.

When Colonel Steve and his little task force homed in on my phone signal and landed in the quarry, they found a dozen half-starved civilians, two guards and a mad monsignor. I didn't ask what happened to them. I don't care.

As mum describes it, the helicopters with their covert ops battle squads landed to witness an insubstantial, ash-caked spectre emerge from a battered caravan, holding his blood-blackened hands up in surrender.

I imagine he looked like the walking dead, although the squad would not have the courage to tell me that. Apparently, the spectre spoke some English gibberish and collapsed. How they could tell it was me I don't know, unless it was something to do with the glamour. They did what they did to the other men in the quarry, carried me onto their helicopter and flew to the naval medical vessel waiting offshore. On the ship, the docs pumped their drugs in and here I was, saved. I had been gone six weeks. Doctor Conor informed me that instead of looking dead I should have actually been dead. God knows what kept me alive.

I have long vowed never to allow myself to get into such a predicament again.

If mum was pleased to see her only son back safe and sound, she didn't exactly go overboard showing it. I was surprised to see her but I subsequently learned we were in a bunker somewhere deep in a secret hospital in Cambridgeshire. She spoke in efficient, unemotional tones; just giving me the facts.

'When Max radioed in what happened, we mobilised. I'd been preparing contingency plans for some time. We were ready to start bombing.'

'Bombing?' I held her hand.

'We couldn't. Until we knew where you were. I mean, you obviously weren't… I mean, we would know that. If you were.'

'What did Max say?'

She didn't react. 'He was so upset, he wanted to mobilise his whole army. His people. Imagine that, the whole American Atlantic Fleet, ready to invade France for you. An American fleet in the Channel.'

I heard the inflection in her voice. I knew what she was thinking. About the American Atlantic Fleet mobilising in the English Channel.

'Don't you do anything to Max,' I insisted. 'Or Felice.'

I lay back and stared at the expensive oak panelled ceiling. 'I don't want you touching them. In fact I don't want you doing anything without telling me. In fact, from now on you don't do anything without my permission.'

Mum loomed over me. I felt vulnerable, all this stuff sticking out of my arms. Perhaps she realised that I wasn't the same Anthony who had gone over in that boat.

'I need to get out of bed,' I said.

'Don't tell me you're growing up,' she said. She looked round the room, as if someone might be listening. 'He has some of his people here now. You know, Americans. Military. He has bodyguards. His own subjects.'

'Do nothing,' I told her. Something occurred to me. 'What happened to Channon? His other bodyguard?' The beautiful Channon.

'Max gave her up to our people,' she said. 'I wasn't there but I think they threw her overboard. In the end.'

'About Max,' I told mum. 'Do nothing.'

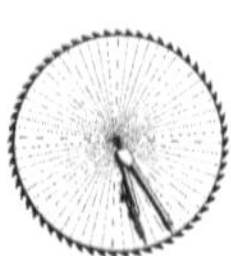

Channon. The lovely Channon. It was about now, as once again I lay in a hospital bed with nothing to do but think, that I understood that my relationships with women were not always entirely successful. That they would never be successful. Channon. Toni. Was I only going to be turned on by women I didn't possess? Then there was Penny (I had almost forgotten her yet at the time been so much in love), even little Alison Locke who gave me her life so willingly. The names were becoming interchangeable; their commonality endorsed by their tendency to die horribly. I began to understand that the only real relationships that would work with me would be the most shallow. If nothing else, at least the lady in question would walk away alive. I understood the future was going to look very lonely. I had no idea then how lonely. No wonder I was so pleased to see Emma. If only that had worked out. I think I would have been happy again. I think that would have done me.

I was a new Anthony! Up and running in a couple of weeks. No more hospital beds for me. Clearly, my body was used to being on the brink of death. Malnutrition and a busted rib was nothing. I had matters of state to attend to.

I arranged a briefing in my drawing room. I liked South African Rodney's décor: all tasteless paintings of the veldt, Zulu spears and a miniature stuffed gazelle standing in a corner. I felt very… elder statesman. I even had a butler serving us drinks on a silver tray. He was a small, silent man with little round spectacles who stood in the corner at attention like butlers are supposed to.

Max was excitable. When he walked in, he seemed ten years older. He was wearing the same old crumpled liberal college professor clothes. Less than a father figure; he now resembled a grandfather. There were tears in his eyes as he rushed to embrace me.

Mind, I looked a little different myself. Gone were the t-shirts and pot belly. Apart from the odd bandage, I was smart and sleek in my dark designer jacket and jeans. The starvation and enforced labour had built me up. I even had a faint six pack. I was not going to get sand kicked in my face. 'You look incredibly well,' Max said.

'I guess the outside world agrees with me.'

He had three men with him. In uniform. Bodyguards. He saw me look at them.

'You want them outside?' he asked.

'If you're okay with Jeeves here?' I jerked a thumb at the butler.

'Fine. Whatever suits you, Anthony.'

'The hall will be fine,' I said and watched Max wave a hand and three suspicious burly men walk out.

Max clicked his laptop and a fifty-five inch LCD screen on the wall hummed into life. He was going full Angstrom PowerPoint. He started his presentation. I saw he was truly horrified by the events in Europe. He personally suffered over every burnt body. I think Max took the exterminations as a personal affront.

'Satellites have been tracking extended lines of people moving into France from Spain, Italy and Germany; even Scandinavia and the fringes of some of the Balkan countries. The lines get longer every day. An exodus, if you like.'

'More like the Pied Piper.' I quite liked the Pied Piper line. I had been practising it.

'She wants them burned on her own soil,' said Max. 'Utterly psychotic.'

'How long before she gets everyone?' I asked.

'She's not going to stay in France,' said Max.

I sat back. Let that sink in. As he intended. I tried not to give away what I was thinking; a new experience for me.

'You're right,' I said at last. 'We need to act. What have you got in mind?'

Max nodded at the big television he had set up. Sweet little graphics of Europe popped up; full of arrows and letters.

'The joint chiefs are planning an invasion scenario right now. They're waiting in the study for you to sign off. In brief: we start with carrier-borne missiles, with airstrikes to nullify their air power. We send in the Blackhawks and hit that village hard straight away to make sure we take down Target One. Hopefully we will hit the lady herself. Maybe they are stupid enough to have kept her in the church. Once that has been expedited, the second wave is a seaborne invasion. That should only be a backup. You and I move in to recondition the remaining population. We share the continent equally, assuming you agree to my regeneration strategy. I want everything to be fair between us. Our troops, in theory, will work only as reorientation guides. End of story. We take Felice Beata out of the equation and an entire population is instantly saved.'

'Won't the French have thought of this?' I asked.

'Well, this is Plan A. If the first strike fails, and the French air force resist, we'll be into full-scale aggression. In that contingency we have to assume their nuclear potential is mobilised.'

'Which means all-out war,' I said. 'And your fleet sitting in my back garden.'

For an instant, Max looked thrown. He shook his head. 'Not at all. I've been over this. Your Royal Navy assumes executive command of the operation. I will personally stay in the UK, to share the risk. Call it… I don't know. Atonement. For the mistake in France.'

He looked at me expectantly. I think he was genuinely afraid. Scared he had overreached himself.

'I believe you, Max,' I said. 'You never know: the first strike might work. I mean, they were pretty disorganised over there. It's got to be worth a try.'

Max could afford to be nice, now he had got his way. 'Anthony, I don't mean to be facetious but I've got to say, the experience over there appears to have done you some good.'

I smiled. 'Why thanks, Max. Let's have some tea.'

I waved at the butler who rang a bell.

'I feel bad for Felice,' I said. 'I mean, she's just a senile old woman. It's not really her fault.'

'It's her life against the millions she's in the process of exterminating,' said Max.

I agreed. 'Are you sure that when she goes we can just walk in and, you know, get them for ourselves? I mean: how do we know that's what happens? I mean, you had that girl in, where was it, Miami…'

Max nodded.

'Is that what happened after you disposed of her? You could get her people?' I asked. He winced at my clinical method of expression.

'The minds of those she had glamoured were free. The effect is terminated on the death of the Siren.'

'So you just re-zapped them?'

Max smiled. He had always found the zap word amusing. 'That's right. Really, I had to. The shock of the glamour suddenly disappearing is profound. You know what happens. The trauma induces huge mental damage. I had to re-imprint the people in Miami to keep them safe. What is done cannot be undone.'

The butler poured my tea into nice austere governmental-looking cups. I had chosen them to give weight to the meeting. To make this a formal occasion. 'So you just went in and took them.'

Max looked puzzled. 'In a way. Listen, Anthony. I don't want to be king of Europe. I don't want to be king of anywhere. That's not what I'm about. We are shepherds, not tyrants.'

I nodded at the butler. 'Thanks Max.'

Max sat back just as the butler unwound the cord from under his gloves. He pulled the leather strap tight and wrapped it round Max's neck.

The butler was calm as he pulled the cord tight. His spectacles glinted in the soft light. Max kicked his feet and dropped his tea cup. The china shattered on the wood panel floor.

The noise must have alerted Max's bodyguards as, outside the door, I heard silenced pistols and thumps as my hidden guys took them out.

Max stared at me and his eyes grew larger and larger. His tongue squeezed out of his mouth, leaking drool.

My chest was tight. I had the perverse feeling that he was playing; that Max was holding his breath. He grabbed his assailant's wrists and tried to free himself. A waste of time: my butler was small but super-strong. That's why I had picked him.

When the job was done, the butler nodded. He went to the door and let Colonel Steve in. 'All done?' I asked.

Colonel Steve handed the silenced pistol to the butler, who unloaded the clip. 'Oh yes.'

Max sat in his chair. He seemed to be observing me through wide, blood-filled eyes. Colonel Steve, the butler and me took a moment. In fact, we *shared* a moment: a brief pause to absorb the momentous nature of my orders. The calm before the storm. You could say: we communed. 'Let her in then,' I told the butler.

He walked to a pair of expensive wooden double doors. Mum walked in; dressed formally; like Maggie Thatcher. She stopped, stunned, and looked at Max in his chair.

'I have to do this quickly,' I told her. 'You stay here.' I nodded to my colleagues.

'Anthony,' she asked. I stopped. There was a new tone to her voice; one I had never heard before. It was… respect.

'Yes, Mum?'

'That phone number. The one on the cell phone. The other Siren's number. Was it… was it his? Was it Max's number?'

I never told her. I smiled and rushed from the room. To this day I have never told anyone.

Max's joint chiefs were in the study. Obviously, his death had cut into their military composure. When Colonel Steve and I found them, they were howling in grief and confusion. I quickly put a stop to that. They were my men now and I needed them.

The doctors were ordered in. They had been waiting upstairs. My newly appointed chief doctor Conor made his entrance with his crack team of medics and psychologists. Their purpose was to ensure that I successfully re-glamoured those that had once been under Max's control.

Now calm and smiling, the joint chiefs marched out to their waiting cars. They had work to do. So did I.

Luckily Max's technological savvy meant I could sit in a single chair, look into a camera and have an instant link to every important individual in his organisation. I spent an hour sat in the chair, spelling out the plan and glamouring. It's not as easy as you might think; re-imprinting the whole of the United States of America. It had taken an awful lot of planning. The ones I zapped had their instructions to rebroadcast my links across their very efficient mass media. My experts predicted only ten per cent of the American people would be lost before I could reach them.

The power in my head loved it. The beast was hungry. After the weeks of terror and frustration, this was the real recuperation. That last half hour was the equivalent of making love to three voracious women at once. Using the glamour pumped endorphins into my system, just like after vigorous exercise or great sex. No wonder I felt good.

A naval officer saluted in front of me as we reached the street. 'Sir,' he said to me, 'we've been monitoring the American fleet. No reported hostile movements.'

'Yeah, well keep monitoring,' I replied. Not that that would make any difference. If I hadn't zapped the fleet, we were finished.

Only now did the euphoria of my mammoth zapping session start to wear off. I staggered against the back of the waiting Bentley. I stared at my distorted reflection in the polished black bodywork. I had done my bit. The rest was watching and waiting. Other people could handle the operation from now. The street was suddenly empty. There was no one about. No one at all.

My first plan, my first real big, wide-ranging plan, was complete. The immensity of the situation hit me and I felt sick. I pressed my hands onto the car, breathing heavily.

I heard footsteps on the pavement.

No.

No more. I wasn't going to be this sick, passive fool any more. I was different now. I was in charge. I stood up straight.

The naval officer stood watching me. He was hesitant; worried about my wellbeing. I would have to learn what these gold bands round their uniform wrists meant.

'Open the car door please,' I asked. I felt faint; blood rushing in my ears.

The officer obeyed.

The Bentley interior was exquisitely fashioned; textured patterns weaving in and out of each other. A single line ran through the whirls and swirls. It seemed to make sense of the whole design; gave it shape. In my confused state, I was hypnotised by its luxury.

'Your mother is asking for you, sir,' said the officer. 'Would you like to see her?'

'No,' I said and got in. The driver gunned the engine and drove me away.

Chapter 34

So without wanting it or doing anything much to get it, I inherited half the Earth.

I gave Max a decent burial. It was the least I could do. After all, he was my friend. More importantly, he was one of us: a Siren.

I didn't waste much time feeling guilty. I liked Max but he was asking for it from the day he turned up. Of course he was. Coming over here alone and unprotected; that was beyond reckless. What did he expect?

Mum had been right. As soon as I got the glamour, there was only one course open to me. Total power or nothing. It took six weeks in France for me to work it out.

Mum and I took an open-topped bus done up as a hearse to Max's funeral.

Thousands of pink faces looked up at me, mouths open, arms waving, making all that noise they make when you let them. I knew at last that I didn't give one shit. Well, what was the point in pretending? Nice idea but simply no longer true. They were them and I was me. If I learned anything I learned that. It really is all about me.

The bus reached Parliament Square and the noise was inhuman. So much cheering; so many voices. I stood and looked out over my people. They were like flowers in a field. You looked at one individual: saw the head, hair, eyes, mouth, teeth. Unique; different.

However, the mass was an entirely new entity; the individuals within creating a new dense body. I studied one then the next one and the next until I realised the details weren't important. They no longer mattered because from the top of the bus they were all the same.

Only one thing mattered, and that was that I lived. And I could only keep living by keeping the people mine. After we got to Mayfair from the funeral, the war people told me an F-87 stealth bomber had successfully dropped and detonated a tactical nuclear bomb onto the Autoire Valley. A covert specialist insertion stealth squad of US Special Forces, who had dropped in to observe the valley, confirmed ten seconds before the bomb exploded, that Felice Beata was still inside the same church. Those Europeans really were as stupid as they looked. I got what was left of them.

Mum changed. She knew her time was passing the moment I flexed a few muscles in the power department. I had by now got bored of Rodney's gaffe and decamped to Buck House and was busy making myself completely safe. I took the safety plans she had spent a year devising and modified them with extra paranoia. Months went by without me hearing from her. As far as I knew she was still shacked up in Saint James's with Sammy Krystle. She deserved a rest. I owed her everything. But she had been a little too quiet when I was lost in France.

My people checked out the post-Max situation in the USA. It was all going to plan. They had their time of turmoil and anxiety and chaos but from LA to New York, Seattle to Miami, my pre-recorded image and voice brought calm and order back to their lives. The survivors were incredibly grateful, so I am told. Quite obviously I wasn't going to go out there myself. If I had my way I would never leave London. And I always had my way.

My aim was still to leave the running of everything mundane to someone else. I never asked to be in charge and I didn't want it. The glamour existed for one reason, so Max had insisted: to bind humanity and stop them exterminating each other. Fair enough, in

Europe this hadn't quite worked out that way but, well, I flattered myself I now had the place running smoothly.

I got directly involved as little as possible. I'd done my part. I was the centre and everyone else could work around me. The worst thing I could do was interfere, so I didn't.

A few months later I moved out of Buckingham Palace. The place was so big and empty I felt disconnected from the rest of the world. Isolation was not what I was after. I like people and I wanted to be around them. Buck House had never featured in my dreams. That was never where I had wanted to live. Something much more modest would suit me better; so I moved to my present apartment in Bankside, just next to the Tate Modern.

I had architects convert one of those luxury glass and steel riverside blocks into the kind of home my imagination had always hankered after. I had the basement garage ripped out and converted into a gymnasium. One of my vows since escaping France was to get my body into excellent shape. I installed a gunnery range. It was always useful to learn new skills. Needless to say, Anthony Graves started out as a terrible shot. He couldn't hit a barn door. At first.

Slowly, the trusted advisors bothering me about oil imports or pollution in the Thames or whatever else, dropped off. I didn't really care and even if I did what the hell did I know? I wasn't an expert. If any of these situations got too difficult a few phone calls would soon put them to rights. The human race had a hymn sheet now, a purpose. And that purpose was to get on with it and leave me alone. I wasn't mad and I wasn't a dictator and I wasn't shovelling them into ovens. What more did they want?

I was surprised when mum called me. To my shame, she had dropped off my radar.

That would be because of my new girlfriend. Have I told you about Gina? Gina rolled up outside my apartment block one morning and announced herself. I would have been hard-pressed to miss her as she stepped out of her limousine stark bollock naked. Who said the glamour robbed people of their individuality?

Gina was a singer who had been married to a footballer and charmed her way through the checkpoints to win me over. Girls. Yes, girls.

I hadn't thought about girls for a while. Those thoughts about Toni and Penny and Alison and so on. They just wouldn't go away. I have heard fear and injury can do wonders for the sex drive, but not me. Crisis and drama have the opposite effect on the Graves libido. When I saw Gina I realised: I just needed the perfect woman, and here she was.

When mum said she wanted to see me, I brought Gina along. I knew mum wouldn't like her but sometimes you just have to live with it. Gina was tanned and sculptured and had a lovely tasteful tattoo of a gecko just above her right buttock. Mum should understand I needed someone just as much as she needed Sammy Krystle.

Christmas was on the way and at six the city was dark. You could see the stars a lot better now in London; now I'd laid down some ground rules about pollution.

Mum was waiting for me on her roof terrace. Gina and I were escorted into a small but tastefully furnished lift; surfacing in a grotto ringed with fairy lights and warmed by a batch of those patio heaters that they used to stick outside pubs. They gave the terrace a warm Christmassy glow. There were too many garish colours for my taste: purples and blues and livid greens. Carefully arranged underlit pot plants gave the stone flags a touch of unreality.

Gina looked great in the light, though. She was wearing this artificial fur coat I'd given her; designed by somebody Italian or other. Underneath: a little black dress, very Audrey Hepburn. My choice. Luckily, Gina was cool with being advised. She had been in a girl band and treated like shit so what I asked of her was a walk in the park (her words).

Mum was sat in a simple steel-frame chair. She was looking out over the city. The Thames gleamed below and I remembered, just out of the blue, the night I had spent with Max on Primrose Hill.

'Hi Mum,' I said. 'This is Gina.'

Mum turned. I couldn't read her expression.

'Hi Mrs Graves,' said Gina.

'How's Sammy?' I asked. We sat down. Gina rummaged in her handbag for those awful cigarettes she insisted on smoking. I had often thought about making her stop, but somehow I liked them. I liked the way they made her voice sound. Anyway, they kept her thin.

'He's dead,' said mum. She waved at a tray on a table. 'Wine? Tea? Something else?'

Her voice was so neutral it was disturbing. A little bit of me inside quailed, but I stayed quiet.

Gina, on the other hand, acted like she'd been shot. Her gold Slim Line lighter was paused between hand and mouth. 'Oh… my… God…'

'So what happened?'

Mum sat back. 'Seems getting himself freed from your influence wasn't quite the success we had imagined. He hung himself. I found him in the en-suite.'

There were tears in Gina's eyes. She leaned forward to touch mum's wrist. 'I'm so sorry,' she said. 'I just want you to know: I'm there for you.'

Mum looked at me.

'You don't like her?' I asked. 'Gina. My mother doesn't like you. Go away.'

Gina dropped her lighter and cigarette. 'Oh God, I'm so sorry, Anthony.'

She raced across the terrace. She didn't exactly throw herself over. It was more of an elegant, gymnastic leap over the railings.

Mum and I sat in silence. I still didn't know her. Not at all. She was a new creature, something else that appeared when I did. We were the last two unclouded minds in the UK. Probably in the western hemisphere. The others I could get, but my own mother? Perhaps that was why I had stayed away.

'You want me to try another one?' I asked. I didn't know what else to say.

Mum's eyes were shards of ice in the night. Her breath steamed. 'You want to know why I… have helped you? All this time. Why I protected you?'

I nodded. 'Okay.'

Still she couldn't cry. The breaths were quicker but there were no tears. 'I was… am… afraid. Of you. My own son. I could see straight away what you would have to do. And I didn't care as long as you didn't get me. I felt like I was in one of those dreams when you're running and running and the bad man is right behind you. Well, you've been behind me, whispering in my ear. You take. You consume. You took your father. You and all your kind. If you didn't get me, one of the others would, so I had no choice. I hoped that by helping you… I would be spared. I didn't care if you got everyone else. I just didn't want you to get me.'

She stood up. 'So now you know. God, I could smoke one of her cigs.'

I handed her the packet.

'Why are you telling me now?' I asked. 'You're safe. I don't have any need to…' Yeah, not the most tactful piece of reassurance. But it was still reassurance.

'No, Anthony. You do need to. Since, since Sammy went… I can't hide any more. I can't hide hating you. You aren't my son. Not since the day that filth got into you. You're something else. And soon I won't just be thinking that, I'll be doing something about it. You understand?'

Shit, tears were welling in my eyes. Whatever had happened, whatever I had done, this was still my mum talking. 'Please. Don't,' I said. I didn't want to hear this. Ever.

Mum was suddenly tender. 'I've wanted to tell you for a long time. I'm sorry.' She touched my hand. 'You were my son and I loved you.'

Suddenly, I was afraid. Stupid I suppose. What was she going to do? I mean: what was she going to do right now?

'Don't worry,' mum said, reading me straight away. 'It isn't going to come to that. I have a plan.'

Maybe she had stuck explosives all over the roof. Perhaps we were back to the sniper idea. I stood up, ready to run; ready to call for help. If only I had kept Gina around. She was pretty useless but at least she would have fought like the devil to protect me.

'You know you could stop me at any second,' she said. Mum lit the cigarette and took a puff. 'You never seemed to think about taking me over. I never knew why. And still all the while you had me terrified. I knew one day it would be my turn. It had to come. One awful day your voice would come worming into my head and that would be that. I would be gone.'

Suddenly, I realised her words were slurring, that she was losing focus, willing herself to speak. 'Mum, what have you done?'

'You could get inside my head with a thought and all that hate, that terror, would be gone.'

'No, mum. I couldn't, not you.'

'You don't have any choice.'

I had that sick feeling again. The feeling I remembered as powerlessness. Events were going to unfold as they unfolded. Mum was wearing a dark green coat and jeans. She had got rid of the finery.

'I want to pity you,' she said. 'I used to. You don't have any choice either, you know. You had to become what you now are. That doctor, what was his name… Angler? He thought the same but he also thought he could keep you as you were. As Anthony.'

Her eyes had a glazed look; something artificial was seeping into her brain.

'You're a force of nature, Anthony. A program, like winter or, I don't know, giving birth. And the boy you were before? Well.'

'Listen,' I said. 'What about what Max said? We could be the future. I, we, can be the way forward and that. For people and the world. We could save the planet. Be its caretakers.'

She smiled and I had to turn away. 'What you've done is frozen the world,' she said. 'Built a tomb; a pyramid. Engraved and carved in Anthony's image.' She giggled dreamily. 'Only this time no archaeologists will come and dig it all up in a thousand years because there won't be any more archaeologists. Because of you.'

'Mum, what have you taken?'

'You barely care *now*. Not about me and certainly not anyone else. How long before even that has gone? And you can't help it. With what happened to you, you have to become the creature you need to become to survive. It's just a matter of time.'

I stood up. Anger was balling up inside me. Anger and something else. The fear, the terror of being alone. I could see the years, the decades stretching ahead and no one to talk to. No one to be with.

'Listen, Mum, you know that won't happen. I'm still me. I'm still Anthony. Me and you, we've got everything. You could go away somewhere. Scotland. I'd leave you alone. I would. Remember Keano? Maybe he got away. I let him go. Maybe he found some Pacific atoll where no one can find him?'

'No, Anthony. You wouldn't. Finally, you would come for me.'

I took a step forward. She backed off, holding up an arm. Something in her system was coming to the boil. She was clumsy, fighting drowsiness. The wind gusted up on this freezing roof and she was so woozy she toppled.

'What are you doing?' I asked.

A funny smile came to her lips. 'I want to go off the roof. Any moment. And you can stop me. You'll have time to stop me. I got the doctor to mix up a cocktail, injected myself. To deal with any pain.'

'Don't be so bloody stupid. I wouldn't…'

'Why not? Why wouldn't you? Listen, Anthony. If you still have anything of my son in you, you won't stop me. I can't… I refuse to go on, waiting for the day.'

She was the one with the drugs but I went woozy. My legs melted beneath me. 'Please, Mum. I can't go on without you. You've done everything.'

She shook her head. She looked like she was about to fall asleep. 'Doesn't matter. I am… just part of… process. I think we've done well, you and I, don't you? We hid and kept you quiet and waited until there were none left. We got the whole world. Don't stop me. I don't want to be like them.'

I wanted to tell her I loved her. But you can't, can you? I mean, some people seem to say it a hundred times a day until the word is meaningless, but not the Graves family. I doubt if I ever told her.

'What about the others?' I said instead. 'The Sirens. How am I supposed to deal with them?'

'No,' said mum. 'There is only you. I've been completely wrong. I have betrayed my own species. We should have destroyed you when we could.'

And she ran over the lip of the roof to that black twinkling sea. And she was right. I had plenty of time to stop her. But I didn't.

Chapter 35

Two years later, somebody invaded. That would make it two years ago. I think that's when they came.

I spent those initial two years drunk. Drunk pretty much all of the time. I was in a dark place. After mum's death, I put the whole of the western world into mourning. A blight of depression descended on my half of the globe. Spontaneous demonstrations of keening and wailing kicked off everywhere, especially in the US, where she had never even been. San Francisco renamed itself after her. (Although: 'San Graves'? Really?)

What happened to mum made me think. And I didn't want to think any more. So I watched a lot of TV, played computer games, neglected my health and stayed indoors. London was ticking over. I didn't want to know. Days blurred up, each one the same. Alcohol reduced the world to a manageable, human level. Drink kept reality in perspective. I seriously considered the possibility of going back to work but I knew I wouldn't see it through. What was the point? It wouldn't have been real. Sitting and drinking was, well, it was all I could be bothered with.

The first news of the invasion came when one of the girls in the apartment said there was an admiral buzzing my downstairs buzzer; wanting permission to come up. He was insisting urgency was required. It would bloody have to be required to disturb me in my misery. The girl asked if she should tell this admiral to piss off.

Perhaps the novelty appealed because the next thing I remember is two American uniformed military chaps standing in my front room enquiring about my health and telling me I didn't need to panic. The elder was a bald, tough looking old buzzard who turned out to be this admiral of which my girl had spoken. Admiral Franklin R. Futz of the United States Navy saluted me.

The admiral took off his cap. 'Sorry to bother you, Anthony, but we have a situation. May we appraise you?'

'Feel free to appraise me of anything you like, Admiral old fellow.' I smiled, enjoying this. Whenever I spoke to Americans I could never resist the urge to act all upper-class stiff upper lip. I held up a bottle half full of spiced rum. 'Be my guest, chaps.'

Admiral Futz nodded and his junior, the equally impeccably groomed Commodore Bob D'Amato, cleared the empty bottles and joysticks off my expensive living room table. Bob plonked a laptop in their place. I was uncomfortably reminded of the time when Doctor Angler had come to my house in Croydon, all those centuries ago.

'These are satellite surveillance images, Anthony,' said the admiral. 'The Mid-Atlantic Ocean. 2200 hours GMT yesterday.'

The picture on the screen was a neat little grid full of white lines and numbers. The digital ocean painted a neutral grey. A grey void spotted with thick black blobs.

'Ships?' I asked.

'Convoys,' said the admiral. 'With armed fighter escorts.'

'Convoys? Plural? As in: more than one convoy?'

'Commodore D'Amato here is OC Intelligence.'

D'Amato took his place in the spotlight. He looked like a man who had been waiting for this moment all his life. He was an efficient, sleek-uniformed officer with steel specs and a thin moustache the Americans seem to favour. 'Can't believe I'm finally meeting you, Anthony. An honour to serve.' I guess he would have spelled that: *honor*.

D'Amato pressed a computer key and a list of names began to scroll down one of the screens. 'Ship registrations are Arabic, Chinese, Indian, Malay, everything. We even have eight of our own decommissioned aircraft carriers; God knows how they got them afloat. Super tankers, frigates, container ships, ferries, pleasure boats. There's every conceivable kind of vessel coming our way.'

'A meticulous operation,' said Futz. 'All this was routine shipping until three days ago, when simultaneously they all altered course.'

D'Amato flashed up some impressive graphics. Big digital blobs covering a blue background. They swirled a bit and joined up.

'This fleet is led by three super tankers and protected by what seems to be the whole Indian Navy,' he said. 'We're getting intel reports most of the civilian traffic was requisitioned via Dubai through third party intermediaries. No traces. This is some serious covert long-range planning. Our Intel in the area didn't pick up anything.'

'Weapons. They're carrying weapons, right? Missiles, bombs, all that?'

Futz coughed. He was suddenly coy. 'Our forces under Mr Angstro– under the previous leadership were quick to neutralise strategic threats. We have been implementing measures for years. He didn't want other powers using nukes on us. These boats are full of people. It's a battering ram.'

I looked at the officers. I needed a drink. Another drink.

'You're joking.'

They weren't, obviously. Joking wouldn't be in Futz's nature.

I was getting bored now. Bored and irritated. These bastards had frightened me. So far I hadn't heard anything to warrant getting me out of my home. I had been happy tucked up in my apartment block. 'So, sort them out,' I said.

D'Amato looked at the Admiral and I knew they were going to say something awful.

'We don't know if we can,' he said.

'You… you don't know?'

The Admiral took a deep breath. 'We simply don't have the ordnance to hit or sink them all. They have too many ships. And some serious air cover.'

'You attacked them already?'

Futz looked almost hesitant. 'In self-defence only. They engaged our reconnaissance aircraft in hostile action as soon as they approached.'

'And now you tell me? What's taken you so long?'

The Admiral seemed puzzled. 'The Prime Order.'

I felt disquiet. Should I know this?

'The Supreme Exec Committee wouldn't give me the veto so I took it upon myself to visit you today. I'm sorry, Anthony. Mr D'Amato agrees with me. I may have disobeyed you.'

D'Amato unclipped an automatic pistol. 'We stand ready to take our own lives.'

'Never mind that! Put it away! What the hell is a Supreme Exec Committee? What's a Prime Order?'

The officers looked at each other. Futz didn't even seem relieved as he re-holstered his weapon.

'We operate under a strict mandate,' he said. 'The Prime Order is: you are never to be disturbed in defence matters. Your personal directive to the Supreme Commander. 18th June Twenty–'

'What? I said that?'

'However, as you also ordered that you be the sole initiator of aggressive action, the SEC was set up to rule on interpretations. Until now, the protocols have never been tested.'

'They failed,' said D'Amato. 'Alerting you is the safest course of action to protect you.'

I fell back onto my large leather sofa. What was going on out there? What world did they live in? How was it these people existed?

I threw the glass away. It shattered somewhere near the television. Never mind another drink. I had to clear my head of the alcohol fumes. I was back in the shit.

'Okay. We'll talk about that later. What about these bastards in the sea?'

D'Amato continued. 'They have limited air power but what pilots they have are suicidal. In our first engagement, their planes simply targeted our planes and blew themselves up.'

'They don't expect to survive,' Futz butted in. 'We have three submarines tracking their fleet. We act now and we can reduce their numbers by sixty per cent. No more without tactical nuclear weapons and they're too close to our shores for that. We can't risk…'

I couldn't believe it. 'What do you mean you can't get them all? You're the biggest fucking navy in the world!'

Admiral Futz remained calm. 'Anthony, I'm sorry but the numbers…'

'What numbers? How many boats are there?'

'Eighteen thousand six hundred and thirty-two,' said D'Amato. 'Originally.'

I dropped the bottle. I stared at my officers. 'Eighteen thousand? How… how can there be that many boats in the world?'

They looked at me. They wanted me to give an order.

'What do they want? And where are they headed?' Although I already knew.

The Admiral nodded. 'Here.'

Eventually, I asked: 'How many people?'

The Admiral stated the figure. Perhaps a big number needed a big rank. 'We estimate that fleet could bear a carrying capacity of some two million people.'

'We have a week,' said D'Amato.

I felt none of that old panic that once would have gripped me. The fact that two million soldiers were heading my way with the express purpose of killing me was just another piece of news. I was ready.

I okayed more air strikes. Every plane, every warship, every scud missile capable of getting to them was launched, from both sides of the Atlantic. The carnage was incredible. Surveillance aircraft provided footage; lit up in night vision green. Flares, fire, explosions, bursting metal and bodies by the ton; all toppled into burning water. Ships cracked and shattered and split; their human cargo spilling into the pounding sea in great packets of humanity. The water, soaked in oil, burned in a fury of flame and smoke. Horizon to horizon was a cauldron of death; a victory phrase from the papers the next day. They weren't wrong.

However, through giant burning waves, the ships kept coming.

I had to admire their bravery, especially when I was informed that this gigantic invasion fleet was a diversionary force. They were not intended to be anything but a distraction.

My air marshals arrived one day to tell me that twenty air liners, including three Boeing 747s, had been hijacked and flown straight at

London and no prizes for guessing their intention. This was the real attack. Someone knew Anthony Graves was in London and they really wanted him dead.

According to Admiral Futz, the opposition hoped we had committed so many defences into stopping the fleet one of the stolen aircraft would find a hole in our protective net. An Airbus nearly did, getting as close as Berkshire. The pilot managed to avoid the barrage of fire from pursuing Tornado fighters before finally being hit by a surface-to-air missile and crashing into Reading. That was a relief.

After six days I was given the bad news. Despite its secondary nature and the carnage wreaked upon it, the mauled remains of the gigantic enemy fleet would inevitably reach the UK.

I went on television and explained the situation. I asked for volunteers to defend me. The reaction was unanimous. Spontaneous marches, loyal civilians, snaked out from all the major cities and headed towards Wales, identified as the most likely landing zone. From Edinburgh to Grimsby to Manchester to Birmingham they went. Smaller boats were launched from all the ports to harass the ragged invasion force before it reached shore. Fishing boats and pleasure cruisers, dinghies and cross-channel ferries; they rammed into that ragged, battered fleet. A fleet that just would not sink.

This time the cameras fully caught the brutality of the fighting. The sea churned with oil and blood. Ships were boarded and the fighting went hand-to-hand. English men and women, many still in their work clothes, fought with guns and swords and clubs and any tool that human beings have traditionally employed to hit each other. The media claimed the fighting was so fierce you could hear the battle in London, but I never did.

Wreckage was examined; intelligence gleaned and a point of origin seemed to be located: papers written in the mountains of Pakistan were found in many of the boats. As to the Siren behind the invasion, my intelligence chaps never found out. To this day I have no idea. No demands were ever issued and no transmissions were made. The invading force, the biggest in history, just came. And despite all our best efforts, despite everything we threw at them, that fucking fleet landed. At Swansea.

Actually, I had a great view of the landings. The army stationed a camera unit in a heavily protected concrete bunker on the shore. At first there was very little to look at. We had cleared the beaches. The distant tide lapped gently in a grey light. The only moving objects were the grey Welsh sea, the occasional gull and, every now and then, a crew member sorting out some technical glitch with the camera. We had discussed setting up automatic cameras but a crew would provide a bit of flexibility in the coverage of the event. They had orders to remain filming until overwhelmed.

Tired of just hearing reports, I had decided to be flown to the action. Well, near it: a field east of Bristol just off the M4, a couple of hundred miles away from any actual danger. My people needed me to stay safe. I wanted to be a good role model.

A young blonde woman, presumably a runner, appeared on camera to give us a smile and a thumbs-up. I ordered the generals to get her airlifted off the beach. Call me soft, but I liked her.

Finally, a thick wall of oily smoke appeared on the horizon. It grew closer and bigger until it blotted out the light. I got quite frightened. Without warning, there was the sound of a ship's horn and a huge civilian tanker burst through the fog and ground itself onto the beach. Spray and shingle and sand erupted as it ploughed forward. The noise overloaded the camera microphones. In a wall of feedback the ship drove into the sand at incredible speed and, with a gigantic shudder, stopped. Explosive fire burst from its hulk. Bodies toppled over its decks. I shrieked.

I looked around. I was still inside the tent, all openings blacked out so we could see the LCD screen, a big screen they used to use to show important football matches.

One of the generals asked if I was all right. I told him I was fine. Now it had started, the invasion was exciting rather than frightening. I knew already I would watch it all again once it was all over.

We cut to a helicopter view. RPGs with their filthy plumes blasted up at us from the other boats. Other ships were looming out of the smoke now, covered in scurrying black smudges. Those aboard were fighting each other to get onto the beach. The helicopters were called off ready for the air strike and we cut back to the beach camera.

The invaders poured out of the grounded ships. They didn't look much like people any more. They were stripped and filthy, smeared with blood and draped in weapons. I heard the screeching of deafening aircraft engines. Blossoms of mud and sand began flowering up across the screen. The black invaders scattered and fell apart, exterminated as they landed, pounded back into the boiling sea. The wall of smoke parted like curtains under the concussion to reveal exploding boats, foam-lashed sand and hundreds of people tossed high into the air.

The cold, unflinching camera sets everything in an electric present tense. I am on that beach; observing. The teeming horde of humanity spills from the wrecks into churning blood-washed surf. They remind me of ants pouring out of their mound of earth.

The machine stands its ground as the first attacking wave flies off. The beach seems to shake with expended energy; recovering from a dreadful trauma. At last, there is movement again. Smudges focus into screaming men, women and children: the few that the impartial forces of probability have decreed will survive the initial carnage. Without pause or hesitation, they charge over the gouged bodies of their colleagues towards the film unit. The image judders under the weight of the invading force. The crew, my crew, screams and the camera is knocked over, its cracked lens facing the smoke-wreathed sky.

At this point when I replay this footage, as I often do in my screening room, I find a couple of long seconds that I cannot understand. The sky fills the screen, shapes shake the camera but suddenly the sound on the microphone clears and over the clamour I hear something very strange. It must be a glitch because for a few moments there is nothing but the sound of laughter. One person, I can't tell if it's a man or a woman, but somebody, somewhere laughing. I don't like the sound. It is wild, unhinged and there isn't an ounce of humour. I wince. Always. I can't bear to listen. Who the hell is it?

Hearing that laugh for the first time in my darkened army tent, I remember I experienced an unbidden urge that suddenly manifested in my stomach. It too was a laugh: a mirthless complementary chuckle. A giggle that forced its way up and out of my throat and felt more powerful and scarier even than the glamour. And the name of that laugh was madness.

I keep watching. The screen cuts to the observational helicopter camera. A second wave of ground attack aircraft scream out of clouds and are gone in less than a second. There is a beat and then a line of liquid fire that cuts surgical incisions through advancing lines on the beach. I can see the concrete bunker, swarming with people. The fire grows awesome and huge in the lens and then we cut to a harmless blue screen.

I am back in the tent. I am safe. A very tempting cooking smell wafts in from the kitchen area.

'Shit!' I recall shouting. Not exactly dignified. Very Anthony Graves.

Admiral Futz returned a clipped smile. 'Efficient,' he said.

We hit them for two days solid. I am told the mass of earth shifted by the shelling surpassed Flanders in the First World War.

Despite that, some of the enemy kept coming. Ships continued to land up and down the coast, enough to matter. Some even escaped Swansea. They had nothing but rudimentary weapons but they would not give in. I wasn't surprised. With war on this planet, morale was no longer a factor.

By now we were wondering just what kind of mind would initiate such a wasteful method of attack. My psychologists could only speculate that this Siren was a child, insane or very, very ignorant. Perhaps he was some peasant in a remote Indian village? Maybe he was a mountain-dwelling Afghan teenager? A cloistered and clothed-up Muslim bride? Whoever, they needed to shoot their advisors. If I had been them, Anthony Graves would be dead by now. My guys suggested I return to London as the final mop-up got underway. I agreed. They were landing in the Bristol Channel and that was just too close.

I lifted off just as a fleet of ground attack jets were flying over to drop lines of incendiary bombs on the enemy. I saw the red glow rising up in the night sky. The Severn Bridge was an inferno.

Back in London, at the Admiralty, my generals took me to the mess for briefing and a meal. I asked to be served only what my soldiers on the ground ate. I had seen in a film that this is what leaders did to command the respect of their men. I don't remember whether I liked the food or not.

As I ate, my generals filled me in on the enemy progress. I tried my best to understand the terminology.

I was shown footage, which at least gave me some sort of frame of reference. Ninety per cent of the fleet had been sunk at sea. That was sixteen thousand ships and one million eight hundred thousand people burned and sunk and drowned. Even now, years later, the sea is so thick with debris and wreckage we have been forced to close the shipping lanes.

Once at the River Severn, the mauled and mutilated invasion force ran into my civilian militias. The generals and admirals had suggested we save the professional army for a last ditch defence of London, if required.

My call to arms had gathered a huge block of people. There were few weapons but that was compensated for by sheer weight of numbers.

The ten thousand or so remaining invaders got across the burned ruins of the Severn Bridge and straight into a two mile thick wall of defending bodies. Within less than a day every enemy soldier was dead. They made a good account of themselves I am told. Over a million of my own were gone; including those sunk and shot down at sea. We never needed the professional army. The invasion was over.

There was talk of retaliation, of retracing steps and exacting revenge. They talked about nipping the next one in the bud. I told them not to bother. I knew the Siren responsible had already given me their best shot. What did they have left?

Besides, I hadn't lived this long by getting all proactive. Doing nothing was precisely what I was best at. You never knew: at some future point, I might need this anonymous Siren for company.

The incident was a refreshing overhaul of my defences. I found the experience personally refreshing as well. It reminded me there was a world outside myself. London was much emptier, for although few actual Londoners had been part of that militia, I chose not to let those that went return. I preferred a more spacious city. I liked more room.

Months later, the generals came to the apartment and gave me the final score. All our planning had come off with a top class success rate. Our armed forces were basically intact and not a nuclear weapon had been fired. I praised them, which they liked.

Our civilian losses were high, well over a million dead and another half a million that probably wouldn't survive the gruelling reconstruction, body burying and living in the countryside without aid or shelter. That was regrettable, but we needed to keep the military at full strength. I promised a number of commemorative events to honour their sacrifice. We decided it was best for the wounded not to hang around and use up resources, so that actually did push us over the two million mark.

I was saddened to hear that Commodore D'Amato had been killed: right at the end his intelligence jet was knocked out by a surface-to-air missile fired from the ragbag army.

As for the invaders, well, there wasn't a single survivor. Not one. Doesn't take a genius to work out they had been given strict instructions concerning capture.

I understand that the loss of life was appalling, although these days I find it increasingly hard to believe that the invasion really ever happened. It was such a long time ago. A feeling of disconnection is to be expected. After all, I only saw it on television.

Chapter 36

I have been giving this story the once over as the pages ease themselves onto the printer tray. Correct me if I'm wrong but I have a dark feeling that perhaps it is possible I don't come across particularly well. These are my words; this is my writing but what I read is unforgiving. The chapter describing my early life before the glamour has disappeared entirely.

This guy, this Anthony Graves, he's like a passive, harsher, stupider version of me. I must have made a mistake. I must have written it wrong. When I'm back in London I'll gather some top authors to have a look over the text. Help me work out where I've made the mistakes.

Until I read it, I was enjoying myself. I've enjoyed writing by the sea. There was something satisfying in watching the chunks of my life fossilised in ink. If it hadn't been for the content and everything about me, finishing would have given me a real sense of achievement.

I don't know how but it's like the writing is judging me. I thought I was writing to the other Anthony, the one in the parallel universe, but I'm starting to suspect it's the other way round. I suspect he is sitting in his comfortable, normal parallel universe and judging me.

I have to face facts. I haven't treated my subjects as well as I could. It's been difficult.

I have made a decision. I'm going to kill myself. I am going to kill myself tomorrow. Shouldn't be that difficult. After all, I have just read about how so many other deaths, suicides or otherwise, have been caused by my hand. It's all there in the book.

I'll stop writing soon. Well, tomorrow in fact. I've finished printing. (I'll do this current paragraph back in London. Store the file on the cloud. Oh, and the memory stick just in case.) I won't miss the writing.

I pile my few personal belongings into the Aston for the drive back to London: water bottle, iPad, packet of Marlboro Lights (yes, sorry). I look back at the cottage; my Sussex writer's retreat. It's a nice spring afternoon and the gardeners have done a marvellous job. That dappled grey stone gleams in a fresh sun. A sea breeze ripples the hedges. Nature is at work. For reasons not entirely clear to me, before I go I decide to destroy the place.

My guys in the marina drive a shotgun down and I spend a pleasant hour shooting the cottage up. With the small rooms still ringing with noise and foggy with cordite smoke, I build a fire on the kitchen flagstones. I find an old can of paraffin in the shed and off we go.

The flames take hold of the old wooden beams and I watch until the roof collapses. I don't know the meaning of this destruction, the symbolism, but I'm sure the critics and professors of literature to whom I bequeath this book will.

I drive to Chichester railway station. I was going to say goodbye to my people at the palace but time is running along.

I blag a laptop on the train and write a bit more, trying to make sense of what I've done here. The ream of paper bearing my life story sits in a bag on the seat next to me. Three hundred and sixty pages of double spaced Times New Roman.

I am disappointed that a reader will learn very little about the real me. All you will get is the fiction. The Anthony Graves represented is a passive, dull, even sadistic character. I don't know much about writing but I do know you're supposed to make the main guy as energetic and active as you can. This Anthony just sits back and lets everyone else sort out his problems. He ends up ruling the place by luck, hiding and ending up the last one in the game. No one is going to know anything about what I was really like, all the innovative and creative things I did. And when I'm gone, that knowledge is going to be important.

So let's make some amends before I go. Anthony. What was he like? As a human being? Let's get some questions down, maybe that will help.

What music does Anthony like? Not really bothered. No, I can't say that. Let's put: The Beautiful South. No, that's rubbish; I come across like an accountant. Favourite food? Oh man. Come on.

This writing, it's hard. I'm boring myself.

Put some facts down. That's what I'm going to have to do when I get back to London. Enough. Save and close the word processing program. Not now. Not when I can catch up with episodes of Sherlock on the iPlayer all the way to Victoria.

Jesus Christ I am so sick of the whole fucking country. For example: the manager at the marina. Was there any need to call me to ask if I needed the power boat back to London? I mean, come on! Duh! I was *at the train station*. I was *getting on a train*. Then the dullard put Chris the boat pilot on. Chris wanted to know what *he* should do. I told him to drive out into the English Channel and sink the frigging boat. Then I told the manager to burn his stupid marina down. And he could stay inside and eat a banana while he was at it. What do they want?

Tell me, book: is it just me?

I try and take stock of my achievements. I read somewhere that this is a positive mental exercise.

What did the glamour really get me? Okay, I claim the willing obedience of some three hundred million people here and in America. That's a plus. However, the curse of the glamour appears to be that if I try and actually do something with them, I'll end up killing a large percentage. So, I can rule the world as long as I don't actually do anything.

My purpose here appears to be that of a queen bee. I'm the biggest bastard in the hive and everything revolves around me. My subjects are the workers and fliers and drones collecting the pollen and making the honey and going the extra mile to keep me fat and happy and content. I don't work. In fact, the less I interfere the better. My job is just… to be. Just sit in the middle of the hive and let them get on with it.

Friends? Forget it; you're the biggest and there's only room for one. Companions? Lovers, even? Loads but none of them provide love. Not really. The other Sirens? They are out there somewhere.

Obviously the most important aspect of a suicide is that it shouldn't hurt. Not at all. If pain is involved then I think it's a safe bet Anthony Graves will be unlikely to see his intention through. In fact, you can take that as a given.

I've spoken to Conor on the phone and he has a number of suggestions. Once he had got through the grief when I told him what I have determined to do. The daffy bastard made me cry. He loves me, you know.

I did have the idea of going out in a blaze of glory. I thought I would dose myself up so my body was completely numb then gather my guns together, get up on my apartment roof and let rip. I would release them all from my influence. I figured I would have been able to take a fair few down before they overwhelmed me. Before they tore me apart. That would be a fitting, poetic end to my reign. But in the end, I couldn't face that. All that hatred suddenly let loose. I would prefer to go out without any fuss. Or is it just too much effort?

I'm back in my apartment now. Six years I have been in charge. Seven years since the start of this little joke on the world.

I have stopped wondering why. Although two hundred people simultaneously getting the glamour was interpreted by so many to be a deliberate indication of intention, I don't think so. Did somebody pull that trigger? Evolution? Aliens? God?

If this was god's answer, he didn't really think it through. Why dole out the glamour so randomly? Couldn't we Sirens have been just a little bit prepared? Why didn't somebody tell us what we were supposed to do? Would that really be too much to ask?

I look over the freshening Thames, at London living its life, and realise there was no reason at all. The Sirens happened because things happen.

I try to convince myself that I'm going to kill myself tomorrow because I feel guilty about all the bad deeds I've committed. That the world will be better off without me.

But it's not that. Finally, it's not that at all. I just can't stand being on my own any more.

The book has done me in. It has brought home just how lonely I am. The Emma experiment was doomed from the start. There is no one for me. We Sirens cannot have equals.

Funny, out of all of my old friends I miss Toni the most. She was a sly dog and you couldn't trust her an inch but that's what I liked about her. I wish she hadn't fallen apart as she did. I wish Major Pete hadn't murdered her. I wish Felice hadn't got her. I wish I hadn't let her go. Yeah, I wish a lot of things.

I think back to that house we took over in Hammersmith. The fun we had when I first had the glamour. Yeah, those were good times. The best. We were wicked.

Early this morning, I went out and wandered the streets. I went over the Millennium Bridge, past St Paul's, up to Bank and turned left to Holborn. I walked through busy, busy streets and all the people knew who I was and they all said hi. I don't understand why I felt even more alone.

I walked all the way to Euston and went up in the tower to my old office where the whole thing kicked off. The tower is now a shrine to my divine origins so the council have left the offices untouched. The guard let me in and activated the lifts. Instinctively I reached for my magnetic plastic pass to open the security turnstile but of course… just stupid.

Up on the twenty-second floor there was the same old view. London stretched out like a living map. Familiar but now utterly strange; my memories just an old film. Dust caked the terminal where I had been sitting when the glamour popped into my head.

This is the geographical position in time and space where me and my projected reader Anthony parted company; the bifurcation, the crossroads, the parting of the ways.

The people down below still travel to work, drive cars, eat in the restaurants, watch TV, procreate. Only now they do all these things for me and, correct me if I'm wrong, they seem a hell of a lot happier.

I haven't been that terrible, surely. I'm not Felice shovelling them into ovens, or whoever it was in Pakistan who sent two million over to die for nothing, or Max who threw away a whole population, or Paula in Florida who burned cities to the ground. I just got on with my life and let the people get on with theirs. I haven't done anything except give the people on this planet a reason to live.

But my book tells me different. If I was that other Anthony reading what I had written, I come off like a monster, just as mum predicted. I'm the villain.

So sod it. They can have their lives back. Perhaps another Siren will move in and take them straight away but at least it won't be me. Maybe they'll go crazy in some other way. I have a theory that most of the glue I have poured into their heads will clear. London, you will continue. I allow you to continue.

After lunch, Conor arrives with an expert anaesthetist and together they lay out the options. I witness a PowerPoint demonstration concerning the death of Anthony Graves.

I choose drugs, nothing flashy. The anaesthetist recommends the safest cocktail and I go with his suggestion. There is a long scientific name to what they will inject.

I shake the anaesthetist's hand. I then warn Conor that he must be ready for the disorientation my death will undoubtedly trigger. He tries to talk me out of my decision. He begs me to stay alive. I thank him but explain that there is no choice.

As he and the anaesthetist leave, I catch a glimpse of myself in the hallway mirror. You know, I'm looking pretty bloody good. I think of the pudgy slob I used to be and decide that whatever being a Siren means, physically the process has done me the world of good. I am beautiful.

My last evening passes with another grand sunset over my capital. Boats full of mourners-in-waiting move silently up and down the Thames. I watch the landscape from my roof until it's too dark to see. My chef Jamie prepares a really top class meal. Lobster and a top notch wine. I hope when he's free again he won't think too badly of me. The meal is delicious. Jamie clears away the dinner plates. I thank him.

I retire to my couch, power up the laptop and here I am again, writing. My final entry.

I'm not worried.

Yes, I'm scared, I'll grant you that, but scared is different. I'm good at scared; I'm the world's expert in scared.

I've polished off the Château Lafite '42, another vintage bottle less in the world, so writing this is getting tricky. I've got a wall of warm cotton wool growing in my head that's stopping the thinking process rather nicely. Conor comes into the room, holding the case containing the phial and syringe. He smiles, like a sympathetic family lawyer; a kindly uncle.

I just want to get these few words out of the way. Now that I'm running out of time getting my thoughts down seems important again. Conor sits next to me on my black leather couch. He rolls plastic gloves over his manicured hands, opens the case and attaches the needle to the syringe. Soon he'll be flicking the tip and squirting liquid out.

I'm looking at myself in the little hand mirror I've popped on the glass table next to the empty bottle of wine. I still look good.

I wonder how *you* look, Other Anthony. Are you tucking up in your little Croydon bedroom after a bland supper with mum and dad and the same old telly and maybe a DVD from Amazon for later? Have you had your teeth capped and your hair highlighted and your nose straightened and your ears pinned back like me? Did you do anything special today? Couple of cans of Stella and work in the morning? Is there any way you think you could ever turn into me?

If you did, would you now do what I'm doing?

I think that's why I have been writing. To answer that question. Other Anthony: what would you do?

Words on a screen. Other Anthony: this book is for you.

And for you who find me in the morning: yesterday you were mine. I had you and today I gave you back. This book is for you too.

Conor is ready. I have to roll up my sleeve. By god, Other Anthony, I'm ready.

Chapter 37

The strangest thing has happened.

You will recall me telling you how good I was looking, just how young and healthy and fit I was. You remember. I am no longer ageing. In fact: the reverse.

Conor has confirmed the diagnosis. According to all the tests, I am in perfect physical condition. I conducted my own compare-and-contrast test: I looked at some old photos. It's true.

I am thirty-eight years of age. Only I look like I did when I was thirty. Which just happens to be the age I became a Siren. I haven't aged a day. Look at the photos if you don't believe me. Isn't that the most fantastic news?

Of course, my unique biology meant more medical tests. I wasn't too happy about that — I've had enough of hospitals — but Conor convinced me. After a couple of days prodding and poking he told me my body has somehow stabilised at the optimum physical stage of the human adult life span. The cells regenerate to replace wear and tear. Apparently, I am not going to get any older.

Obviously you understand what this means. It means I was wrong. There is a reason I am a Siren. I am here for a purpose. I am meant.

Now I understand where I was going wrong. I was working to the wrong timetable; rushing through life. I have all the time in the world. I am going to go on.

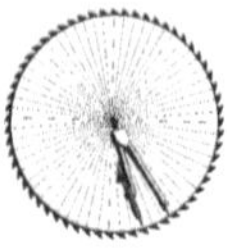

This is my last writing. No more after today. I've got things to do. I'm busy.

Tomorrow I fly out to New York.

It's high time I went to America. There's a lot of people there and they've never seen me. They have a right to meet the man to whom they have dedicated their lives.

They are going to use their superior resources to find my purpose. I intend to isolate the reason I have been given the glamour, why I was chosen.

And when I've done that, I'm going to visit the Empire State Building and the White House and Disneyland. I already have a list of Hollywood actresses to accompany me.

The research will begin at the UN Building. My advisors are continuing Max's work on tracking down the remaining Sirens. I want to know their names, where they live, how many people they have and how we can neutralise their threat. I don't want any more surprises like the invasion. I don't have time.

Doctor Conor is the man to thank for stopping me killing myself. He has, over the years and without my knowledge, been increasingly surprised by my physical progression. At first he wasn't sure what to make of the results, assuming that more exercise and a better diet was the reason for my youthful looks. He held off telling me what he suspected but when I revealed my intentions to do away with myself he decided he had to let me know. His nerve failed him up to the moment I asked him to stick the needle in. I actually have a sneaking suspicion he would have said anything to stop me killing myself. That's how much he loves me.

I am excited, for the first time in years. Something is coming; some great revelation is on its way. I have no idea what it might be but there is no doubt in my mind I am here to make the world ready.

I find it odd to think that Felice might have been right. That this senile hairy-chinned witch with her dreams of salvation was correct.

I often picture her sitting in that cold church rocking back and forth in her little wooden chair. Had I not nuked her, she would not have died either. She would have remained an arthritic ninety year old crone. Just in case though, I've sent people in to that radioactive hole to check we have definitely cremated the bitch.

I have other theories about Sirens; lots of them. One I keep to myself is that ultimately there is meant to be only one. It seems two hundred were chosen but only one can be last Siren standing. As my changing biology suggests that naturally we're going to be around for some time, there will be only one method to whittle down the numbers. Barring accidents, the ultimate Siren will have to destroy the others. Pure Darwin; kill or be killed. I am sure I'm not the first to understand this theory so I have to keep on my toes. Those who are left will be cunning and clever and wily. The strongest will work with each other, at least for a while. I have some advantages: I have the entire technological resources of the Western Hemisphere and its peoples at my command, which makes me the strongest. I am also in my right mind. Overall I am confident of victory.

I spend my last night in the apartment. Yes, another last night. To be honest I'm getting tired of London… and before you say it, no, I am certainly not tired of life.

If I like the look of America I may stay there. In fact, I know already I will. Travel will do me good. Not forever of course. I'm a Brit at heart. However, I am already working on ways of organising my work force to begin reshaping the UK into a country more to my liking. I can't carry on with the population blindly muddling their way through their lives. They deserve a bit of purpose. They deserve an aim in life. Let's get them building, doing something useful. Let's all help build a better Britain.

The world has changed. All this pretending that it hasn't and trying to keep society the same as pre-Siren times is pointless. I just got depressed. The challenge is to build something new and, I believe, something wonderful. So my citizens: it's off to work we go.

And one day, I will be back to see what you've come up with. Can't say when. I have time.

I have plans.

There's a final surprise. I am tapping in these last notes on the laptop while my staff pack my bags when who should turn up but the most eminent clergymen in the country.

The Archbishop of Canterbury, the Head of the Catholic Church in the UK, the Chief Rabbi and the President of the British Muslim Association have come to discuss my deification.

I blame myself. Since I announced on TV that I have ceased ageing (resulting in more than a few spontaneous festivals in my honour, I modestly assure you), the religious leaders worldwide have been in turmoil.

'We have happily all reached one inevitable conclusion,' says the Archbishop of Canterbury, as my butler pours them tea one by one.

'A very happy conclusion,' says the President of the British Muslim Association.

'We believe that you, Anthony, can only be the son of God. Quite probably, in fact, a manifestation of God Himself.'

The Head Cardinal smiles and nods his assent. They are in accord; pleased. I wonder if they have drawn straws to see which one would tell me.

What do you say to being officially pronounced a god? Six years ago I would have needed therapy. Now, despite some embarrassment, I smile and accept the compliment.

Look, I'm not going all Felice. There's nothing wrong with my brain. But something did happen to me all those years ago.

Let's face it: I do have a miraculous power. Two! Or perhaps they are facets of the same phenomenon. We don't need the glamour any more so can we really say the establishment of immortality at this exact moment is merely coincidence? Somebody is up there pulling the strings. Who's to say I'm not the son of god? You?

'That's terrific news,' I tell the religious leaders. 'What do you want to do about it?'

The leaders look at each other. The Chief Rabbi says, 'We believe the way forward is to unite our beliefs. Combine our different practices and rituals into one solid creed. We have already made significant progress with the general restructuring.'

'There are one or two matters of difference,' says the Head Cardinal. 'Icons, symbols, dietary requirements and so forth but we would hope to consult you if our discussions get bogged down. If you are amenable, Lord.'

'The wonderful truth of the matter is,' says the Hindu guy I probably didn't mention before, 'now that we have positive proof of the revelation of your Divinity, great leaps of accord and understanding have already occurred. You have united the human race.'

Beaming grins all around.

'That's great news, guys,' I tell them. 'But you know I have a plane to catch.'

I scram out of the apartment pretty quick. My butler bundles the bags down the stairs and out to the waiting cars. I leave them to smile at each other. Thing about religion, it's best left to the experts.

We drive through London. I tell the chauffeur to take the long way round. I want to see my city as I have made it, for the last time. My mobile phone beeps but I turn it off. I don't want to speak to anybody, not just now.

We pass along the Embankment. The Thames is flowing faster these days, probably something to do with me. The city buildings possess a shining quality that reminds me of the London buried in my memory. A child's memory of dense, ultra-real, mysterious architecture, buildings you would never see anywhere else glowing with neon lights and populated by incomprehensible, busy people. The bridges are lined with those people now. They're watching me leave. These people, my human beings, they make no noise. I am leaving them for another continent. I guess they're wondering if I'll ever come back.

I think of the thousands of London miles I travelled here. The commute, the shopping trips, the drinking trips. Just like millions of other people doing just the same. Hundreds of years of history soaked into the buildings and the pavements and the river, distilled to this moment. The moment I leave.

What was it my mum said about building a pharaoh's tomb? A legacy to myself? Stasis?

She was wrong, because now I know there is a reason for this madness. I have purpose. I may not know what this purpose is, but there is no doubt if I can get everyone here pulling together, I soon will.

I have weird dreams. These are new. I dream I am the other Anthony, this made-up one I've been writing to. I dream that getting the glamour and becoming a Siren never happened. In this dream the revelation I wait for is the realisation that I will wake up at home in Croydon, on a Monday morning, about to get up and go to work.

In fact, I had the dream last night again and jumped awake. I sweated and gibbered until my consciousness caught up with the real world. I am this Anthony; the real Anthony. I am safe Anthony.

London flashes by faster as we reach the A4 at Hyde Park and head west to Earl's Court and Knightsbridge. I am out of the centre. Goodbye!

Still, there are plenty of the other bits of London left. I think how big the city is; how many people still live in it who I know nothing about. How did they ever manage without me?

Heathrow is as big and unwieldy as ever. I guess I could move the airport closer, or convert the City Airport. However, as no one except me travels by air any more, I can't really see the point. Perhaps I'll get someone to come up with a decent architectural solution.

My driver cruises through the gates straight to the runway. A single 747 sits on the tarmac. Conor and my other necessaries are already waiting. They stayed over in a hotel last night.

I've had the aeroplane checked and double checked. Imagine the shame if I've come all this way to end up crashing into the Atlantic because some dodo forgot to bolt the wings on properly. What a way to go. I'm a god for Christ's sake. That really wouldn't do.

Still, I'm a bit apprehensive as I step out of the car and the pilots and crew greet me. They all look impressively seasoned with their healthy air crew tans and uniforms. They look brighter and stronger than us normal folk and I find that reassuring.

As we're on the subject: did I mention my old friend Keano? Did I tell you I had been worried about him? In my imagination he had found his way to a desert island or Pacific atoll, still free of my influence, or worse, under someone else's. No, there was nothing to worry about. As I prepare for the flight, my people call to tell me that only a few days after I let him go, Keano was at a service station in Scotland and accidentally got himself glamoured. He can't remember the details but I am assured he is very happy.

I think I might ask Conor for a pill. I'm a bit hesitant about telling these super impressive air people I've never flown intercontinental before. I feel foolish and naïve. A touch of the old Anthony.

'Ready?' asks Conor.

'Yeah. Looking forward to going.'

'Good,' he says.

I think I'll replace Conor with one of those American physicians when I'm over there. He's okay and everything but aren't these Yank doctors supposed to be the best in the world?

Conor ushers his medical team up the steps of the plane. My chauffeur reverses the car and drives away.

The pilot shakes my hand. 'A pleasure to be flying you, sir,' he says. 'Captain Anthony Marshall.' He looks at me, overawed and a little afraid.

'Funny, that's my name too,' I reply, to forestall any discomfort. 'I feel a lot safer knowing that.'

'Thank you, sir. When you're ready…'

'You go on,' I say. 'Start your pre-flight checks. I'll be up in a second.' He nods and trots up the ladder steps.

I take a look round. Not much to see here, just a scarred airport road with little green plants growing in the cracks. There are a few unimpressive stubby aerials and the clustered buildings of the control tower. In the distance some trees cower under a big grey sky. England: in all its sensible, polite glory, waiting for me to go.

Actually, I won't ask Conor for a pill. I don't want anything to fuzz the old head up. Funny, since the new discovery I have stepped up my health program. No more drinking; serious exercise and a proper diet, stripped down to the bare nutrition. Why? I don't know but I guess I can keep the illusion that I've earned this new good health. No, I don't want anything messing up my head. I'm excited about all the work that lies ahead of me. The UN is going to be packed for the conference. I'm going to be really busy.

The 747 engines whine with pent-up potential energy.

There's so much to do. After all, I'm not getting any younger.

THE END

About the Author

Without considering himself a science fiction writer, Simon Messingham is the author of eight novels for the BBC's Doctor Who range. His many awards include the British Fantasy Society Short Story Prize and, in 2015, Best Comedy at the Limelight Film Festival for his short film Not My Wife. He co-wrote the BBC cult comedy series Tales of Uplift and Moral Improvement starring Rik Mayall. He lives with his family on the south coast of the UK, where he spends too much of his time working in an office and attempting to finish a feature film before he gets old and dies. Sirens is his first original novel. Simon's web series Making Beach can be found here:

makingbeach.com

About the Publisher

Derelict Space Sheep is an Australian micropublisher eyeing off the Southern Cross and drawing power from several backyard Hills Hoists in full flap. Our publishing ethos favours both British humour and her stewardship of the English language, with a nod to Australian sensibilities and our convict heritage. If you've enjoyed this publication, please take a moment to post a review to Goodreads or elsewhere. Request a copy from your local library. Recommend the book on social media. Befriend us online!

derelictspacesheep.com

www.ingramcontent.com/pod-product-compliance
Lightning Source LLC
Chambersburg PA
CBHW030820310726
48980CB00006B/569/J

9781925270044